T4-ADK-827

Running for Home

Brenda Dawson

WestBow Press
A DIVISION OF THOMAS NELSON

Copyright © 2012 Brenda Dawson

All rights reserved. No part of this book may be used or reproduced by any means, graphic, electronic, or mechanical, including photocopying, recording, taping or by any information storage retrieval system without the written permission of the publisher except in the case of brief quotations embodied in critical articles and reviews.

Scripture taken from the New King James Version. Copyright 1979, 1980, 1982 by Thomas Nelson, inc. Used by permission. All rights reserved.

WestBow Press books may be ordered through booksellers or by contacting:

WestBow Press
A Division of Thomas Nelson
1663 Liberty Drive
Bloomington, IN 47403
www.westbowpress.com
1-(866) 928-1240

Because of the dynamic nature of the Internet, any web addresses or links contained in this book may have changed since publication and may no longer be valid. The views expressed in this work are solely those of the author and do not necessarily reflect the views of the publisher, and the publisher hereby disclaims any responsibility for them.

Any people depicted in stock imagery provided by Thinkstock are models, and such images are being used for illustrative purposes only.

Certain stock imagery © Thinkstock.

ISBN: 978-1-4497-4007-8 (sc)
ISBN: 978-1-4497-4008-5 (hc)
ISBN: 978-1-4497-4006-1 (e)

Library of Congress Control Number: 2012902527

Printed in the United States of America

WestBow Press rev. date: 3/28/2012

Prologue

The old horse stood dozing in the sparse shade of an oak tree. A spring breeze gently ruffled his still long coat of red winter hair. He swatted his tail lazily at the few flies already buzzing in the warm weather of early March. He had seen many springs, a fact that was obvious by the way he looked. He wasn't sway-backed or broken down, but his knees were large with age and arthritis. His back sometimes became stiff and caused his gait to be rough. None of this mattered to him now as he sank deeper into sleep. In his dreams, he was running and turning, running and turning, running and turning...

Michael got off the school bus and watched it leave a dusty trail as it lumbered down the worn, dirt road. He stood there a moment and thought about how much his life had changed in such a short time. Time usually moved slowly in the life of a twelve year old, but it seemed like he had been riding in a time tunnel lately, speeding along so fast that it sometimes felt as if he couldn't hold on any longer. Two weeks ago he had been in foster care in Detroit, Michigan, and now here he was in a little country town in Tennessee. Talk about culture shock! He had lived his whole life in a big city with lots of different people. He hadn't ever had a family that he could remember. He had been told that his Dad took off before he was born, and that his Mother had been on drugs and had died of an overdose when he was almost three. That was when he had first been put in foster care. The state picked out who he would live with, and it usually didn't work out.

He had had eight different foster homes. That was almost one a year. Some of the people had been pretty nice, but some of them weren't. When he was six years old, he found out that the people who took him were paid money to be his foster parents. That was when he decided he must really be worthless if that was the way he had to get a home. Not too long after that he began to, (what was it they called it?) act out his frustrations. All he knew was he was MAD. The older he got the madder he got, and that's when he began to be shuffled in and out of all those foster homes. He never really let anyone get close to him, because he knew they wouldn't be around for very long. Finally even the state ran out of foster homes, and he was to be sent to a juvenile facility when someone found a relative of his Mother's in Tennessee. Once the people had been contacted about him and agreed to take him, Michigan couldn't send him to them fast enough. Turns out it was his Mother's aunt. Her name was Maggie Hayes and she lived in Cedar Grove, Tennessee with her husband, Joe. No one had been able to find them sooner, because they had been living overseas with Joe's job when Michael's mother died. They had been back in Tennessee for five years now, since Joe had retired. Their son, Chuck and his son Max also lived with them. Chuck's wife had died in a car accident about ten years ago. Maggie kept Max, who was also twelve years old while Chuck worked as a truck driver, and part-time youth minister at their church. They all lived on the family farm. It wasn't a big farm, only about forty acres, but to Michael it seemed huge. He was used to apartments and pavement. He had never even had a dog, much less all the animals that were on the farm.

Michael shook his head as if to bring himself back to the present. He still didn't know how he felt about being with another family, even if they were really his family. He also didn't know how they felt about him being there. They were nice enough, but everything was still new and weird. He reminded himself he had been through this before, and it was just a matter of time until he was sent packing again. With those thoughts, he started to become angry. He began walking down the road to his Aunt's house. He hadn't gone far before he saw the old red horse standing under the tree in the pasture beside the road. Michael picked up a rock and threw it as hard as he could at the horse. He heard a thud and saw the horse jump as the rock hit his back leg. For a moment he felt great satisfaction that he had hit his target, and something else was experiencing pain as real and strong as his. As he watched, the horse held his injured foot off the ground, and he saw blood begin to appear from the cut the rock had made. His satisfaction quickly evaporated and he was filled with guilt. He looked around quickly to see if anyone had seen him. When he was sure there was no one around, he hurried over to the fence to get a better look at the damage he had done. As he saw Michael approach, the old horse's eyes grew wide, and he quickly limped off.

Michael stood there for a while watching, wishing he could take the throw back. He didn't like the way hurting the horse made him feel. Oh well, he thought as he continued his walk home. It was just one more thing to be mad about.

Chapter 1

Sparks Twister Doc, or Doc, as he was called, had been roughly awakened from his slumber by the sharp and immediate pain in his back ankle. It was his first barrel ankle. It was the ankle that he planted in the dirt, and then used to push off on his way to the second barrel when he was competing against the clock at rodeos and barrel races.

Doc was a registered American Quarter Horse. He was a beautiful red, sorrel color with a wide blaze down the center of his face, and two, big, white stockings on his back legs. In his prime, he had been an example of the perfect quarter horse. He was heavily muscled from his chest to his hip. He had a shorter top line than his bottom line. That meant his back from his withers to the point of his hip was shorter than the distance of his belly from the back of his front leg to the front of his back leg. Both of these things were important. To be a good barrel racing horse, the muscle was needed to push off from a barrel and accelerate at lightning speed to the next barrel. The difference in the top and bottom line gave a horse the ability to be fluid and quick in his turns.

Doc wasn't just a good barrel horse, he was a champion barrel horse. He was the horse that all the other barrel racers hoped would stay home. When they saw him step out of the trailer they knew the best they could hope for was second if Doc had his customary blazing run. When he ran, he was a sight to behold. It was as if he knew he was a star. He would enter the arena with his neck arched and prancing with his powerful muscles coiled to begin his run. Doc didn't so much run barrels as he attacked them! From the moment his partner gave him the reins and the cue to go he flattened his ears back next to his head, and leaped to his task. If the barrel hadn't been an inanimate object and had been able to see the ferocious red giant hurtling toward it, the barrel would have either taken flight or died from fear. Once Doc had begun his pattern, as the three barrel cloverleaf is called, he seemed to inhale the barrels with his turns, so that if the spectators blinked they missed it. Every run was a war to Doc and he always intended to win. So much so that if he didn't people who knew him couldn't believe it, and couldn't rest until they figured out to their own satisfaction what had happened. Doc was a barrel running machine.

Doc didn't run alone. He had a great partner, and he loved her. Oh, he didn't like her much at all at first. He didn't like any humans at that time in his life. He was three years old when he met her. At three years old he was already massive in size, though not as big as he would be, and intimidating to most riders. The human who owned him at that time had bought him as a two year old and sent him to a barrel horse trainer in Texas. Doc had liked Texas. The lady who broke him to ride and trained him for barrels had known how to read a horse and get the best out of them. She wasn't mean or heavy handed when she worked with him. Doc flourished under her guidance, and the trainer immediately recognized what an equine athlete she had in her barn. She tried to buy him from the man who owned him, but he was not for sale. Like any good trainer, she knew that Doc's owner had too much horse for his riding ability. When she tried to explain that to him and suggested an older more seasoned barrel horse, the owner would not hear of it. He told her he could ride anything on four legs, especially if a woman could ride him. Instead of letting the trainer help him and Doc, the owner decided it was time for him to take over. The man never stood a chance.

Even though Doc was a green two year old with just ninety days of professional barrel training, he was already very strong and quick as a cat. So quick that the first time the man attempted a barrel run on him, Doc jumped out from under him as soon as he started to the barrel.

The man was left sitting on his backside in the arena dirt. The laughter of the crowd stung him, and from then on he was determined to make Doc pay for his embarrassment.

Doc had only done what had been asked of him, and could not understand what happened when his owner took him back to the horse trailer. He began to yank on Doc's reins, cutting his tongue with his bit. Then he took a riding whip and began to beat Doc with it. For the first time in his life, Doc felt fear of a human. He had always been trusting, and thanks to the trainer in Texas, he had never experienced this kind of abuse.

That night began the worst year of Doc's life. Things only got worse as Doc's fear of his rider caused him to overreact to the man's every move. Always, Doc was blamed for his rider's inability. The man began to use harsher and harsher bits and equipment on Doc. He put a bicycle chain over his nose and a chain behind his ears to keep his head down. Never did he realize that the fault was not Doc's. The punishment Doc endured at the man's hands was beginning to take its toll. Doc's tremendous athletic ability was overshadowed by his fear of doing something wrong. He began to balk at entering the arena and rear if he was pushed to go in and run. Finally, everything came to a head one night at a barrel race in Kentucky.

Doc had a new severe bit in his mouth that caused pain without any pressure on it. Along with the other things the man had put on Doc to control him, the new bit was more pressure than Doc could stand. When it was time to go in the arena and run, the man grabbed Doc's mouth and spurred him hard, because he was anticipating Doc's refusal to enter. The sudden onslaught of pain caused Doc to rear so high that he fell over backwards. The man had fallen off and was not hurt, but the accident had scared Doc as never before. The next thing Doc knew, he had been yanked to his feet, taken back to the trailer, and tied securely to the side of it. Doc watched wide-eyed as the man approached with an axe handle.

As he drew his hand back to strike Doc, a girl's voice spoke, "Excuse me, sir but I've been admiring your horse. Can you tell me something about him?"

The man stopped and looked at her. She was tall and slim. She had long brown hair and crystal blue eyes. Her blue shirt was tucked into her jeans and secured with a belt and a buckle that had a barrel racer on it. Her cowboy hat sat back on her head and had the task of securing all that shiny hair. She looked about sixteen, and the man immediately thought that perhaps he could unload this horse he had come to hate.

"Sure," he said. "What do you want to know?"

"For starters, how old is he, and how is he bred?"

This was a good sign the man thought. She didn't just want to pet the horse, she was showing genuine interest in him. "Well, he's just a baby, only three years old. As for his breeding, he's Doc Bar and Poco Bueno bred ,and if you know anything about quarter horses, little lady, you know it doesn't get any better than that. By the way my name is Brian Adams, and what would yours be?"

"Susan," she said, "Susan Bradley." Susan hadn't missed the condescending way that this Brian Adams had spoken to her. That was okay. Let him think she was a "little lady" who didn't know about anything about horses. That would suit her just fine. In truth, she knew quarter horse bloodlines all the way back to the foundation horses of the breed, and while this horse was well bred, there were too many outstanding quarter horse sires to say there were none better.

She had liked the looks of this colt from the first time she had laid eyes on him a month ago. She had made it a point to try and find out as much as she could about him. What she learned, she didn't like. Brian Adams was the kind of man that gave barrel riders a bad name. People who used his training tactics seldom won anything, made a bad impression on people who saw them ride, and worst of all ruined a lot of good horses. If she had her way Brian Adams would never touch this colt again.

"Well, Susan Bradley, why are you interested in my colt?" he asked.

Susan chose her words carefully. She knew the kind of person Brian Adams was. As long as you stroked his ego and made him feel in charge you could deal with him. After all, wasn't that what got this colt in trouble? Every time Brian rode him, his ego was bruised and he definitely was not in charge.

Even though Susan had no intention of leaving this trailer without Doc's lead rope in her hand she replied, "I just thought I might be able to talk to you about him, but if you're busy I don't want to bother you. I can come back later." There, she had thrown the ball back in his court and put him in charge. It worked like a charm, as she had hoped it would.

"That's fine, little lady. I've got time," he said.

The negations began and $2,500.00 later, Susan had bought herself a horse.

Chapter 2

Michael was almost at the gate that led to his Aunt's yard. It was an inviting scene, with its green grass and flowering spring bushes along with tulips and buttercups coloring the landscape. As he entered the gate Michael stopped, closed his eyes, and breathed deeply. Partly he wanted to take in the crisp, fresh smells of spring, but mostly he was trying to calm his unease about going in the house. His anger had dissipated as he walked the dirt road home. He had real guilt feelings about hurting the horse, but right now that was being overshadowed by his nervousness. He hadn't lived with his aunt and uncle long enough to feel comfortable around them.

Actually Michael didn't know how to feel comfortable around anyone, because the only person he had been around long enough to know was himself, and right now he wasn't too sure about that. He knew his behavior had not been very good in all those foster homes, but that was because he always felt unwanted except for the paycheck the foster parents got for putting up with him. But his behavior had never been cruel, and he had never wanted to hurt another person or animal.

Ever since he had thrown that rock his stomach had been in knots. He was worried about what he had done, and what would happen to him if he lost this place to live. He hadn't let anyone know how scared he was at the prospect of going to the juvenile facility. He knew that if he blew his chance with Aunt Maggie and Uncle Joe, he would go there for sure. This was it, his last chance. If Michael had known how to pray he would have been doing some serious talking to God, but since he didn't he took a deep breath and opened the screen door to Aunt Maggie's kitchen.

The scene that greeted Michael was certainly one that he wasn't used to seeing. There was his aunt bending over the oven door putting an apple pie in the stove to cook for tonight's supper. One thing was for sure, he had been eating like never before in his life! He was used to corndogs and frozen dinners, pizza, and fish sticks. Every night since he had been here there was a home cooked meal.

No that wasn't right, to Michael it was a home cooked feast. There was fried chicken, pot roast, ribs, meatloaf, salmon patties, chicken and dumplings to name a few. Some of these like the salmon patties and chicken and dumplings, Michael had never even heard of much less eaten. There was creamed potatoes, fried squash, pinto beans, white beans with something called ham hock(whatever that was), and vegetables to name a few, and Aunt Maggie always made a pie or cake to top off the meal. So far, Michael had not found one thing that he did not like, a fact that was not lost on Aunt Maggie.

Aunt Maggie looked up and smiled outwardly, but her heart broke at the look on Michael's face. When she was a little girl the man who lived on the farm next to her father's always used to kick his old dog whenever the dog crossed his path. The animal was terrified of his owner, and she was reminded of the look in the old dog's eyes when she looked into Michael's. Maggie B. Hayes (the B was just an initial not a name, a fact that annoyed her to no end) was a born lover. She loved kids, old people, animals, her family, her church, and God. It was criminal that a child so young should be so scared. Well, Aunt Maggie said to herself, between me and God we'll change all that. She knew it would be a long road to get Michael's eyes to sparkle the way a twelve year old boy's were supposed to, but she had nothing but time and so did God. Aunt Maggie had never met an animal or human that she couldn't love back to life.

"Well, how was my new favorite boy's day today?" Aunt Maggie asked as she peeped over the top of her nose glasses that she had put on to set the oven temperature for her pie.

For a moment, Michael was terrified he was going to cry! He never cried, not in all the terrible foster homes he had been in, not when other kids punched him, or made fun of him for being the new kid, or not having a Mom or Dad. He always told himself that if he cried they won, so he NEVER cried. Why did the way Aunt Maggie looked at him and asked him about his day make his eyes start to fill? Michael quickly looked down and made a big deal of putting his backpack on the bench by the back door.

"It was okay," Michael said. He knew he wasn't telling the truth. The other kids at school were not sure yet what to make of him. Most were just curious, but some were eager to make the new kid's life difficult. He talked differently than they did, and he dressed differently than they did. His baggy jeans and loose tee shirts were the style in all his other schools, and Michael liked the way they hid how skinny he was under them. He was plenty tall enough for his age, but he had always been thin.

"Okay isn't too bad for just a few days at a new school," Aunt Maggie said. "By the time you've been here a few months you'll feel just like you've been here all your life."

Michael's heart leaped in his chest. Did she realize what she had said? If she did, did she mean it? It sounded like she thought he wouldn't be leaving! Calm down, Michael told himself don't get your hopes up. Not yet anyway.

Michael needed to change the direction of his and Aunt Maggie's thoughts so he said, "Something sure does smell good. What are you cooking?"

Aunt Maggie smiled broadly as she took off her nose glasses, "Tonight we are having tenderloin and homemade biscuits, gravy, creamed sweet potatoes, green beans, and apple pie, so I hope you're hungry". Aunt Maggie loved to cook, but she loved to watch her family enjoy their meals better. She had noticed that when Michael first came to them mealtimes were confusing for him. She soon picked up on the fact that he wasn't used to the food they ate in the South, and she also discovered that he apparently was not used to the whole family sitting down at the table for a meal. She delighted in the fact that Michael had gone from a hesitant taster of her meals to one of her biggest eaters. She didn't say anything to him about his table manners. She was wise enough to know that when he realized he would always have a full plate and a family to eat his meals with, the problem would take care of itself. Aunt Maggie giggled out loud when Michael licked his lips and swallowed hard as she recited the menu.

"Why don't you go upstairs to your room, change your school clothes, and get a head start on feeding the livestock. Chuck picked Max up early from school for his dental appointment. They should be home anytime now, and the sooner all the chores are done the sooner we can eat. Joe had to go to the feed store to get chicken feed. We have to keep my hens happy so I'll have plenty of eggs for baking," Aunt Maggie said as she got out her biscuit board and rolling pin.

"Yes mam," Michael said as he raced up the stairs of the old farm house. Funny he'd never heard yes mam, no mam, yes sir, and no sir until he came down here, and certainly his new family hadn't told him to say it. He had heard Max answer his Dad and Aunt Maggie and Uncle Joe that way. For some reason, he liked to say it to Aunt Maggie. He especially liked the way it made her smile. Michael didn't know it, but Aunt Maggie had already begun to crack his hard protective shield.

Chapter 3

The old, red horse kept picking up his right back leg and sitting it down. Sometimes, he even stomped it on the ground hard in an effort to ease the discomfort. It felt like he was being stung by bees in his ankle. The blood continued to pour from the cut because a horse's lower leg has many blood vessels, and an injury in this area causes more bleeding than in other areas less richly supplied with blood. The blood was also drawing flies to the wound, and the flies began to torture Doc with their hunger to make a meal of it. If Susan had been there she would have washed his injury, held his foot, and then kept pressure on it until the bleeding had stopped. But Susan wasn't there. She hadn't been there in a very long time.

The thoughts of the one human that Doc had loved above all else, made the old horse sad for things long past. Things he knew in his heart he would never have again. It had been ten years since he had smelled her scent on the way to the barn to see him. She smelled like the new spring flowers. Her voice was always soft, and she never hurt him. She was patient with him when he couldn't understand what she wanted from him, and when he did finally get it, she couldn't praise or pet him enough. He had especially liked the carrots and cookies she always seemed to have in her pocket for a reward.

Doc had his last treat form Susan ten years ago. They had gone into the arena to run barrels that night, and she had just disappeared. He had never seen her again since. For a long time he ran the pasture searching for her. A few times he thought he saw her at the barn and went flying, nickering to her, only to find she was not there. He still looked for her sometimes, but he never ran anymore. Even a horse can become disappointed and lose hope. The pain in his leg had turned to a dull ache. The old horse lowered his head, closed his eyes and began to dream.

Susan couldn't wait to show her Dad the three year old she had bought from Brian Adams. She knew Adams thought he had taken her, but that was alright because she knew it was the other way around. The man didn't have a clue about what caliber of horse he had. She knew though. Her Dad had trained horses all his life and had made sure she knew horses. It didn't take much encouragement. She had always loved horses. Her Mom used to hope she would outgrow it, and her Dad was afraid she would. It was a good thing she didn't, because when her Mom got sick and died horses were the salvation for both of them. Her Dad couldn't teach her enough, and she couldn't learn enough. They worked hard each day until when darkness fell and it was time to leave the barn for the empty house, they were both too tired to think. They just fell into bed and started all over again the next morning. It took a year before the hurting stopped enough for them to slow down, and enjoy their horses, each other, and their memories. Susan's mother was always afraid she would get hurt with the horses, and her father was convinced that she never would. Susan's dad used to tell her Mother "Tammy, that kid can ride anything with four legs."

It was true. She was a natural rider. She was balanced in her seat when she was on a horse. That meant that the zipper of her jeans was always dead center of her horse's back. She kept her weight on the balls of her feet in the stirrups, with her feet parallel to the horse's body, and always, always kept her heels down. By keeping her feet parallel to the horse's body her legs were not twisted, and her knees did not hurt. Keeping her heels down kept her foot in the stirrup and let her use her legs as signals for her horse. Under her Dad's guidance she became aware of how she could help or hurt a horse with her riding.

This knowledge equipped her to see the problem with Brian Adams and the big sorrel.

Susan was eighteen when she bought Doc, and she had big plans for him. She was going to use all her skills and her Dad's experience to make a great barrel horse out of Doc. She knew she would have to untrain a lot of negative things he had been taught. It was always harder to get a horse to let go of things caused by punishment, or abuse, or just plain stupidity. Horses weren't really so different from people. A person can be told fifteen good things about themselves and one negative thing, and you can be sure that person will focus on that one negative. Susan knew Doc had a lot of negatives to forget thanks to Brian Adams.

Susan turned the big diesel truck onto the road, across the railroad tracks, and into the driveway of the farm where she and her Dad lived. She pulled up to the barn as her Dad came out of the tack room. She quickly parked the truck and trailer and jumped out to meet her father.

"Dad, you're not going to believe what I've got," Susan said excitedly.

"Well, let's have a look," Robert Bradley said smiling.

Susan quickly untied Doc from the tie inside the trailer. She knew never to open the back doors of the trailer before untying a horse's head. A lot of good horses had started to back out of trailers, found themselves tied at the front, panicked, and hurt themselves badly. She had seen everything from cut heads to bleeding back legs. That was not going to happen to Doc. As she opened the trailer doors and climbed in to lead Doc out, she watched her Father's face carefully. Susan knew she could count on his expression to tell her what she hoped she would see in his assessment of her purchase. A wide grin began to spread across his face, and Susan knew she had won his approval.

"So, Dad, what do you think?" she asked.

"I think I'll have to see him move, see what kind of attitude he has, and how he's bred before I know for sure, but right now just looking at him, I like him," he answered her.

Doc had been taking in his new surroundings. He felt relief that the person who hurt him so much was not there. At the same time all his senses were on high alert, because he was in a new place with new humans, and he had no trust in any of them. Doc raised his head high, smelled the air for any scents he could recognize, and opened his eyes wide to search for potential danger.

He didn't have long to wait. No sooner had he begun his check than a huge, screaming, dragon began to snake its way along the edge of the pasture, billowing black smoke on its way to devour him! In utter fear for his life, he jerked back on the lead rope with everything in him and tore free of Susan. She was no match for the red giant, and only let go of the lead rope when it burned her hands as Doc took flight.

"Noooo!" Susan screamed as Doc ran down the road. When he saw the railroad tracks he was scared to cross them, so he ran down the middle of the tracks to escape the monster that was after him. To her horror, Susan saw the oncoming train begin to close the distance between her horse and the engine. The engineer was frantically blowing his horn in an effort to scare Doc off the tracks. It was impossible to stop the train with so much weight behind it, so Doc's only hope was to jump off the tracks. Susan saw that it wasn't working! The last she saw of her horse, he was just barely in front of the train when he disappeared around a turn in the tracks. With her view obscured, she could only shudder when she thought of what she would find when the train was gone.

She began to run praying over and over, "Please God, please God, please God."

Chapter 4

Joe opened the back door, and entered the kitchen. He stood over six feet tall, and weighed two hundred and fifty pounds. His weight was a bit of a problem for him. Well it actually wasn't a problem for him, but it definitely was for Miss Maggie and his doctor. Since they seemed determined to let how much he weighed bother them so much, he figured he didn't need to worry about it. Joe never worried about anything. He didn't worry about donuts, candy, pies, cookies, or cakes. If it was good and he wanted it he ate it. It was a habit that drove Maggie crazy! When Joe would come home with goodies, she would immediately tell him he had to stop eating all those things and lose weight. Joe always countered with it was her fault for being such a good cook, and he only bought things to help good causes like bake sales and the Girl Scouts with their cookies. Joe had it figured out where it was his duty to buy this stuff. Somebody had to help these causes and he was prepared to sacrifice himself. He had even been known to invent a good cause to go along with a muffin or two. He knew he wasn't fooling anybody, especially his wife.

Maggie turned and looked over her shoulder, as she was putting her biscuits on the pan to go in the oven with floured fingers. She always smiled when she saw the big man. He was the light of her life. He had made her happy every day since she had met him. She always told people that Joe had made her laugh every single day that they had been married. It made her life with him a real treat. Joe had on his usual checkered flannel shirt with his denim overalls. Since he had retired,

Maggie joked with him it was his new uniform. Joe didn't care. Overalls were not only comfortable, they also never cut into your waist when you ate just a little too much.

"Hey, good looking," Joe said, "where is everybody?"

"Well, Chuck and Max are still at the dentist. Actually, they are probably on their way home by now. Michael has gone to the barn to feed so we can have supper when Chuck and Max get here."

"Do you think it's a good idea to turn that boy loose with the stock? After all he didn't even know what a barn was when he got here two weeks ago. I declare, I've never seen a kid so bumfuzzled by farm life," said Joe.

"Oh, don't be so negative, Joe. He's come a long way in two weeks. We've got twelve years of misery to remove from his memory, and I intend for us to do it. It breaks my heart that we weren't there for him when his Mother died," said Maggie. "Besides, I think he's starting to like going to the barn. When I told him to change his clothes and go feed, he couldn't wait to get out the door. We'll make a country boy out of him, yet."

"You're probably right," said Joe, "I've learned not to argue with you about kids and animals."

The kitchen door opened again, and in came Chuck and Max. Chuck was tall like his father with the same blue eyes, and brown hair. He was strong and broad, but his midsection in no way resembled Joe's. Joe liked to tease him and tell him that one morning he would wake up and his belly would be just like Joe's. He said it was the Hayes' curse. When Chuck was a little boy, he used to check his belly the first thing every morning. Now that he was older, he no longer believed the curse business. He just did all those stomach crunches because he wanted to! Where Joe ate whatever he wanted, Chuck was a health nut. He didn't like things like broccoli, but he ate them anyway. He worked out at the gym every chance he got, and would ride a bike or run five days a week. Joe said if he had to do all that he'd just as soon die a little quicker, and enjoy his life a whole lot more. It was a running battle between the two of them. Chuck never won, but he never gave up either.

Max stood beside his father with a very lopsided grin due to the shot of Novocain that the dentist had given him in order to fix a cavity in his tooth.

"Helwoo Gwanny Maggie," he drooled, "I hawd a cabity."

"I can see that," Maggie laughed. "Why don't you go to the barn and help Michael feed, and maybe your mouth will wake up so you can talk better and eat your supper?"

"Otay," said Max.

Chuck watched his son go out the door. He was the same age as Michael, but Michael was much taller. Where Michael's eyes were serious, Max had eyes that danced with mischief. More than once, Chuck had been sent a note by Max's teacher for a behavior conference. It was always for the same thing, and every time Chuck would come home and have the "you are not the class clown" talk with his son. It was usually good for about three months. They were presently on the second month since the last talk. Chuck knew as surely as the sun rose in the east, that he would get another summons from Max's teacher. There was no way to keep Max from being a clown, look at his grandfather. Joe always told Chuck if that was the only problem he had with Max, then he was a lucky Dad. Silently, Chuck agreed with his father.

Max rounded the corner of the barn and saw Michael bending down to gather the eggs from the nests Joe had made for Maggie's chickens. What he saw made him quickly duck back behind the side of the barn. Max smiled a huge drooping grin, as he poked his head around far enough to see the big red rooster begin dropping his wings, fuzzing up his feathers, scratching the ground and drawing a bead on Michael's backside. Roho, as they called the rooster, wasn't about to put up with this newcomer stealing his hen's eggs. This was his barnyard and he was going to make sure Michael knew it. With that thought in his little bird brain, the attack began!

Michael didn't have a clue that the rooster was anywhere around, or that he would object to him being in the henhouse if he had known. What he did know was that a weight hit him in the back, and before he could react he was being flogged with great big rooster wings, and being stuck by something very sharp in the back! He also felt the top of his head being pecked very rapidly and none too gently!

"Ahhhhh," screamed Michael as he turned on his back, grabbed the still very angry rooster by the neck, and rolled around furiously on the ground, "Help, help! Get him off!"

This only seemed to further incense the rooster. How dare this newcomer grab him by the neck? He'd show this boy what a rooster could do! Roho immediately went into overdrive with his wings. If it was possible to fan a boy to death with feathers he was going to do it. Michael turned loose of the rooster's neck to grab his wings. He was being flogged so hard and fast he couldn't open his eyes to see how to escape from Birdzilla! This freed Roho's head to continue pecking at whichever part of Michael he could hit.

"Ow, ow, ouch, quit, stop, get off," wailed Michael, "HELPPP!"

By this time Max was rolling on the ground laughing and drooling at the same time. In the middle of his misery, Michael realized he was not alone.

"Max! Max! Do something," he yelled.

Max heard him, but he was laughing so hard he couldn't breathe. It was clear to Michael he was on his own. While he was trying to cover his head without letting go of Roho's wings, his hands slipped and Roho took flight. He flew a short distance away, and began to scratch the ground and look at both boys as if getting ready for round two. Max and Michael both looked at each other, jumped up, and took off to the house. The egg gathering could wait until after supper when they were armed with Miss Maggie's broom.

Chapter 5

Robert Bradley shook his head as he rubbed is hand across his face. He was worried that the train had run over the new horse his daughter had bought. He had to admit he was a beautiful animal. Susan had been determined to buy him as soon as she set eyes on him. The more she found out about him the more she knew she had to have him. He had spent a long time teaching her the ways of horses, and how to train them to become your partner instead an unwilling mount. Horses had been their salvation when Tam had died. Well, horses and God. He didn't know how he would have coped with the death of his wife and the responsibility of a young daughter if he hadn't had his faith and been able to pray for strength and help.

Robert began to pray now, "Please Lord let that horse be alive, but if he isn't give my daughter the strength to deal with what she finds left of him."

He knew what a tender heart Susan had and that if Doc was dead she would take it hard. He went to his pickup, got in and began to drive slowly down the road beside the tracks hoping for the best.

Susan was getting very tired. She was running beside the tracks begging God to save her horse. She didn't know why she had such strong feelings for him already. It didn't make sense. She hadn't even ridden him yet, but she knew he was meant to be her horse. She had been running about a mile in the deep limestone rocks the railroad put beside the tracks to keep the sparks from the wheels and brakes from starting fires. The rocks worked well for that, but they were awful for running. She was watching for Doc's hoof prints, and was relieved that she could track his flight this far with no sign of blood or an accident. His hoof prints were about a foot deep in the loose rock so she knew he was running hard.

Every turn in the tracks she held her breath just knowing that when she rounded the curve she would find Doc, and it would be bad. So far so good but how far could a horse out run a speeding train? She was approaching another turn. The tracks were up about fifteen feet higher than the fence and pasture that ran along side it. As Susan turned the curve her heart caught in her throat! She was petrified by what she saw! The hoof prints disappeared, and the barbed wire fence was torn as if a huge animal had been thrown through it! Had the train sent Doc hurtling down the bank and broken the fence? If so, he had to be torn to pieces!

Robert kept creeping along the road in his pickup. He had seen no sign of Susan or the horse. He continued to pray for God's help. He felt sure he was going to need it when this thing played out. He was already thinking about getting one of his neighbors who owned a backhoe to come and bury the horse once they found what was left of him. It was a bad way to end what his daughter had thought was a good day.

Susan went crashing down the side of the tracks, sliding in the loose rocks She lost her balance, and slid the rest of the way down on her backside. She came to a stop where the fence was broken. To her dismay, she found a lot of red hair stuck to the sharp barbs on the wire. Susan hated barbed wire! It was only good for maiming a horse. She had seen horses that had to be put down because of massive injuries and infections from barbed wire cuts. She looked wildly for any sign of Doc, but other than the hair on the barbs there was nothing.

Then she saw it, hoof prints in the pasture leading up the hill. She scrambled up the hill scanning the pasture as she ran. What she saw made her suck her breath in with an audible gasp! Standing at the very far end of the pasture with his head arched and his tail held high was Doc! He looked beautiful! How could that be? As relief flooded through her, she saw the reason for Doc's impressive pose. A very angry longhorn bull was not happy that Doc had entered his domain.

Doc was in a pasture that belonged to their neighbor, Mr. Tanning. He had purchased the bull as a novelty. The huge horns on the bull made him a very formidable animal. As she watched, Susan saw the bull lower his head and proceed in Doc's direction. This was just great, she thought. I find my horse alive after he out runs a train, and now I have to figure out a way to save him from a 2,000 pound bull with horns the size of a small house! She looked quickly around for a weapon, and found none. The only thing she had was the lead rope she had grabbed when she ran after Doc. It would just have to do the job.

Susan began running, yelling and twirling the heavy snap end of the lead rope over her head. It never entered her mind that she barely weighed 110 pounds soaking wet, and that if the bull decided to go after her she had no place to hide because she was in the middle of an open pasture. There weren't very many things Susan was afraid of, and she didn't doubt herself now.

The big bull heard a commotion and turned to see the source of the noise. He was greeted with the sight of a wild, screaming, human with a whirling snake coming out of her head. The longhorn had never seen anything like this. He spent a few seconds sizing up the creature rapidly closing the distance between them and decided to let it eat the horse instead of him. With that decision made the bull spun around, snorted, threw his tail up in the air, and ran out of sight.

Susan saw the bull take off and had just a moment of relief until she turned her attention back to Doc. Apparently he had never seen such a sight as she had presented either. With his head and tail still high, he began to trot a high stepping gait that looked quite showy. Susan began to walk calmly in Doc's direction whistling and talking softly. Doc continued his high-step away from her until he looked up and spied the retreating bull. This made him stop and reconsider his choices, the bull or the crazy but small, human. He decided on the human. He stopped and waited for Susan to get close to him. She very slowly and easily walked up to him. She kept her eyes on the ground and did not look into Doc's eyes. Her father had taught her this trick. A horse is a prey animal and making eye contact with a potential predator will cause them to take flight every time. It was just instinct. If she and Doc had known each other better she wouldn't have had to avoid eye contact, but they had just made each other's acquaintance. It worked beautifully. Doc still had his halter on, but his lead rein was long gone. Susan was glad she had grabbed the spare lead as she took off after Doc. Not only had it proved a good weapon, but it allowed her to go around her horse checking for injuries from his wild escapade. She couldn't believe what she found. Doc, for all of his adventure, only had one small scratch from the barbed wire on his chest! Susan said a silent prayer of praise and thanks to God for His hand in sparing Doc.

Susan reached up and petted the broad space between Doc's eyes gently, "Welcome to your new home Mr. Big. And please, don't scare me like that again!"

Susan put her hand on Doc's shoulder, and began to walk him back to the barn. Robert Bradley pulled over to the side of the road when he saw his daughter leading the big red horse across Mr. Tanning's field to the gate that joined their two pastures. It was nothing short of a miracle to see the big horse in one piece after outrunning a train. He too, said a prayer of thanksgiving for God's help. It just proved again how no request was too small or insignificant for God to handle, even a runaway horse.

Chapter 6

Michael lay in his bunk staring at the ceiling. He shared a room with Max. This was nothing new. He had shared rooms with other kids in foster homes. What was new was the way Max had welcomed him. He had actually seemed happy he was there. Michael had to admit to himself that it was a good feeling. He hadn't felt wanted very often in his life. Out of the darkness came a giggle that erupted into full scale laughter.

"What's so funny?" asked Michael.

"You and Roho," giggled Max.

"It wasn't too funny from my point of view," answered Michael.

Max kept laughing "Ow, get him off," he said mocking Michael when he and the rooster were fighting.

"Okay. Just wait until he jumps on you," said Michael. "See how much I help you."

"Come on," Max said, "I was just joking. Besides, he has attacked me. He's attacked everybody except Granny Maggie. Everything loves her, even that ornery old rooster."

"Why do they keep him?" asked Michael.

"Papa Joe likes to hear him crow in the mornings and he causes a real ruckus whenever a fox or a possum gets in the henhouse looking for a chicken dinner. When Dad or Papa Joe hear it they get their gun and take care of it. Granny Maggie likes her chickens and her eggs," answered Max.

"You mean they shoot a gun off outside?" asked Michael incredulously.

"Well duh," said Max, "where do you think the henhouse is?"

"No, that's not what I mean," replied Michael, "In Detroit if you heard a gunshot, you heard the police sirens a minute later. You could go to jail for shooting a gun."

"Uh, Michael, in case you haven't noticed, you're not in Detroit anymore. You're in the country in Tennessee. Everybody knows how to handle guns down here. Dad says that's why you don't have as much crime and people getting accidentally shot and killed."

"Because you can shoot wherever you want?" asked Michael.

"No," Max said as he patiently tried to explain, "it's because most everybody knows how to shoot a gun ,knows they have to respect what a gun can do, like kill you, and most crooks know if they break in somebody's house down here they will probably get shot. That's why we don't have so much crime as big cities. Crooks are lazy, but most aren't stupid."

"Wow. Sometimes I feel like I'm in an old western movie," said Michael. "Things are so different from what I've always been used to."

"Is that so bad?" asked Max.

Michael thought for a minute before he answered. He went over the last two weeks quickly in his mind. Actually, it had been the best two weeks he had in a long time. He could go outside anytime he wanted. There was grass, and trees, pastures, and woods to explore. He had never had that before. And there was Max. He really liked Max, and he hoped Max liked him. Everyone was nice to him. That REALLY never happened before. Oh, some people had been okay to him, but never had he been in a foster home where everybody seemed glad to have him there. Maybe the best thing of all was Aunt Maggie. She always smelled so good. He knew because she was a big hugger (boy, he wasn't used to that). When she wrapped her arms around him in one of her giant hugs, he liked the way she smelled and how good it felt to be hugged. The last few times, he had wrapped his thin arms around her and hugged her back. That was an awesome feeling!

"No," Michael said quietly, "it's not bad at all."

"Good," said Max, "I think its pretty cool having you here. Now go to sleep."

Joe was already in bed watching the late news, when Maggie climbed into bed beside him.

"You know, Joe, we may have to do something about that rooster."

"What do you mean? I like old Roho," said Joe.

"I don't want him to hurt anybody. Didn't you see the scratches on Michael's arms?" said Maggie.

"Maggie, if that boy can't keep a rooster from flogging him, he'll never be able to stand up for himself. That's why farm life is good for a kid, especially one like Michael. Don't you worry about him and that rooster. In no time at all that rooster won't be so quick to jump on him, unless I miss my guess. Remember he has Max to show him how to be a country boy," said Joe.

"Huh," sniffed Maggie, "fat lot of good that did him today. Max was too busy laughing to help Michael."

"Now Maggie, Michael isn't a baby, he's a twelve year old boy. You don't have to be so protective of him. You're like an old mother hen with a new chick," said Joe.

"Joe, that child has been through no telling what, and he still has a sweet spirit. I don't know what I would be like if I had lived my first few years like he has, and I intend to make his life here with us a good one."

"I know, sweetheart, I want to help him, too. But, I think we can do it without killing old Roho," laughed Joe, "even if a big pot of chicken and dumplings would be pretty tasty."

"I declare, Joe, I don't know if you married me for love or for my cooking," Maggie said indignantly.

"That's me, Joe Hayes, man of mystery. Always keep 'em guessing. That's my motto. Wanna fight about it?" joked the big man.

Maggie swatted his arm, "There, good night," she said smiling. He always made her happy. A fact she was sure to mention to the Lord every day as she said her prayers.

Chapter 7

Doc tried to put his weight on his wounded back ankle. It had been four days since the rock had been thrown. His ankle was twice the normal size, and when he walked he carried it. The pain had intensified over time instead of getting better. Susan would have fixed it by now. How he missed her! He missed getting in the trailer and going to new places to run. He missed being brushed, and stroked, and petted. He missed his big clean stall in the barn. He hadn't been in that stall for ten years now. Hardly anyone ever even came to check on him in the pasture anymore. Doc finally gave up and lay down. His left back leg was so tired from bearing all his weight that he had to get some relief. His head dropped, and once again, he was dreaming.

Susan pulled her pickup and trailer into the parking lot on the rodeo grounds. Doc was doing awesome the last three weeks! She'd had him almost three years now, and he just got better and better. She had never had a bond with a horse like the one she had with the big red sorrel. Once he had gotten used to her way of riding and training he tried harder than any horse she had ever ridden. He had the biggest heart and he gave her all of it every time she asked. They had brought home the first place check from the barrel races in the last three rodeos. It had amounted to a sizeable purse. So far this year they had won almost $8,000 and it was only the beginning of March.

It was a good thing that Doc was having a breakout year. Susan and her Dad had earned their living by breaking and training colts for people. For some reason, there hadn't been many this year. Maybe it was still a little too early in the year, but whatever the cause, their income had dwindled to a fraction of what they were used to. Her Dad liked to remind her that the Lord would provide for them. He always had. Susan's faith told her the same thing. It was just that the electric company, the gas company, the feed store, and other necessities weren't willing to wait on the Lord.

Doc began to paw impatiently because the trailer had stopped and he wanted out. Susan couldn't help but smile. The big guy knows where he is and what he's here to do thought Susan.

She crammed the gearshift in park, and jumped out of the truck.

"Okay Mr. Big I hear you," she said as she untied his lead line from the trailer.

She went around to the back and opened the door for him to come out. After she had Doc unloaded and tied to the trailer, Susan went to find out when she and Doc were supposed to run and pay her entry fee. On her way to the stand, she ran into another barrel racer who was a friend of hers. She didn't see her very often because she lived in Alabama, but sometimes they wound up at the same rodeo or barrel race. Her name was Tessa Jackson, and she rode a big iron gray quarter horse that was Doc's main competition when they found themselves running together. His name was Chicka Moz, and he was as big as Doc. He hadn't been running barrels as long as Doc, but he was getting better every time Susan saw him run. Her eyebrows drew together in a frown. Why did Tessa have to pick this rodeo? She really needed to win some money to help with bills.

"Hey Suzy," yelled Tessa, "it's good to see you! You left that big sorrel at home, I hope."

"Are you kidding? I can't go anywhere without my main man," Susan laughed as she gave Tessa a hug. Tessa was about four inches taller than Susan. She had coal black hair, eyes so brown they looked black and beautiful skin that always looked tan. Her father was a Native

American, and it showed in her refined features. When she came flying into the arena all dressed in black on that gray horse with the black mane and tail, they were so striking that you would catch yourself watching the picture they made instead of the pattern they ran.

"Just my luck," moaned Tessa, "I drive five hours to the same rodeo you enter with that red tornado. Can I pick them or what? I don't guess he's gotten fat or sick has he? At least then I might have a chance."

Susan laughed, "Nope, he's just fine. At least he was when I left him at the trailer. I'd better get back and check on him. I'll probably see you in the warm-up pen."

The warm-up pen was where the barrel racers warmed up their horses before they ran. A horse like any other athlete needs to warm up their muscles and tendons before they run. Any rider who didn't properly warm up their horse was risking a season ending injury to their mount. Susan had seen it happen, and she always made sure Doc had at least thirty minutes of walking, trotting and loping circles in both directions. They were lucky at this rodeo because this one had an actual arena to use. Some places the best you could do was try and find a grassy spot with no holes in it.

Susan didn't know it, but she was being watched on her way back to her trailer. The person watching her had an ugly sneer on his face. He didn't like this young woman and he hated her horse. His sneer changed to a sly smile as he realized an opportunity had presented itself to him. It was an opportunity of which he was going to take full advantage.

Chapter 8

Michael was sitting at the breakfast table half asleep It was Saturday morning, and he had discovered that no one slept in on Saturdays or Sundays at Aunt Maggie's and Uncle Joe's. At least if he couldn't sleep he could eat. He was fast becoming a big eater, and he had even gained some weight. Maggie smiled when she looked at him. His pants weren't quite so baggy and his arms no longer looked like toothpicks sticking out of his shirt sleeves.

"Well boys, we have to go and hoe out rows for Miss Twilla Batson's beans," said Uncle Joe. "You know how picky she is so eat up, because we're burning daylight."

Here was another saying that Michael had never heard before. It seemed that every time he thought he had heard them all Uncle Joe would come up with one more.

"Why are we hoeing rows and who is Miss Twilla?" asked Michael.

"Well," began Uncle Joe, "Miss Twilla is an older lady who lives alone on her family farm just down the road about two miles. She has about twenty cats and she tries to put out a garden come spring time, but she isn't able to do it by herself. She won't let anyone help her, so Miss Maggie lets on like she needs some of her beans. In exchange for us doing most of the work, Miss Maggie gets some beans, cans them, and gives them back to her for her to have through the winter."

"Why are we doing all this if she just gets everything she gives us back?" asked Michael.

"Because, if we didn't she would have a hard time getting enough to eat. She is in her seventies and has almost no money except a small pension from a factory job she once had. This way she can feel like she is helping us while we help her," said Aunt Maggie. "The Bible says, we are to love our neighbors as ourselves. We certainly have enough to eat, so we need to make sure Miss Twilla does, too."

"What does the Bible say about loving grumpy old ladies that fuss all the time and don't even say thank you for what you do?" asked Max.

Aunt Maggie giggled and said, "It says the exact same thing. Remember to always be respectful and mind your manners. That means all three of you."

Joe looked up as if he was offended at Aunt Maggie's words, but his eyes were full of mischief as he said, " Don't worry honey, she scares me too much not to be nice."

Michael heard the click, click, click of toenails on the hardwood floor, and he knew that Norm was on his way to the kitchen. Norm was a Jack Russell terrier, but in no way was he the standard Jack Russell terrier. He was about a foot tall, with short white hair, and big black spots on his ears and over one eye. That part was typical of a Jack Russell, and that was where Norm's similarities with the breed ended.

Jack Russell's are known for being fearless, and willing to take on anything in a fight no matter what or how large. Not Norm. Norm's back legs were fused so that they always moved together. When he scratched one ear with his back foot, both back feet scratched. One just scratched air. When Norm walked, he hopped with his back feet much like a rabbit. The really amazing thing about Norm was that he could fly when he ran, and he ran a lot.

Norm wasn't the bravest dog and when he was scared, he would dive under Aunt Maggie's bed at ninety miles an hour. From that vantage point he would proceed to bark. Norm's bark was different, too. He didn't really bark, he just woofed a lot. A full fledged bark might have attracted too much attention to him. If he was really scared, Norm wouldn't make a sound under the bed and might spend the whole day there until he felt it was safe to come out. Sometimes Norm could just see something and he would head for cover. If Uncle Joe had one of his guns out, for whatever reason, Norm went under the bed. He didn't like the sound they made, or thunder made, or if he forgot and tore into the garbage, and Aunt Maggie said "Norm, what did you do?" straight under the bed he went. With all his little quirks, Norm was a dog that everybody loved. He was so funny, that everyone loved to see him coming and play with him. Michael was no exception.

Michael had never had a pet of any kind, and he thought Norm was awesome. Norm had taken to sleeping with Michael in his bed at night, and the little dog had no way of knowing the amount of peace and comfort Michael felt with his presence. Norm hopped through the kitchen door and into Michael's lap.

"Can Norm come, too?" asked Michael.

"Oh honey, I don't know," said Aunt Maggie. "He might be trouble with Miss Twilla's cats."

"I'll help watch him, Granny Maggie," said Max.

"Please can he come?"

"Oh, alright, but if he causes trouble, I warned you," said Maggie.

"Load up boys, we've got work to do," said Joe.

"Can we ride in the back of the truck," asked Max?

"Sure, it's just a couple of miles away and it's all on the dirt road," said Joe. "We'll be home in plenty of time for supper, Maggie."

Michael wasn't too sure about the job they were about to do. He had never done farm work and it must be going to take the whole day to do it.

On the way to Miss Twilla's house he asked Max, "Is it really going to take all day to get the garden work done?"

"Naw," said Max, "We may be gone all day but if we are most likely it'll be because Papa Joe finds somebody to talk to."

Michael breathed a sigh of relief. He didn't know how good he would be at farming. Uncle Joe was turning into the driveway of a house that had flowers everywhere! There were old buckets, tin cans, old sinks, an old watering can, an old watering tub, and even an old washing machine that all had flowers sprouting from them. Michael had thought Aunt Maggie had a lot of flowers, but Miss Twilla had her beat. The house was an old one with a small front porch that had a swing and more flowers on it, along with about five cats that were napping in the sun.

Max leaned over and told Michael, "Miss Twilla has one cat named Sweetie Pie. DON'T touch it. It's the meanest cat you've ever seen, and the biggest. I tried to pet it once and it scratched and bit me before I could pull my hand back. Sweetie Pie is also Miss Twilla's favorite cat. I think it's because they are both grumpy. Oh yeah, Sweetie Pie is solid black, so stay away from any black cat and you should be okay."

"Thanks for the heads up," said Michael. "Is that Miss Twilla?"

"Yep, that's her," said Max.

Michael took in Miss Twilla's appearance as he climbed out of the bed of the pickup. She didn't look seventy, but then he wasn't sure what seventy looked like. She got around O.K., she wasn't all bent over, and she didn't look sad or tired. She was a tall lady, with lots of gray hair that stuck out in all different directions as it escaped from the bun that tried to contain it on the back of her head. She wasn't exactly fat, but she sure wasn't skinny either. She had on a dress with an apron over it like she had been baking, and she had on black lace up shoes with a heel on them that looked very uncomfortable. When she started to speak, Michael was sure they must have hurt her feet because you couldn't be as fussy as she was without a reason.

"It about time you got here Joe Hayes. I've been waiting all morning for you and Max to show up. Who's this new boy you brought with you? You know I don't like strangers on my place!"

"Now Miss Twilla, settle down and don't get yourself so upset. You know what happens when you get upset and we don't want that do we?" asked Joe.

Michael leaned over and asked Max, "What happens when she gets upset?"

Max giggled, "She faints. Just passes smooth out. Kinda like one of those fainting goats or a possum. Craziest thing you ever saw."

"Wow, what do you have to do if she konks out, call 911 or something?" asked Michael.

"Nope, we just fan her until she comes to. It's usually not too long," said Max.

While Joe and Miss Twilla talked, she held the screen door open. Sweetie Pie saw her chance to escape to the back yard. There was a mockingbird that had been dive bombing her lately when she strolled outside, and she planned on having poultry for lunch. As Sweetie Pie went by the side of the house on her way to the backyard, she heard "woof" and stopped for a moment. When she was sure that it was not a problem for her she continued on her mission to find the bird.

Norm had been left in the pickup with the windows down while Joe and the boys were on Miss Twilla's porch. Norm loved to "chase the kitty" at home. It was a game Max taught him. Max would say "chase the kitty, Norm" and he would run and jump on the barn cats. He didn't do anything to them. He just jumped on them and held them down. The cats didn't do anything to Norm because they knew he was harmless. When Norm spied Sweetie Pie his 'woof' meant the game was on!

Sweetie Pie had made it all the way to the back yard and was in a crouching position to hunt the bird. Norm jumped out of the truck window and went running after the cat. As he came around the corner of the house into the backyard, he saw the cat already getting low to the ground for him to jump on it. Sweetie Pie saw a new victim. She loved to put dogs in their place almost as much as she loved hunting.

As Norm was almost to Sweetie Pie she flipped over on her back. At the instant Norm jumped on her, she popped out her claws, much like someone flipping open sixteen switch blade knives. Norm got close enough to Sweetie Pie to go airborne. It was always at this point that the barn cats would lie still and wait for Norm to jump on them, because he would sit on them for a minute, then jump off and go on to another victim. Unfortunately for Norm, Sweetie Pie had no intention of playing dead. Instead she intended to make Norm dead or at least very beat up. As Norm landed on her, Sweetie Pie immediately closed all four paws around Norm's fat little body and dug all sixteen of her claws as deep as they would go into Norm's flesh. At the same time she managed to turn Norm upside down so that she was on top of him, not only sinking her front claws into both sides of his head, but she was also raking his belly with her claws on her back feet.

For a split second, Norm was in shock. This never happened when he played "get the kitty". Didn't this cat know how to play? As soon as Norm asked himself that question, Sweetie Pie answered with hissing, spitting, growling, and more claws! At that point, Norm's brain began to send the message PAIN! Once that registered, Norm began to yelp, howl, bark, and honest to goodness cry like a little puppy! This only served to incite Sweetie Pie to attack with more gusto, and victorious cat screams.

All the commotion caused everyone on Miss Twilla's front porch to run to the back yard to see what was wrong. The sight that greeted them was straight out of a Saturday morning cartoon show. Norm and Sweetie Pie appeared to be suspended in mid air as they went round and round with Sweetie Pie intent on murder and Norm just trying to get loose of all those teeth and claws. The sounds coming from the tangled mass of dog and cat were awful.

"Oh Lord help us," cried Miss Twilla, "your dog is killing my Sweetie Pie." Nothing could have been further from the truth, but before anyone could say a word, Miss Twilla hit the ground like a ton of bricks. She was smack in the middle of one of her fainting spells.

"Uh-oh," said Uncle Joe as he took off his hat and began to fan Miss Twilla. Michael and Max sprang into action at the same time. Both tried to go to Norm's rescue. Sweetie Pie saw two new victims. Max reached them first and before he could grab Norm, Sweetie Pie had jumped on his arm and clawed her way to the top of his head. Poor Max was spinning, swinging his arms over his head, and screaming "get it off" at the top of his lungs. Michael did his best to help, but every time he was ready to grab the cat Max moved and Michael would swat him instead of Sweetie Pie. Poor Max wasn't just being cut to pieces by cat claws, he was getting some pretty good sized bumps on his head from Michael's help.

Suddenly Michael had an idea! If he could just pull Max's tee shirt up over his head then he could trap the cat in Max's shirt. Now that he had a plan, Michael set to work putting it in action. It took a minute to grab Max's shirt tail with all the spinning and flailing of his arms Max was doing, but Michael was able to execute the plan and trap the cat in the shirt. Once he had the cat trapped, Michael saw the one drawback to his plan. Max was trapped inside his shirt with a very angry cat that he really couldn't get rid of now!

"Michael, what are you doing?" yelled Max.

"Sorry Max. Don't worry I've got another idea," said Michael.

"That's what I'm afraid of," yelled Max as he continued to spin and holler as Sweetie Pie renewed her attack.

Michael made a frantic grab for Max's tee shirt and caught the bottom of it. He pulled with all his might and the shirt popped off a bleeding and scratched Max while trapping Sweetie Pie inside. Michael held the shirt and cat for a second while Sweetie Pie assessed the situation. The way she saw it, she had two down and one, namely Michael, to go. Michael realized he was to be the next victim about the same time that Sweetie Pie did. He couldn't get rid of the shirt fast enough. He threw it into the air as fast and high as possible.

At that exact moment, Miss Twilla came to. Uncle Joe had been fanning like a madman. As Miss Twlla's eyelids fluttered open, Uncle Joe gave a sigh of relief. Unfortunately, his relief was short lived because the first thing Miss Twilla saw was Sweetie Pie flying through the air with her head sticking out of the neck of Max's tee shirt!

"Ahhh, my cat," was all she managed to get out before she passed out again.

"Oh no, not again," wailed Uncle Joe as he began to fan.

Michael looked at Max. He looked like he had been thrown into the world's biggest thorn bush. He had scratches everywhere, even on the tip of his nose.

"Uh Max, I think the cat won," said Michael.

"I told you, that's the meanest cat in the world. Where's Norm?" said Max.

In all the excitement, the one who had started all this had been forgotten. Both boys began a frantic search for the little dog. They called and called. Another of Norm's habits was to hide and not come out if something scared him, and Sweetie Pie hadn't just scared him, she had given him a near death experience! They continued to search while Uncle Joe continued to fan Miss Twilla.

Aunt Maggie heard the pickup turn into the driveway. Her boys had been gone all day, and she was sure they would be tired and hungry from all the garden work. She smiled as she thought how happy they would be to be finished with the bean rows. She heard the screen door open and she turned to see Norm with what looked like red dots all over him come flying in the door and run under her bed. Next, came Max who was so covered with scratches and cuts he looked like he had been fighting a buzz saw. Max went running up to his room saying he didn't want supper. Michael and Joe came next. They both looked worn out!

"Honey, have I got a story for you," said Joe. "Oh yeah, we didn't get any garden work done, and don't be counting on helping Miss Twilla with her beans this year. She said if we came back on her property, she was going to call the sheriff."

Aunt Maggie looked at Michael and all he could do was shake his head!

Chapter 9

Susan looked up on her way back to her truck to see Doc pawing hard and fast at the trailer. Doc was always very calm at the trailer. She couldn't remember him ever pawing and appearing so upset. She hurried to Doc and put a reassuring hand on his neck.

"Easy Mr. Big, what's gotten into you?" Susan asked as she continued to calm him.

Doc was scared! He had picked up a scent on the wind with his nostrils that he had not smelled in a long time. It was a scent that still had the power to terrify him. He wanted to break free of the trailer and run as fast as his legs would carry him to get as far from the scent as possible. Every time he had smelled the scent he had been hurt, so he associated it with pain. Only Susan's presence kept him from fleeing, and he had no way to tell her of the danger they were in.

Doc had stopped pawing, but it was evident that he was still nervous for some reason. Susan quickly took a mental inventory of Doc's physical condition. When she could find no cuts, bumps, or bruises she knew he hadn't hurt himself by being so agitated. What was the reason for him to be so upset? She kept her hand on Doc but turned to scan the area around the truck and trailer. What was that? She saw a movement on the other side of her truck. It looked like someone was crouched over and running away!

"Who's there?" She yelled.

Susan didn't wait for an answer. She quickly ran to the back of the trailer so that she could see down the other side of her pickup. Again

Running for Home

she thought she saw someone move, but it was dark enough to make her doubt that she really had seen something. In any event, it was enough to make her uneasy. Doc never acted up at the trailer and she was not in the habit of seeing things that weren't there. Susan walked all the way around her trailer, and could find nothing unusual. Why then did she still feel so nervous? She went back to Doc and stood by him. He had begun to calm down some, but he still wasn't himself. She knew her horse well enough to know that something was wrong, but she had no idea what it was.

"Dear God," Susan whispered, "keep Your mighty hand on Doc and me, and protect us from whatever might try to harm us. Please let us be safe and successful tonight, because You know how much Dad and I need a check to try and keep our dream alive. In Jesus Name, Amen."

She felt better immediately. Once again, she was so grateful for her faith in God and His love for her. Susan was always in prayer to God. God had helped her through the death of her Mother, and enabled her to be there for her Dad, even though she had only been fourteen at that time. She had grown up going to church and being taught about God's love for His children. Her faith had become even stronger when she had to have God's help to get her through those tough times. She didn't know how people made it without being able to talk to God about everything in their lives. She liked to think of the Bible as her handbook for living. A person could find the answer to any question they might have just by reading it.

Susan leaned her head on Doc and thought about the plans she and her Dad had for their farm. After her Mother had died, her Dad had seen a program on TV about how working with horses had helped prisoners turn their lives around. The horses were their responsibility and they developed a relationship with them that changed their lives for the better. The prisoners in the program were much more successful in their lives when their sentences were completed and much less likely to return to lives of crime. That same night while Robert Bradley watched the late night news, there was a story about the high percentage of young inner city teens that were getting in trouble at an early age. These teens often didn't become better. They usually became worse, and eventually most grew up and went to jail.

Robert Bradley decided right then that if horses could help save people's lives, why wait until they were adults. Why not try to save them when they first got into trouble as kids? Robert talked to Susan about his idea, and she thought it was great. They had the farm, a great barn, and some good horses. All they needed was a bunk house for the kids to stay in while they were there. At least, that was all they thought they needed. That had been two years ago, and they were still trying to get their plans off the drawing board. They hadn't counted on all the red tape involved. They needed all kinds of licenses, permits, and code requirements to be able to take troubled kids in and help them. Every permit, license, and code inspection had a fee to go with it. That was the problem. Especially since they didn't have the usual number of colts in training to help pay for things. Oh well Susan thought, all we can do is try and ask God for help. Maybe He is trying to teach us patience. She smiled when she thought of her Dad. Patience had never been his strong point.

"Okay Doc, how about we settle down and do the job we came here to do?" Susan said as she patted him on the shoulder. She went to the tack compartment of her trailer, and reached in and got her saddle blanket and placed it on Doc's back. Next, came her barrel saddle, breast collar, and then she put Doc's protective boots on to give his legs and tendons extra support. When all this was done she put on his bridle, and swung up on his back.

She never got used to the feeling of power she felt when she was on her horse. He was so strong and fast, but he was also so easy to control. She could ride him with just two fingers on the reins. She had a very gentle bit in his mouth, unlike the one that Brian Adams had told her she would need. Over the last three years, they had truly become a team. She could shift her weight in the saddle and Doc would feel it and respond accordingly. It still surprised her that Doc was so intimidating to a lot of people to ride. It did take someone who knew how to ride to stay on his back because he was so quick.

Running for Home

Susan heard the rodeo announcer begin to welcome the crowd over the loudspeakers. She knew it was only about ten minutes until the grand entry of all the contestants into the rodeo arena. All the contestants were expected to participate and most had to carry a flag of some sort to make it a real show for the crowd. Doc was always a crowd favorite. Whenever he heard the music begin to start the program, it was almost like someone told him "YOU'RE ON!!" He would arch his neck and prance like he was the star of the show. Susan couldn't help but laugh every time they went around the arena. Doc seemed to enjoy the whole thing more than the crowd! It wasn't unusual to hear ohs and ahs whenever they passed people in the crowd. Sometimes people even followed them back to the trailer to pet Doc. Talk about one, big, red ham, Doc was it!

"Come on Doc, let's go do your stuff," Susan laughed as she walked him to the gate to get their flag. Tessa was there too with Chicka-Moz who was not nearly as happy about carrying a flag as Doc. The big gray horse blew loudly and ran sideways as Tessa tried to calm him and not drop her flag. Susan steered Doc beside her hoping that he would help Tessa settle her horse down. It worked, and before Tessa could even say thanks the gates opened, and the rodeo grand entry began. All the horses would lap the arena. Then they would perform a serpentine pattern around some of the riders stationed at the four corners of the arena, and finish by filing out. This required all the horses to go past both sides of the bleachers two times before they made their exit. This was nothing new, Susan and Doc had done it countless times. Because it was so routine, Susan was not prepared when Doc suddenly reared and ran sideways out of line and into the center of the arena.

"Easy Doc," said Susan, "what's gotten into you?"

If only he could have told her! Doc was going by a section of the crowd when the same scent that had terrified him earlier had come to his nostrils again. The fear was so real that he had to move away from the danger. It was all Susan could do to get him back in line with the rest of the grand entry. He did not want to go close to that section of the crowd again. Doc stayed nervous and when they circled back by the place again, Susan had to use all her skill to keep Doc from bolting and exiting the arena.

As the grand entry finished and left the arena, a conversation was being carried on in the stands about Doc and Susan.

"Well, well, it looks like a skinny girl can handle a horse that turned you every which way but loose," laughed a short, stocky, man with red hair and a big round nose.

"Shut up Carl, if you know what's good for you," said Brian Adams. "That horse is an idiot. Anyone could see that by the way he acted up just now."

"If he's such an idiot, how come he's rated the top horse in this barrel race?" asked Carl.

"I don't know. Maybe he hasn't had any decent competition. Whatever the reason, just wait until he runs tonight before you bet any money on that nag. I've got a feeling he won't even place," Adams said. He didn't add that he intended to make sure that Doc and Susan would lose.

Chapter 10

Michael sat in the back seat of the car on the way to church with Uncle Joe, Aunt Maggie, and Max. Chuck had gone earlier because he was the youth minister, and he wanted to get his materials organized before his Sunday School class got there. Although Michael had been to church with his new family a couple of times, it was still a fairly new experience for him. He had never been to church in his life before coming to his Aunt and Uncle's home. The first time he went, he had no idea what to expect. He didn't know if it would be loud or quiet, if it would last a long time or a little while, would he stand up or sit down, would he be able to talk or not say a word? It turned out that it had been all those things.

When he got to church, he went to a class for his age group with Max. It didn't last too long. There was talking to other kids and in class, then a bell rang and they were dismissed. After about a fifteen minute break when everyone visited and found a place to sit in the church auditorium, the church service began. There was singing and beautiful music that Michael liked a lot. There were announcements about people in the church who were sick or in need of help. There was a sermon delivered by the preacher, Brother Evans, that was sometimes loud and sometimes not (Bro. Evens seemed pretty excited about what he had to say).

After that, they passed around what Michael thought were crackers and grape juice, but not everybody got to drink it. Then they passed around plates that people put money in, and Michael thought he could take some out if he needed it. When he reached in for a fist full of dollars, Max whacked him on the arm and whispered that withdrawals were not allowed. During this time everyone would stand up and sit down whenever the person on the stage told them to. It seemed to Michael that he would just get to sit down and he would have to stand again.

That had been his first Sunday experience at church. This was his third time to go to church and things didn't seem so foreign to him now. He had even gotten to know a few people at church and they always seemed happy to see him. It was another thing he was not used to, but it was a nice thing and he liked it. Michael was staring out the back window of the car when he saw the old red horse lying on the ground close to the fence. He sat up to get a better look. He hadn't seen him since he had thrown the rock and hit him. He felt relieved when he saw that he was resting and appeared to be fine.

"Looks like Old Doc is taking a nap in the spring sun," Uncle Joe said.

"It still makes me sad every time I see him and think about what happened," said Aunt Maggie.

"I know," said Uncle Joe," Susan has been gone ten years now. That doesn't seem possible. Time has a way of getting away from you."

"I just wish time had made things better, but it hasn't," said Aunt Maggie. "Robert used to be the first one at church on Sunday and couldn't do enough to help people, now he never sets foot in the church door. Whenever anyone tries to talk to him about coming back to church he gets angry and tells them to mind their own business. I don't think I've ever seen anyone more bitter."

"I know Miss Maggie, about all we can do is pray for him. God can get things done that we can't," said Uncle Joe.

Michael wondered who Susan was and where she went. He figured it must have been the Robert man's wife. She must have taken off and left him with a bunch of kids or something. That kind of thing happened all the time in his old neighborhood.

"You would think Robert would take better care of Susan's horse, because she loved him so much," said Aunt Maggie.

Running for Home

"You've got to remember that Robert blames that horse for Susan not being here," said Uncle Joe.

Yep, thought Michael, that proves it. The man's wife must have taken off. Maybe she even rode away on her horse if he was mad at it. They were pulling into the church parking lot so all thoughts of mysterious neighbors ended. Michael saw Chuck and waved. Chuck had found an admirer in Michael. Chuck was everything that Michael wished he could be. He was big and strong. He was happy and had lots of friends. He didn't appear to ever be afraid of anything. That was what Michael yearned for the most, to not be afraid of people, of things, of not having a home.

Chuck saw Michael and waved back at him. He didn't know what to expect about Michael when he heard he was coming to live with them, but he found he liked the little guy. He knew Max liked Michael, and it was good for Max to have a buddy his own age living at the farm with him.

"Are you guys ready to do some work?" asked Chuck when Max and Michael walked up.

"What kind of work Dad?" asked Max.

"Helping set up for puppet skits for the five year old class. The youth group is doing a puppet show about Noah's Ark for them this morning so let's get going," said Chuck. With that, both boys followed Chuck to the storage closet to begin getting what they needed for the puppets.

The sermon was over, church had been dismissed, and the Hayes family with Michael was walking down the front steps of the church to go to their car. They met a friend of theirs, Al Norton, on the way out.

"Hey Joe, did Robert Bradley get in touch with you?" Al asked.

"Nope, I haven't seen him," said Uncle Joe, "what's he want?"

"I'd rather not say. I'll let him tell you. I just wanted to warn you so you wouldn't be caught off guard. Gotta go, the wife's in a hurry to get to her mother's for lunch," said Al as he walked away.

"Well don't that beat all," said Uncle Joe. "What could Robert Bradley want to talk to me about?"

"Who knows," said Chuck, "I didn't know he ever talked to anyone."

"Oh well, let's get home. I need to get my roast out of the oven," said Aunt Maggie.

"I never keep good food waiting," said Uncle Joe, as they all got in the car and started home.

Uncle Joe pulled into their driveway at the same time Robert Bradley drove his truck in and got out. It was easy to see Robert was not happy.

As the Hayes family got out of their car, Robert approached them pointing a finger that was shaking with anger at Michael and said, "Joe Hayes that little punk you brought down here is causing trouble, and you owe me $743.00."

Chapter 11

Susan was puzzled. She had owned Doc three years now, and he had never acted like he did in the arena for the grand entry. She was worried that something physical might be wrong with him. He was sweating and still agitated. As she dismounted and tied him to the trailer, she began to be afraid that he might be on the verge of colic. Colic is very serious in a horse because of the potential for death. Colic can be a blockage of the horse's intestine, or it can be a portion of the intestine has become twisted. Colic is incredibly painful, and some of the first symptoms are sweating, being agitated, kicking at their belly, trying to lie down and roll, and not eating or drinking. Susan had a good friend whose horse had died as a result of colic, and since then the thought of losing Doc the same way was scary. She did know that most colic cases could be cleared up with a shot to stop the pain, and she always had one with her. When the horse is no longer in pain, if the intestine is not twisted, relaxing the horse's muscles will sometimes stop the colic. Susan had a wonderful veterinarian, Dr. Russell, who told her if a shot of the pain killer did not work, get to a vet fast.

Susan loosened Doc's girth on the saddle, and stood back to check him out. He was pawing in the gravel beside the trailer. Did that mean he had a stomach ache? She decided to get her shot and have it ready just in case she needed to give it to him. As she went around the trailer to get into the tack compartment where she kept her medicines she stumbled over something on the ground. Puzzled, she stooped down to see what it was. She reached down and picked up a rubber mallet.

It was like a huge hammer, but instead of being metal it was made of hard rubber. Susan frowned as she realized the mallet had not been there when she had been saddling Doc earlier. If it had, she would have already tripped over it, because it was right in front of the trailer door where she kept her saddle. Something was definitely strange about this barrel race. Her horse was not acting right, she kept seeing things that weren't there, and now she was finding things that had no business being where they were. All of Susan's senses were telling her to be on guard for danger. She didn't know what the danger was, she just knew it was real.

Once again, Susan did what she always did when she needed help. She began to pray. "Father, I feel afraid and I need Your protection and strength. I know that with You watching over me and giving Your angels charge over me I will be safe. Please take care of me and my horse, in Your Son's Name, Amen."

There, she felt better already. She took a deep breath and got the shot ready for Doc in case he got worse. She pitched the heavy mallet into a deep gully that ran next to the parking lot. She threw it with all her strength to help release her frustrations with everything that had been happening since she unloaded her horse at the rodeo. What was that! Susan stood stock still. She didn't even breathe. She could have sworn that she heard a loud grunt when the mallet hit the ditch. She waited a long time and heard nothing. That's just great, she thought, now I'm hearing things too!

Susan went back to the side of the trailer where Doc was tied, and was happy to see that he was no longer pawing. He also seemed calmer, even though his eyes were still wide and he kept flaring his nostrils scenting the wind. Maybe he smelled a coyote or something, Susan thought. He did seem calmer now. She decided to put his bridle back on him and ride him around the rodeo grounds in an effort to calm him and be sure he was alright.

"Come on Mr. Big, let's go for a ride and settle both our nerves. We've got a job to do and we need to stay focused," she said as the big red horse put his head down and gave her a shove with his nose. Susan giggled and marveled that her horse could always make her smile. She tightened his girth again, swung lightly into the saddle, and rode away.

Brian Adams lay in the ditch with one hand over his mouth to keep from making a sound. The other hand was over his ear that was throbbing and aching as it turned very red and hot from the impact of the rubber mallet hitting it. He had been hiding behind Susan's horse trailer with the rubber mallet. He knew it would take her a little while to get to her trailer after she left the arena for the Grand Entry Parade, because all the riders would have to get clear of the alley way that led into the arena. He knew he could count on her being in a horse traffic jam long enough for him to put his plan into action.

It really wasn't much of a plan. He was going to hide behind Susan's trailer, and after she had tied her horse and walked away, he was going to hit Doc in the left front knee with a rubber mallet. He was going to use the mallet because it wouldn't break the skin and cause an open wound that Susan would notice. He picked the left front knee because Doc would have to make two turns on that inside knee for his second and third barrels. He was going to make sure they didn't take any money home from this rodeo.

The problem with his plan was that he again underestimated the giant red horse. He didn't count on him having such a fit. What could have made him act so stupid? He had heard him pawing and snorting as he crouched on the other side of the trailer. Instead of just tying him and walking away, that skinny girl had stayed by him, petting and talking to him, trying to settle him down. Just when he thought she was going to leave, he realized that she was about to go to the back of the trailer. And she would see him!

Adams had looked for an escape and found none. His only hope was to jump into the drainage ditch that ran beside the horse trailer. It was deep and dark and he didn't think Susan would see him. He had dropped the mallet and dove into the darkness. He hit with a thud and landed on a big rock with his ribs. He had been doing his best not to groan with the pain in his ribs when the mallet landed on his head, hitting his ear with enough force to make him see stars. He couldn't help the grunt that escaped his lips between his fingers that were supposed to hold back any sound. He was in such pain that he barely heard Susan ride away. When he was sure she was gone, he stood up to leave. At least, he tried to stand up. The rock in his ribs made him walk all bent over, and the pain in his ear caused him to hold his hand to it and tilt his head. Brian Adams looked like a grotesque gnome as he scrambled out of the ditch on his way back to the stands.

It had been almost an hour since Susan and Doc left the trailer and they were up next to run barrels. Tessa and her gray horse had made an awesome run. They had clocked a time of 16.45 seconds, and were in the lead so far. Susan was the last one to run. That was both good and bad. You knew what you had to do to win, but sometimes the pressure got to you. Susan couldn't let that happen tonight. She and her Dad had too much riding on Doc's big strong back.

Doc knew what was about to happen too. His warm-up was finished and he was waiting for his turn into the arena to run. As Susan sat on him, she could feel his giant heart beating through her saddle. Doc wasn't scared or nervous; he was pumped and anxious to get at those three barrels. He didn't have long to wait. The rodeo announcer was on the loudspeaker saying, "Ladies and gentlemen direct your eyes to the alleyway for our last barrel racer. This cowgirl and her horse are presently leading in the standings on our rodeo circuit. Don't blink or you might miss them. Susan Bradley and Doc come a ridin!"

With that, Susan leaned forward on Doc and gave him the cue to go. Doc responded like a well oiled machine. His ears flattened as he made his first leap into the alleyway. He continued to pick up speed and accelerate on his way to the first barrel. When his shoulder was even with the first barrel, he slowed just enough to plant his back feet under him as he passed the barrel with his body, and roll back to his right as he again accelerated on his way to the second barrel. Susan had a good feeling because Doc had just swallowed the first barrel. Her job was to stay centered and balanced, help him slow up enough to make the turns, and be ready and set for the next barrel. Doc got to the second barrel and made an equally beautiful left turn and then seemed to explode toward the third and last barrel. Susan knew she had a good run going and got to the third barrel before she was ready for it. She lost her balance just enough to make Doc stumble as he rounded the last barrel.

Susan couldn't believe what she had done. She knew the stumble was her fault not Doc's. Her heart sank as she looked up to send Doc home, as it was called when the last barrel had been turned and you were running to the finish line. Before she had time to worry further, Doc picked himself up and seemed to know he had time to make up. The big, red horse appeared to literally fly to the finish line. He was running so hard that he ran all the way down the alleyway and almost back to the trailer before he could stop. Susan had been trying so hard to get him stopped that she hadn't heard her time. Oh well, she thought better luck next time. She didn't even bother going back to the alleyway to see who had won. She was so deep in thought about how to pay some bills and taking care of her horse that she didn't hear Tessa walk up.

"Way to go," said Tessa.

"Wow, I've never known you to kick a girl when she's down," said Susan.

"What are you talking about?" asked Tessa.

"Just my awful barrel run," said Susan.

"If that's awful, I'll gladly swap with you," answered Tessa, "your 16.00 flat beat me and Moz."

"What!" said Susan," Doc ran a 16 flat?"

"Yep he did. Even with him stumbling half way around the last barrel. That's some horse you've got there, my friend."

Susan looked up at her horse and smiled, "You said it Tessa. He's a gift from God, and he sure helped the Bradley family out of a tight spot with that run."

Brian Adams managed to catch up with his friend just as the barrel race was over. It had taken him that long to be able to walk halfway straight.

"Hey Brian, I thought you said that nag wouldn't win anything. They just announced that he set a new arena record, and won first place," Carl said. "Hey what's with you? You look like somebody gave you a cauliflower ear. I never saw an ear that red before, and why are you all bent over like that?"

"Shut up Carl. You talk too much," said Adams as he hobbled to his seat.

Chapter 12

"What on earth are you talking about, Robert?" asked Maggie.

"I'll tell you what I'm talking about," said Robert as he turned an angry face to look at Maggie. "That kid both of you brought down here threw a rock at Doc, cut his leg, and now infection has set in so bad the vet doesn't know if the horse will make it. Not only that, it cost me $743.00 to find out my horse will probably die." Robert was so angry that he almost yelled while he was talking to Miss Maggie.

That was more than Joe could take. It was one thing to yell at him. He was a man, and a very big man at that who could take whatever anyone sent his way. It was bad enough that Robert was accusing Michael of causing trouble without any proof, but when Robert raised his voice to Miss Maggie that was the last straw. The big man practically leaped toward Robert. He began to poke him in the chest with his big finger and tell him exactly what was going to happen if he didn't get off his property immediately, but he had better be very sure he apologized to Miss Maggie before he left. To emphasize what he had said, Joe doubled up his fist, and raised it in the air so that it was level with Robert's jaw.

Just then, the sheriff pulled up with his blue lights flashing. He didn't know what was being said, but he could tell from the body language that a fight seemed certain between the two men. Sheriff Dawson Laws was a good and fair man. The people of Cedar Grove respected him and knew they could count on him in times of trouble. None of the small town sheriff stereotypes applied to Daws as he was affectionately known to the town. Daws Laws was the good guy lawman that every town needed and few were lucky enough to have.

Daws shoved his car in park and jumped out, saying "What's going on here fellas?"

Michael had been standing behind Aunt Maggie listening to everything that Robert Bradley was saying about him. Everything had been going so good here, and now it was all over. His last chance to have a home and family was gone. All because he had thrown a stupid rock at an animal he never expected or really wanted to hit. Suddenly, Michael saw the blue lights of the police car! All the color left his face as he froze in fear. He knew about police cars, and where they took you. He knew that from his old neighborhood in Detroit. It was starting to happen! He had been told that if he messed up here he would have to go to a juvenile detention facility. That meant the same as prison for a twelve year old boy. He could barely get his breath. Michael did the only thing he knew to do. He ran! No one noticed that he had gone. The argument between the men had everyone's full attention.

Michael ran through the kitchen door intent on going out the side door of the porch so he wouldn't be seen making his escape. On his way through the living room, he saw Norm sitting up and looking at him the way a dog does turning his head back and forth as if trying to understand what was happening. Michael felt tears sting his eyes as he looked at the little dog. He loved Norm and the thought of being taken away from the farm, the family, and Norm was too much.

Michael ran to Norm, scooped him up, and briefly buried his head in Norm's fur. He sobbed loudly for the first time in a long time. He had been hurt before, but this time it was too much for him to stand. He knew he had to hide, but where? While he was thinking he brushed his hand across his face, held Norm even tighter, and began to run again. He made it out the side door, and headed for the barn. He would have to find a place in the barn to hide until dark, otherwise he would be seen either going down the road, or walking across the newly planted hay field.

Running for Home

As soon as Michael went through the big barn doors, he saw Roho, the rooster, standing in the barn's hallway. Michael knew if Roho started after him, the rooster would begin crowing and making so much noise, that the sheriff would find him. He quickly climbed the ladder to the big hay loft, which was very difficult carrying Norm. When Michael got to the loft, there was hay stacked everywhere in the barn. This was good thought Michael, because he should be able to find a good hiding spot in the middle of all the bales of hay. He was a professional at hiding. That was another skill he had learned in his old neighborhood. When you were small and had no one to protect you on the streets, it didn't take long to learn to hide where you wouldn't be found.

Michael quickly moved some bales of hay around so that he had a small cave in the middle, and when he pulled the bales back in place he couldn't be seen. Now all he had to do was wait until dark so that he could run away. He wondered where he would go, what he would do for food, for money. Michael worried about all the things a twelve year old should never have to worry about.

Since all he could do was sit and wait for dark, Michael became very sad. He looked at Norm, and the little dog looked back at him with eyes of love. Michael had longed for that look all his life and had never really known it, but he knew it now because Aunt Maggie looked at him like that too. Well, that was over. When she found out what a horrible person he was and the bad thing he had done, she wouldn't want anything to do with him again. Michael didn't know how many times his heart could break. He thought it could never happen to him again, but it was happening again, only this time it hurt the worst it had ever hurt.

He couldn't stand it any longer. He bowed his head and cried silently in Norm's fur. The little dog turned to lick the tears from Michael's face, but that just made them fall faster. Michael was desperate for someone to help him! In his misery, Michael thought about the Sunday School lesson and how the teacher had told them that you could always talk to God, and He would hear you. Michael had wondered about that because, his life had been so bad that he felt like God pretty much didn't care about him. He didn't even know how to pray. He had heard Uncle Joe say grace at supper, and had heard people say prayers in church, but he had never just talked to God. Now seemed like a good time to start, because it was the only thing he had left to do. Michael raised his head and looked at Norm. His tear stained face would have broken Aunt Maggie's heart if she had seen it. It was a face that was so desperately alone and sad.

"Norm," Michael whispered, "I don't think God much cares for me but the way I see it, He's my only hope, so here goes. God, if you really do care for me like Aunt Maggie has said, please don't let me go to jail, let me stay here, and don't let them find me and Norm. In Jesus Name, Amen. There Norm, I think maybe God heard me."

Just as Michael began to calm down and feel a little better, he heard the barn door open and footsteps start up the ladder to the hay loft!

Chapter 13

Susan was preoccupied on her drive to the big barrel race in Mississippi. She was so lost in her thoughts that she missed her turn on the interstate highway, and didn't know it until she had gone a good twenty miles out of her way. When she realized what she had done, she was aggravated with herself because she was already running late when she left home. Now she was going to be pushed to get to the arena in time not to miss her class.

She had been thinking about how she and her Dad had finally almost, made their dream to help kids by using horses come true. They had worked so hard. It seemed like every time they thought they were done with all the paperwork, codes to satisfy the state, and the building requirements, something else would come up. Now all those things had been completed. They were only waiting to pass inspection by the state to begin to take kids in who needed a second chance.

Susan sighed as she thought how it had taken them four years to accomplish all that work. They had done most of it themselves. Her Dad was good at building things, and she was good at helping him, and doing all the leg work the city and state required.

She smiled as she thought about how Doc was good at finances. He had paid for most of the things they had needed. In truth, none of it would have been possible without Doc. Susan and Doc had been together five years now. She had never had a horse like Doc, in fact very few people ever get to have a horse like Doc. He was big, beautiful, fast as greased lightning, and a champion. He was the best barrel horse wherever they went. He had brought a lot of money to the farm with his winning runs.

The barrel race they were going to tonight was a 4-D barrel race. That meant there were four divisions that paid money, with each division having five paying places. The winning first division run tonight was paying $12,000.00. Doc had been winning the 1-D money almost every time they ran. Susan was hoping that he would do the same for them tonight. It would give her and her Dad a nice nest egg in the bank to help with any unexpected expenses in case they had overlooked something

Susan saw the lights of the arena long before she got to the parking lot for the trucks and horse trailers. As she approached, she saw that the barrel race had already started. She wasn't surprised, but it did make her a little nervous. She didn't like to cut things this close. She still had to unload Doc, saddle him, go and sign up in her class, and warm the big guy up for his run. Oh well, she thought, first things first. She would just do everything at warp speed.

As she was backing Doc out of the trailer, she heard a familiar voice.

"Well, you did make it after all. I was beginning to think you weren't coming," said Tessa as she rode up on her big gray, Chicka-Moz.

"Hey buddy," said Susan, "you wouldn't believe the trouble I've had getting here. First, I'm late leaving home, then I totally forget what I'm doing and miss my exit on the highway. I went a good twenty miles out of the way and had to drive like a manic to get here as quick as I did. Sometimes I think I have a five year old brain in my twenty three year old head!"

Tessa laughed, "Are you sure you want to run? You look pretty stressed to me. I think you need to just sit this one out and relax."

"Thanks for your concern," Susan smiled back, "but Doc and I didn't almost break our necks coming all this way to sit and watch you take home the big money on that gray horse. We plan on giving you a little competition."

"Great," Tessa groaned, "but we better quit jawing and you better get signed in so they will know you are here and can tell you when you run. I gotta go finish my warm up, because Moz and I only have about twenty minutes until we run. Seriously, good luck."

"Thanks and right back at you. I'd rather get beat by a friend any day," said Susan. She watched Tessa and Moz ride away still struck by the pretty picture they made. The announcer's voice spurred Susan into action as he announced a rider's time on the barrel pattern. She quickly tied Doc to the trailer, gave him a pat, and set off at a jog to go and enter.

Susan and Tessa didn't know that a man had been lurking in the shadow of an adjacent trailer listening to their entire conversation. Brian Adams had continued his obsession of blaming Doc and Susan for his inability as a rider and his lack of character as a person. Adams spent more and more money on good horses only to fail because he refused to take advice from trainers, control his temper, and admit that he was at fault not the horse. A lot of people knew that he had owned Doc first, and remembered how he had been unable to handle the big horse. To make matters worse, that skinny girl had been able to take his horse and turn him into the kind of barrel horse he had always wanted. He continued to take a lot of flack from other riders about what a good horse he let get away.

He was going to make sure he didn't hear anything about what a good run that horse made tonight. He patted his shirt pocket to be sure the syringe was still there. He had gone to a vet and told him he needed a tranquilizer shot to keep in his trailer just in case he ever had an accident and needed to tranquilize his horse to get him out of the trailer. This wasn't an unusual request as most good horsemen kept these shots in their trailers. A horse is an awful big animal for a person to try and help if it is panicked by a traffic accident. The tranquilizer makes it possible to get a horse out of a bad situation without them hurting themselves or their owners.

But Brian Adams didn't want the shot for his trailer. He wanted it for Doc. He couldn't believe his good luck because Susan was running late and wouldn't have time to ride her horse very long to warm him up for the barrels. That was good because he needed her to run pretty quick

Brenda Dawson

after he gave Doc the shot so Doc wouldn't begin to feel the effects of it in time for Susan to realize something was wrong. Adams saw that now was his chance! Susan was leaving in a hurry to enter, and that left Doc alone at the trailer. He began to ease toward Doc.

Doc threw his head in the air. He was alarmed by a familiar scent that always upset him. He caught a movement at the front of the truck and saw the object of his terror. He began to move back and forth on the end of his lead line, but he was tied and could go nowhere. He stopped and began to paw in huge, stomping, strokes throwing gravel high in the air with his hoof.

Adams saw the big horse react and suddenly wasn't to sure he wanted to get close enough to give him a shot. He swallowed his fear when he thought of how much he hated the horse and his rider. He quickly ran up to Doc and jabbed the needle deep in his muscled neck pushing the plunger of the syringe down and delivering to medicine to Doc.

When Doc felt the sharp stab of the needle, he reared as high as the line tied to the trailer would allow. Where was Susan? Doc was terrified! He tried to come down on he man hurting his neck. Again, he was hampered by being tied to the trailer, but he did manage to crush the man against the side of the trailer.

Adams saw what was going to happen but could do nothing to stop it. Just as he finished giving Doc the shot he felt a crushing pain in his left shoulder where it made contact with the trailer. He dropped the needle, grabbed his left arm and ran back into the shadows. He had done what he set out to do, but not without dislocating his shoulder. He wouldn't be riding in tonight's barrel race, but at least he would have the satisfaction of watching Doc make a really bad run. At that thought he was able to smile, even though he was in extreme pain.

Susan came rushing back to the trailer. She was in a big hurry. She only had time to saddle her horse before she had to make her run. She hated that because she always warmed Doc up for at least thirty minutes before he ran. Like any athlete, he needed time for his muscles to get warmed up and ready for him to do his best and avoid injury.

"Okay, Mr. Big, we've got our work cut out for us. I'm sorry big guy, but we'll have to run without warming you up."

Susan looked at Doc as she threw his saddle on his broad back and noticed that he had been pawing at the trailer. She frowned because he usually never got upset at a barrel race. Maybe her nerves had caused him to feel uneasy. She quickly finished tying her cinch and put his bridle on. As she swung up on his back she heard her name being called by the announcer as the next to run. She put her cowboy hat down tight on her head and sent Doc toward the entry way of the arena at a trot.

Doc was having a hard time making his legs do what he was telling them to do. He felt like his body was too heavy for him to move and like he was trying to walk through molasses. He couldn't see well either! What was wrong with him?

Susan stopped at the arena gate and waited for her name to be called. She surveyed the arena and noticed that the ground was very deep and that the barrels were metal. She frowned briefly because metal barrels could leave a nasty bruise if you hit one with your leg. She would have to make sure she didn't hit one. Anyway, with Doc that wasn't a problem.

The announcer said, "Susan Bradley on Spark's Twister Doc is our next contestant. Bring him on in Susan!"

With that, Susan gave Doc the signal to go. He didn't have his usual burst of power, but they were headed to the first barrel. Susan asked Doc for more speed, but he could barely manage to go as fast as he was, and to make matters worse he was having a hard time keeping his feet under him. As they approached the barrel, Susan sat down in her saddle to get ready to make the turn. She knew something was not right with her horse and had already made her mind up to pull up once they got around the first barrel, and take Doc out to see what was wrong with him.

She didn't know that the powerful drug that Doc had been given was kicking in with its full force. Doc was doing everything he could to stay on his feet, but the big horse couldn't outrun the effects of the drug. He also couldn't manage the tight turn around the barrel in the deep dirt of the arena. Just as they were even with the barrel, Doc lost his footing and went down hard. Susan went down even harder and hit her head on the rim of the metal barrel. She lost consciousness immediately. Doc staggered to his feet. He saw Susan on the ground, but his legs would not move to take him to her. In his drugged state, he was only aware of flashing lights, a loud siren, and someone taking Susan away.

Chapter 14

Michael sat up straight in his hay cave and strained his ears to hear. Maybe he didn't hear someone climbing the ladder. Maybe it was just his imagination. Maybe it was an animal. NO! It was a person climbing the stairs to the hayloft. What was he going to do! He looked around wildly for some place to go, something to do, but found nothing. Michael's heart was beating so hard from fear it sounded like a sledge hammer hitting an anvil in his ears. He was holding his breath, and holding Norm so tight the little dog began to squirm. The footsteps were in the loft now. At first the steps went away from him and Michael began to hope that they would just keep going.

What was that! Oh no, the footsteps were once again coming in the direction of his hide out. They were getting closer, and now it sounded like they had stopped very close to him. Michael was as still as a mouse and as quiet as one too, but he forgot about Norm. Norm had heard the footsteps just as Michael had, and he also knew they were getting too close for comfort. Being the excellent guard dog he was (when he was not hiding under Aunt Maggie's bed), Norm let out a ferocious "woof". Michael quickly put a hand over Norm's nose, but the damage had already been done. Michael had cowered down as low as he could go into the hay, when he saw the bale of hay in front of his hiding place begin to move.

Chuck stood in front of Michael looking down at him, and thinking how much Michael looked like a small, trapped animal. He reached out his hand to help Michael out of his hole in the hay.

"Hey buddy, what are you doing up here in the hay?" Chuck asked.

"I'm running away," said Michael, "at least as soon as it gets dark I am."

"Why?" asked Chuck as he sat down on a hay bale next to Michael.

"You know why. You heard what that man said, but I didn't do it," Michael said. He felt bad about lying to Chuck, but it was the only thing he thought he could do. He really liked Chuck and didn't want Chuck to not like him anymore.

"I heard Mr. Bradley just like you did, but I didn't hear anything that was worth running away. When trouble comes to someone in this family, we face it by trying to do what is right to fix the situation. We also make very sure that what we do is what is right in the sight of God. When you tackle a problem that way, you can't help but take care of it," said Chuck. "You said you didn't hit Mr. Bradley's horse with the rock, and since you have been living with us, you haven't given me any reason not to believe you, so if you tell me you didn't do this thing, I'll believe you."

Michael looked up at Chuck and swallowed hard. Now what was he supposed to do? He had never been so trapped by his words as he was now. Chuck had said he believed him. If he told him the truth now, Chuck would think he was a liar. Chuck had been right. He had never lied to him, until just a few seconds ago. How could he take back what he had said? What was he going to do? A huge black hole of fear opened up in his chest and threatened to suffocate him. Before he could think any more thoughts, Chuck stood up and took his hand.

"Come on buddy let's go get this thing taken care of," said Chuck.

Michael followed Chuck like a zombie down the steps of the hayloft, through the barn, and back to the house where Aunt Maggie, Uncle Joe, Mr. Bradley, and the sheriff were still standing and talking. No one was shouting now, but Uncle Joe and Mr. Bradley didn't look very friendly. As they approached, Michael heard the sheriff talking.

"Now, Robert, I understand why you are upset, but you can't come on a man's property and begin accusing his family of things without proof."

"That's telling him Daws. I want you to escort him off my place. Nobody talks to Miss Maggie like he did. He's just lucky you got here when you did or I would have taught an old dog some new manners," said Uncle Joe as he shook his fist for emphasis.

"Now Joe, you stop talking to Robert like that. You two used to be great friends, and there is no call for either of you to be acting like two bantam roosters in a barnyard," said Aunt Maggie.

Robert snorted his agreement with Aunt Maggie and soon wished he hadn't because, she turned her attention on him!

"And you, Robert Bradley, what do you mean acting in such a way on Sunday, the Lord's day when you should have been in church with us like you used to be. Was any of this so urgent or bad that it couldn't have waited until tomorrow or at least been handled in a more civil manner? The very idea! The sheriff having to come to my house just as I'm getting home from church. I hope you are proud of yourself," said Aunt Maggie as she looked Robert in the eye and shook her head sadly.

Robert Bradley had the good grace to look ashamed of himself when Aunt Maggie put it to him like that. Aunt Maggie was a true southern lady, and his rude behavior was wrong.

"I'm sorry Miss Maggie, but I'm out a lot of money because of what that kid did, and I need to know what you are going to do about it," he said.

Chuck spoke up, "Mr. Bradley, I've talked to Michael, and he tells me he didn't throw the rock that injured your horse. He has never lied to me and I believe him, so unless you can prove otherwise he isn't the one who did this." Chuck put his arm around Michael's shoulder and pulled him close to his side.

This had the effect of pouring gasoline on a fire just as Aunt Maggie had calmed Robert down. He became so angry again that he practically sputtered, "I got proof, and I'll be back with it in the morning along with the sheriff. You Hayes are going to pay for this!" Robert said as he spun on his heel, jumped in his pick-up and slammed the door.

As he was speeding out of sight, Sheriff Laws said, "I'm sorry folks, but it looks like I'll be seeing you again tomorrow. Let's try to figure this out without so much emotion."

" Dad-burn it Daws, Bradley could make a preacher cuss," said Uncle Joe.

Aunt Maggie put her hand on Uncle Joe's chest and said, "I think that's an excellent idea," she said. "Now Daws won't you stay and have Sunday lunch with us. I have plenty of biscuits and homemade blackberry cobbler."

"Now that's an offer I can't pass up," said the sheriff.

Michael had an awful feeling in the pit of his stomach. It wasn't hunger. He was wondering how he was going to be able to eat with the sheriff sitting at the table with him, and he was wondering how he was going to get out of the mess his lying had gotten him into.

Chapter 15

The grandfather clock in Aunt Maggie's living room chimed three times. Michael counted them just like he had been counting them all night. He was in bed with his eyes wide open staring at the ceiling. He heard the gentle snores of Max across the room in the other twin bed. Max had been on his soap box after dinner when the sheriff had left. He was angry that his new cousin and friend had been wrongly accused of hurting Mr. Bradley's horse. He kept telling Michael to "just wait", and "don't worry", and "Dad and Grandpa Joe will take care of that Robert Bradley".

Michael knew that Max was trying to make him feel better, but all of his encouragement had the opposite effect. It only served to make Michael feel worse because now he had not one but two major problems. He had hurt the horse even though he didn't mean to, and he had lied to Chuck when he hadn't wanted to. He had been going over and over it in his mind all night long trying to figure out what to do.

Every answer he came up with always came back to the same thing. He had to make things right. He was sorry about the horse, but he was sorrier about lying to Chuck. Chuck was someone he looked up to, and he wanted Chuck to like him. Once Chuck found out he had lied to him and let Chuck stand up to everybody about Michael being innocent, he knew Chuck would hate him and want him gone.

Just thinking about it made his heart race like he had been running for miles. Where would he end up? What would happen to him? Every thought and every question brought a feeling of fear and panic. Michael was so worried that he literally began to shake. A movement under the covers brought his attention to Norm. The little dog was sleeping with him, and he could tell something was wrong. He inched his was up to Michael's face and started licking his cheek. Why couldn't people be like Norm and love him no matter what?

Michael finally knew what he had to do. He had known it all along, but he just couldn't make himself do it. He had to go to Chuck and tell him everything. It was the scariest thing he had ever had to do, but there was no other way. How was he going to get the courage? Suddenly he remembered what Chuck had said to him. "When trouble comes to someone in this family, we face it by trying to do what is right to fix the situation. We also make sure that what we do is right in the sight of God."

Michael kept thinking about that. Finally, he couldn't stand it any longer. He threw his covers off, grabbed Norm, and quietly left the bedroom. After he had closed the door, he tiptoed down the hall to Chuck's bedroom door. It wasn't closed all the way so when he opened it, no sound was made. Michael paused a minute, and swallowed hard. He must have squeezed Norm tighter because a small complaining 'woof' escaped and caused Chuck to sit bolt upright in his bed.

"Who's there?" asked Chuck.

"It's just me," replied Michael.

"What the," exclaimed Chuck, "it's almost four in the morning. Are you sick or something?"

"Yeah," said Michael'

"Well, which is it," asked Chuck, "sick or something else?"

"Both," said Michael as Chuck turned the lamp on beside his bed.

"Okay pal, you're going to have to explain that one to me." Chuck sat up on the side of the bed and patted the spot beside him for Michael to sit down.

Michael clutched Norm even tighter. The little dog was his security blanket and his source of courage. He had never been so scared. He couldn't keep from shaking, and when he spoke his teeth chattered as if he was cold.

"YYYou seeee I I have ttto tttell you something I I I," he stammered.

Before he could go on, Chuck stopped him. He gently put his big hand on Michael's shoulder, "Its okay Michael you don't have to be afraid to tell me anything. Now take a deep breath, relax, and let's talk."

This had the effect of stopping the shaking, but tears silently began to stream down Michael's face. He dropped his head, and said, "You're going to hate me when I tell you this, but I didn't tell you the truth about Mr. Bradley's horse. I did throw that rock, but I didn't mean to hurt him. I'm sorry I lied to you, but I was afraid. I'll pack my stuff and be ready when the state people come to pick me up in the morning."

"Whoa there, Michael. I think you are getting a little ahead of yourself. If you want to leave we won't keep you here, but if you think we are going to send you away for a mistake, you are wrong. We all make mistakes, Michael. None of us are perfect. That's the great thing about having a family, you've always got someone to turn to when you need help."

When Michael heard Chuck's words, the dam broke, and he began to sob uncontrollably. Chuck was not prepared for the torrent of emotion that was pouring out of such a small little body. He put his arm around Michael and tried to comfort him, but he wasn't having much success. Michael's sobs had awakened Aunt Maggie, who came rushing into the room tying her bathrobe.

"Gracious me, what's wrong," she asked as she looked worriedly from Chuck to Michael to Norm.

Chuck told her what Michael had told him because Michael couldn't stop crying long enough to talk. When Aunt Maggie figured out what the problem was she took charge of the situation. She sat down by Michael on the bed and put her arms around him. Michael grabbed onto Aunt Maggie like a drowning man would grab a life preserver. He sobbed and sobbed until he was physically spent. Michael laid his head in Aunt Maggie's lap and she stroked his hair until he fell asleep. Aunt Maggie motioned for Chuck to go, and she stayed with Michael. She continued to stroke his hair, and pray over him as the sun began to shine and signal the start of a new day. She smiled to herself as she thought about how it really would be a new day for Michael. It would be the day that he found out that a family doesn't leave you.

Chapter 16

Robert Bradley was fuming. He had hardly slept a wink last night. He had been too angry. He was not a liar, and that was what had been implied at the Hayes' house when Chuck said he believed what that kid had said about injuring Doc. Well, he was going to prove to everybody who was lying and it sure wasn't going to be him. His truck practically slid sideways as he turned into Al Norton's driveway. He began to honk the horn to get Al to come outside. It worked.

"Dad-burn it Robert, what's got into you?" asked Al who was more than a little irritated at being honked at so loudly and early on a Monday morning.

"Get in the truck. I need you to go with me to Joe Hayes' house and tell him what you told me about that kid injuring Doc," said Robert.

"What!" exclaimed Al.

"You heard me. I went over there yesterday with the sheriff and told them what had happened, and they didn't believe me. I told them I'd be back today with my witness and the sheriff, so get in because we have to go and pick up Sheriff Laws next," said Robert.

"Thanks a lot," said Al, "when I told you about what I saw I never intended to have to get in the middle of you and Joe Hayes. If I had thought that would happen, I'd have kept my mouth shut."

"Well, it's too late for that now. The cat is out of the bag. I've already told Daws Laws we would meet him at his office to go to see Joe, that you were my witness, and would tell him what you told me. Now come on," said Robert.

Al Norton was not happy as he grabbed the door handle of the pick-up and yanked it open. Robert Bradley had given him permission to turkey hunt on his property, and although the season didn't open until the end of March, he had been out scouting for turkeys so he would know where to hunt when he had seen Michael. He knew Michael hadn't seen him because he had been wearing full camouflage and been sitting under a tree in a pasture on the opposite hill. He had seen the school bus let Michael off and watched him start down the road. Al saw him stoop down, grab a rock, throw it, and hit the horse. He had recognized him as the kid who had just come to live with Joe and Miss Maggie.

He felt a twinge of guilt now for telling Robert. The poor kid had been bounced around all his life and if anyone could help him it would be Miss Maggie. Like Robert said, the cat was out of the bag now. Robert had been fit to be tied when he had talked to him about how much the vet bill was on his horse, and how he just didn't have that kind of money. Robert had said he sure wished he knew how old Doc had gotten hurt, and before he thought about it, Al had told him he knew. Now look where he was, on his way over to big Joe Hayes' house with Robert and the sheriff. This was not a good way to start a week!

They arrived at the sheriff's office and didn't even have to get out. Daws was in his car waiting on them.

"Hello boys, I called Joe and told him we would see him this morning so let's get going because he's expecting us," said Daws, as he pulled out of his parking lot.

Robert fell in behind him, and in no time they were getting out at the Hayes house. Miss Maggie greeted them at the door, smiling and asked them to come in for some coffee and pound cake.

Al Norton suddenly felt like his day was taking a turn for the better because he had eaten Miss Maggie's pound cake before, and was more than happy to accept her invitation. Daws Laws was also smiling and looking at the steaming cups of coffee and large slabs of the moist cake on plates just waiting for them to sit down and eat. Robert Bradley felt himself softening for just a moment, but he caught himself in time to protest.

"Now Miss Maggie, we're not here for coffee and cake. We're here to settle what happened to my horse once and for all! I brought my witness!"

Al could feel his delicious piece of cake slipping away. He really wanted that cake and coffee. Why, it was barely 6:30 in the morning, and Robert had honked him out of his house before breakfast.

"Now Robert," Al said, "there's no reason to be rude to Miss Maggie's kind offer. We have plenty of time to straighten this out, maybe even while we have coffee and pound cake."

"That sounds like a plan to me," said Sheriff Daws.

Robert had the good sense to know when he was outnumbered, and grudgingly sat down at the table.

"That's better," said Aunt Maggie, "we're all friends and neighbors and there is no need for anger between us. Don't you agree, Robert?"

Robert had just put a delicious bite of cake in his mouth and still had the fork between his lips when he looked up at Miss Maggie. He made quite a sight. His wispy gray hair was thinning, and at the moment was standing straight up on his head, because he had just taken his hat off. Nobody kept their hat on at Miss Maggie's table because it was considered rude, and it was obvious that Robert hadn't combed his hair before he put his hat on this morning. The smiles Robert's comical picture elicited broke the tension of why the men were there. Just then Joe came into the kitchen followed by Michael.

"Robert, we owe you an apology," he said. "Michael came to us and told us what really happened. He lied because he was afraid, and I don't guess I can blame him. You and me did cause quite a ruckus and get the sheriff to jump in between us. I'd have probably done the same thing if I had been in Michael's shoes. That doesn't excuse what Michael did, and we are going to make it right. Now, what's it going to take to make you happy?"

This was not what Robert had been expecting at all, and he was unprepared for Joe's question. He thought a minute and said, "I need to have the vet bill paid."

"That's fair," said Joe.

"And I need someone to come and help take care of Doc. The vet said his leg has to be taken care of twice a day. He has to be kept in a clean stall until it heals, and the stall has to be cleaned twice a day to keep the chances of infection down."

"That's fair enough, too. We have talked to Michael and he is very sorry about what he did, and he wants to make it right. Now, he doesn't know anything about horses, but Robert, you have forgotten more about horses than most people ever knew, so I figure you can show Michael what he needs to do," said Joe.

At that Michael swallowed hard, and his eyes grew large at the thought of Mr. Bradley being his boss. He didn't know which was scarier, horses or Mr. Bradley?

Robert Bradley looked from Miss Maggie, to Joe, to Michael, and back to the sheriff. He didn't know what to say. Everything he came over here to fight about was dropped in his lap along with some great tasting food. Robert Bradley knew he had just been made an offer he couldn't refuse.

"Fine. Have the kid at my place this afternoon about 4:00 after he gets home from school, and I'll show him what to do."

"His name is Michael, Robert, and I know I can trust you with my nephew. He's a good boy. You'll see that the more you get to know him," said Aunt Maggie.

"Well, according to the vet, he'll be coming over for a long time," said Robert.

Michael took a deep breath, swallowed hard, and for the millionth time he wished he could take that rock throw back.

Chapter 17

Michael sat at his desk and watched the clock on the wall of his schoolroom. It was almost 3:00. He had been dreading 3:00 all day. He usually couldn't wait for dismissal from school, because he was always anxious to get home. That's funny he thought to himself, I think of Aunt Maggie's as home. He smiled to himself. It felt good to think of some place as home. His thoughts came back to more serious matters. He was worried about going to Mr. Bradley's house this afternoon. What if Uncle Joe left him there alone with Mr. Bradley? What if Mr. Bradley decided to beat him up for hurting his horse? He had been around plenty of grown-ups who liked to beat on kids. He knew Mr. Bradley was already mad at him. What would he do if it was just the two of them?

Suddenly the dismissal bell rang, and Michael was on his way to the parking lot to meet Uncle Joe.

"Hey Michael, over here," yelled Chuck.

Michael jogged to Chuck's truck, "I thought Uncle Joe was picking me up. What happened?"

"Nope, you're stuck with me. Miss Maggie thought it would be better if I went with you for the first day since Joe has a tendency to be a little hot tempered. I have to admit I think she is right. Now hop in and let's beat most of this after school traffic."

Michael did as Chuck said but he really didn't mind if they were caught in traffic. It would just make them a little later getting to Mr. Bradley's which suited him fine.

"Are you going to drop me off and come back to get me later?" Michael asked. He had to know if he was going to be alone at the Bradley farm.

Chuck's next words caused Michael to feel as if an elephant had gotten off his chest, "No, I think I'll hang around and see how you doctor a horse. I don't know much about horses, but I think they are beautiful animals. Maybe I'll learn something."

Chuck had been watching Michael and could tell how nervous he was, so he wasn't about to go off and leave him until Michael felt comfortable at the Bradley barn. He reached over and ruffled Michael's hair, "Don't worry, Mr. Bradley is really a good man. I know all you've seen of him is his temper, but it'll be okay I promise."

Michael wasn't sure about things being okay, but he was glad that Chuck was staying with him. Chuck started talking and telling him about Mr. Bradley.

"Mr. Bradley and his wife, Tamara, grew up here in Cedar Grove. They lived on the farm where he still lives now. Mr. Bradley was a horse trainer and farmer. He always said he couldn't make a living just being a farmer or a trainer but if he did both, he could, so he trained horses and raised corn, wheat, and hay. He was best at breaking young colts. No, wait, he always said you don't break a young horse, you teach and train them. I guess he was one of the first people to think that way. It sure must have worked because people were crazy about the way their horses turned out when Robert got through with them. He always had a long waiting list of people wanting him to train their horses.

Mr. Bradley and his wife had one child, Susan. They used to go to church with us. Every Sunday when I was little we either had Sunday lunch with the Bradley's or they ate lunch with us. Susan was the apple of her parent's eyes.

Actually everybody was crazy about her. She had the biggest smile and sweetest heart of any girl I've ever known. Boy, could she ride a horse. She definitely followed in her Dad's footsteps where horses were concerned. In fact, her Dad said she was going to be better than he was with horses, and that's saying something. I guess things started to go bad for Robert when his wife got sick and died. I think she had cancer. I know she was sick a good while before she died, because your Aunt Maggie was always taking food and going over to sit with Mrs. Bradley when Mr. Bradley had to be gone for a little while. Susan was just like all the rest of us and was crazy about Miss Maggie, as she called her. We had several prayer services for Mrs. Bradley, but in the end God's plan for her was to go home."

"Wasn't she at home already?" asked Michael.

"Going home is figure of speech, Christians use when a Christian dies. It means the person who dies has gone home to heaven," explained Chuck.

Michael thought for a moment. Heaven wasn't a new word he had heard at church, but the concept of heaven was. He thought heaven was just the top of the sky, but that wasn't what Chuck was talking about.

"What is heaven, Chuck?" asked Michael.

"Oh Michael, it's more wonderful than anything you can imagine. The Bible says it has streets of gold, and there will be no sorrow or sadness only joy and happiness. Think of the most beautiful place you have ever been, the best day you have ever had, the best you have ever felt both inside and out and that isn't even half of what is waiting for us in heaven."

"If it's that good why people don't just kill themselves and go there?" asked Michael.

Chuck grinned, "It doesn't work that way. First you have to obey God and do what He tells us to do. You can't kill yourself and go to heaven. God wants us to live out our lives for Him. He has a purpose for all our lives. We have to try to fulfill that purpose and help other people in the process. Think of going to heaven as going home to be with someone you love after being on a journey."

"Well, how do you know what you are supposed to do to obey God?"

Chuck grinned again, "That's easy, God gave us an instruction book. It's called the Bible, and everything we need to know is written in it. Here's our turn."

Chuck turned the truck off the highway, and across a railroad track. They turned in the first driveway past the tracks, and went down a long driveway that ended at a barn. Just beyond the barn was the house. The barn was huge. It looked like it could hold hundreds of bales of hay and lots of horses. It also looked neglected, like no one ever fixed anything up or took care of it.

As Michael and Chuck got out of the truck and walked into the hall of the barn, Michael noticed that almost all the stalls were empty and had cobwebs everywhere like nothing had been inside of them for a very long time. Some of the stall doors were hanging by only one hinge, and some of the boards in the stalls were rotten and broken. It was also very dark and it smelled stuffy. This barn didn't feel like Uncle Joe's barn.

Uncle Joe's barn was alive with chickens ducks, cows, dogs, and cats. It was an inviting place to be, especially to a twelve year old boy. Not this barn. Compared to Uncle Joe's barn, this one was just plain spooky.

They kept walking all the way down to the end of the hallway to the last stall on the left. The light was on in the stall, and Michael could see the horse and Mr. Bradley inside. This stall wasn't like the others. It was clean with lots of soft bedding. There was hay in the hay feeder, a big bucket of fresh water and a feed bucket on the wall in the corner. Mr. Bradley didn't hear their approach, and was bending down looking at the horse's swollen leg muttering to himself.

"Hello Mr. Bradley. Michael's here to start his new job for you. If it's alright with you, I'd kinda like to hang around until he's finished. I just might learn something myself," said Chuck.

Mr. Bradley straightened up somewhat stiffly and said, "Makes me no never mind. I was just deciding what I was going to do. I called the vet out like I told you, and the only thing he said he could do was give me a $575.00 bottle of antibiotics and tell me he couldn't do anything else. The rest of his bill was just to get him to come out to the farm and look at the horse."

It was obvious that Mr. Bradley thought he hadn't gotten his money's worth or much help. He turned back to look at Doc again.

Michael quickly took in Mr. Bradley's appearance. He was about Uncle Joe's age, but there was an air of despair about him, like he hadn't been happy in a long time. Funny, thought Michael, I know how that feels. It made Michel uneasy to remember just how bad it felt to be that sad. He still had to pinch himself to be sure Aunt Maggie, Uncle Joe, Chuck, Max, and everything else here in Cedar Grove were real and he wouldn't lose them like he had lost everything before. Michael began to think that maybe Mr. Bradley wasn't so much grumpy as he was unhappy. Suddenly, Mr. Bradley didn't seem quite so scary to Michael.

Chapter 18

Michael heard the beep, beep, beep of the alarm clock and quickly roused from his deep slumber to shut the alarm off before it woke Max. It was 4:30 a.m. and time for him to get up to go to Mr. Bradley's and take care of Doc's foot. It had been two weeks since Chuck had taken him to the barn for his first lesson in veterinary medicine.

It hadn't gone too well the first time. Mr. Bradley had shown him how to wash Doc's injured foot with a hose for twenty minutes. This had to be done twice a day. The cold water helped to reduce the swelling and also helped to wash the cut out cleanly so that no dirt or debris was stuck inside to cause more problems with healing. After the water bath, Michael was shown how to apply a salve that Mr. Bradley mixed up on his own. Since the vet hadn't given him much encouragement on getting Doc well, Mr. Bradley had decided to use the skills he had developed from years of working with horses to help Doc. After the water, Michael would disinfect the cut with iodine, and then apply the salve. That was the plan, but for the first two days it didn't work too well.

Michael had never been around a horse in his life, especially one as large and intimidating as Doc. Even with a badly infected foot, and very sick, Doc could still move fast enough for Michael to be startled and jump. This in turn, caused Doc to jump even more. It became a dangerous situation for both horse and boy. Mr. Bradley almost told Michael to just forget about helping and go home, but he didn't. He really didn't know why he didn't except that for the first time in a long time he seemed to have a sense of purpose. He needed to help Doc even if he still blamed the horse for the worst thing that had ever happened to him, and he needed to help Michael learn how to be around a horse and not get hurt. He didn't admit to himself that he almost looked forward to Michael coming each day.

With Robert's guidance, Michael learned how to move slowly and in a way that wasn't threatening. He told Michael that horses are prey animals and that the first response of a prey animal is to run from fear and danger. Even if Doc couldn't run on his hurt foot it didn't change the fact that when he felt scared by Michael's actions, he still tried to take flight.

He also told Michael that horses look to humans for leadership much the same way that in a herd of wild horses, they look to the stallion as the herd leader. With that in mind, when Michael became nervous or uneasy he tried very hard not to let it show and upset Doc. Michael didn't know if he could control his emotions enough for Doc to remain calm, but after trying it a few times and seeing the dramatic difference in the horse he was very pleased and encouraged.

Robert also told Michael that horses are much like little kids. When a child runs to their parent scared and crying, the parent calms them and tells them the are safe, and the child quits crying. If the parent had gotten upset and been afraid too, the child would have only gotten worse. The same thing works with horses. When people stay calm around frightened horses they settle down. If people yell and scream at them, the horses think something bad is going to happen and really act up. This caused a light to go on in Michael's head! He had never thought that an animal would react to his actions. It reminded him of all those foster homes when he was mad all the time, because he just knew the people would kick him out. That was what he had been doing, reacting to the people where he had been placed.

For the first time in his life something was looking to him for help and security. Now that he knew how to help Doc, he was determined to be good at his new job. He knew what being scared felt like, and he was going to make sure Doc wasn't scared of him. He watched and listened to everything Mr. Bradley did and said. He tried his best to exactly imitate his movements and his calmness. He learned how to put a halter on Doc, get his lead rope and take him outside his stall to hose down his injury by himself. The first few times it took all his will to not shake when the big horse made a sudden movement or seemed to get too close to him. Gradually, he became more comfortable and so did Doc. Now he looked forward to going to the barn. Doc was once again working magic only this time not with barrels, but with the heart of a wounded child.

Michael pulled on his jeans, grabbed his book bag, and went downstairs to the kitchen. As usual, there were wonderful smells coming from there. Aunt Maggie was up and cooking his breakfast. She had decided that she would take him to Mr. Bradley's in the mornings. She would leave him while she went back and got everybody else up and fed breakfast. Then Uncle Joe would pick him up at 7:30 and take him to school. Aunt Maggie insisted that he eat a good breakfast before they left so Michael slid into the chair at the table with his mouth already watering. He had bacon, eggs, biscuits, jelly, and orange juice. While he was eating, Aunt Maggie was wrapping up at least four biscuits and bacon to take to Mr. Bradley. She said she had to cook anyway, and she doubted that Robert ate like he should living by himself as he did. Aunt Maggie sure loved to feed folks.

Maggie was smiling to herself as she thought about the new jeans, shirt, and boots Michael was wearing. She had hoped Michael would change his baggy clothes for some better fitting ones, but she was amazed when he asked her if he could maybe get some western jeans and boots like Chuck wore. She knew she could thank a big red horse for this change, too. She had seen Michael go from being downright afraid of Robert and his horse to talking about Doc and how he was doing. He also mentioned Robert often and would tell her some of the things he was teaching Michael about taking care of horses.

Once again she was amazed at the way God works. He had taken a boy from an inner city, plopped him smack down in the middle of the country, and used an incident of harm to accomplish so much good. Here was Michael coming alive on a farm, going to a man's home that had lost everything from hope to his belief in his God, and both of them were learning from each other and enriching each other's life.

She knew that if anybody had asked Robert about Michael he would have told them Michael was just making up for injuring Doc. He wouldn't have let on that he even liked Michael, but Maggie knew differently. In the two weeks that she had been taking Michael to Robert's, she had noticed that he had gone from being an old sour-puss to sometimes almost smiling when they pulled into his drive. That was one of God's wonderful ways, thought Maggie, turning a mess into a blessing.

She finished wrapping up Robert's breakfast about the same time Michael finished his.

"There, I'm ready to go if you are," she said.

Michael downed the last of his orange juice and grabbed his backpack as he said, "Yes maam, we're burning daylight."

Aunt Maggie smiled and said, "Now that sounds familiar, but the sun is just starting to rise I guess we're almost burning daylight."

Michael was out the door and heading to the car. Maggie smiled as she watched the newest cowboy in his boots and jeans. It was quite a change from a scared kid in baggy pants. Yep, she thought, God sure does good work.

Chapter 19

Doc was sleeping in his stall when the sound of a car door closing woke him. His head came up and he stretched his neck and back to throw off the last cobwebs of slumber. He listened intently for a sound that he had come to know. There it was, the footsteps of the boy who had been taking care of him. Doc was beginning to look for him to come and get him out of his stall to take care his wounded foot. At first, the boy made Doc so nervous that he tried to get away from him. Every move Doc made caused the boy to jump and that made Doc move even more, but whatever it was that had been scaring the boy went away and now when he came, Doc could relax. Doc didn't realize that he had been what was making Michael nervous. When Michael had been with Doc at first it was a case of the scared leading the terrified.

Doc walked over to his stall door. The door was only about four feet high. It was a half door and Doc could stick his head out to look down the long hallway of the barn. Sure enough, there was the boy coming toward him with a smile on his face. It had been a long time since Doc had been cared for in a stall on a daily basis. For the last ten years, he had weathered all the seasons in the far back pasture by himself with little shelter and some hay during the cold winter months. He didn't understand at first what had happened. He had always been in a nice big stall. The same stall as a matter of fact, that he was in now. Every morning very early, Susan would come to the barn to feed him with her happy greeting of "Good morning Mr. Big". It was a ritual that was a part of his everyday life. After she fed him and gave him time to eat,

Susan would get him out of his stall. They would usually go for a ride on the trails that wound their way around their farm. It was beautiful with streams, deer, and wild turkey for companions. There were steep gullies to climb, fallen trees to jump, and big hills to hurry over. Doc loved ever minute of it.

What Doc didn't know was that Susan was keeping him in condition so that when she asked him to run barrels, his mind was clear from the relaxing rides, and his body was fit and strong from the terrain of the trails. Susan knew that once a barrel horse knew the barrel pattern and knew his job when he entered the arena, he didn't need constant working on the barrels. Doing so had ruined many good barrel horses. Horses, her father used to say, were like little kids with short attention spans and easily tired of too much work. To keep a trained barrel horse sharp and perform well, you kept their mind clear and their physical condition excellent.

Robert Bradley always said the best way to condition a horse was on trails. Not dangerous trails or rough trails, but trails with enough varied terrain to work all their muscles, expand their lung capacity, and get their heart rate really pumping. Susan found that once again, her father knew what he was talking about. The only time Doc saw a barrel now was when they were competing. It was almost like a treat for Doc to run barrels by doing it this way. He never tired of the game it became or grew to dread entering the arena the way he had when Brian Adams owned him. Every aspect of his life had improved when Susan got him.

It had been that way until she had left him so long ago. With each passing day that he was back in his stall he seemed to remember more and miss her more all over again. He had taken to lifting his head in the air and breathing deeply to try and catch her scent again. It was something he had stopped doing a long time ago.

Michael reached Doc's stall door. He reached up and began to stroke Doc's wide blaze down the center of his face. Michael found that being around Doc was fast becoming one of his favorite things to do. The big red horse made him feel like he was doing something good. He was the cause of the injury that had given him the job at Mr. Bradley's barn, and for that he was truly sorry. He had apologized to Doc every time he tended the wound from the rock. As much as he hated what he had done to the big horse, he was so grateful that he was the one caring for Doc. Getting to know the horse and how to handle him had given him a tremendous boost of confidence like he had never had before. Michael had always been dependent on everyone he lived with in all his foster homes. He had never had a say in any aspect of his life. Now, he was responsible for another living creature. A big, beautiful, imposing creature that seemed to like him and was willing to trust him to do the right thing. He was going to make sure he didn't let Doc down.

"Hi big guy. Where's Mr. Bradley?" Michael asked. When he had gotten out of Aunt Maggie's car the barn lights had been off. They were usually always on. Aunt Maggie didn't want to leave Michael but he had assured her that he would be fine, and he knew where the light switch was to light up the barn until the sun was high enough in the sky to do it for him. Aunt Maggie finally agreed to go, but she wasn't happy about it. It made Michael feel good to have someone who worried about him. It was yet another thing that he was experiencing by living in his new home. For what seemed like the millionth time Michael prayed that God would make this home last.

"Here I am, boy. What's that you got in that sack?" asked Robert.

"Oh, here, Aunt Maggie thought you might like some of her biscuits with bacon on them," said Michael as he thrust the sack out to Mr. Bradley.

That was what Robert had been hoping to hear. Everybody knew that Maggie Hayes made the best biscuits in the county. In his opinion, they were the best anywhere. The crisp, fried, bacon was an added bonus. Robert's mouth was already watering at the thought of his breakfast feast. It was working out pretty well with the boy coming over two times a day, especially since he knew what to do and how to do it. He found himself looking forward to Michael coming, but he told himself it was only because it meant less work for him and he got care packages from Miss Maggie.

Robert had slept later than he meant to. He hadn't even had his morning coffee. A fact he intended to fix immediately since he had bacon and biscuits to go with it.

"Do you think you will be okay down here without me? I have some things to take care of in the house for a little while," Robert told Michael.

"Sure Mr. Bradley. Doc and I will be fine," said Michael. He knew what Mr. Bradley had to take care of, and it was in the sack he was holding. Michael may have been twelve, but he wasn't stupid, plus he knew how good Aunt Maggie's biscuits were.

"Alright, be sure you do everything just like I've taught you. I'll be back to check on you before you leave." With that Robert turned and began to walk briskly up the drive back to his house.

Michael watched him leave with a grin on his face, and then he turned back to the big, red horse. Just as he bent over to pick up Doc's injured foot, he was pushed face forward into the bedding of Doc's stall! Before he could move he felt the point of something cold, sharp, and metal between his shoulder blades!

Suddenly, he heard a voice say, "If you don't want to be slit open like the horse thief you are, you won't move."

Michael had never felt more scared or alone in his life!

Chapter 20

Aunt Maggie was finishing her breakfast with the rest of her family. She was studying her almost eaten egg with a frown on her face. Uncle Joe looked up and smiled.

"Are you mad at that egg, honey? If you are, just bite it again and then it should be all gone, and so will that frown you've got on your pretty face." Uncle Joe still thought Aunt Maggie was the most beautiful woman he had ever seen. He smiled at her as she looked at him.

"Oh, Joe, I just can't get rid of a bad feeling I got when I left Michael at Robert's barn. It was dark and I didn't want to leave him there, but he insisted he knew where the lights were and what to do. I want him to become confident and sure of himself, so I left him there like he wanted me to, but it just doesn't feel right," said Aunt Maggie.

"Now sugar, I know you and I also know what a mother hen you can be. That's not a bad thing, but sometimes you have to let a kid stand on his own two feet. It does them a world of good. Even if they make a mistake, they can learn from it and not do it again. Shoot, I ought to know I've made enough mistakes in my time. He'll be fine. I don't think he will get into any trouble at Robert's barn. We don't exactly live in a high crime area where Michael is likely to get attacked or beat up," laughed Uncle Joe.

"I don't know Joe, I just feel that something isn't right," said Aunt Maggie.

"Well, if it will make you feel better I'll go on over there and stay until it's time for him to go to school. I can't have my best girl wearing a frown. I'm finished with my breakfast anyway, and a mighty fine breakfast it was thank you very much," laughed Uncle Joe.

"Would you, Joe?" asked Aunt Maggie feeling better already. She knew if anything was wrong, Joe would take care of it.

"You betcha sweetheart, I'll be back after I take Michael to school with a full report," he said as he bent to kiss her bye.

Joe went out, got in his truck, and started over to the Bradley barn not knowing what was happening to Michael.

Michael was not about to move. A million thoughts were racing through his head. Who was this person? What did they think he was doing? Why would they threaten him for taking care of Doc? Most importantly, what was he going to do to get out of this mess alive? While he was trying to formulate a plan, he heard footsteps approaching. Please don't let it be another crazed killer!

The next thing he knew, he felt the knife leave his shoulder blades. He still didn't move until he heard, "Charlene Nicole, what do you think you are doing?"

It was a woman's voice and a very angry woman at that. Michael rolled over and took in a scene that would have been comical if he hadn't been so humiliated. He got his first good look at his assailant. It was a girl! She looked about ten years old with wildly curly, red, hair and thick coke bottle glasses. She had on jeans, boots, a tee shirt with a barrel racer on it, and she still held the weapon. It was the pitch fork that Michael used to clean out Doc's stall twice a day. No wonder it felt so sharp against his skin. The lady had the girl by the arm, and the expression on her face let the girl know she was not happy. For the first time, Michael really looked at the lady. When he did he didn't see anything else. She had beautiful shiny black hair, big dark eyes, and the prettiest skin he had ever seen. She was beautiful. He didn't know who she was, but he knew he liked her already. While he was taking this all in, he became aware of Mr. Bradley, and even Uncle Joe. Now, what was Uncle Joe doing here so early?

"Mom, don't call me Charlene. You know I'm supposed to be called Charlie!" said the girl.

"Right now young lady, I think you better be quiet and listen to me. This young man is working for Mr. Bradley, and you owe him an apology. Now put down that pitch fork, help him up, and apologize."

Michael wished the ground would open up and swallow him. He had never been so embarrassed in his life. Not only did this girl knock him down and scare him to death, but he had to be saved by her mother. Now she was trying to help him get up! Michael brushed her hand aside, got to his feet, and glared at her.

"What's the big idea?" he asked her.

"I'm sorry," she said, "but when I found you in Doc's stall, I thought you were trying to steal him. Everybody knows Doc was Susan's horse."

Michael looked up at Mr. Bradley and saw him grimace at the girl's last words. Before he had time to think about it, Uncle Joe said, "Robert, what's going on here?"

"Don't get your hackles up Joe. This here is Tessa Jackson and her daughter Charlene."

Before Robert could continue Charlene interrupted with, "My name is Charlie."

"Excuse me," said Robert, "Charlie. Tessa was a good friend to Susan and to me, after Susan was gone. She needed a place to keep her horse, that big gray over there in the stall across from Doc's, so I told her to bring him here. They got in kinda late last night, and I didn't have time to tell them about Michael coming to care for Doc until we heard the commotion coming from the barn. That was after Charlie had gotten the drop on Michael with the pitch fork." Robert tried to keep the amusement out of his voice, but he wasn't completely successful.

"Well", said Uncle Joe, "Charlie sure makes a big first impression, right Michael?"

Once again, Michael wanted to be anywhere except where he was at the moment. "Yes sir, if that's what you call attacking somebody while their back was turned." Michael didn't want them to think she had gotten him down fair and square. She had cheated!

"Charlie, don't you have something to say to Michael?" said Tessa.

"Do I have to?" said Charlie.

"If you want to be able sit down for supper tonight, the answer is yes," said her mother.

Charlie lowered her head and a barely audible "sorry" came out.

"Oh no, that's not good enough. I mean a real apology Charlene," said her mother with added emphasis on Charlene.

Charlie obviously knew how far to push her mother and this time she said, "I'm sorry I thought you were a horse thief, and threw you on the ground, and made you lay there in the stall, and not move, and scared you to death, and had to have all the grown ups come and save you."

That was just great! As if he didn't feel silly enough already, Charlie's apology managed to put everything he was feeling into words in front of everybody. How was he ever going to live this one down? At least Max hadn't witnessed his humiliation. That would have been too much.

"Hey Michael, you got sawdust all over you!"

Michael closed his eyes and groaned. Correction, Max had seen everything. He just didn't see Max because he was behind Uncle Joe. Michael had a feeling it was going to be a long day at school.

Chapter 21

The April breezes were blowing the leaves of the big maple tree outside Michael and Max's bedroom. It was a moonlit night, and the leaves made slow, moving, shadows on the ceiling that would normally have put Michael quickly to sleep. Tonight, Michael's eyes were wide open. He kept replaying the events of the day in his mind. Just as he had feared, by second period at school, Max must have told everybody about "Charlie" getting the drop on him and having him face down in the stall with the pitch fork in his back. The first fifty times some kid came up behind him and stuck their finger or pencil in his back and said "stick em up" in a high little girl voice, he had been able to try and laugh it off, but by the time the last bell rang to dismiss school, it was all he could do not to clobber somebody!

He had been riding the school bus to Mr. Bradley's farm in the afternoons to take care of Doc and clean his stall. Uncle Joe or Chuck would pick him up depending on which one showed up first about 6:00. The school bus was turning on the road where Mr. Bradley lived and slowing to let him off. As Michael was going down the steps to exit the bus, he was hoping with all his might that Charlie was not at the barn. He had gotten in the habit of looking forward to going to the barn and being with Doc. If that red headed demon was there it was going to ruin it for him. He walked down the hall of the barn to Doc's stall and there was no sign of her! He looked quickly over to the stall where the gray horse had been and it was gone! Maybe they had moved. Suddenly, things were looking up.

Michael went happily into Doc's stall and patted him on his massive neck. Since Michael had been caring for Doc he had been brushing him every day, and it showed in the way his red coat glistened. When he had first been put in the barn his coat was rough and dull. With the grooming and shedding of his winter coat, Doc was shining like he did when Susan took such good care of him.

Michael had no way of knowing that Doc looked for him to come each day. Animals seem to have an internal clock and Doc was no different. Twice a day, morning and afternoon, Doc knew about the time that Michael would be there and began to watch for him. He had begun to neigh or talk softly to Michael when he saw him. Michael had been surprised the first time it had happened, but now he liked for Doc to talk to him. As Michael patted Doc's neck the big horse nuzzled him on his arm. Michael reached into his jeans pocket and pulled out the carrot strips that had been in his lunch sack Aunt Maggie had made for him. It wasn't that he didn't like carrots, he knew Doc liked them more. Doc immediately saw the treat and made short work of it. Michael smiled and began to brush Doc before he took care of his foot. It was a quiet time that both horse and boy enjoyed together

"Well, I see you're back."

It was a simple statement, but one that made Michael grit his teeth. He stopped brushing, turned around, and there SHE was!

"For your information, I am here every day, morning and afternoon," Michael said turning away to dismiss Charlie. Charlie was not one to be dismissed.

"Oh, I know. I know all about you. I know you just moved in with your Aunt and Uncle. I know that you threw a rock and really messed up Doc's leg, you jerk." Charlie added the last part with great emphasis. "What did that horse ever do to you? If I was him, I'd stomp you into a greasy spot." With that, Charlie pushed her coke bottle glasses back up on her nose, and crossed her arms, waiting for an explanation.

That did it. She had hit a nerve. The problem was that she was right. Michael had already told himself everything she had just said to him, but he sure didn't appreciate hearing it again from her! Michael turned around, stood up very straight and said, "I think you need to mind your own business, Charlene." He had deliberately used her full name because he knew she didn't like it. Michael did not know her well enough to realize what using her full name would do to her.

Michael had never seen a sight quite like the one Charlie presented. Her whole face turned the color of her hair, and she jumped straight up in the air. When she came down she started jumping and kicking in his direction, all the while shouting, "KEE AAHH" over and over again. The next thing he knew she began to spin along with the jumping, kicking, and shouting. Michael instinctively jumped back and into Doc's big broad side. Doc was also looking wide eyed at the wild creature that was coming toward him. Doc turned quickly to put his head in the back corner of his stall. When he did, since Michael was leaning against his side, it propelled Michael straight into the red tornado. Michael was losing his balance and beginning to fall forward. As he did so, Charlie was in the middle of a major kick with her brand new, pointed toe, cowboy boots. The toe of Charlie's boot made contact with Michaels head, and suddenly everything went black for Michael as he fell to the ground in a heap and did not move.

Charlie and Doc both stood perfectly still. Doc waiting for what she was going to do next, and Charlie waiting to see if Michael was going to move. When it became apparent that Michael wasn't moving, Charlie said, "Oh no, Doc, I've killed him. Boy am I gonna be in trouble now."

Charlie tried to think what to do next. Maybe she could hide the body. Maybe she could bury him under the big dirt pile at the back of the property. Maybe she could just leave and no one would ever know she had been there. While she was trying to figure out what to do next, she heard voices, lots of voices. They were coming this way. Now what was she going to do? Charlie began to think fast. Suddenly, she remembered the little old lady that used to be their neighbor. Her name was Mrs. Brewster. She used to fall down sometimes and when she talked, it seldom made sense. Charlie and her Mom used to check on her a lot, before she moved in with one of her children. What was it her Mom told her was wrong with Mrs. Brewster? It was something that sounded strange to her. It was something like dominoes, or detention. No, that wasn't right. The voices were coming closer! Quick, she had to remember! Then she had it. Charlie ran into the hallway of the barn and saw Mr. Bradley, Uncle Joe, and her mother.

"Come quick. Michael has demonia," she said while she waved her arms wildly. Charlie was nothing if not dramatic.

"What on earth are you talking about?" asked her mother.

"It's Michael, he just fell over like Mrs. Brewster used to do," said Charlie as they all stood for a minute talking in the barn's hallway.

"Charlie, Mrs. Brewster was eighty four years old. She used to fall because she couldn't walk too well any more," said Tessa.

"Oh no Mom, I'm sure it's the same thing because remember how she used to say things that didn't make sense. Well, I wouldn't believe a thing Michael tells you, because he has that same stuff. You know, its called demonia," Charlie finished with a very superior look on her face for her diagnosis of Michael's problem.

"Charlie," her Mom sighed, "He can't have the same thing. You are talking about a condition called dementia. It's something that only older adults can get, not twelve year old boys." While they were talking, they made their way to Doc's stall. When Tessa looked over the door and saw Michael out cold on the floor of the stall her eyes grew wide and the first thing she said was, "Charlie, what is going on?"

Chapter 22

Michael kept watching the play of the shadows of the leaves on the ceiling of his bedroom. He gingerly reached his index finger up to the big knot just above his right eyebrow to touch it. As soon as his finger made contact with the golf ball size knot he grimaced. Now, what was he going to do? He knew he was going to have a big, black, eye by morning. It had already started to turn a deep shade of purple by the time he went to bed in spite of Aunt Maggie's best efforts with an ice bag. Today had been bad enough with all the joking about Charlie getting the drop on him. How was he going to stand it when everyone found out his black eye came from the same girl?

Max hadn't been any help. He just giggled and told him, "If I were you I'd pretend to be sick until it went away and stay home from school. If it helps any, I promise I won't spill the beans about this. Sometimes guys have to stick together."

Michael began to think about what he and Aunt Maggie had talked about after he got home. Everyone else had finished their supper and gone their different ways, and Michael and Aunt Maggie went into the family room. Aunt Maggie had sat on the sofa and told Michael to put his head in her lap so she could hold an ice pack on his injured eye. Michael liked the feeling of having his head in her lap and someone taking care of him. It was something that had rarely happened in his young life. They had a long talk about Charlie and all the things that had happened to him since she had showed up. After Aunt Maggie had told him some of Charlie's story, he wasn't quite so ready to strangle her the next time he saw her.

Aunt Maggie told him how Charlene was named after her Dad, Charles. Her Dad had left them and married another woman who had a son. Charlene had been about seven years old when he left, and she felt like his leaving was her fault. She thought he left them because he wanted a son instead of a daughter, so she began to call herself Charlie and insisted that everyone else do the same. Her Mother tried to make her see that she was wrong to think that her Dad had wanted a boy instead of a girl, but Charlie wouldn't listen. It was the only explanation that made sense to her. How else could her father just up and leave them. She decided that if she got rough and tough enough, he would come back.

When her Mother saw how Charlie was being affected by Charles leaving them, she put Charlie in martial arts training thinking it would develop discipline and focus in her life and keep her from getting into scrapes at school. Charlie loved it and became very good at it. The problem was she became too good. She kept getting into trouble at school only now she could really beat up the other kids. That was why they wound up in Cedar Grove. Tessa had decided the best way to change Charlie's behavior was to go somewhere different and get a new start. That was also why they were keeping their horse at Mr. Bradley's farm, and the reason Michael had met Charlie.

"Why is she still so mad, Aunt Maggie? I never had a Dad and I wasn't that mad about it?" said Michael.

"I know, sweetie. You deserved a Dad, like all children do. God's plan is for a child to have a loving mother and father, and that's what is best for any child. The problem is a lot of adults don't think about their children before they think about themselves, and they make some very bad choices without understanding how a child sees things. Charlie's problem is that she feels rejected by her father, like he just threw her away. It caused a hurt in her heart that may never heal. Acting like she does, in a very strange way, is her way of dealing with her feelings. She can't beat up her father like she does kids, even though that's really what she wants to do. So she gets into a scrap at school and feels better for a little while, but before long the feelings of rejection come back just like water begins to boil every time you put it on the stove. Her father's desertion doesn't ever go away or stop hurting so she finds a way to release some of the pressure. The problem is it isn't the right way."

"I feel bad for her because of what her Dad did to her, Aunt Maggie, but why did it have to be me that she decided to use for a punching bag?" asked Michael.

"I don't know the answer to that, honey, but I do know what God's answer would be for how you should treat Charlie," said Aunt Maggie.

"Yeah, I know how I'm going to treat her," said Michael, "I'm gonna knock her head off first thing the next time I see her."

"Will that make you feel better?" asked Aunt Maggie.

"Boy, will it. Maybe I'll be able to walk through the halls at school without everybody laughing at me because I got a black eye from a girl."

"You know, she isn't very big, and she is two years younger than you are. Do you think that will make the other kids think better of you for beating up a little red headed girl with glasses?" asked Aunt Maggie.

Michael got quiet and his eyebrows drew together in a frown, as much as the swelling over his right one would allow that is, while he thought about what Aunt Maggie had said. The idea of being known as the guy that beat up a little girl at school was not very appealing. He hadn't thought of it that way. In his mind, she was Hurricane Charlie, and she had gotten the better of him twice. Aunt Maggie had painted a picture of the way he would be seen if he went through with his plan. This was not working the way he intended for it to.

"Uh, when you put it that way, it makes me look pretty bad doesn't it, Aunt Maggie?" said Michael with such a look of defeat that Aunt Maggie had to stifle a smile while she held the icepack on his eye and stroked his head.

Michael just wished he could stay there forever, with his head in her lap and her stroking his hair. He didn't think anything had ever felt so good in all his life. However, he knew that tomorrow he would have to face Charlie again and he really needed a plan. Her Mother had been so angry with her when she found about what had happened, that for Charlie's punishment, she was going to have to do Michael's chores at the barn for two weeks. Michael hadn't wanted her to, because he liked the time he spent with Doc all by himself, but her Mother insisted. They finally decided that Michael would continue to take care of Doc and spend time with him. Charlie would have to clean the stall and wash the water bucket, not only for Doc, but for Tessa's gray horse, too. That meant that the first thing in the morning, he would see Charlie again, at least with his good eye.

Michael thought a minute and then asked, "You said you knew what God's plan would be for me to handle Charlie?"

Aunt Maggie just smiled and nodded.

"What is it Aunt Maggie?" asked Michael.

"To be as nice to her as you possibly can," she said.

Michael's eye got very big, the other one was too swollen to open wide, and said, "Oh no, just look at me, Aunt Maggie."

"I am and I see somebody that I think is very special. I see a boy who has had too much heartache for his twelve years, but who has become one of my favorite people. You have a good heart Michael. You can understand some of the problems that Charlie is having, because she feels so rejected. In her case, it comes from her own father, not foster parents. She needs our help, Michael, not our anger."

"How do I do that when I'm so mad at her?" asked Michael.

"Well God tells us in the Bible to repay evil with good. Would you say that Charlie had done evil to you?" asked Aunt Maggie.

"Boy would I," said Michael.

"The Bible also says that if you do that, you will heap coals of fire on the heads of people who were mean to you."

"Now you're talking. I'd like to set her head on fire," said Michael.

"It's a figure of speech, honey. It means that if you repay good for bad, the person who was bad will feel ashamed of themselves and hopefully they will learn a lesson and not act that way again. In that way, you will have helped them to be a better person," said Aunt Maggie.

"Can I think about that for a while, Aunt Maggie," asked Michael. He wasn't quite ready to give up on knocking her head off.

"Of course you can, honey," smiled Aunt Maggie.

Michael's eye was starting to get heavy with sleep. The one that Hurricane Charlie had kicked had already swelled shut. He had been thinking about what Aunt Maggie had said. It was going to look bad if he beat up a little girl with glasses. Even if he knew she was a demon, no one else would. He sure didn't want to keep on like he was going. He was getting pretty tired of her making him look so bad. Maybe if he did what Aunt Maggie said, she would change. One thing was for sure, he certainly didn't want to have to spend the next two weeks around her the way she was now. It looked like Aunt Maggie's solution was the only one he had. It wasn't the plan he would have picked, but at least it was a plan.

Chapter 23

Michael heard the alarm clock buzzing. It was 4:30 a.m. and time to get up and go to the barn. He kept reaching for the clock to turn it off so that it wouldn't wake Max, but he couldn't see it. His good eye was buried in the pillow and his Hurricane Charlie eye was not about to open so he could see. Finally, he managed to knock the alarm clock off the bedside table with a crash. Oh well, so much for not waking up Max!

"Good grief Michael," said Max, "I'm trying to sleep! I'd give you a black eye if a little girl hadn't already beat me to it."

Michael heard the giggle but it still rubbed him the wrong way for Max to bring it up.

"Max, you promised not to say anything about Charlie and my black eye at school. You weren't just kidding were you? You really won't say anything will you?"

"Course not buddy," said Max still giggling, "but we aren't at school now. You didn't think I'd let you off completely did you?"

Michael groaned, partly from what Max had said but mostly from sitting up so quickly in bed, and causing what felt like a 50 pound hammer to start beating on the inside of his head!

"Ow," he said as he sat up and swung his feet over the side of the bed, "I think my head is going to explode! I guess I can handle it here at home if you'll keep quiet at school. Now go back to sleep. I'll see you later." With that Michael dressed quickly and went downstairs.

Max lay in bed laughing to himself. Most kids would have been mad at being awakened so early, but Max was always looking for something to laugh about. This was going to be a gold mine. Michael and Hurricane Charlie, as they were all beginning to call her, were going to be one joke after another. Max smiled to himself as he thought of something else. Michael had said he could handle being teased at home. It was the first time he had called their house his home. Yep, he could handle having a brother, too!

Aunt Maggie was just going to the foot of the stairs to call Michael when he came down.

"Oh my," she said as she got her first look at Michael's eye after it had swelled more overnight. "How does that feel?"

"Not too good, Aunt Maggie. I've got a headache something awful."

"From the way it looks, I can believe it," she said.

Michael hadn't seen himself yet because he didn't want to turn the light on in the bedroom with Max trying to sleep. He went over to the mirror in the hallway and got his first look at the damage overnight from Hurricane Charlie!

"Aunt Maggie," wailed Michael, "I look like some kind of mutant from a horror movie!"

Aunt Maggie didn't answer right away. She had to agree with Michael, but she couldn't let him know it. Not only was his right eye swelled so big that the swelling reached from his hair line to his lower cheek, but the blue, black, and purple colors of the bruising covered almost the whole right side of his face. That has to hurt, Aunt Maggie thought to herself.

"After you eat your breakfast, I'll give you something for your headache. I don't want you to take it on an empty stomach."

She looked at Michael and knew what he was thinking. It was going to be hard to explain his face at school.

"You know Michael, I think it would be best if after you take care of Doc, you come back home and put ice on your eye again today. We need to get some of that swelling down, and since today is Friday, there won't be any school tomorrow so we can ice it down tomorrow, too. By Monday your eye should look a lot better."

A flood of relief washed over Michael. He had been dreading going to school today, and after he got a look at himself he didn't know what he was going to do. His relief was short lived though, because he knew that even if it looked better by Monday his eye would still be black, and he would still have to answer some questions about it.

"What am I going to say when the kids ask me what happened to my eye?"

"Well, I think the truth is always best," said Aunt Maggie

That was just what Michael was afraid of. Even if Max did keep quiet, his eye was still impossible to miss. Michael sat at the table and put his head down on his arms. Even that hurt.

"Tell them that you were taking care of a big horse that ran into you and caused you to fall and hit your head. It knocked you out and when you came to, you had a major shiner. That is one hundred percent true. You don't have to say a word about Charlene."

Michael jumped up, and hugged Aunt Maggie. What she had said was true, but he hadn't thought of it that way. Even though his head was pounding, he kept on hugging her. She always knew how to make everything better!

The medicine Aunt Maggie had given him after breakfast had begun to work and the pain in his head was getting better, except for when the car hit a bump in the road. They were on the way to Mr. Bradley's barn and he would have to see HER! Aunt Maggie had made Mr. Bradley his usual sack of bacon and biscuits, and she had suggested that he take some to Charlie. Michael hadn't wanted to, but he couldn't tell Aunt Maggie that, so he had Charlie's sack too. What he really wanted to do was throw them at her, but he knew that would disappoint Aunt Maggie, so he couldn't do it. They were tuning into Mr. Bradley's drive and the lights were on in the barn. As Michael opened the door to get out, Mr. Bradley walked up to say hello to Aunt Maggie.

"Morning Miss Maggie is that some of your mouth watering biscuits and bacon I smell?" he asked. Before she could answer, Mr. Bradley got

Brenda Dawson

his first look at Michael's face. "Land sakes, boy, it looks like you've been fighting a buzz saw! I don't think I've ever seen an eye swell up that big. And just look at the color on that thing. If it's this purple in the barn light, I can't wait to see it in daylight. Take this as a lesson, boy, watch out for women!" Mr. Bradley finished off with and emphatic pat on Michael's back that made his head begin to pound again. Robert Bradley scooped up his sack of breakfast with a smile on his face as he told Miss Maggie thanks and good bye. He began to whistle as he walked back to his house for his coffee to go with his biscuits.

"I'm glad somebody got a laugh out of the way I look," said Michael sarcastically.

Aunt Maggie sat behind the wheel of the car with a thoughtful look on her face.

"Well if that doesn't beat all. I haven't seen Robert that happy in years. Michael I think you are good for an old grump," she finished with a smile.

"Thanks, I think. I'll see you later Aunt Maggie," Michael said as he shut the car door.

Aunt Maggie pulled away and Michael began to walk down the hallway to Doc's stall. He had the sack of bacon and biscuits for Charlie. He suddenly felt very foolish taking her something to eat with his face looking like Quasimodo's because of her. He got to Doc's stall and looked in. Doc nickered softly to him when he saw him. His stall was clean but there was no Charlene. Maybe she had come and gone. Maybe he wouldn't have to see her, and give her the biscuits Aunt Maggie had sent. Maybe....

"Don't get that stall dirty. I've already cleaned it. And don't mess up that clean water. I just put it in there. Be sure you shut the stall door good when you leave, because I don't want to get in trouble for something else you've done."

Well guess who, Michael thought as he gritted his teeth and turned around. Before he could say anything, Charlie got her first look at him and fell over laughing.

"Wow, you look horrible. No, I mean it you are just plain scary. If a little kid sees you they will have nightmares for weeks. Man, I'm glad I don't look like that. I bet you face never goes back the same as it was before. I bet you'll always be all squinty eyed," Charlie finished with a flourish.

"Do you always make people want to choke you when they see you or is it just me? I swear, you could make a preacher cuss." Michael had heard that one from Uncle Joe once when he was mad at Roho the rooster for chasing kittens.

"I'd say you better think about that choking thing, because you've only got one good eye left, and I'd hate to have to make it swell shut, too," Charlie said as she took a step toward Michael.

That did it! It was more than he could take. He had tried to be nice. He had brought her the biscuits like Aunt Maggie wanted him to, and all she could do was start mouthing off at him. Michael threw down the sack, cocked his head so that he could see her out of his good eye, and attacked. He didn't realize that his perception of distance would be off with just being able to see out of one eye. He lunged at Charlie and grabbed for her. He just knew he had her but he missed. Charlie jumped out of the way, but she was so busy laughing at Michael that she forgot the wheel barrow she was using to clean the stall was behind her, and she fell. Michael saw his chance and quickly got Charlie in a head lock.

Once he had her all he wanted to do was make her give up and promise to behave. He just didn't count on Charlie not giving up. She was fighting for all she was worth. When she realized she couldn't hit him with her fists, she began to bite his arm that he held her with for all she was worth. Not only that, but she was kicking his legs, and yelling like a wild animal. Michael was beginning to think something was seriously wrong with this kid! His head was killing him again from all the exertion, and he just knew he could feel drops of blood coming from the bites on his arm. He wanted to let go but didn't know how. Maybe he could talk to her.

"Charlie, Charlie, listen to me. Charlie will you stop! Be still and I'll let you go."

For a moment, Michael thought he had made progress because she quit fighting. Just as he was about to release the head lock he had on her, she started again, with more fury than ever. By now they were rolling around in Doc's stall, and covered with sawdust. Above all the commotion, they heard a very stern woman's voice say.....

"Charlene Nicole Jackson, what is going on now?"

Both fighters looked up to see Charlie's mother looking like only a very angry mother can look. Charlie quickly let go and swallowed hard.

"Uh, we, we, uh, we were, uh," stammered Charlie.

"Hello Mrs. Jackson, "Michael said. "Charlie was just showing me how to get out of a head lock. Right Charlie." Michael looked at Charlie with his good eye and tried, unsuccessfully to wink.

Charlie looked puzzled at first but quickly said, "Yeah, that's right. Just like they taught us to in Karate class. What are you doing here Mom? I thought you wanted me to ride to school with Michael's uncle."

That was news to Michael, who thought oh, that's just great.

"Miss Maggie called to tell me that Michael wasn't going to school today because he has a terrible headache. Looking at him, I can see why. I'm very sorry about your eye Michael. If Charlene gives you any more trouble just let me know. I promise to take care of it for you," Tessa finished with a withering look at Charlie.

Now was his chance! He could really get her now! He'd make her pay! Just as he was getting ready to tell her mother everything, Michael turned and looked at Charlie. He had never seen a more pitiful sight, except for maybe when Max got in the fight with Miss Twilla's cat, Sweetie Pie. The look Charlie gave him was begging him to keep silent.

Michael heard the words coming out of his mouth, but he couldn't believe what he was saying, "It's O.K. Mrs. Jackson, we were just clowning around."

"Yeah, Mom that's right we were just clowning around," Charlie said nodding her head violently for emphasis, and hoping her mother was buying their story.

Tessa frowned briefly, but then she said, "I think you two had better finish your chores and quit playing. What's this?" she asked picking up the sack of biscuits.

"Oh, I brought Charlie some breakfast from Aunt Maggie," said Michael. He didn't add that he was hoping she would choke on them.

"How nice. Charlie you need to take a lesson from Michael on how to be a friend. Thank you Michael for being so thoughtful. Now you two get busy," with that Tessa walked off.

Michael and Charlie sat in the stall and looked at each other for a minute then Charlie said, "Why did you do that? You could have gotten me in a lot of trouble, but you didn't. What's up with you?" Charlie was looking at him and trying to figure him out.

"Look Charlie, you don't have to be mean all the time. Sometimes you can be nice to people. I know that's probably news to you since every time I've seen you, you have caused trouble."

"Well you made me do it," Charlie shot back.

"Whatever," Michael said as he got up and began brushing the sawdust off.

"Did you really bring me some breakfast?" she asked as she crossed her arms and looked at him.

"Yeah, I did. It's some of Aunt Maggie's biscuits and bacon. Do you want them?" asked Michael

"Are you kidding me? You probably spit on them just so you could laugh when I ate them."

"I didn't spit on them Charlie. Do you want me to eat one to prove they are okay?"

"That won't prove a thing, because it will be your spit. If you didn't do that you probably wiped them on the bottom of your shoe, or you probably.........."

"THAT'S IT," said Michael. "I don't care if you eat them or not. Just shut up!!!"

With that he turned to Doc and began to take care of his leg. The next thing he heard was the sack rattling, as Charlie dug in to her breakfast. Michael just shook his head silently and thought how right Mr. Bradley had been when he told him to "Watch out for women". He could have used that advice before one of his eyes was swelled shut.

Chapter 24

Doc was in horse heaven. He was knee deep in fresh green grass that was tender and sweet. He grazed eagerly, enjoying the late April sun warming his now glossy red coat. He raised his head and looked for the boy that he had come to love. Michael was lying on his back in the soft grass, looking through half closed eyes at the brilliant blue spring sky. He was watching fat, puffy, clouds being chased by the warm winds. Doc had more confidence in Michael than he had in anyone since Susan. She was still a memory for the giant red horse, although it was a distant memory. He didn't think he heard her or saw her sometimes anymore. He still occasionally raised his head and drew in big breaths of air to see if he could find her scent. He never did, but he couldn't quit trying. Michael was here and he was real. He brushed Doc, made his foot feel better, fed him and cared for him. Doc had come to love the attention and the boy.

Michael was also enjoying his day. It had been a half day at school for the teachers to have a work day. Michael had gotten to the barn at 11:30, when the school bus dropped him off. He happily found that he was by himself today at the barn. Mr. Bradley had left to go to town for some kind of business, and Charlie wouldn't be there until about 4:00 because she went to the elementary school, and the teachers there weren't on the same schedule as the teachers at Michael's school. It was just him and Doc. Today was the end of the two weeks that Hurricane Charlie had to work off her punishment for knocking him out. His eye had pretty much healed with only a small amount of purple left above his eyebrow. He had told the story at school just like Aunt Maggie had suggested, which was all true, it just left Charlie out. Max had kept his word and not mentioned anything about his "accident". It had all gone much better than he had thought it would. He had been stuck with Charlie for the past two weeks, but even that hadn't been as bad as he was afraid it would be. She was just as bossy as ever, but somehow it didn't make him want to strangle her as much as it had before. He ignored her most of the time, which usually just led to more lectures from her. She sure did like to talk a lot.

Michael felt warm breath on his neck and looked over to see Doc's muzzle. The big red horse had come over to him. Michael's heart jumped, but not from fear. He really likes me, thought Michael! Michael didn't sit up. He just kept lying in the grass, but he did reach up and stroke the big horse between his soft brown eyes. Doc didn't move either and the boy and horse enjoyed a moment of silent communication. They were two creatures who had been thrown away, but had found each other, a fact that strengthened the developing bond between them. With one last push against Michael's neck Doc resumed his meal of the soft new grass. Michael gave a sigh of contentment. His life in the city seemed years away instead of a few months. He didn't think he could ever stand to go back to that life. He hoped and prayed he never had to, and each day that passed made him feel more secure in Cedar Grove.

Michael turned his head to watch Doc as he ambled around the pasture grazing. His foot was healing well. Mr. Bradley said a horse needed to eat what God intended for them, so he told Michael to take him to the pasture and let him graze. They had been coming outside for a week now and Doc was looking good. That was what had Michael worried. He had become very attached to Doc, and dreaded the time when he would no longer be needed to take care of him. Mr. Bradley hadn't said anything about him not coming to the barn yet so maybe he hadn't noticed how good Doc was doing. Funny thing about Mr. Bradley, he didn't seem so grumpy anymore. In fact he had started smiling pretty often. Whatever had caused the change, Michael was glad. Uncle Joe was right when he said it was just as easy to smile as it was to frown, besides, it made people wonder what you had been up to. Since Uncle Joe called himself a "man of mystery", Michael guessed he should know.

Michael's attention was captured by the sound of Doc lying down in the soft grass and rolling in it for a good scratching. Michael rose up on his elbows to watch. He had seen Doc do this before, but he was still amazed by how agile the big horse was with everything he did. All of his movements were smooth and fluid. Doc had finished his roll and was just lying in the grass with his legs tucked under him.

As Michael watched him, he began to wonder what it would be like to climb on that big broad back. He had never ridden a horse, but it must not be too hard because lots of people do it and all you have to do is hold on. Michael's over simplified idea of horsemanship gave him courage. He got up and began to walk over to Doc, talking softly to him. Doc watched him approach with interest, but he did not get up. When Michael reached him, he began to stroke and talk to Doc as he positioned himself beside the horse to climb on his back. Michael didn't stop to think that he had no saddle or bridle. Even if he had, it wouldn't have made any difference because he was just going to sit on Doc. He wasn't going for a ride today.

Michael had no way of knowing that Doc's only experience with being ridden bareback had been a bad one with Brian Adams. When Adams had first gotten Doc, he decided to show his horsemanship skills and jump on the young horse bareback in front of his cronies. Doc wasn't even broke to ride. When Adams climbed on his back and kicked him hard with both feet, he was terrified and did what scared horses do. He tried to get the scary thing off his back by bucking and promptly launched Adams in the air like a missile. His reward had been a beating by Adams that Doc did not deserve. Susan had never ridden him bareback because she had heard what Adams had done and knew horses remember negative experiences much longer than positive ones.

Michael kept stroking Doc and talking to him. Doc seemed completely comfortable with Michael standing so close when he was on the ground. Lying down is a vulnerable position for a prey animal, and it doesn't take much to make them get back on their feet. Instinct has taught them that they have to be ready at all times to run from danger. This was yet another indication of how much the horse trusted the boy.

Michael eased himself to Doc's side and gently put his leg over his back. As Michael sat upright on Doc's broad back he didn't move, because he was so amazed at how big Doc was from this vantage point. He had not imagined how warm and soft Doc's back would feel underneath him, or how massive the muscles in his back would be when he felt them with his legs. Doc didn't seem to mind Michael sitting on him at all. He turned his head to look at Michael but there was no sense of unease in the horse's expression. Michael gradually began to relax. He stroked Doc's big neck, and talked to him just like he always did only now he was actually on his back! It was one of the best experiences Michael had ever had. How could anyone who had ever been on a horse once not want to do it all the time he wondered to himself?

Michael progressed from just sitting to lying down on Doc's back. The warm spring sun began to work its magic and both horse and boy began to doze. They presented quite a picture, the horse resting his nose on the ground with his eyes closed, and the boy sprawled out on his back napping.

If Michael had been an experienced horseman, he wouldn't have gotten on the back of a horse lying down, loose in the pasture, with no halter or bridle, much less have fallen asleep. Doing that sort of thing is setting yourself and your horse up for a bad experience. Horses are very light sleepers and easily startled when they are asleep, and Doc was no exception.

Charlie had gotten to the barn at 2:00 instead of 4:00, because her mother had taken her to a dental appointment to see if she needed braces. She hadn't needed braces, and she got out of school early so it had been a good day for her. Her mother had dropped Charlie off at the barn to do her chores while she went to the grocery. Charlie knew that Michael would be there, because he had rubbed it in that she had a full day of school. She couldn't wait to tell him he was wrong again, and that she didn't have to have a "metal mouth".

She was starting to think Michael was not so bad, but boy, she had to tell him everything to do. How in the world he would have made it at the barn without her she didn't know. He was just lucky she had come along when she did. Oh, she knew their first couple of meetings with the pitch fork and the black eye hadn't exactly been good, but he had brought it all on himself. She was beginning to think she would be able to get Michael where he would be alright on his own at the barn, but it was going to take a lot of work on her part. On top of that, Michael usually didn't even thank her when she had to point out all of his problems to him. Some people just didn't appreciate all the hard work other people did for them. Charlie was something of a legend in her own mind.

She had been in the barn and found that both Doc and Michael were missing. She knew that they had been going to the grassy pasture, so she set out to find them there. When she got to the pasture, she could not believe her eyes! Michael was asleep on Doc's back while he was lying in the grass. Good grief, didn't he have a brain? What if something scared Doc and he jumped up and took off, then where would Michael be? It was a good thing she had gotten there when she did. She immediately began to run, yelling and waving her arms to wake Michael up.

Doc was awakened suddenly. He didn't know what it was at first, but then he saw IT! It was that wild thing that had been spinning and kicking and making those sounds in his stall that day, and it was coming right at him! Doc completely forgot that Michael was asleep on his back. All he could think about was escape. He jumped up so quickly that Michael only had time to open his eyes. He didn't have a clue about what was going on. He just knew he had to hold on tight. He clamped his legs as tight as he could around Doc's broad sides and grabbed his mane in both hands, all the while still not completely upright on Doc's back.

The sudden pressure of Michael's legs on his bare back caused an instant flashback to Doc's bad experience with Brian Adams. Now he had two things to try to escape from, a creature running at him and one on his back. Doc started to run and buck at the same time. When Charlie saw what was happening, she stopped and watched. She saw Doc bucking and Michael riding him for a little while at least. The pasture had a hill in it that led to a valley below. Charlie watched Doc disappear over the hill. The next thing she saw was Michael in the air back at the top of the hill. She only saw him for an instant before gravity took over, and he again disappeared from view. Oh great she thought, just what I was afraid would happen. You just can't save some people from themselves. Now I'll have to go pick up the pieces and see if I can teach that boy something about horses. Charlie sighed and began to walk calmly to find Doc and Michael. There was no need to hurry now that Michael had gotten himself in another mess. Yep she thought, this boy is gonna take a lot of work.

Chapter 25

Michael opened his eyes to find himself flat of his back. He was watching stars dance around his head just like on cartoons when somebody gets hit over the head with an anvil. For a minute he couldn't breathe and that was scary, but he also couldn't figure out what had happened. Slowly as he sat up he came to realize two things. One, he was sitting in the middle of a briar patch, and two he had come off of Doc. He must have had the breath knocked out of him, because it was becoming easier to breathe now. He looked down at his arms and found dozens of small red thorns sticking out of them. He was pretty sure he had as many in his back that had gone through his shirt. Thank goodness for denim jeans, because the thorns didn't seem to have penetrated them.

Michael looked around for Doc and saw him standing about fifty feet away looking like he didn't know what had happened either. Michael called softly to him and Doc started to come to him. Suddenly Doc threw his head in the air and snorted. He turned and ran away a safe distance, before stopping and looking back like he had seen a ghost.

"Well, I see you're not dead. I don't think I've ever known anyone more accident prone than you are," announced Charlie as she pushed her glasses back up on her nose.

"I don't know what happened," said Michael.

"What do you mean, you don't know what happened? Don't you remember anything?" asked Charlie.

"No, I don't. One minute I was asleep, and the next minute I'm hanging on to Doc's mane, then I'm sitting in the middle of a bunch of thorns. I can't figure it out. It's like I was abducted by aliens," replied Michael as he began to pick out a few of the many thorns.

"Humph," snorted Charlie, "if they had, they would have brought you back before you tore up their space ship."

"What's that supposed to mean?" Michael asked as he frowned.

"Oh, nothing, but I can tell you exactly what happened. I saw the whole thing. You were all stretched out on Doc's back sleeping while he was lying down in the grass. Did you have a bridle on him? No! Did you have a saddle on him? No! Did you even have a halter and lead rope on him? No! Honestly, what were you thinking? That was really stupid," said Charlie feeling very superior.

"Doc wouldn't hurt me. Something must have scared him, but what?" asked Michael.

"So you really can't remember anything?" asked Charlie.

"I just told you I didn't," said Michael losing his patience with her.

"Well, like you said, something must have scared him, but who knows what, especially a crazy horse like that one," said Charlie.

"Shut up! You don't call Doc crazy. He's smarter than you are, Charlene," said Michael as he moved to defend himself, knowing what the reaction would be to him using her full name.

Michael wasn't disappointed. Charlie immediately lunged for Michael. Since Michael was already on the ground, he tripped her with his legs and watched her fall. When she hit the ground face down, and he moved quickly to sit on top of her to keep her from getting up and starting her karate moves. As Uncle Joe said there's more than one way to skin a cat, even though Michael wasn't quite sure what that meant.

Charlie was so mad she was spitting, "Get off me you big cow. I can't breathe!"

"No, not until you promise to behave and take back what you said about Doc," said Michael.

"You know you aren't supposed to call me anything but Charlie. Now I'm gonna black your other eye! See if I ever try to help you again, and that horse is crazy. My Mom said so. Do you want to call her a liar?" yelled Charlie as she squirmed trying unsuccessfully to get away.

"Look, if you don't want to be called Charlene, don't be saying bad things about Doc. If you'll call a truce and tell me what you meant about Doc I'll let you up. Deal?" asked Michael.

"Oh no, you're not getting away with that. I tromp all the way down this field to wake you up, trying to help you and this is the thanks I get. I don't think so. Just tell me what you want to swell up this time. Your other eye, your nose, or maybe your whole big, fat, head." Charlie was wiggling and squirming with a vengeance now and it was becoming harder and harder to keep her down.

"Okay, how about I promise not to call you Charlene anymore," said Michael.

"That's not good enough," spat Charlie.

Michael had begun to process what she had said about tromping down the field to wake him up.

"Wait a minute, did you say you were coming down to wake me up?" asked Michael.

Michael's words cut through the red haze of anger Charlie was feeling. She knew she had to change to subject, or he would think she had scared Doc. She might have scared him a little, but not much.

"I'm suffocating, your jerk! Okay, truce. Just let me up and no more Charlene stuff!"

Michael moved and Charlie jumped up. Michael couldn't help laughing because she had dirt clods stuck in her glasses.

"What's so funny?" she demanded.

"Look at your glasses," said Michael.

"I can't, if I take them off I can't see," she said.

Michael felt guilty for teasing her about her name and her glasses. He reached up and pulled the dirt off her glasses. Charlie looked at him like she didn't trust him.

"There," said Michael, "now tell me why you called Doc crazy."

"Because he is. He killed Susan, who was my Mom's friend," said Charlie.

"Are you talking about Mr. Bradley's daughter?" asked Michael.

"Well duh, who do you think I'm talking about?" asked Charlie.

"Then you're wrong. She's not dead she just went away," said Michael.

"Where did you get that idea?" asked Charlie.

"Because, Aunt Maggie talked about how long she had been gone. She said it had been ten years. She didn't say she was dead," said Michael.

"When she said that she meant she was dead. Trust me I know the whole story. My Mom was there and she saw the whole thing," Charlie said, once again feeling very superior with her knowledge.

"Okay, so let's hear the story," said Michael.

Chapter 26

Aunt Maggie was in the kitchen cooking her family's supper. It was one of her favorite times of the day. Things were starting to slow down in the late afternoon. Her whole family would be home before long and seated around her big table. She would catch up on everyone's day, and get to see them eat a hearty meal. Tonight they were having ham, creamed potatoes, green beans, and canned tomatoes from last years garden, gravy, homemade biscuits, and cherry cobbler. She was just putting the finishing touches on the cherry cobbler when suddenly the back door flew open with a crash, and in came Joe followed by Norm, who promptly ran under the bed.

"My gracious Joe, what in the world is wrong?" asked Maggie.

Joe was so angry the veins in his temples were standing out and Maggie could have sworn he had smoke coming out of his ears!

"Those dad-blamed emus of the Johnson's are out again, and they are ruining my freshly sowed garden! Not only that, they attacked the dogs and almost scared Norm smooth to death. They look like chickens on steroids. I've never seen such a mismatched put together critter. Where's my gun? We're having us some emus for supper tomorrow night. I've had it with them. The last time they got out they ran through my fence and then all my cows got out. I like to never caught them because they were so spooked they were heading for the hills!"

"What's all the hollering about?" asked Max who had been in his room upstairs.

"Emus," roared Joe, "and there's about to be three less of them around here as soon as I get my shotgun."

"Now Joe you can't shoot the neighbors animals," said Maggie trying to reason with him. "Why don't I give the Johnson's a call and have them come and get them?"

"Go ahead, but they better hurry because as soon as I get my gun, I'll have the problem solved. Ah-ha there's Ol Lucy. Come to Papa baby we got work to do."

Joe had named all his shotguns Lucy from the time he was a kid in the country. When Joe grew up, hunting was something farm families did. Joe was an excellent shot and he had taught his son and his grandson to respect guns and to use them safely.

"Besides, Sam Johnson told me if they came over here again to shoot them on the spot and that's what I aim to do." With that Joe stormed out the door almost as fast as he came in.

"Uh-Oh Granny Maggie what do we do now?" asked Max with a worried look on his face. Max hadn't seen Grandpa Joe this mad in a long time.

"I'm going to call the Johnsons, you go and keep an eye on your grandpa," said Maggie as she was looking in the phone book for the number.

"Okay," said Max, "Norm, come on boy let's go!" Norm wasn't about to go back outside. He had already seen death in the face of the emu that almost caught him and stomped him. There would be no more monster birds for him today as he snuggled deeper under the bed.

Emus are huge birds that the Johnsons had decided to raise for their meat. It was supposed to be very good for people and very healthy. The problem was Sam Johnson's wife, Sally. She had named all the emus, petted them, and refused to let Sam sell them for their meat. That wasn't the only problem. Sam hated the emus, and the emus hated Sam. Poor Sam was stuck with huge birds that kicked like mules, stomped whatever came into their pen, had giant claws on their big feet that had more than once ripped his pants, and now had decided to terrorize the neighborhood. Sam was thoroughly sick of herding emus. He had had to replace two dogs, three cats, and a pot-bellied pig that they had done in. His neighbors were good people, but they were quickly joining his "I hate emus" club. That was why he had told them to just shoot them. If Sally wouldn't let him get rid of any emus, maybe some of them would disappear, and he wouldn't have to answer to his wife.

Joe Hayes was a man on a mission. He was normally a fairly easy going guy, but when Tyrannosaurs Rex with feathers started to destroy his farm a man had to do something. Ol Lucy would be just the answer to his problem, or at least that was what Joe thought. There were some emu facts that Joe didn't know. One was that their feathers were so thick that buckshot from Lucy would not penetrate them. Joe also didn't know that emus can be pretty nasty when they are mad. They like to use their feet and legs to stomp, kick, and rake their claws. Joe was about to learn all of this.

"There you are, you ugly buzzards," Joe said as he found them busily scratching up his freshly planted corn. He stopped long enough to check to see if Lucy had any bullets. Just his luck, the chamber was empty. As he was getting his bullets and starting to load his gun, the big male emu spotted him and started for him. The emu had no fear of people because Sally petted him, and Sam ran from him. He was an emu bully who just loved to chase big humans, small or large animals, or just anything that got in his way.

Joe was still working with his bullets when what felt like a semi truck ran over the top of him. Lucy, bullets, and Joe went flying through the air. When he landed, Joe just had enough time to jump out of the way of a second attack. He didn't make it without losing the whole side of his pants leg, however. When Joe stood up, and saw his pants and the trail from blood running down his leg from the emu's claw, he turned another whole shade of red with anger. That blasted bird had tried to kill him on his own property! Not only that, Lucy was in two pieces. This emu was gonna pay. Joe began to chase the big bird with the intention of strangling his long neck with his bare hands.

Max rounded the corner of the field just in time to see his grandpa jump on the back of a running emu .Wow! He didn't know Grandpa Joe had it in him.

"Yee-Ha, ride em Grandpa Joe," Max hollered, "show him who's boss."

Joe barely heard Max. He had his hands full of emu feathers, and he was also fast discovering riding an emu wasn't easy. He had belly flopped on its back. His hands were holding onto the wings and the rest of him was pretty much bouncing on the big bird's back with every step the animal made. The emu was not happy to have Joe aboard, and was taking evasive maneuvers to remove Joe from his back. Since Joe had no emu riding experience, it didn't take long for him to hit the ground. He landed face down in his newly plowed garden dirt. He didn't get up very quickly and the emu turned back for round two. Joe looked up just in time to see the bird coming, so he decided to tackle him. No bird-brained bird was going to get the better of Joe Hayes! Joe got in his tackling stance as the monster bird came by. He made a successful jump and this time he had the bird by his big, long, neck.

When Joe had grabbed the bird's neck they had both fallen to the ground. The problem with holding an emu neck is that there is not much to hold onto. It's very long and skinny, and a good grip is almost impossible. Joe was determined not to let go, but it became a challenge. The emu squirmed and almost got to its feet, but Joe managed to wrestle it back to the ground. In the process Joe's shirt got ripped off by the emu's claws, and Joe has some big, red, scratches down his back. The emu didn't escape the battle totally without some scars of his own. In the process of trying to keep him on the ground, Joe was grabbing anything he could to accomplish that purpose. The emu had several large bald spots on his back where Joe had pulled out handfuls of feathers.

The two combatants continued to roll around on the ground for what seemed to Joe like an hour, but in reality was only about three or four minutes. It was amazing how tiring a good fight could be! Joe was getting worried he would have to give up and lose the fight when he heard the most wonderful sound.

"Grandpa Joe, I'll help you," said Max, as he got ready to jump in the fray.

"Max wait," said Joe, "I've got a better idea. Go to the barn and get my ropes. We're gonna hog tie these things. Just hurry. I don't know how much longer I can keep him down." As if for added emphasis, the emu rolled Joe over so that he came up sputtering garden dirt. It was not Joe's best moment.

Max headed for the barn at a dead run. He was almost there when he saw his Dad. "Quick Dad, you've got to help me. Grandpa Joe is fighting an emu, and the emu is about to win. He sent me to get his rope. He says we're gonna tie that thing up."

Chuck knew his father. He was a big, strong, man who hated to lose any kind of battle, but what Joe didn't acknowledge was that he was no spring chicken. Chuck smiled to himself at the "chicken "part since Joe was rolling around on the ground with one at that very moment. Anyway, Chuck knew Joe wouldn't give up, so he'd better hurry and help end the war of the birds.

"You get the rope and I'll go help Joe," said Chuck as he took off at a run.

He was not prepared for the sight that greeted him. He couldn't help but laugh. There was Joe covered with dirt from head to toe, pants legs ripped, as well as his shirt, and there was an emu that seemed to be suffering from a severe case of emu mange. Great clumps of feathers were missing. About that time Joe looked up, and Chuck got another laugh. Joe had a mouthful of feathers!

"I'm glad you think this is funny because I sure don't," yelled Joe. "Now get down here and give me a hand with this bird monster!"

Chuck decide the best way to help was to jump on the bird's head and try to cover his eyes. Maybe if he couldn't see, he wouldn't struggle so hard. Chuck did just that, and it did seem to take some of the fight out of the emu. By this time Max had arrived with the rope.

"Okay Dad, what's the plan with the rope?" asked Chuck.

"We're gonna tie his feet together. He's just about killed me with those dad-blamed turkey toenails," sputtered Joe. "Max, you swap places with Chuck. Sit on this buzzard's head to keep him down, and Chuck, you tie his feet together."

Max and Chuck quickly changed places while Joe kept a death grip on the emu's neck. Joe also had his legs wrapped around the emu. One thing about Joe, when he decided to do something, he gave it all he had. Chuck got one leg tied with the rope, then used the rest of the rope to catch the other leg. He had seen what those legs had done to Joe, and he knew he had to be careful. When both emu legs were securely tied up, all three of them jumped up to see if the ropes would hold and keep the big bird on the ground. It was almost like watching a bird rodeo where the ropers wait to see if they would win the contest with their roping skill. The emu struggled for a few minutes, then conceded defeat. It just lay on the ground panting, but it also gave Joe a very evil eye and angry growl.

"Ha! Take that you big, ugly, buzzard. You didn't get the best of Joe Hayes. It appears you didn't know who you were tangling with," said Joe as he stood over the big creature.

Chuck almost laughed again, because it didn't appear that Joe had known who he had been "tangling with" either. His shirt and pants were torn, he was covered in dirt, mud, and some emu feathers, and between the two adversaries, Joe was the only one bleeding. As Joe continued to gloat, Sam Johnson pulled up in his truck.

Sam got out of the car and began to apologize profusely, "Joe I'm sorry. Every time I think I have those birds fenced in so they can't get out, they manage find a way out. I sure hope they haven't torn anything up or hurt any of your animals." What Sam was really thinking was he hoped he didn't have to replace any more livestock or pets. These emus were getting very expensive.

"Well, no real harm done I guess. They did wreck my garden that I just planted," said Joe.

When Sam looked at Joe, he began to think maybe his emus had caused some harm after all. Joe looked like he had been hit by a train!

"Joe, are you alright?" asked Sam as he took in Joe's ragged appearance.

"Sure I am Sam. It'd take more than a giant bird to get me down," replied Joe a little indignant that Sam thought he couldn't whip a bird in a fight. "Now, let's go tie up the other two." Joe was going to show Sam how to handle these offending critters.

"Wait Joe, you got the one that matters," said Sam. "This one is the ring leader. The other two just follow him wherever he goes. I'll let the tailgate down on my truck and we'll put him in the truck bed. The other two should follow the truck back home. We just have to figure out how to load him in the truck."

"Well, that's no problem," said Joe, "Chuck, you and Max go get one of those big heavy poles out behind the barn."

Max had visions of Joe clubbing the bird with the pole to put an official end to the contest. "Uh, Grandpa Joe, are you sure you want to do that?" asked Max.

"Well sure I am, now go get that pole."

Maggie had to stay in the house until her cobbler came out of the oven She had called the Johnson's and Sally had assured her that Sam would be right over. She had wanted to go see what was happening with Joe and the birds, but she hadn't heard any gunshots so she hoped the birds had gone to visit someone else. She heard the timer on the stove go off, and she hurried to get the pie on the cooling rack, then ran out the back door. It didn't take her long to get to the field where Joe had said the emus were. What she saw stopped her dead in her tracks.

Chuck and Sam Johnson each had one end of a very long pole with an emu on it hanging by its trussed up legs. The big bird didn't seem to be shot anywhere. It just had lots of feathers missing. Maggie thought to herself that emus must molt or shed their feathers like her chickens did, because there were big bare spots all over the emu where its feathers were missing. Sam and Chuck were walking toward Sam's truck with the bird while Joe and Max brought up the rear. Joe had a big smile on his face like he was very pleased with himself. Maggie knew that look.

It was the look her husband always had on his face when he emerged victorious from one of his escapades.

By looking at him, Maggie had to wonder if he really was the victor. His clothes hung in rags, he was covered in mud and scratches, and he was carrying Lucy in two pieces. What on earth could have happened here? While she watched, Chuck and Sam hoisted the bird into the back of the truck with a lot of grunting and straining. Joe did his part by telling them how to do it. Once the emu was loaded, Sam got in and began to slowly drive away. When the other two birds realized that their leader was leaving them, they began to run to catch up with the truck. After they caught it, they slowed their pace to a trot and began to follow Sam home.

Joe walked over to the spot where Maggie was rooted to the ground taking it all in and said, "Miss Maggie I sure hope supper's ready, because I've worked up one big appetite. It's not everyday a man has to show a giant bird who's boss. Come on, sweetheart, I'll tell you how I did it while we walk to the house." With that, Joe put his arm around Maggie and began his epic tale of bird battle.

Chuck and Max looked at each other and laughed. They knew this was a tale that would be retold often and would probably get bigger with each recounting.

Chapter 27

"Well," began Charlie, "Susan and my Mom were in Mississippi at a 4-D barrel race."

"What's a barrel race and what does 4-D mean?" asked Michael.

"You mean you don't know what a barrel race is?" said Charlie. "I declare, sometimes I forget how stupid you are."

"Never mind the insults, just answer the question," said Michael.

"A barrel race is just what it sounds like. It's a race with 3 barrels set up in a triangle or cloverleaf pattern. Each rider has to go around the barrels one at a time without knocking any of them over. The rider with the fastest time wins. A 4-D barrel race is one that has four different divisions of winners. Each division usually has a first, second, third, fourth, and fifth place. Susan and my Mom used to be in the first division, because that's the best and the fastest horses."

"I get the barrel race, but I still don't understand the 4-D thing," said Michael.

Charlie rolled her eyes and said, "Oh brother! If the fastest time anybody ran at a 4-D barrel race was 16.2 seconds, that would be the first place in the first division, and the four next fastest times, would be the other four places. Have you got that much?" demanded Charlie.

"Yeah, I think so," said Michael.

"Now," began Charlie like she was talking to a three year old, " The second division first place winner would be the fastest time one second slower than the first division, so if the first place time was 16.2 seconds, the first place time in the second division would be a 17.2 second barrel run. The first place time in the third division would be two seconds off the winning first division time or 18.2 seconds."

"I get it now. That means the fourth division winning time would be 19.2 seconds," smiled Michael feeling like he had just unlocked the mysteries of the universe.

"Finally," said Charlie very dramatically. "Each division has five winners so it would be five winners in the 16 second range, five winners in the 17 second range, five winners in the 18 second range, and five winners in the 19 second range. That way there are lots of chances to win. That causes more people to enter, which means more entry fees to add to make more prize money. Now can I go on with the story?"

Michael just nodded.

"Okay, so like I said, Mom and Susan were in Mississippi at a 4-D barrel race. Mom said Susan was late getting there. She missed a turn or something, so she didn't have much time to see when she would be running and get her horse ready. Mom just talked to her for a little while and the next thing she knew, she heard the announcer call Susan's name as the next contestant. Mom said it was awful. She said Doc acted funny from the time he went into the arena. He was wild eyed and all over the place. Mom said he was one of the fastest horses she had ever seen."

"I bet he was," said Michael as he looked with admiration at the red horse grazing a short distance away.

"No dufus, being so fast wasn't a good thing that night because he was out of control. Mom said she could tell Susan was trying to pull him up, but Doc wouldn't listen to her. He just kept running wide open. He was running so hard and fast that he couldn't make the turn at the first barrel. He fell down hard and Susan's head it the rim of the metal barrel. Mom said Susan was knocked out immediately. The ambulance came into the arena and carried Susan to the hospital. My Mom went in to get Doc and take him to the trailer. She said he must have hit his head too, because he was acting like he was having a hard time walking. She said by the time she got him to the trailer, he could barely walk.

She put Doc and Moz up and went to the hospital to check on Susan. When she got there they told her Susan didn't make it. The doctor said she had died instantly. My Mom had to be the one to tell Susan's Dad. She said he took it real bad. He first said he was going to shoot Doc for killing he daughter, but Mom reminded him of how much Doc meant to Susan and that she wouldn't have wanted him to do that. Mr. Bradley brought Doc home that night and threw him in the far back pasture. Mom said she didn't think he had anything else to do with Doc until you hurt him when you threw that rock," finished Charlie with a sigh of superiority.

Michael winced when she reminded him of what he had done. Now that he knew Doc, he felt even more guilty for hurting him. "I guess that explains why Mr. Bradley is so grumpy."

"Mom said he practically became a hermit. He didn't go anywhere or see anybody. He let his farm run down. He had been working hard on it to turn it into a place where kids that needed help or didn't have homes could come and live and learn how to do better. Mom said that was why Susan was in that barrel race. It paid $10,000 in prize money and that was going into their fund for fixing up the farm for kids."

Michael was quiet. He was absorbing everything that Charlie had told him. It explained a lot about Mr. Bradley. He wasn't just a mean old man. He was a sad and lonely man. Michael knew how that felt. Shoot, that was the way he had felt most of his life until he came to Aunt Maggie's house. He had almost been one of the kids that Mr. Bradley and Susan were trying to help. Maybe he could help Mr. Bradley. Michael had found out how good it felt to not have dark clouds over his head. He thought Mr. Bradley deserved the same thing.

Chapter 28

Michael got out of Tessa's truck and closed the door.

"See you later, loser," yelled Charlie.

Michael didn't respond. He just grinned to himself as he heard Tessa scolding Charlie for her choice of words. Tessa had given him a ride home. Aunt Maggie had called her, and said they had chickens out or something like that, and would she mind dropping Michael off when she picked up Charlie. That was just fine with Michael. He still thought Charlie's mother was the most beautiful lady he had ever seen. Sometimes he wondered how Hurricane Charlie could even be related to her. They sure were different!

Michael smelled the wonderful smells of supper coming from the kitchen as soon as he opened the back door. Everybody was already seated at the table and eating. The sight that greeted him was a surprise. The sight of Uncle Joe to be exact. There sat Uncle Joe with a long red scratch down the left side of his face, red scratches on both arms, and a huge knot right on top of his head! The knot was very visible because of Uncle Joe's receding hairline. Actually, most of his hair had vanished, but Uncle Joe still called it "receding". He always said "God thought I was so good looking he needed to give me more room for my face and less for my hair".

"What in the world happened to you?" asked Michael in disbelief.

"I've been fighting monster chickens," grinned Uncle Joe, "and you should see what they look like."

"Nonsense Joe," said Aunt Maggie, "they were emus and they belonged to our neighbors. I'm surprised they weren't upset with you for plucking their birds."

"Now sweetheart, I didn't start that fight, but I sure enough finished it. Sit yourself down, boy, and I'll tell you all about it."

"How did you get that great, big, knot on your head, Uncle Joe? It looks like it would hurt," said Michael.

"Naw, it takes more than a goose egg to hurt me. I got it when I was choking down one bad emu. I had a hold on his neck. The trouble was, his neck was about three feet long, so wherever I grabbed it he still had plenty of neck left to try and peck me with his great big emu bill. That's where I got the lump. Felt like somebody hit me in the head with a hammer, but it didn't slow me down. You see, it happened like this. I got that emu in my sights and decided he needed a dose of good ol Joe medicine…"

As Uncle Joe launched into his adventure, Max kicked Chuck under the table. Chuck looked up at Max and they both began to chuckle as the story was already getting bigger and so were Michael's eyes.

Aunt Maggie just shook her head and smiled as the big man she loved so well was telling Michael what had happened. One thing about living with Joe Hayes, her life was never dull. He always saw everything as fun and an adventure. Funny, she thought, he had never outgrown those two character traits, and she was very glad he hadn't.

As Joe's story and supper both ended, Joe told Max and Chuck he wanted them to help him check the fences that the emus came through to be sure none of them were torn down. He told Michael to give Miss Maggie a hand with cleaning up after supper since he had been working outside at Mr. Bradley's most of the day. That was fine with Michael because he liked to be around Aunt Maggie, and he had some questions he wanted to ask her about what Charlie had told him.

"I'm sorry you got stuck with kitchen duty, honey. I know it doesn't seem very manly compared to fixing fences," said Aunt Maggie.

"Oh, that's okay. I don't mind," said Michael as he began to clear away the dirty dishes. "Can I ask you something, Aunt Maggie?"

"Of course you can," she replied with a smile. "What is it?"

"Well, Charlie and I were talking today, and she said that Mr. Bradley hated Doc because he said Doc killed his daughter. Is that true?"

Aunt Maggie sighed and said, "I'm afraid so, sweetie, although I think Robert just needed something he could blame for all the hurt he suffered at losing the last of his family. You see, his wife had gotten sick and died several years earlier. He still had his daughter to think of so he had to keep going for her sake. They became quite a team. They were both excellent with horses, and people were always wanting them to train their young horses and help them with their riding skills. They added onto their barn, and boarded people's horses, along with the horses they trained for people. Robert farmed to help make ends meet. He put out corn and oats, and he cut all their own hay and baled it. He usually had extra hay to sell to folks who needed good hay to get their stock through the winter. Susan gave riding lessons and she also competed in barrel races. I don't know much about barrel racing, but she had a reputation for being very good at it. She won quite a bit of prize money, or so I heard, with Doc.

My oh my, did she love that horse. Robert used to laugh and say that if she had to choose between Doc and him, she would choose Doc every time. It was something so see her ride him, since he was so big and she was so small. Oh, she was tall enough, but in comparison to Doc she looked like a fly sitting up there. They would take off running at full speed and you could hear her laughter as she rode across the pasture. She used to say that she knew there would be horses in heaven because she couldn't be happy there without them. I suppose she's up there riding her horses right now, because the Bible says there is only happiness and contentment in heaven."

"Charlie said something about Mr. Bradley planning on making the farm a place where kids with problems could go. Is that true?" Michael asked, once again thinking to himself "kids like me".

"Yes, it was Robert's plan before Susan died. Once she was gone it was like all the life went right out of him. He stopped going anywhere, he stopped seeing people, he didn't farm anymore, and he stopped going to church. He used to be in church every Sunday. He especially loved the singing. He has a beautiful bass voice. I don't guess he ever sings anymore. It's sad, he has such a musical gift from God and he isn't using it. He's even mad at God. I just wish he could be reached some how to know how wrong he is to feel that way," finished Aunt Maggie.

"I think I would be mad at God, too Aunt Maggie. I mean Mr. Bradley lost everything he had for a family. I've heard the preacher say in church that God can do anything. Well, He should have helped Mr. Bradley and not let his family die," said Michael feeling very sad for Mr. Bradley.

"Oh honey, it isn't that simple. Of course God can do anything, but sickness and death are not from God," said Aunt Maggie.

"I don't understand," said Michael with a confused look on his face, "if those things don't come from God where do they come from?"

"Well you've been to church with us enough to know about God. God loves us and only wants what is good for us, but He also gives us the freedom to choose to follow Him and his laws or to follow another path."

"I still don't understand. What other path?" asked Michael.

"It's a path that is led by things that are bad for us. Things that will harm us and keep us from being happy and content. Just as God is in heaven, the Bible tells us that Satan is in charge of the earth."

"Do you mean the devil? I heard Chuck talking about him in one of the youth classes he taught. Where did he come from and why doesn't God stomp on him and get rid of him if he's bad?" asked Michael.

"Yes, the devil and Satan are the same thing. Originally, Satan was the most beautiful angel in heaven. All the angels worship God and do whatever He tells them to do. Satan, who was called Lucifer in heaven, decided he was greater than God and should be worshiped. God sent him away from heaven and cast him to earth, where he still is today, if you believe the Bible and I do," said Aunt Maggie.

"Since Satan can't harm God, he wants to hurt God by making His children, the people on earth, follow him instead of God. Satan's ways and plans are always bad for people and keep them from being happy and content. That is why God lets Satan rule the earth. He lets his children choose to follow His ways to happiness and heaven or to be led astray by Satan," said Aunt Maggie.

"So are you saying that Mr. Bradley's wife and daughter were following Satan?" asked Michael.

"Oh, my stars no, honey. I can see I'm making a mess of this!" exclaimed Aunt Maggie. "Let me try again. God does not promise us a life free from pain, sickness, death, or even sadness. What He does promise us is the strength to get through the hard times we face in life if we rely on Him, do His will, and talk to Him in prayer. We are all going to be sick sometime, and we are all going to die someday, but we don't have to be sad and hopeless about it. With God's help, we can make it through anything and still find joy in our lives. That's what the devil wants to stop. He wants us to be sad, hopeless, bitter, and mean."

"Because Susan and her mother both died, it doesn't mean they weren't good people. Like I said we will all die someday, but what is sad about their deaths is that Robert turned his back on God just when he needed Him the most. You've been around Robert enough to know he isn't content with his life or happy in any way. When someone who follows God's law dies, we know it's only a matter of time before we see them again in heaven. Don't you think that would make Robert happy if he could just remember that instead of being mad at God?"

"Yes mam, I guess so. It's a lot to try to figure out," said Michael.

"Sweetie, that's an understatement. I hope I haven't completely confused you, but if you have any more questions just ask me, or Chuck. After all he's the youth minister and he lives right here. Isn't that handy," smiled Aunt Maggie. "Now I guess we better get these dishes cleaned up."

Michael took the dishes to the sink for Aunt Maggie to put in the dishwasher. All the while he was deep in thought. What Aunt Maggie had said would explain a lot of things. The way he understood it, God didn't cause bad things to happen. God just made sure He was there to hold your hand through the bad things if you wanted to reach out and take it. Michael could see how knowing that God was there to help you would keep you from being afraid or like Mr. Bradley, angry. Mr. Bradley had to know this stuff if he went to church so much. Michael wished there was some way to remind him. What was it Aunt Maggie had said about prayer? She said it was the way we talked to God, and made our requests known to Him. Maybe if he asked God to help Mr. Bradley remember, He would and Mr. Bradley wouldn't be so grumpy and sad. I can at least try Michael thought. What have I got to lose?

Chapter 29

Michael slowly came awake. He stretched his arms and legs while he twisted his body first one way then the other. He kept his eye closed and smiled as he became aware of the fact it was Saturday and there was no school. What a great way to start a day, almost. A sound began to penetrate his contented thoughts that immediately made his eyes flash wide open! No, it couldn't be! Not in his own house, not on a perfect Saturday, it just wasn't supposed to happen. He listened more intently. Sure enough, he had been right the first time. He was hearing voices, and the voices he was hearing were Hurricane Charlie's and Aunt Maggie's! What in the world was SHE doing here? One thing was sure, he was going to find out. He jumped out of bed and danced around on one foot while he was trying to hurry and get his jeans on. The noise he made caused Max to wake up and squint a sleepy eye at him.

"What's going on? Can't a guy sleep late on a Saturday morning?" asked Max.

"You better get up fast, because you won't believe who I think is in the kitchen," said Michael as he continued to get dressed at warp speed. His head was stuck in his tee shirt while he waved his arms to try and settle it around his neck. Just then the door to their room burst open.

"Well, just lookee here," said Charlie. "One clown is trying to figure out how to dress himself while the other one has a really bad case of bed-head. Now where is your camera when you need it? Oh yeah, this is just the kind of dorky room I figured you two would have. Clothes all over the floor and stupid hunting pictures on the walls. Who's your decorator, Smokey the Bear and the thrift store down the road? Man, this place even smells like a dorkey room. Ever thought of trying to figure out how to open a window and let in some fresh air?" Charlie finished her tirade with a very self satisfied smirk, and leaned against the door frame.

Max didn't appreciate her bed-head remark and frantically tried to smooth his hair down with his hands. When this didn't work and he heard another giggle from Charlie, that was it. On the nightstand next to his bed were two tennis balls and a football. He reached over, grabbed one of the tennis balls, and aimed it at Charlie's head. As soon as he threw it he heard a thud followed by and loud "Ow". She immediately disappeared down the hallway, and both boys heard her go down the stairs to the kitchen.

"Uh-oh," said Max, "she's headed to the kitchen. This ain't gonna be good. I just hope Papa Joe isn't down there."

"How come?" asked Michael.

Before Max could say a word they both heard a very loud, and very angry, "Boys, get down here NOW!"

"That's why," said Max as he scrambled out of bed and into his clothes. "Papa Joe has this thing about boys hitting girls. It's been nice knowing you Michael." Max looked like a man on the way to the electric chair.

"Wait a minute, Charlie is the one who started all this. Uncle Joe will listen to us," said Michael as he tucked his shirt into his jeans.

"That's where you're wrong. Grandpa Joe said that when he was growing up boys were not allowed to hit girls. It just wasn't right, and that's the way all the men in his family were going to behave. According to Grandpa Joe hitting women is a sorry way for any man to act and he won't stand for it. Like I said, it's been nice knowing you."

With that, they hurried to the kitchen when another bellow came from below.

They both tried to get in the doorway of the kitchen at the same time. The result was that they got stuck for a minute. It gave them time to take in the scene before them. Aunt Maggie was holding a wet cloth on Charlie's left eye and shaking her head sadly at them both. Uncle Joe was standing beside Aunt Maggie with his arms folded across his chest and the maddest face Michael had ever seen on anyone. Michael heard Max swallow hard and whispered, "Max I think you're toast."

"What was that?" asked Uncle Joe as he turned a fierce gaze on Michael.

Now it was Michael's turn to swallow hard, "Uh, nothing Uncle Joe I was just hoping for some toast for breakfast. That's all."

"You two will be lucky if you get bread and water after the way you treated this sweet little girl," roared Uncle Joe. Both boys visibly jumped at the sound of his voice. As Uncle Joe glared at them and Aunt Maggie was looking at them with a mixture of hurt and disappointment, Charlie took the opportunity to make a face, stick out her tongue, and grin at them.

"She's not a sweet little girl," blurted out Michael trying to get them to see how Charlie was using the situation, by pointing and gesturing toward her.

Before Uncle Joe and Aunt Maggie could turn all the way around to her, Charlie had quickly gone from gloating to a pathetic, teary eyed, victim saying, "Miss Maggie I can't see too good out of my eye. Will I be blind?" as she dissolved into tears.

"There, there, sweetie. Of course you won't be blind, It's just bruised, that's all," said Aunt Maggie as she comforted her.

Max and Michael looked back up at Uncle Joe's face, and both of them knew that they were looking at the face of doom.

"I won't stand for a boy hitting a girl in my house. It's just not right, and Max you knew that. Michael you might not have, but you do now. I'm normally a pretty easy going fellow but this crosses the line. You may as well get ready for your punishment."

"But Uncle Joe, she started it," protested Michael.

"Did she hit one of you? No, don't answer that because it doesn't matter if she did. Max tell Michael the rule about hitting females," ordered Uncle Joe.

"No matter what, there is never a reason to hit a girl," said Max dejectedly.

"Good. Now that that is clear, you boys can forget about breakfast. I need one more fence checked that those blasted emus might have gone through. I want both of you to take the fencing tools, hammers, and bush cutters and check the whole fence at the back corner of our property. You'll have to cut out some bushes that are grown up in the fence to be sure it isn't broken down. That pasture fence covers about thirty five acres so maybe it will give you plenty of time to learn what I expect of you boys."

"Yes sir," said Max. "Can I have the key to the four-wheeler so we can load up all the equipment?"

"Nope, you'll need to carry all of it. There's nothing that helps a memory like good honest work and a lot of sweat. Now I don't expect to see you two until you come back and tell me you are finished checking the fence." With that Uncle Joe turned back to Aunt Maggie and poor, injured Charlie.

As the boys were heading to the shed to get the fencing tools, Max told Michael, "You don't have to help me. Go back and tell Grandpa Joe you didn't have any part in causing Charlie to lose her eyesight."

"I'm the one that caused enough commotion for her to come up to our room. If I had been quieter, maybe none of this would have happened. Anyway, I do owe you one because you didn't tell anybody at school about what Charlie did to my eye. Besides, I'd rather be out here with you than back there with Charlie."

"Thanks, I just hope you still feel that way after we've been over thirty five acres of fence. I guess we've got everything so we can get going." said Max.

Both boys were loaded with tools, hammers, wire, and brush cutters. Uncle Joe sure knew how to prove a point. It got more ingrained with every acre. They had checked about twenty acres and were just getting ready to follow the fence down into a secluded clearing when they heard what sounded like a gunshot about twenty yards in front of them. They couldn't see because it was just around some of the dense brush that

Uncle Joe had told them about. Max and Michael hit the ground and didn't move. As they looked at each other wide eyed, they heard the thud of what sounded like very big boots just beyond the brush coming in their direction!

Chapter 30

Joe watched the boys leave the barn with the tools he told them they would need to repair any breaks they found in the fence. He almost relented and got the four-wheeler for them when he saw the difficulty they were having carrying everything. No, he told himself, they needed to remember this particular rule, and there was nothing like sweat to keep a memory sharp. He shook his head as he turned to look at Miss Maggie and Charlie.

"I declare, Maggie, I don't know what got into those two, but I can promise you they won't need to be rocked to sleep tonight. When they get through checking fences, I've got some hay bales that need moving and the barn needs cleaning out. I know Michael has to go to Robert's today, so Max can just go with him. I can't stand rude behavior in boys toward females. Especially uncalled for behavior."

"Don't you think you're being a little hard on them Joe?" asked Maggie. "They really are good boys."

"Yes, they are, but the reason they are is because they know there are consequences for behavior that is not allowed. To my way of thinking, they earned these consequences, so they are going to have to take their punishment."

Hurricane Charlie had been listening to the conversation between Joe and Maggie. Miss Maggie was still holding a cool, wet cloth on her eye. When she heard everything that was in store for Max and Michael she began to feel bad for her part in their trouble. She had gone up to their room uninvited. How was she supposed to know they were such grumps when they first woke up in the morning? All she was trying to do was offer a little advice on how to make their room look better and smell better. They just took it all wrong. She might have overdone it with her injury. Actually the tennis ball had barely grazed her eye, but by the time she got to the kitchen she had rubbed it hard enough with her fist to make it look very red and watery. When Miss Maggie had been checking her eye, she might have let her believe it was a little worse than it actually was.

Charlie might be a pain, overly dramatic, and known to sometimes stretch the truth, but she didn't like feeling guilty and responsible for the punishment Max and Michael had gotten. The truth was that she had started to think that Michael was okay. He had saved her when they were fighting and her Mom appeared. When he told Tessa that they were just playing around you have knocked her over with a feather. After all, she had blacked his eye and put a pitch fork in his back. How was she going to fix this? While Joe and Miss Maggie were talking, she thought frantically about what to do. There was only one thing she could do.

"Uh, excuse me, Miss Maggie, I need to tell you something."

"Sure, honey, what is it?"

"Well, I think my eye is okay now, why don't we let Max and Michael off the hook," said Charlie.

"If that don't beat all," said Joe to Miss Maggie, "that sweet little thing is trying to keep those two from taking their medicine." Joe bent down to Charlie and said, "Honey, don't you worry about them, I'll take care of Max and Michael." With that he patted her head while muttering" bless your heart" mostly to himself.

This wasn't working. Charlie took a deep breath and blurted out, "I'm not really hurt and I might have said some things that I shouldn't have." When she looked up at Joe and Miss Maggie they were both looking at her like she had two heads.

Now it was her turn to wilt under Joe's stare. "How about you tell us what happened," he said.

Charlie swallowed hard, and to her credit, told the truth, the whole truth, and nothing but the truth. When she had finished, she looked up at Joe and Miss Maggie and added, "I'm sorry. I was mad at Mom because she is doing this school thing and I don't get to be home with her on Saturdays. I've told her Dad will be back, then everything will be just like it was before and we will be a family again. It just makes me so mad that she won't believe me. I know he's coming back to us." By this time there were big tears running down both of her cheeks, and Miss Maggie's heart was breaking for her. Joe hated for anybody to be so sad, especially when there was nothing he could do to make things better.

"Oh sweetheart, I'm sorry you are so upset, but don't be angry with your Mom. She just wants to improve herself. She told me she had always wanted to be a nurse. Think of it like your Mom is making her dream come true. Remember, it's not permanent. It's just for a short while. I'm looking forward to having a girl in the house. Why there's nothing but boys around here. I'm very outnumbered as you can see," Miss Maggie reached out and swept Charlie into a big hug.

"Please don't make Max and Michael do all those things. It was my fault, not theirs," said Charlie.

"Well," said Joe, "it won't hurt them to take care of the fence. They didn't have to get mad and throw something. I tell you what, I have to go into town and run some errands for Miss Maggie, but when I get back, how about we get in the "mustard machine" and go find them?"

"What's the mustard machine?" asked Charlie. Charlie was about to find out.

The mustard machine, also known as the Joemobile, was an old 4-wheel drive Ford Bronco. Joe had bought it used about fifteen years ago. It was his hunting, fishing, and farming vehicle. It was the exact same color as the mustard that you put on hot dogs and hamburgers, bright yellow. It had a bullet hole in the hood that had missed all the vital parts of the motor. Joe said it made for a manly vehicle. It was loaded down with camouflage hunting clothes, fishing gear, some empty soda bottles and under the front seat was a plastic shoebox full of candy bars, moon pies, cookies, and peanut butter and crackers.

Joe said it was for emergencies so that if the mustard machine broke down, he wouldn't starve to death. Miss Maggie liked to point out that

Joe could probably go for several days without food and still be just fine. It had a hole in the floor where Joe had shot at what he thought was a snake, but it turned out to be a rubber snake one of his hunting "buddies" thought would be a good joke. Joe said that was fine, because with two bullet holes, there was no way his Bronco would be mistaken for a sissy ride. Joe loved to drive the mustard machine. He would take off through woods, down creeks, up steep hills, and through pastures. He just locked in the four-wheel drive and kept going. The only thing Joe thought was wrong with his mustard machine was the rear window had gotten rolled down and would not roll up. It made for some pretty chilly rides in the winter time.

When Joe got home, he climbed behind the wheel and fired up the engine. As soon as it turned over, Joe began to smile. He knew that one day he would try to start his Bronco and it wouldn't start. As a matter of fact every time it did start he was relieved to know that it wasn't dead yet. He reached up and patted the dashboard, put the car in gear and pulled up to the house.

"Let's go girls," he yelled.

"I'm not going Joe, but Charlie is. Here she comes," said Miss Maggie.

"Climb in here young lady and let's go find those two knuckleheads," said Joe. With that Joe took off across the pasture, bouncing and bucking over all the rough spots. Charlie reached down and fastened her seatbelt without having to be told. Joe was grinning from ear to ear, and having a ball. Charlie was holding on and trying not to get hit by fishing rods and empty soda bottles. She didn't realize it, but she was grinning too!

Chapter 31

"Somebody's shooting at us!" exclaimed Max.

"Why?" asked Michael incredulously.

"Now how am I supposed to know that?" said Max more than a little irritated at the question and the situation in which they found themselves. Then in true Max fashion, he piped up, "I guess we're just too good looking."

"This isn't funny, Max. I don't really like being on my belly in the grass while there are bullets flying all around me. What are we gonna do now?"

"Okay, one more time, how am I supposed to know what to do? On the plus side, we've only heard one bullet. Maybe whoever it was has gone," said Max as he continued to lay low and keep his head down.

Their brief period of hope ended as they once again heard what sounded like very big boots stomping in their direction.

"Come on Max, let's belly crawl into that ditch over there. Maybe we can hide under those big weeds," said Michael.

"Good idea, we're sitting ducks out here," said Max. Both boys began to crawl on their stomachs to the nearby ditch to take cover under the weeds. As they crawled, they were conscious of each and every briar that was growing abundantly along the ground and sticking in their arms and bellies.

"Ow," whispered Michael, "why do there have to be so many thorns around here?"

"I don't know, but which would you rather have, a bullet hole or some briars to have to pick out? I'll take the briars, myself," said Max.

Max and Michael had almost made it to the big weeds when they heard some very loud and very close laughter. They froze, face down on their bellies afraid to turn around because they knew the gunman had caught them!

"What in the world are you two doing?" asked Joe.

"Looks to me like they are practicing being snakes since they are crawling on their bellies," giggled Charlie.

"Shut up," said Max quickly, "Papa Joe get down! Somebody is shooting at us. We heard a gunshot."

"Boy, that wasn't a gunshot, it was the old mustard machine backfiring when I turned off the key. Just a small protest on its part I reckon," said Joe. "Where were you two going on your bellies anyway?"

"The mustard machine!" said Max.

"Backfiring!" said Michael.

"Yes," said Joe, "Now where were you going?"

"We were trying to hide in those weeds," said Michael as he pointed and looked in that direction. When he did, he got his first close look at the "weeds". What he saw made him suck in his breath, and exclaim, "Uncle Joe, what are you doing with a marijuana patch!"

"What am I doing with WHAT!" exclaimed Uncle Joe.

"A patch of wacky backy, giggle weed, Mary Jane," began Charlie feeling very superior with her knowledge of slang for marijuana. Unfortunately for her, she was stopped with a chorus of "shut up" from all three males listening to her.

Michael was surprised at Uncle Joe who had just violated one of his very own "rules for females". He had yelled at Charlie and told her to "shut up". He looked up at Uncle Joe to point out his mistake, but thought better of it since Uncle Joe's face was a funny purple color, and the veins in his neck looked like they were close to bursting.

"Boy, what makes you say something like that? If this is your idea of a joke, we need to discuss your sense of humor cause I ain't laughing," warned Uncle Joe.

Michael swallowed hard, suddenly wishing he hadn't mentioned the marijuana. However, it was too late now. Michael began to stammer,

"Tho, tho, those weeds over there are not just weeds. They are marijuana plants. I know because I've seen marijuana plants growing from before, when I lived in Detroit."

Uncle Joe walked quickly over to the tall weeds and began a close inspection of them. He wasn't very familiar with marijuana because he had no reason to be. He didn't like drugs or what they did to people, but he came to the conclusion that Michael was right. These were great big marijuana plants that some low down dirty dog had planted on his property!

Not only had they planted them on his property, they had cultivated the ground around them, had put plant food stakes, and milk jugs full of water at the base of each plant for feeding and watering them. If Uncle Joe's face had been purple before, the knowledge of the extent of the criminal activity that was going on at his farm made his face look dangerously close to exploding! As he surveyed the plants, he became aware of a path through the tall grass that led to the edge of his property. He began to follow it and what he found made him even madder, if that was possible.

Charlie, Michael, and Max had stayed put while Uncle Joe was doing his inspection. It seemed like the safest thing to do, given Uncle Joe's present frame of mind. It proved to be a wise decision, because the explosion they heard coming from Uncle Joe should have had a mushroom cloud over it.

"Oh man, I don't know what he found, but it's got to be pretty bad. I think we should just wait for him to come back here. I sure don't want to go see what's wrong, do you?" asked Max.

Michael and Charlie both nodded their agreement quickly, but they didn't have long to wait. Uncle Joe came barreling back, yelling at the top of his lungs, "Do you know what those sidewinders did?" Before any of them could answer, he continued, "Those stinking low life's cut my fence, my good wire fence. My cows could have gotten out. Can you believe that somebody would do that to another man's property? Just wait till I get my hands on them. I'll teach them not to mess around with Joe Hayes. Why when I'm through with them there won't be enough left of them to think about a marijuana crop much less come on my property and tear up a man's fence."

"Uh, Grandpa Joe," said Max, "why don't we take their marijuana plants. They cut our fence."

"Good idea," said Joe, "I'll not have this poison on my farm!"

With that he began to pull plants out of the ground by their roots. The three kids didn't move, they just watched a very angry Joe Hayes take out his fury on some very unfortunate plants. When he had finished, it looked like a pot tornado had come though the field, uprooted them, and thrown them down.

Joe stood up, took off his hat, and wiped his forehead on the back of his hand. As he looked around at the carnage he had caused, a satisfied smile began to show on his face.

"Okay you three, here's what we're going to do…."

Now what was taking Joe so long? Maggie loved him with all her heart, but that didn't keep her from becoming exasperated with him. He had a habit of getting involved with things and forgetting the time. She needed him to go back into town for her. She had forgotten that her chickens were out of feed. As she looked out her kitchen window for what seemed like the hundredth time, she saw a cloud of dust with a yellow center coming down the dirt road. It's about time, she thought, but as she continued to watch, she began to frown. Now what on earth has that man got flopping out of the back of the mustard machine?

Joe was smiling ear to ear as he bounced down the dirt road with his haul hanging out the back window that refused to raise up. Joe was so excited that he was driving like a mad man. Just wait till Miss Maggie sees this! Everything he did involved thoughts of Miss Maggie. He thought he saw her peering out the kitchen window, but he couldn't be sure because he was making too much dust on his wild ride to get home.

Joe's wild ride wasn't lost on his three passengers. Charlie was in the front seat with her seat belt on, but that didn't convince her she wouldn't go airborne at any second. Both boys were in the back seat, and every big bump in the road caused them to be bounced so high that they hit their heads on the roof of the car. There were no seatbelts in the back seat, and there were definitely no shock absorbers on the mustard machine. An added benefit of no shock absorbers was the feeling of your stomach jumping up in your throat when you hit a really big bump. Between Joe's satisfaction with his own personal drug bust and Max, Michael, and Charlie enjoying the ride of their lives, all four occupants were grinning ear to ear as they came to a roaring stop in the driveway by Maggie's kitchen door. Before the dust could settle, Joe had jumped out of the vehicle and begun to call for his wife.

"Hey good looking, come and see what I brought you."

Miss Maggie came though the screen door, waving her hand in front of her face to try and clear some of the dust away so she could see. "My heavens, Joe, what have you got in your car?"

"Now honey, you know the mustard machine is not just a car. It's a ride," said Joe as he grabbed Miss Maggie's elbow to steer her around back to see what he had.

"A ride is an understatement," said Michael, "I've been on roller coaster rides that weren't that scary."

Max nodded in agreement, and for once, Charlie didn't say anything but she did look a little green.

Joe proudly presented his cache to Miss Maggie, "Look here sweetheart, I've made my very own drug bust. Yep, that's right just me and the kids. What do you think about that?"

"I think you need to explain what you are talking about. I don't see any drugs. Just some very big weeds."

"Those very big weeds are the drugs! Its marijuana and it was growing in our back pasture. The crooks that were growing it cut our fence so they could tend their crop without having to climb through the fence. I had the last laugh, though, because I took all their pot. Yes sir, not one single plant left."

"Now Joe, you know two wrongs don't make one right," said Miss Maggie as she looked sternly at the big man.

Michael leaned over and asked Max, "What does that mean?"

"It's one of Granny Maggie's sayings. It means just because one person does something wrong, it's no excuse for you to do something wrong," answered Max.

"I didn't do anything wrong, honey. I just made a citizen's arrest so to speak of an illegal substance. Why I had impressionable children present, and it was my duty to do the right thing and remove this stuff," answered Joe in his most heroic tone.

"Now we have to be on our way. We are going to take this to the sheriff and let him know what has been going on out here."

Miss Maggie still wasn't sure about Joe's explanation, but she didn't how she could argue with what he had just said. "Hold on just a minute, Superman, Charlie has to stay with me because her Mom could come to pick her up before you get home. Oh, I need some chicken feed from town as long as you are going that way. I'm all out."

"You got it darlin'. Load up, boys, we're headed to Daws Laws office."

Both boys jumped in the back seat to get the most out of the ride again, and they were off in another cloud of dust.

Charlie just stood there shaking her head and said, "Does he always drive like that, Miss Maggie?"

"Not when I'm with him, but I'm not so sure when he's on his own. Sweetie, my Joe is a fifteen year old trapped in a grown up's body," said Maggie, but she was smiling as she said it.

The mustard machine roared into town with its prize waving in the breeze. As the boys watched the sheriff's office go by they looked at each other wondering where they were going.

"Uh, Grandpa Joe didn't we just pass the sheriff's office?" asked Max.

"Yep, we're gonna get Miss Maggie's chicken feed first. Besides I want to show my buddy, John Hill, what we've got. He manages the feed store. Here we are boys. Hop out," said Joe as he shoved the car in park.

John Hill was on the sidewalk in front of his store as Joe and the boys parked and got out. John smiled as he saw Joe approach. One look at Joe's face told him he was up to something.

"Hi, Joe, what's new?" asked John.

"Just walk to the back of this fine automobile, and I'll show you," answered Joe.

As John rounded the car's fender and saw what was in the back, his eyes grew large and the first words out of his mouth were, "Have you lost your mind? Get that stuff off my property. Don't you know you could get me in a lot of trouble if the law comes by and sees this parked here? Why there's no telling what could happen or what kind of fine I could have to pay. I'm telling you Joe, get that out of here."

By this time, poor John Hill was almost in the middle of a fit. He knew Joe Hayes was one of those people that could get by with anything. Unfortunately, he was not. The thought of that much marijuana being found in his parking lot conjured up all kind of images, and all of them were bad.

"Calm down, John. You'll have a stroke. Don't you want to hear the story of how I got it?"

"NO, I don't care. I just want it gone!" With that John turned and walked back in the store.

"Come on, boys, let's go find Daws Laws. Some people just don't have any sporting blood," said Joe.

They went back to the sheriff's office only to find it locked with a sign that said "Back soon, Daws".

"Now what, Grandpa Joe?" asked Max.

"Well, we'll just go to old Daws Laws house. We'll make a home delivery."

When they got to the sheriff's house, no one was home.

"Now if that don't beat all. Most lawmen spend their time trying to find this stuff, and here we are trying to find one to give it to. We'll just leave it here for the sheriff. Give me a hand boys," said Joe as he backed up to the sheriff's front porch.

Brenda Dawson

Daws Laws pulled into his driveway. It had been a very busy day, and he was looking forward to relaxing in his easy chair. Now what was that on his front porch? It looked like a bunch of plants. As he approached, he recognized the plants were marijuana. As he was looking at them, he saw a note with his name on it attached to his door. He opened it and began to smile as he read: "I've been out doing your job for you. Couldn't find you at your office so I made a home delivery. Joe Hayes." He knew there would be a story to go with this that would be worth the listening.

Chapter 32

Doc was looking over the half door of his stall expectantly. It was past time for the boy to come and get him. He had begun to look for Michael. Not in the same way he looked for Susan when she had been there. No other human could take her place, but this boy had become important to him. He had something and someone to look forward to now. Doc didn't know what he was experiencing was love. It was what made life good for man and animal. Without it, life was devoid of color, meaning, and purpose. Without love, one's world was a very dark place.

Doc wasn't the only one looking for Michael. Robert Bradley was watching the clock and getting more aggravated by the minute. Where was that kid? He should have been at the barn an hour ago. It was the middle of June and Michael had been coming to take care of Doc for almost eight weeks now.

Since school was out for the summer, Joe had been letting Michael ride the four-wheeler through the back roads to come to the barn. It was a situation that Robert didn't like one bit. Joe should know that those four-wheelers could be dangerous. Why it seemed like you were always hearing about somebody getting hurt or killed on one of those things on the news. Michael was a city kid. He didn't know how to handle equipment like a boy who grew up on a farm. Robert made up his mind that he was going to have a talk with Joe about this four-wheeler thing. He looked at his watch again, and walked to the window to see if he could see Michael coming across the pasture. There was still no sign of him.

Robert had begun to care for Michael much like Doc. Robert had been in a dark place in his life for a very long time. He had begun to feel that life was not worth living. Who could have known that one kid and one rock would change his life like it had. Before Michael had started to come to his barn, one day was just like the next. There was nothing or no one to make a difference. Robert didn't realize that his bleak life was of his own making. When his daughter had died, he had tuned his mourning and grief into his way of life. One day became the next, and the next, and the next, and he sank deeper and deeper into his dark pit. If it hadn't been for Michael it may never have changed. Robert got up in the morning now eagerly looking for Michael. He told himself it was for Miss Maggie's bacon and biscuits, but he knew that wasn't the truth.

Robert heard something and walked to the window again. He let out the breath that he didn't know he had been holding as a feeling of relief flooded over him. Michael was coming across the field and going to the barn. Robert hurried to get his hat and meet him.

As Michael got off the four-wheeler Doc neighed a loud greeting to him.

"Hello to you, too, big fella," said Michael as he reached for the big round cake box Aunt Maggie had sent with him. She had given him instructions to be careful and not drop it on the way over. It contained one of her famous butter and cream cheese pound cakes still hot from the oven.

Robert got to the barn and spoke sharply to Michael, "Boy where have you been? Don't you know you are almost an hour late?" Michael had no way of knowing his anger was caused by worry.

"I'm sorry Mr. Bradley. Uncle Joe's green beans had to be picked for Aunt Maggie. She wants to can them tomorrow. She said Miss Twilla doesn't have her garden this year and she wants to can some beans for her. She started to send you some, but she said she thought you would rather have a pound cake so she made you one. It was still baking so I had to wait on it. Here you go," said Michael as he handed the warm cake box to Robert.

Running for Home

Robert suddenly felt bad for the way he had spoken to Michael. The kid was late because he was doing something for his Aunt Maggie, and she was doing something nice for him.

"Oh, that's okay," said Robert as he awkwardly patted Michael on the back, "Did you say that cake is still hot?"

"Yes sir. Aunt Maggie said to tell you to take it in the house and take the top off the cake box to let it finish cooling."

"Well, I guess I better do what Miss Maggie says. You go ahead and take Doc out, and I'll check on you later," said Robert. He could already taste the warm cake with a good cup of coffee as he hurried off to the house with his prize.

Not even Robert's sharp words could dampen Michael's day. He loved his life with Aunt Maggie and the rest of the family. He especially loved the way he got to do things he had never done before, like ride the four-wheeler and take care of Doc. He was still worried that Mr. Bradley would tell him to stop coming, but he hadn't mentioned it yet. He even had started to like Mr. Bradley after he found out why he was so grouchy.

Michael still didn't know a lot about God. He knew that Aunt Maggie said that when you prayed, you talked to God and told him everything that was important to you, and asked God for his help. Lately he had started to ask God for help to stay with Doc and for Mr. Bradley's happiness. Michael just wished he knew how to tell if God was listening. Michael decided God must not have heard him yet, because Mr. Bradley had been so fussy with him when he got there. Oh well, he guessed it wouldn't hurt to keep trying, because Aunt Maggie sure thought God answered your prayers.

Chapter 33

Michael sat on the big, flat rock in the middle of the creek watching Doc paw and splash in the cool water. This was something else he had never done before he came to Cedar Grove, play in a creek. Mr. Bradley said that water was good for any kind of injury so he should take Doc and stand him in the creek to let the cold water and the current take the soreness out of his leg. Michael didn't know about the creek at the back of one of Mr. Bradley's pastures until he started taking Doc there, and now it was one of his favorite places. There were huge, old trees that shaded parts of the water, and there were big, flat rocks in the creek that were perfect for sitting or walking.

Michael was on the rock with his jeans rolled up to his knees so they would stay dry skipping rocks. He didn't even have to hold Doc's lead rope, because the big horse loved the water and would stand in it until Michael led him out. Michael still thought Doc was the smartest horse in the world. Of course his knowledge of horses was limited to Doc, but that didn't matter to Michael. As he looked at him, he again wondered what it must feel like to ride such a huge animal. He wished Mr. Bradley liked him well enough to teach him how to ride, but he didn't think that would ever happen. Before he could give riding any more thought, he felt a sharp sting in the small of his back.

"Ow," said Michael as he turned to see what had happened. "Charlie, I should have known it was you! Why'd you throw that rock at me?" he demanded.

"Because you looked like a big old toad sitting on a rock and I was trying to make you jump in the water like a good frog should," she said.

Michael drew back to let a big rock fly in her direction.

"Wait! I was just joking. Good grief, don't you have any sense of humor? I was just going to splash you to get your attention and my arm slipped when I threw the rock. That's the truth. Mr. Bradley sent me to tell you that he had to go into town to the grocery store, something about needing coffee. He said for you to rub Doc down, go ahead and feed him, put him in his stall and he would see you tomorrow."

Michael wasn't sure about the rock slipping part, but he was glad to get Mr. Bradley's message.

"Okay, I guess," he said, "Come on Doc. Time to go for your afternoon brushing." Michael reached out and clipped the lead rope to Doc's halter, then walked on the rocks back to the bank leading him.

"Why don't you ride him out of the water? His leg is healed enough for that," said Charlie.

Michael looked at her, and for once she didn't seem to be trying to start something with him.

"Because I don't know how to ride a horse," he admitted.

"I can teach you," said Charlie.

"Yeah, right. Like I would trust you. Every time I'm around you bad things happen," Michael said rubbing his back.

"Look I can't help it if you are accident prone. You know some people are just clumsy. I think they are born that way. Maybe you are one of those people and you can't help it. Anyway, I promise I can teach you to ride. Did you forget my Mom is a champion barrel racer? She's taught me everything she knows so I'll just teach you," said Charlie pushing her thick glasses back up on her nose.

Michael looked at her to try and see if she was up to something, but she looked like she meant what she said. Her Mom was a barrel racer. He knew that much was true. He had seen some barrel races on TV recently, and he knew that to do that you had to be a good rider. He had never seen Charlie ride, but it made sense that her Mom would teach her how. Michael narrowed his eyes and looked at her.

"Do you promise you are telling the truth?"

"Yes, you big chicken," she said.

"Okay, when do we start?" asked Michael.

"How about right now?" said Charlie

"What are we gonna use for a horse?" asked Michael.

"Oh I don't know, maybe the one at the end of that lead rope you're holding! Duh!" said Charlie.

"You mean Doc? He's almost well and I don't want to hurt him. Besides, what will Mr. Bradley say?"

"You won't hurt him. You aren't going to do anything today but just walk him in the corral at the barn. Mr. Bradley won't say anything because remember he's gone to town. Now do you want to learn how to ride or not?"

Something didn't feel right about what Charlie was telling him. He didn't want to make Mr. Bradley mad at him, but he really, really wanted to know how to ride a horse.

"Okay let's go."

They walked Doc back to the barn, and put him in the corral. Charlie went to get her Mom's saddle out of the tack room. She told Michael they didn't need a bridle, they could just use the halter and lead rope. Charlie came back with the saddle but she couldn't find a saddle blanket. She said they didn't need one of those either. Michael thought they were sure missing lots of stuff, but Charlie said she knew all about it and not to worry.

They managed to get the saddle on Doc's back, and then Charlie took over.

"Watch carefully how I put the saddle on," she said. "You have to put it in the center of their back then tie the girth with the strap on the saddle, like so." Charlie looped the strap two times through a ring on the saddle and said, "All done."

"Will that stay? Don't you tie a knot in it or something?"

"Well, I guess suddenly you know how to saddle a horse better than me. I'll just stand back and let you do it," with that Charlie put her hands on her hips and stepped back.

"Don't be so sensitive," said Michael, "I was just asking. What do we do next?"

"Well, we tie the lead rope in both sides of the halter to make reins and you climb on." Charlie fixed the lead rope and motioned Michael to get on Doc's back.

It took several tries, but Michael managed to get in the saddle. He felt like he was sitting on a mountain and began to rethink Charlie's idea. Doc was so big and tall, and the ground looked a long way down. Michael swallowed and said, "Now what?"

"Now we have to work on how you sit in the saddle. You are supposed to grip with your knees and legs. Don't worry about keeping you feet in the stirrups because all good riders don't even need stirrups. Now do what I said, pull your feet and legs up high in the saddle and squeeze. That way when your horse moves, you are ready for it."

Michael did as she instructed, but it felt very uncomfortable and off balance.

"Are you sure this is right?"

"Yes, you just aren't very good at it yet. Now take the rein, and hold it very high in the air. That way your horse knows you have the reins, and you are in charge."

Michael did as she said. He wondered if he could ever get used to such a strange position. This didn't look like the way the riders on TV had been sitting on their horses.

While Charlie had been giving her lesson, and Michael had been doing what she said, Doc had been getting nervous. Whatever Michael was doing on his back did not feel right. The saddle was pinching him without a saddle blanket, and for some reason Michael was pulling his head very high up in the air. Doc began to move and shake his head to try and get Michael to release some of the pressure from the reins.

"Charlie! What do I do now? He's moving," yelled Michael forgetting Mr. Bradley's rule of never yelling around horses.

"Don't ask me. I didn't tell you to make him move. If you're not going to listen to me and do what I say, I quit." With that Charlie stomped off and left Michael and Doc in the corral.

Robert Bradley had gotten almost all the way to town when he remembered he had not told Charlie to give Michael Miss Maggie's cake box back. It was worth turning around and telling Michael himself, because Miss Maggie might just give him a refill. He still had to go back to town to get his coffee, but a man had to know his priorities. Just as he tuned in the drive and glanced toward the barn, he slammed on the brakes. There in the middle of his corral sat Michael on Doc with the weirdest form he had ever seen anyone have on the back of a horse.

Chapter 34

Robert got out of his truck and hurried over to the corral. His thoughts were going a hundred miles an hour! What was that boy thinking? Was he trying to get himself killed? Didn't he know Doc could hurt him? What in the world made him get in such a strange position in the saddle, because you couldn't sit on a horse like that without trying? Robert's thoughts were stopped abruptly when he looked at the saddle girth and saw it had come loose and was dangling under Doc's belly. The only thing keeping the saddle on Doc's back was Michael sitting in it, and he was doing a lousy job of that.

As Robert got to the corral gate, he got his first look at Michael's face. The boy was so scared he couldn't move which in this case was a good thing, because any movement on his part would send the saddle and him crashing to the ground.

"Michael, listen to me and do exactly what I say. Don't make any sudden movements, but slowly lower your hands and legs, and relax them."

Michael grabbed onto every word that Robert said like a drowning man grabs a life preserver. He very slowly did as Robert said, and was relieved to notice that Doc calmed instantly.

"Now Michael," said Robert, "I'm going to open the gate and come into the corral. Just sit still and wait for me to get to you." Robert didn't add that he and Doc didn't much care for each other, and that he was worried Doc might shy away from him. If he did the saddle was sure to move enough to frighten the horse and make him buck or run away.

Either way Michael stood a very good chance of getting hurt. These thoughts caused Robert's heart to beat fast and his hands to shake. It was a physical reaction to a strong emotional fear. Robert said a quick prayer for Michael's safety without even realizing it.

Robert quietly opened the gate and began to walk slowly and easily to Doc calling his name and saying "whoa" softly and repeatedly. Doc was thoroughly confused by this time. Nothing had felt right to him since Charlie had begun to saddle him. The only reason he had not exploded was his trust in Michael, and he was doing some strange things on his back. No one had ridden him but Susan since he came to this farm, and that had been a very long time ago. He had certainly never had an inexperienced rider on his back, or his saddle and bridle in such an unusual manner. Horses are creatures of habit, and anything new is usually pretty scary to them. Doc was no exception. As he watched Robert approach, his eyes got wide and he began to move away.

Robert watched Michael begin to shift to the side in the saddle. He knew he had to act now or Michael might suffer a bad fall. He reached out quickly and grabbed Doc's halter. The giant horse startled at the movement just enough for Michael and the saddle to hit the ground in a heap. Since Robert had a hold on Doc's halter, there was no danger of Michael getting stepped on or kicked by Doc trying to get away from the scary situation he saw on the ground next to him.

"Easy boy," Robert told the big horse quietly. Even though he had strong feelings against Doc, he was still a good horseman and instinctively quieted the animal. As Doc began to settle down, Robert looked at Michael. He was on the ground with one leg still over the saddle, looking like he had just escaped death.

"Boy, are you alright?" asked Robert.

Michael could only nod. For some reason his voice didn't seem to be working.

"Well, that's good because you've got some explaining to do. You never take a man's horse for a ride without his permission. I'm going to put Doc in his stall. You dust yourself off and get ready to so some talking!"

Michael got up and began to beat the corral dust off with his hands. All the while he was thinking and worrying. What was he going to do? What was he going to tell Mr. Bradley? Was he going to be in a lot of trouble? What would Aunt Maggie and Uncle Joe do? Would they send him back to Michigan? Would this be the thing that made them do that? What would happen to him now? Would he ever get to take care of Doc again? It suddenly seemed like everything that had become so important to him was within a hair's breath of disappearing! It was all because of one bad choice he had made. Why did he ever listen to Charlie? Even with all the unanswered questions, he knew that Charlie was not to blame. He was the one who had made the decision.

As he finished putting the saddle up, he knew what he had to do. He had to tell Mr. Bradley the truth, and then Uncle Joe and Aunt Maggie. Michael said a prayer, "God, please, don't let me have to leave this place." It was a short, silent, simple prayer that had the power to control his life!

Chapter 35

Uncle Joe put down his fork and licked his lips as the last bite of Miss Maggie's pound cake passed his lips.

"I know that's the best pound cake you've ever made, Miss Maggie," declared Joe as he took a big drink of ice cold milk.

"Oh Joe, you say that about every cake and pie I make. With you, the one you are eating at the time is always the best," laughed Maggie.

"And what's wrong with that? You can't fault a man for being truthful sweetheart," said Joe as he gave Maggie a big hug. "I have to go cut a tree that fell across the fence. It shouldn't take too long. Don't worry I'll have my appetite back for supper."

"I've never known you to not have your appetite Joe," laughed Maggie.

Joe headed to the door. As he opened it he saw Robert Bradley's truck coming down the driveway, with the four-wheeler in the back. "Well, what the….? I bet the four-wheeler broke down." Joe was mostly talking to himself, but Maggie heard him and hurried to look.

"Oh Joe, you don't think Michael had a wreck on it and got hurt do you?"

"Naw, probably just a busted fuel line or something. It's mighty nice of Robert to bring it home instead of calling me to go and get it. Does he seem like he's getting a little more sociable to you?"

Aunt Maggie didn't have time to answer. Robert and Michael were getting out of his truck and coming to the house.

Michael had told Mr. Bradley the whole story. He told him about wanting to learn to ride a horse, about loving Doc, and wanting to still take care of him, and how sorry he was for what had happened. Mr. Bradley had listened to the whole story without saying a word. When Michael had finished, he told him to get in the truck, because he was going to take Michael and the four-wheeler home. That was the last thing that had been said. Now here they were at Uncle Joe and Aunt Maggie's and Michael had a belly full of butterflies. He knew he would have to tell it all over again.

"Hello, Robert. Is everything okay?" asked Joe.

"No I'm afraid not, Michael has some things he needs to tell you," said Robert.

"Well come on in and let's have a listen," said Uncle Joe as he held the door open for them.

Once they were all in the house and seated around the kitchen table, Michael again gave an account of what had happened at Mr. Bradley's farm. When he finished he told them how sorry he was, and how he wished it had never happened.

No one said anything for a little while then Uncle Joe said, "Michael, were you hurt?"

"No sir," answered Michael.

"Robert was anything broken, or was the horse hurt in any way?"

"No to both questions," answered Robert. "I just thought it best to bring Michael home instead of letting him ride that machine since he was a little shaken up."

The last part of Robert's answer made everyone's head come up and look at each other! Was this really the hardhearted Robert Bradley they all knew? A knowing smile faintly touched Maggie's lips. She knew then that Robert cared for Michael. He didn't bring him home in his truck because he was mad at him. He brought Michael home because he was worried about him. Of course Michael didn't know that, but that was okay… Maggie looked at Joe who had a puzzled look on his face about what to do next.

"Robert, since you are the offended party, what do you think we should do?" Maggie asked. She was very interested in seeing what kind of discipline Robert would mete out.

Robert was completely caught off guard. So was Michael, whose first thought was "this is going to be bad".

"Well, well, I don't, I mean, uh, I haven't thought about it," stammered Robert.

Uncle Joe had taken off his hat and was thoughtfully scratching his head, Michael was looking very intently at the kitchen table, and Robert was staring off into space like the answer would come from there. Aunt Maggie decided it was time to play her trump card.

"We understand if you are angry with Michael, Robert and don't want him to come back to your farm. Joe and I will pay off whatever is left of the bill that Michael still owes if you want us to."

All three male heads snapped up at the same time. Joe didn't really want to do that. Michael was afraid they would do that, and Robert was surprised because he had not even thought of that. When Maggie saw Robert's expression, she knew she had been right in her assessment of the situation. Robert did not want Michael to stop coming to help him.

"Now, Miss Maggie, let's don't be hasty. The boy still needs to learn his lesson for hurting the horse, and I'm not that mad at him. He's just now learning how to take care of things at the barn without me telling him everything to do. I think we can come up with something better than that," said Robert.

Maggie had been watching Michael, too. She could tell that he didn't want to stop going to Robert's barn.

"Hmm," she said, "how about we just plan on Michael helping you the rest of the summer. That would finish his vet bill off, and be his punishment for riding your horse without your permission. What do you think?"

Again all three male heads popped up and looked at Maggie, but this time all three were smiling. Maggie was quite pleased with their response.

Robert appeared to giving the idea some serious thought and said, "I guess we could do that. It sounds like what would be best for the boy. Yeah, it's fine with me. What do you think Joe?"

"Oh, it's good with me," said Joe

"Fine, then it's settled," said Maggie. "Michael will continue working for you just as he has been, and he will definitely not do anything without your permission. Right, Michael?"

"Yes mam," said Michael.

Robert got up from the table to leave, but stopped and asked Michael, "Why didn't you ask me to teach you how to ride a horse?"

Again, three heads snapped up, but this time Maggie's was one of them with a very surprised look on her face.

"I didn't think you would want to," was all Michael could say.

"Well, if you still want to learn, and it's okay with Miss Maggie and Joe, I'll teach you," said Robert.

Michael was ecstatic! He was going to learn how to ride and he would have a great teacher. Maggie and Joe were both speechless but did manage to nod their consent.

"Fine then, we'll start tomorrow. No lace up boots. Only pull on boots, and they need to be a half size too big. I don't want any feet hung in stirrups. If your boot is a little too big it can come off if it needs to. Joe, can you help me unload the four-wheeler, and I wanted to talk to you about that thing," said Robert as he headed for the door.

"Uh, sure," said Joe as he looked somewhat confused at Maggie. Maggie just raised her eyebrows and shook her head.

"Michael, come on and give us a hand," said Joe

All three left to go outside, and Maggie began to get ready to fix supper. Her mind wasn't on cooking though. It was on thanking God for sending them Michael. He was proving to be like one of the stones that he had told her about skipping in the creek. He had landed in their house, but he was making ripples that spread out and touched others, like Robert. She had been praying for Robert for ten years. She had even begun to sometimes think Robert was a lost cause, but she knew with God, there were no lost causes. There were only roads people took that caused them to be lost from the purpose God had for them. Continuing to pray for someone was much like a search party never giving up looking for someone who was lost in a wilderness. Michael and Robert both needed a purpose, and it was beginning to look like they might have found it in each other. Maggie smiled to herself as she once again thought God's timing is always perfect.

Chapter 36

Michael had been too excited to sleep much last night. He kept waking up thinking about how he was going to be riding Doc! When the alarm clock finally went off at 5:00, he jumped out of bed a full hour earlier than normal. It brought a moan of protest from Max, who rolled over and put his pillow over his head.

Michael dressed quickly and went downstairs to the kitchen. Aunt Maggie looked up in surprise at the early riser.

"Goodness, Michael, you're up with the chickens this morning. Why so early?"

"Today is the first day of my riding lessons. I mean my real riding lessons, and I don't want to be late."

Maggie had put her apron on and was just starting the breakfast biscuits. "Michael, sit down in this chair by me. We need to talk."

Michael was instantly on edge. Aunt Maggie or Uncle Joe hadn't said anything to him about what had happened at Mr. Bradley's farm. This must be it, he thought. His heart began to beat fast as he imagined all the possible things Aunt Maggie was about to tell him. Were they going to send him back to Michigan after he worked all summer for Mr. Bradley!

"Uncle Joe and I talked last night about what happened yesterday at Robert's farm," she said.

Oh no! This was it. They had waited to talk about it by themselves, so it must be a big decision. Michael just knew he would have to leave Cedar Grove. He couldn't stand the thought of it. He jumped up and put his arms around Aunt Maggie.

"I'm so sorry for what I did. I'll never do anything like that again, only please, please, let me stay here. I'll work for Mr. Bradley forever if you want me to. Please, don't send me away!"

Maggie was totally caught off guard by what Michael said. It had never entered their minds for Michael not to stay with them. Gracious, when was this child going to accept they were not going to throw him away? As he hugged her, she could feel his body shake with fear. That did it. Maggie quickly dusted the flour off her hands, and wrapped Michael in a big hug. It was the best feeling in the world to Michael.

"Oh Michael, when will you believe us when we tell you that you are part of this family, and you aren't going anywhere. Just because things happen doesn't mean we can't deal with them, and put them behind us, and go on," said Maggie. She held Michael away from her so he had to look at her and continued, "Do you understand me, Michael?"

Michael could only nod vigorously and grab Aunt Maggie in another big hug.

Maggie smiled and said, "Now have a seat. I have some things I need to tell you."

Michael did as he was told and Maggie went back to her biscuits as she spoke.

"I think you know now that what you did yesterday was wrong don't you?" Michael again nodded.

"Good," continued Maggie, "I want you to understand something else. When you work for someone like you are working for Robert, they have to be able to trust you with what they ask you to do. That is what makes a good employee and an honest person. It doesn't matter what kind of job you are doing it's still the same from cleaning stalls to being the president of a company. My Mother always said "anything that's honest is honorable", and that's true. Always be sure you never do anything to break someone's trust in you."

"Do you think Mr. Bradley won't trust me anymore?" asked Michael.

"No, I don't think that. It may take a little while for him to trust you as much as he did, but I think he will. Uncle Joe and I are very proud of you for telling the truth about what happened. We also want you to know that when someone gives you a job, you have to be responsible and do the job well. Okay?"

"Yes Mam," replied Michael.

"Something else. Remember that Robert can be a little grumpy, but don't take it personally. It's just his way."

"I know, Aunt Maggie. I won't."

"Good, now set the table for me while I put these biscuits in the oven and we'll have breakfast."

Chapter 37

Maggie and Joe stood at the kitchen window watching Michael start the four-wheeler and leave for Robert's farm.

"You know Maggie, it was the dangest thing Robert wanted to talk to me about yesterday. He told me he didn't think Michael should be riding the four-wheeler to his barn. He said he would come and pick him up, if need be. I told him Michael was fine with the four-wheeler, but thanks anyway. That didn't satisfy him. He thinks they are dangerous and offered again to come pick Michael up. I finally told him Michael needed to learn to operate different kinds of equipment, and riding over to his farm was good experience. Robert wouldn't shut up about it till I promised to make Michael go no faster than second gear, which is pretty slow. What do you think that was all about?"

"I think Robert is starting to care for Michael. With his history of loss with his family, he is afraid something will happen to Michael. I also think that's why he offered to teach Michael how to ride a horse. He wanted to be sure he was taught correctly so he would have the skills to be a safe rider."

Joe took a minute to think about it and just said a very profound, "Don't that beat all."

Maggie was right in everything she thought about Robert Bradley. Robert had been scared to death when he had seen Michael sitting precariously on Doc's back yesterday. For ten years he had been alone in his house with his memories and grief. After Susan's death some people had come by to see him, but that stopped with time. He couldn't seem to make himself leave his house to go on with his life. Some strange belief made him feel if he did he would lose what little hold he still had of his daughter, and she would be gone. He hadn't changed anything in her room to this day. He would go in there and see a scrap of paper with her handwriting on it or smell her perfume, and for a few brief moments it was like she was still with him. He hadn't done anything because he didn't know which would be more painful, going into her room, or not having her room to go into.

Then he met Michael. When he first heard about what the kid had done, he had been angry. He didn't like to even think about Doc, and now he had to put him in a stall and care for his injury. He made up his mind Michael was just a punk kid from up north and he didn't want any part of him. The only reason he let him on his farm was to work off the vet bill the boy caused. He didn't realize at the time he would have to be at the barn twice a day to show him what to do. He hadn't been getting out of his house for days at a time, and now he had to be at the barn in the morning and evening. He also had to have contact with another human being two times a day.

Robert's problem wasn't that he didn't have a heart. He had just put a brick wall around it so it didn't break anymore. He had always had a soft spot for kids. That was why he wanted to help them before Susan died. The more he was around Michael, the more he liked him. He began to look for him in the morning and afternoon. Robert didn't notice that he didn't go in Susan's room as often as before.

Robert was finishing his second cup of coffee while waiting for Michael. He had a problem that he was trying to sort out. When he had told Michael he would teach him how to ride, he forgot he no longer had a good gentle lesson horse. When Susan had been there they had quite a few to pick from, but since she had been gone, he had sold all the horses except Doc. The only reason he kept Doc was Susan had made him promise to always take care of her favorite horse if anything happened to her. She had been half joking when she said it, because neither of them expected Doc to outlive his master.

The only other horse in the barn was Tessa's gray horse and he was too much for a beginner to handle. Robert decided to go ahead and use Doc for the first few days, because Michael wouldn't be riding until he learned what he needed to know on the ground. Since Michael had been taking care of Doc, the horse was used to the boy and the groundwork should go fine. He would have to find a horse somewhere to borrow that was gentle enough for a beginning rider. Robert caught a movement out of the corner of his eye. He looked up to see Michael bouncing much slower than usual over the pasture to his barn. "Now that's better," Robert said to himself with a smile.

Michael had begun to think he would never get to Mr. Bradley's barn. He wasn't sure but he felt like being limited to going so slow on the four-wheeler was part of his punishment for the whole incident with Doc and Charlie. He made sure he didn't break his "speed limit". He wasn't about to risk doing anything else that might get him in trouble. As he stopped in front of the barn, Mr. Bradley walked up.

"Morning Michael. Go ahead and do your chores. When you finish, come to the house and get me and we'll start your first riding lesson."

"Yes sir!" said Michael as he quickly began to get to work. He could just see himself riding Doc in a little while. Michael wondered to himself if Mr. Bradley would be letting him barrel race by this afternoon. Probably not, he decided, he'll probably save something to teach me tomorrow.

Michael finished his work in record time and ran to the house to get Mr. Bradley. Robert had been watching him all morning from his window and smiled to himself as Michael knocked on the door. Robert opened the door.

"I'm all finished Mr. Bradley."

"Okay, let's go," said Robert as he got his hat. They walked down to the barn. Robert told Michael to get Doc out and tie him in the hallway of the barn. Michael did as he was told, all the while just knowing he was going to be in the saddle soon and on Doc's back.

Robert watched as Michael tied Doc the way he had taught him to when he had been taking care of his leg. He was glad to see that Michael tied Doc at "eye height and arms length" so the horse would not get tangled in the lead rope. Eye height meant that whatever you tied your horse to was about the height of your horse's eye when his head is level with his withers or shoulders. Arm's length meant that you give your horse no more slack in the rope than the length of your arm. That way they don't get tangled in the rope. Michael also used the knot he had shown him that could be untied by just pulling the end of the rope. When Doc was secure in the hallway, Robert told Michael to go ahead and groom him. He wanted to watch Michael do this task also.

"When you are brushing a horse out to ride, you always pay extra attention to their backs and under their bellies. You don't want anything under your saddle that might stick or pinch them," Robert told Michael who nodded and began to brush those two areas of Doc for all he was worth. Michael just knew he would be placing the saddle on Doc in a matter of minutes. When he had finished brushing, he looked to Mr. Bradley for further instructions.

"Good job, boy, now put him back in his stall."

"Huh?" said Michael not thinking he had heard correctly.

"Put Doc back in his stall," repeated Robert.

"But I thought I was going to get a riding lesson. How can I ride him if I put him up?"

"You're getting a riding lesson but your horse is out back. Now put him up, and let's go get on your horse."

Michael was more than a little disappointed. He wanted to ride Doc, not some other horse. He did as Robert said, and the two of them walked out to the back of the big barn. Michael looked eagerly for his horse, but there wasn't one anywhere!

"Mr. Bradley, I don't see my horse."

"Sure you do boy, he's right there under the shed."

Michael looked again closely, but still didn't see a horse.

"Where is it?" Michael finally asked.

"There he is right there. His name is Ol Blue."

"The only thing I see is a blue barrel hanging from ropes," said Michael.

"That's your horse, Michael," said Mr. Bradley laughing and patting Michael on the back.

"Oh, so you're not really going to give me riding lessons. It was all just a big joke," said Michael, feeling like he had fallen for a bad joke.

"No, that's not true. I am going to teach you how to ride but when I get through with you, boy, if you listen and do what I say, you will be able to ride anything you want to. Now come on over here and meet Ol Blue."

Michael noticed a saddle on the ground by the barrel. The ropes that secured the barrel had old pieces of inner tubes tied to them and they were connected to the barrel. There was a handle on the front of the barrel. It was the strangest looking contraption Michael has ever seen.

Robert noted his confusion and began, "Look Michael, we don't start out on a real horse. I need to know that you have some of the basic skills you need to ride before we use a live animal. The whole reason for lessons is to learn and to be safe. A horse isn't a big puppy. A horse is a half ton of power and strength that can hurt you if you don't know what you are doing."

"How is a barrel on ropes like a horse?"

"Ol Blue here has got a lot of folks started riding horses. I taught my daughter with Ol Blue. I can make Ol Blue move by moving the handle in front and by pulling another rope in back. The ropes and inner tubes the barrel is hanging from simulate a horse's movement. That movement can either be a little or a lot depending on how much and how fast I move the handle or rope. You'll learn to balance without the danger of getting hurt on a real horse, and when we are through with Ol Blue you'll know how to sit in a saddle. The first thing I want you to do is saddle Ol Blue."

Michael bent and picked up the saddle from the ground, but before he could place it on the barrel, Mr. Bradley stopped him.

"You're missing your saddle blanket boy. You never ride a horse without a saddle blanket under your saddle, and you always make sure it's a good thick one. One of the biggest mistakes riders make is not buying a good saddle and blanket for their horse. Cheap saddles and blankets are like you wearing cheap plastic shoes. You might wear them for one day and your feet hurt just a little bit, but when you wear them day after day you get blisters and more blisters. It doesn't take long before no one could make you wear those shoes, because they hurt. Cheap equipment is the same for a horse. It doesn't take long for a horse's back to get sore and hurt and then you have a horse that bucks or acts up. That's the only way a horse can tell you something is wrong. Unfortunately, most folks just think their horse is being mean or ornery when that happens. You have to know how to read a horse and listen to what he is telling you."

"Will you teach me how to read a horse?" asked Michael.

"I'll do my best, but most of it comes from spending time with your animal and knowing him. A horse isn't something just to get out and ride and put up. If that's all you want to do, you might as well get a bicycle."

Michael thought about what Mr. Bradley said. He already knew some things about Doc because he had spent so much time taking care of him. He had discovered, accidentally, that when Doc quit eating his hay in his stall, it wasn't because he was full. It was because he was out of water and wanted a drink. As soon as his water bucket was filled he would take a big drink and go back to his hay. Michael felt good because he already knew one thing that Doc would "tell" him.

"Okay boy, watch how I put the saddle on, then we'll take it off for you to practice."

Robert placed the saddle blanket on the barrel telling Michael to be sure he always centered it in the middle of the horses back. Next, he picked up the saddle and carefully set it on the blanket, making sure it was centered also. He told Michael to never throw a saddle on a horse's back. Always pick it up and place it on them. That way your horse doesn't try to move out from under the saddle when you get ready to ride. Next, he showed Michael how to tie the girth that holds the saddle secure. He wrapped the tie strap through the ring in the girth two times, and then tied it. The knot kinda looked like Uncle Joe's tie on Sunday mornings when he finished.

Robert took everything off Ol Blue and said, "Now, you saddle him."

It took Michael three tries just to get the saddle blanket right. When he reached for the saddle to put it on, He knocked off his blanket. Robert just sat on a bale of hay and smiled to himself. It was going to be a long lesson.

Maggie had cleaned up the supper dishes and was just leaving the kitchen, when she heard the four-wheeler stop at the barn. She had saved Michael a plate on the stove. She knew he would be hungry, because he was so late. She was very curious to find out how his first lesson went. Michael came through the screen door looking very tired.

"How did your first riding lesson go?"

"Good I guess, if you call putting a saddle on a barrel about a hundred times a lesson."

"Did you say a barrel?" asked Maggie.

"Yes, Mr. Bradley said I needed to learn some stuff before I use a real horse. Do you know how heavy a saddle can get after picking it up and putting it down for about two hours? Mr. Bradley wants it to be perfect every time, or you have to do it over. The way he's teaching me is nothing like what Charlie said. I don't think she knows anything about horses."

"Well, you know that whatever Robert teaches you is the right way. Just do everything like he says. Your supper is on the stove."

"Thanks Aunt Maggie, I'm starving."

Maggie smiled as she watched him begin to wolf down his supper. Apparently being a cowboy worked up an appetite!

Chapter 38

Michael's heart was beating so fast he was sure his shirt was jumping. He wasn't afraid he was excited! He found himself sitting in the middle of Doc's broad back. He had been riding that barrel for two weeks. He had more blue spots on him than Ol Blue had. He must have landed in the dirt a million times or at least it felt like it. He didn't know you could make a barrel move so many different ways. Every time he was able to stay on it for any length of time, Mr. Bradley would pull the ropes harder so that he had to increase his skill or get thrown. He always got thrown, but he eventually became skillful enough to stay on with the extra force Mr. Bradley used on the ropes.

Robert had been pleased at the progress Michael had made. He had discovered that Michael had a natural sense of balance, which was something that you were born with, not taught. Horsemen called it a natural seat. Robert had agonized over where to get a gentle horse for Michael to ride for his lessons. He had not been able to find one to borrow. He finally gave in to use Doc after he saw how the horse and boy had formed a bond. He made sure that Doc and Michael were in a corral so that Doc couldn't take off with Michael. Michael had assured him that Doc wouldn't do that, but Robert had reminded him that horses were first and foremost prey animals and usually when they are frightened, the fear rules their reaction. It was a mistake many riders made. Robert kept telling Michael that you always have to think one step ahead of your horse. If you see something that looks just a little strange to you while you are riding, it's going to look a lot scary to your horse. Always be ready to calm your horse and ride safe.

Doc was curious. After years of not being ridden, with the exception of Michael sitting on him like a bird on a nest during his lesson with Charlie, here he was in the corral with a rider on his back. It felt strangely good to him. It would have been better if it had been Susan, but it was still good. He had come to love Michael and trust him so he was relaxed and waiting for Michael to tell him what to do.

That was another thing Robert kept telling Michael. Horses are always looking to humans for leadership. You have to give clear signals with your hands, legs, and seat to tell your horse what to do. Michael had learned to lower his hands when he held the reins, because when you raise your hands much higher than your horse's withers, it causes them to raise their heads and not respond as well to the bit. Robert also taught him to use his legs to guide his horse. Horses move away from pressure like we do if someone is pushing us. If a rider puts his right leg against his horse's side it will cause the horse to move to the left. The same thing is true if you use your left leg for pressure, the horse will move to the right. Michael also learned that if you lean forward with your seat, it is a signal for your horse to accelerate his pace, and if you sit down hard in the saddle, it is a signal for your horse to slow or stop.

Michael had learned all these things on the barrel, and now he was going to get to try them on Doc. That was why he was so excited. He was really going to ride Doc today! He looked over at Mr. Bradley standing in the middle of the corral for instructions.

Robert saw the look Michael gave him and smiled to himself. He felt confident that Michael had the skill to ride Doc. That boy had hit the ground so many times on that old barrel that if he hadn't been serious about riding he would have quit. No matter how many times he came off or how hard he hit, he never said a word. He just climbed back on. Robert had to admire the kid's grit and determination.

"Well, don't look at me. I'm just going to stand here and watch you use what you have learned on Ol Blue. Remember Doc is going to be a lot touchier than a metal barrel. Use small cues with your legs first, then you can apply more pressure if you need to. Let me see you walk around the corral, staying close to the fence rail."

Michael took a deep breath and gently squeezed with his legs. He was pleasantly surprised when Doc began to move forward at a walk. He was so pleased that he forgot about guiding Doc with his hands, and they began to go to the center of the corral.

"Bring him back to the fence, Michael. Remember to use your reins and keep you hands low," instructed Robert.

Michael did as Robert said and Doc immediately took the cues and went to the rail at a walk. Robert watched as it began to dawn on Michael that he was riding a living, breathing, horse. Michael had a grin on his face so big it looked like it went from one ear to the other. After he had made two trips around the corral to the left at a walk, Robert told him to turn Doc and go to the right while still keeping him on the fence. Michael thought for a minute, and then he pulled his right rein toward his belt buckle and put his left leg against Doc's side. As soon as Doc felt the change in cues, he turned to the right. Michael only made two mistakes that Robert quickly corrected. He didn't release the rein or the leg pressure as soon as he should have and Doc went in a circle.

"Let go of your rein and take your leg off his side, boy," said Robert.

Michael did and Doc began to go to the right at a walk. After he had made two trips to the right, Robert told him to stop Doc and back him up. Michael set his seat down in the saddle, said "whoa" and then pulled back on the reins for a stop as Robert had taught him. Mr. Bradley had told him it was important to give your horse an idea of what you wanted him to do before you start pulling on the reins. By sitting down deep in the saddle and saying whoa, your horse knows a stop is coming. Michael was delighted to see that Doc stopped almost as soon as he sat down in his saddle. He didn't really need to say whoa or pull back on his reins!

"Wow, did you see that Mr. Bradley? He stopped as soon as I sat back in the saddle! I didn't even have to use my reins."

Robert smiled as he saw how excited Michael was with Doc. It felt good to be working with a horse again. He discovered that he had been away from one of the things he truly loved in his life for too long.

"That's the mark of a trained horse. It's what makes them a pleasure to ride. Susan used to call it power steering," Robert caught himself as he said Susan's name. How long had it been since he had said it out loud? It was another of his ways to hold on to Susan. If he kept everything inside it couldn't evaporate like the morning dew and leave him. Robert looked down quickly.

"Back him up now, boy," said Robert without looking up.

Michael had seen Mr. Bradley's smile disappear. He didn't think he had done anything wrong, but he wasn't sure.

"Did I do everything like I should have, Mr. Bradley? I sure don't want to mess Doc up."

Robert looked up into Michael's expectant face. He knew Michael had no way of knowing his thoughts. He smiled to reassure the boy, and found that it made him feel better, too. Susan had been great with kids. She would have enjoyed working with Michael especially since he was riding her horse. In a strange way, Robert began to feel that she was there with them and it gave him a wonderful sense of freedom he hadn't had in a long time. He smiled again, but this time the smile went up to his eyes and covered his whole face.

"No, you didn't do anything wrong. Now let me see you back your horse up. Remember what to do with your hands, seat, and feet."

Michael lowered his hands, sat deep in his saddle, put some weight on his feet and pulled back on the reins. When Doc moved one step back he relaxed the reins. This was Doc's reward for going back, the release of pressure on his bit. Michael repeated the process for a few more times until Robert told him "good enough".

Michael had never felt so good in his life. He had ridden a horse and not just any horse. It was Doc. Doc had taken his commands and done just what he had been asked to do. He wanted to keep riding and never stop, but Mr. Bradley was telling him that was enough for today.

"Don't worry Michael you can do this every day and before long you will be able to get out of this corral and go out on your own with Doc. You did a good job today, now go unsaddle your horse, rub him down, and feed him," Robert said as he turned toward the gate to leave the horse and boy.

"Yes sir," said Michael as he dismounted. "Uh, Mr. Bradley, thanks. I mean it. Thank you for what you have taught me about riding. Nobody has ever taken that much time to help me with anything before this."

Robert turned and looked at Michael. Susan would have been happy to hear what Michael had said. Once again, he felt her there with them, and he felt that little by little a weight was starting to be lifted from his shoulders. It was a heavy weight and would take a lot of chipping away to get rid of it, but a skinny kid and an old barrel horse just might be able to do it.

Chapter 39

It was the end of September. The night air was beginning to get a little chilly. It made the last days of summer all the more sweet. It wouldn't be long until the cold, gray days of winter would bring rain and some snow. The leaves were turning colors before they dropped to the ground. Michael had never been in the country at this time of year. He had never seen so many leaves turn so many colors. There were trees everywhere, and all of them were "showing off" as Aunt Maggie called it. She liked to say there wasn't an artist anywhere that could paint a picture as beautiful as nature, and nature's glory belonged to God. Michael had to agree, because when the sun was shining through the trees in the woods, all the reds, golds, oranges, and greens were spectacular.

He had been riding Doc almost two months now. He had progressed from the training arena to the trails that wound through the woods of Mr. Bradley's farm. He was happier than he had ever been in his short life. Mr. Bradley had made sure he could ride and control Doc before he let him out of the arena. Michael was a natural at riding a horse, a fact that was not lost on Robert Bradley. Robert also recognized that the boy and the horse had a strong bond that made them work well together.

Michael couldn't believe how free he felt on Doc's broad back. At first, he had been a little fearful to go faster than a trot. Doc was so big and had so much power that he wasn't sure he could control him at a canter. He had been surprised when he galloped him for the first time and Doc had stopped just as easily as he did when he was trotting. It was a thrill that went through his whole body and a revelation that Doc would listen to him and take his commands. Now he looked for places in the trail to let Doc stretch out and run. Doc enjoyed it as much as Michael did. When he felt that Michael was going to give him the cue to run he would begin to prance and arch his neck, as if to say "I'm ready when you are". As Michael began to read his horse and know what Doc was telling him, a new level of confidence emerged in his riding.

When they were out riding the trails, Michael felt an amazing sense of peace. He talked to Doc who seemed to understand every word, and he talked to God, mostly thanking him for his life in Tennessee and for Doc.

School had started back from the summer break. Michael was already dreading when the days became too short to ride after school was out in the afternoon. He had worked off his debt for the vet bill, but now he was working for Mr. Bradley to pay for his riding lessons. Truthfully, neither he nor Mr. Bradley wanted their arrangement to end, and the riding lessons were just an excuse for it to continue. There was another person who didn't want Robert and Michael to part company. Aunt Maggie had begun to see a real change in Robert. She didn't want to risk Robert returning to his hermit like ways.

Michael continued to go and take care of Doc and his barn chores in the mornings after breakfast and before school. He rode the four-wheeler to Mr. Bradley's, and the bus would pick him up there and take him to school. When school was out, he rode the bus back to Mr. Bradley's. He would do the afternoon barn work and ride Doc. When he was done, he rode the four-wheeler back home to Aunt Maggie's. It was a full day and by the time he got in bed at night it was no problem for him to fall quickly and deeply asleep.

"There you go, big guy," Michael said as he put Doc in his freshly bedded stall. It had been a long day for Michael. There had been a test in math, an oral report to be given in literature, and a pop quiz in history. He thought he had done okay in math and on the report, but he was a little nervous about the quiz. He knew he would have to keep his grades up to keep coming to the barn. That was the one thing Aunt

Maggie was very serious about. She said his education was his future and he had to give it his best effort. That was something else he wasn't used to having in his life. Someone who wanted the best for him and cared about the grades he made in school. He found he didn't want to disappoint her with poor grades. Funny, he never cared about his grades before. He was finding he wished he had, because sometimes school would have been easier for him now if he had done better in his other schools. It just meant he had to work a little harder, but Doc and Aunt Maggie were definitely worth it.

He had finished all his chores now and was just getting ready to head home when he heard a commotion coming down the hallway of the barn. Doc spun around in his stall and looked anxiously over the stall door. Michael froze in his tracks in the middle of the hallway as a wild black horse broke loose from Mr. Bradley and came leaping and plunging toward Michael with its teeth bared and ears flattened against its head. Michael felt that he was watching death come straight for him. He tried to make his feet move, but they wouldn't budge. With the black horse bearing down on him, Michael was still frozen in fear. Suddenly, there was a crashing sound and Michael was thrown across the hallway of the barn by Doc's stall door as Doc burst through it!

Chapter 40

Robert stood looking at Doc as he was munching his hay in his stall. He bore little resemblance to the big red monster that crashed through his stall door to intercept the black intruder in his barn. Robert shook his head as he recalled his fear when he realized Michael wasn't moving out of the way of the horse that was coming straight for him. He had been as surprised as anyone when Doc came through his stall door. It was the last thing he would have imagined to happen.

He replayed the scene in his mind as Michael was thrown out of harm's way by Doc's explosion. As soon as he was in the hallway of the barn, Doc flattened his ears against his head, and met the black horse's charge. The sudden appearance of Doc caused the black horse to slide to a stop, spin, and run back toward Robert. Being an experienced horseman, Robert knew better than to jump in front of a terrified horse and try to stop him. Thinking quickly, he opened the door of a long empty stall, threw up his hands, waved his arms, and yelled to divert the horse into the stall. With Doc behind and a scary loud human in front of the horse, the empty stall looked like the safest place to be. As the horse ran in, Robert slammed the stall door shut and once again yelled, and waved his arms to stop Doc from continuing his pursuit.

Doc quickly returned to normal and calmed down. After Robert had made sure no one was hurt and Michael was okay, he told everyone to go home. He would stay in the barn, fix Doc's stall door, and bed down the new horse.

Michael hung back until everyone else had gone. He wanted to talk to Mr. Bradley. Doc had saved him from that strange wild horse. Mr. Bradley had to know now that Doc really liked him if he was willing to break out of his stall to help him. If Mr. Bradley agreed with him and reinforced what he thought, he would know for sure it was true.

"Uh, Mr. Bradley, did you see how Doc jumped in front of that horse to keep him off of me?" Michael asked hopefully.

"Huh, what? Oh, you think Doc did what he did to save you?" Robert asked. When Michael nodded, He just smiled and shook his head. "I hate to disappoint you boy, but that's not what happened."

"Then what did happen?" asked Michael.

"What you just saw was herd instinct," answered Robert.

"But we don't have a herd here. There's only Doc and Charlie's Mom's horse on the whole farm."

"That's all it takes. Horses are very territorial, and they don't take kindly to newcomers. Come to think of it there are a lot of humans like that," said Robert as he thought of his own reaction to Michael when he first met him.

"But that doesn't explain why Doc broke down his door and went after the other horse," said Michael trying to make sense of what Robert was telling him.

"Actually it does. Doc was just telling the new horse you are not welcome here and get out. Charging the new horse was his way of saying that. Anytime you introduce a new horse to a barn you make very sure to keep them separated from the other horses at first. You let them look at each other and get used to seeing one another before you even let them touch noses to check each other out. Even then, there's usually lots of squealing and snorting. After a while, you turn them out together a few at a time until all the horses are ready to accept the new horse. That way none of the horses get hurt. I've seen some good horses ruined for life by being put immediately in with strange horses."

"So Doc just did what any other horse would have done," said Michael sadly.

"I can't really say that, because most horses aren't as big and strong as Doc, and able to destroy a door that easily. But in answer to your question, most horses would not have been happy to see a new horse in their barn."

Michael lowered his head and said, "I better get home, now. I'll see you tomorrow Mr. Bradley."

Robert nodded and watched as Michael walked out of the barn, stopping just long enough to stroke Doc's head. He sure wished he could have told Michael that what Doc did was because he wanted to help the boy, but he knew that wasn't so.

Aunt Maggie finished the last of the supper dishes and turned to look for Michael. He had told them the story of what had happened at the barn. He said he was fine and all the people and horses were unhurt, but he seemed like something was bothering him. Aunt Maggie noticed the porch light was on, and saw Michael swinging on the porch swing. She went outside and sat down by Michael in the swing. She put her arm around him and patted him affectionately on the back. For a while they sat quietly, rocking slowly in the old swing and listening to the frogs and crickets sing the day to its end.

"I've always loved sitting out here in the evenings after the day is done," said Aunt Maggie. "It's so peaceful and quiet, don't you think?"

"Huh, oh yes mam," said Michael absentmindedly.

"Michael, is there something on your mind?" asked Aunt Maggie.

"Do you remember when Mr. Bradley told me he would teach me how to ride? He also told me he would teach me to read a horse? You know, to know what that horse is thinking and why it acts like it does."

"I seem to remember you telling me that," said Aunt Maggie.

"Well, today I thought I knew exactly why Doc did something. I thought I was reading him just like Mr. Bradley said, then I found out I was all wrong. I thought Doc broke down his stall door to help me, but Mr. Bradley said Doc was just done what any horse would do by not wanting a new horse next to his herd. I guess I should just be glad Doc did get between me and that new horse, because it was coming right at me," said Michael.

Aunt Maggie knew what was wrong. Michael wanted to think that he was more than just another human to the horse he loved. She sat quietly for a few minutes, swinging and thinking.

"Michael, where were the other horses Mr. Bradley has at his farm?" she asked.

"He only has one other horse. It's the gray horse that belongs to Charlie's Mom. It was in its stall at the other end of the barn. Why?" asked Michael.

"Well, I'll be the first to admit that I don't know much about horses, but from what you and Robert say, I think maybe Doc did help you, because of what you are to him."

"I don't understand what you mean," said Michael.

"You said the only other horse on the farm was at the other end of barn. I think since you have spent so much time with Doc, and since he isn't ever with the other horse, Doc sees you as his herd. I think he didn't want the new horse anywhere near you. That would explain everything. The herd instinct behavior because he was protecting his herd, you." said Aunt Maggie.

Michael sat quietly for several minutes thinking about what Aunt Maggie had said. A wide grin began to spread across his face as he saw the truth of what Aunt Maggie had told him. He was so happy he jumped off the swing and hugged Aunt Maggie so tightly she couldn't breathe.

"You're the best Aunt Maggie! Thank you, thank you!!"

With that Michael ran in the house calling Norm for their nightly game of tug with and old pair of socks.

Land sakes, thought Aunt Maggie. She didn't think she had ever seen anyone go from down in their shoe tops to on top of the world so fast. She continued to sit on the old porch swing thinking about Michael. Without realizing it, she began to hum her favorite hymn. She always did, when she was content.

Chapter 41

Michael came to a stop at the barn. He was a little later than usual because it was Saturday and he had slept in. He was still early enough that he had to avoid old Roho, the maniac rooster at Uncle Joe's barn, when he was getting the four-wheeler to leave. Roho had been up, crowing over his domain, and ready to flog anyone who got in his way. Michael had gotten away without having a battle with him. He didn't know if Roho was mean or crazy or maybe both. He was just glad that Mr. Bradley didn't have roosters.

Michael got off the four-wheeler and started down the hallway of the barn. He was a bit leery of seeing that black horse again. Talk about mean or crazy! He had never seen anything like the sight of that wild animal coming at him yesterday. He wondered if there were straight jackets for horses. He hoped so, because that horse could sure use one. He thought again about Doc crashing through his stall. He smiled as he remembered his conversation with Aunt Maggie. No matter what Mr. Bradley said, he knew now that Doc was helping him.

He was at Doc's stall. The big horse had his head over the door, whinnying softly. Michael leaned over the door, put his arms around Doc's neck, and buried his face in his mane. Doc put his head over Michael's shoulder, and rested it there. It was their morning greeting, and Michael always looked forward to it. He breathed deeply, savoring the familiar smell of his friend. Suddenly Doc threw his head up and flattened his ears, looking very menacing. Michael saw the reason for

Doc's behavior. The black horse had put its head over the stall door and Doc had seen it. As soon as the black horse saw Doc, it retreated back into the recesses of the stall. When it had gone, Doc returned to his normal self. There it was again, proof that Aunt Maggie had been right. Michael was one very happy kid.

"Are you ready for breakfast, boy?" Michael asked knowing the answer. Doc was always ready for his meals.

Michael made his way to the down the hall of the barn to the feed room. He had to pass the black horse's stall to get there. He made sure he was on the far side of the hallway from the stall door as he walked by. He was expecting the horse to charge at him, and wanted to be well out of reach. As he passed the stall door, he didn't see anything. That was strange. He didn't even hear anything. He inched a little closer trying to get a look in the stall without putting himself too near the door. He looked in the dark stall and still couldn't see. It was early enough for the barn to be dark without the full sun of the day. Michael looked up and down the hallway just to be sure that wild creature wasn't somehow out of the stall and lying in wait for him. When his scan of the area turned up nothing, he peered cautiously over the stall door. It took a minute for his eyes to adjust to the dim lighting, but when they did, what he saw shocked him!

"Morning Michael," boomed Mr. Bradley as he walked down the hall of the barn toward Michael.

Michael jumped like he had been shot. He wasn't expecting Mr. Bradley; he was expecting a horse attack. Michael's violent reaction caused an equally extreme reaction from the black horse. It frantically began to rear and try to climb the walls of its stall. Michael began to run backwards from the stall so fast that he fell and sat down hard in the sawdust. The sounds of the horse in the stall were like someone was in there hitting the walls with hammers.

Robert had watched the whole scene. He knew exactly what was going on, and it caused him to shake his head sadly. He wondered if he had gotten himself into a mess trying to help an old friend.

"What are you doing setting down on the job, boy?" he asked Michel with a smile as he helped him to his feet. Michael's eyes were as big as saucers as he looked up at Robert, then back to the still noisy stall.

"Come with me," said Robert. "If we get out of her sight, that black mare will settle down."

They walked on into the feed room, and just as Mr. Bradley said the horse got quiet. Michael had heard Mr. Bradley say the horse was a mare. He knew that meant it was a female. He was surprised, because he thought it had to be a wild stallion, with the way it was acting.

"That's a girl horse?" asked Michael.

"Yep, that's what a mare is," said Mr. Bradley.

"What's wrong with her? Is she crazy?" asked Michael.

"She has a lot wrong with her, and, yes she is crazy, but it's because she is scared out of her mind."

"What's she doing in our barn?"

Robert smiled inwardly as he noticed Michael had said "our" barn. He didn't take offense, in fact it felt pretty good to think of this old pile of wood that was the barn, as a partnership again.

"Well, she is here because I have a friend I hadn't heard from in years call me the other night. This mare is the last colt that was born from his old stallion. The old horse died and it like to have broke his heart. He had owned the old stud since he was weanling.

The stallion had a successful career on the race track for a short time, until he suffered a leg injury and couldn't race anymore. Frank, my friend, took him home and he became Frank's favorite horse. He let the horse have a year off to heal from his injury and then, even though he couldn't race again, he could be ridden over the farm and on trails. Frank rode that horse everywhere. This mare is the image of her daddy. That's why she is so important to my friend. There won't be any more colts. She is the last one."

"Does he know she is crazy?"

"She hasn't always been like this. Frank said she was the best little filly to ever be on his farm. She would follow you around like a dog, and always wanted to be near you. He said you couldn't go outside without her nickering to you, and running up to the fence hoping for some petting."

Michael thought about the sight of her trying to climb the walls of her stall, and had a hard time thinking it was the same horse Mr. Bradley was describing.

"If she was such a good horse, what happened to her?" asked Michael.

"A bad trainer is what happened to her."

"Why would your friend send her to a bad trainer?"

"Well, he didn't know the trainer wasn't a good one. I used to train all of Frank's horses, but about ten years ago I decided to quit the horse business," said Robert looking down at the feed room floor. He didn't like remembering why he had quit the horse business. "This is the only horse Frank has that I haven't trained. He said he didn't need another horse until he lost his old stallion. He knew I no longer took horses for other people and tried to find someone to work with his young mare. The person he chose told Frank his training methods were much like mine. Going slow and easy with a young horse, building confidence, and when you are done you have a partner instead of just an animal to sit on and ride."

"Then why is she nuts?" asked Michael once again repeating himself.

"Because this trainer wasn't truthful with Frank. He knew what Frank wanted to hear and that's what he told Frank, when he didn't use those methods at all. Instead he was cruel and what you see in that stall down there is the result of those methods," Robert said sadly.

Michael thought about what Mr. Bradley had said, then asked, "What are we supposed to do with her?"

Once again, Robert smiled to himself at Michael's use of "we".

"Well, we are her last hope. When Frank got his horse back she was so abused that he couldn't do anything with her. At first she was so malnourished that she wasn't a dangerous horse, because she was so weak. You see, one of this person's training methods was to withhold food and water to starve the horse into submission."

"Why did your friend let him do that to her?'

"He didn't know it was being done. This trainer lived about 400 miles from Frank. Since it was so far, Frank just told him he would leave her for 90 days worth of training, then come and see where to go from there. Frank called and checked on her regularly and the trainer gave him good reports so he had no reason to think anything was wrong. When he went back at the end of 90 days he was shocked to find his horse was malnourished and abused."

"What did the trainer tell your friend when he came to get his horse and she looked like that?" asked Michael feeling very bad for the horse down the hall. He knew what it was like to be somewhere that people told other people one thing and then treated you different.

"Nothing, because he wasn't there. He took off and left the horse in a pen for Frank to pick up. It's probably a good thing he wasn't there. Frank was so mad he said he would have used some of that guy's methods on him. Anyway, the mare is here because if I can't help her he is going to have to put her down. That's what made me say I'd take her."

"What does put her down mean?" Michael had never heard that term before.

"It means you kill them."

"What! No! Why would you do that?" Michael couldn't believe what he was hearing.

"Because she is dangerous Michael. Remember, a horse is a big animal, and if you have an uncontrollable horse, it can seriously hurt and even kill people. You can't let that happen. If Doc hadn't come through his stall door, she would have run over you last night. I didn't realize until then how truly bad this mare was. I don't know if I can do anything with her, but you are to stay away from her. I'm the only one to be around her. Do I make myself clear on that?" said Mr. Bradley in such a way that Michael replied with an instant "Yes Sir!"

Michael was very glad that he didn't have to feed and take care of the new horse. He had wondered if she would be part of his barn work. Michael remembered something Mr. Bradley had told him, "Didn't you say that a scared horse was more dangerous than a mean horse?"

"Yes, I did. That's just my own personal opinion that comes from years of working with horses," said Robert.

"Why do you think so?" asked Michael.

"There aren't that many truly mean horses. You occasionally find one, but they are rare. There are a lot of scared horses, though. When a horse is afraid, that fear can sometimes override training if the fear is great enough. You expect to be on guard with a mean horse, but with a horse like this black mare, you don't know the things that will terrify her and maybe make her hurt you when she tries to get away from those things. Does that explain it?"

"I guess so," said Michael.

"Okay then. I'm going to leave her in the stall that she is in now. She's three doors down from Doc. That's far enough that they can see each other without being able to kick the stall walls to get at each other. I'm going to cut a door in the back of her stall so she can get out in the corral behind her stall for some exercise. We'll let her stay like that until she starts to come around and trust us a little," said Robert.

Michael didn't say it, but he figured he'd be Mr. Bradley's age before that happened.

Chapter 42

Michael was bouncing over the fields on the four-wheeler heading home. It had been a very good day at the barn. He kept his distance from the black mare as he went up and down the hall of the barn while he was doing his chores. It wasn't a problem, though, because she stayed against the back wall of her stall as if she was trying to hide from everyone. He found himself feeling bad for her. If she had been the kind of horse that Mr. Bradley's friend said she was, she sure had been through some bad stuff to turn out like she was now. He had been in one foster home where he had tried to stay hidden from his foster mother, but it usually didn't work.

He shook his head hard to clear away the bad memories. He looked around as he rode and saw how beautiful the fields and trees were. He would never have believed when he was in that bad foster home he would one day be on a four-wheeler riding it away from a barn with a big red horse in it that he rode and loved to a home that was the happiest one he had ever known.

Michael was suddenly struck by the realization that all the bad foster homes he had been in, served to make his home now that much more special. He knew that Aunt Maggie, Uncle Joe, Chuck, and Max were what a family was supposed to be, and he didn't think he could love anyone more than them, especially Aunt Maggie. She always said that God has a plan for everything, and everybody. She said it said so in the Bible. She said you just had to try to do what God wanted you to do and it would happen. Michael wasn't sure what he had done to get himself where he was now, but he was sure he was going to do his best to stay there.

He wondered if it would work the same way with the black mare. If she got over what had happened to her, would she be even happier at Mr. Bradley's barn than she had ever been before? Michael decided he would have to ask Mr. Bradley about that, because he didn't know that much about horses.

Michael groaned out loud as he stopped the four-wheeler under the shed at the barn. He had forgotten it was Saturday and Charlie was staying with Aunt Maggie while her Mom was taking nursing classes. She was gathering the eggs for Aunt Maggie. When she looked up and saw him, she put down the egg basket, pushed her coke-bottle glasses up on her nose, put her hands on her hips and said, "Well lookey here, the world's greatest cowboy. How many times did you fall off that old barrel today, parrrdner?"

OHHH, Michael gritted his teeth, and clenched his fists at his sides as he said, "Charlie, you know good and well that I'm riding Doc now. You're just mad because you can't even ride a stick horse, so shut up!"

Whap! Michael didn't see it coming, but he felt the warm egg break on his forehead and begin its slimy drip down his face. That did it. He had gotten enough of Charlie! He lunged for her and when he got her she was going to eat one of those eggs! Unfortunately, just as he was about to grab her, the egg got in both his eyes and he couldn't see. The result was Michael landed face down in the chicken coop. Charlie saw her chance. She immediately jumped on Michael's back and began to break the rest of the eggs over his head while he was down on the ground. About that time unknown to both Charlie and Michael, old Roho rounded the corner of his chicken house and saw two intruders smashing his unborn chicks to smithereens.

Roho jumped straight up in the air and came down hard on Charlie's head, who was still breaking eggs over Michael's head. As Roho began to flog and spur Charlie, she began to try and fight the rooster. This caused Michael to get more punches than the rooster. As Roho continued his assault, Charlie fell to the ground beside Michael and both of them began to fight the rooster, who now had the two intruders just where he wanted them on the ground and perfect rooster targets. Roho renewed his attack with a vengeance. Charlie and Michael were getting hit by wings and spurs so fast they couldn't see. They began to roll on the ground in an attempt to escape, but Roho rolled with them. It turned into a whirling mass of Michael, Charlie, and chicken. The screams and squawks were heard at the house.

Aunt Maggie looked at Uncle Joe and they both ran out of the kitchen toward the barn. Aunt Maggie grabbed her broom and Uncle Joe grabbed his shotgun. When they saw the rolling mass of chicken warfare, Aunt Maggie sprung into action. She took aim with her broom and swung as hard as she could. Unfortunately, Michael's behind rolled up where Roho had been and caught her swing.

"Ow," yelled Michael as he felt an unfamiliar attack. Man that rooster was powerful. He really packed a punch.

Aunt Maggie took aim again and this time she caught old Roho in mid air. Roho let out a loud squawk and landed about ten feet away from the rolling mass of egg breaking, chicken coop intruders. With the rooster off of them, Charlie and Michael stopped rolling on the ground and sat up. When Roho saw his targets had gotten still he started to renew his attack. Before he could do more than flap his wings, a giant BOOM rang out as Uncle Joe fired his shotgun at the errant rooster. The shot landed in the dirt in front of the rooster and threw dirt all over him. Roho was scared out of his little rooster mind and began to flap and flutter like he was dying.

Charlie and Michael both couldn't believe their eyes. Uncle Joe had killed Roho! Aunt Maggie spun around and said, "Joe Hayes you've killed my rooster! What on earth are you doing shooting a gun off in my hen house. It will take my chickens weeks to get over this. Just what am I supposed to do for eggs?"

Michael didn't think he had ever seen Aunt Maggie this mad, and she was this mad at Uncle Joe. Joe also saw the fire in his wife's eyes and knew he was in trouble.

"Aw Sugar, I'm sorry. I just got a little carried away. I was just trying to save the children," said Joe thinking quickly. How could Miss Maggie stay mad at him for protecting innocent children? At the mention of the children, both adults turned to look at them. The sight they saw caused them to break into hysterical laughter.

Charlie had her glasses on sideways, chicken feather sticking out of every curl in her hair, and egg yolks up to her elbows where she had been attacking Michael before Roho had attacked them. Michael's hair and face were covered with broken egg slime, which had served to glue dirt and chicken feathers to it as he rolled around avoiding Charlie and Roho. You could only see two eyes through the dirt and eggs. When Aunt Maggie and Uncle Joe finally stopped laughing, Aunt Maggie said, "What caused all of this?"

Michael and Charlie both started to point at each other but had the same idea at the same time. Both of them pointed to the still flopping rooster and said, "HE DID!"

As if he knew that he was being wrongly accused, Roho stopped his flopping, stood up very tall on his little chicken toes, and crowed at the top of his lungs. When he had finished, he turned around and regally strutted away as if all humans were beneath him.

"See Honey, I didn't kill your rooster," said a very relieved Uncle Joe.

"I see that Joe, but no more shooting in my hen house. Michael and Charlie both of you go to the house and get cleaned up. I've never seen two kids is such a shape."

"You heard her," said Joe, "let's go. Don't worry Miss Maggie I'll make sure they do what you said." Uncle Joe was happy to have an excuse to go to the house. He didn't want Miss Maggie to get after him again.

As Maggie watched them head to the house she couldn't help but smile. Of the three of them, she knew which one was the biggest kid. He was carrying the shotgun.

Chapter 43

Robert was doing what he had been doing every morning for the past seven weeks. It wasn't quite daylight yet and he had already been at it for about an hour. He had come to enjoy these early mornings. It brought back so many things he hadn't done in years. He had always loved horses. He loved everything about them, their smell, they way they looked, the way a good horse felt under you when you were riding, but most of all he loved getting to know each horse's personality. Horses were as individual as people, but you didn't know it unless you spent time with them. That's what he was doing, spending time with the Black Mare. He was sitting on his little chair in the corner of her stall, reading a book and having his morning coffee.

When he had first come in her stall to sit quietly in the corner, she had been terrified. She knew she had no way of getting away from him, so she had stayed as far away as the big box stall would allow, turned her tail to him, and watched him nervously for any sign he was coming in her direction. Robert had not even lifted his eyes to look at her for several days. To do so would have been threatening to her, and would probably have caused a violent response. He read his paper and drank his coffee. Sometimes he talked to her, sometimes he sang softly to her, and sometimes he offered a handful of grain, but he never moved from his seat or tried to approach her. She had to make the first move.

It took two weeks, but she did. She came to sniff the handful of feed he was offering her. As soon as she sniffed it she drew back to her corner and waited for Robert to try and catch her. When Robert didn't move, she came back and repeated the same sequence of events. This happened many times before she became brave enough to take a few grains of the feed and retreat. When Robert still didn't try to touch her, she came back for a little more, then a little more, until now she was eating feed from his hand.

The Black Mare was still wary of Robert, but she had begun to be curious about him. She didn't like humans anymore. She had trusted them at one time, but then humans had taught her differently. They had hurt her and scared her so badly she wanted no part of them. This one in the corner of her stall was different from any before. He didn't do anything except make soothing sounds and give her grain. He never tried to catch her. She would watch for some sign of danger from him, but there wasn't any. She began to take some tentative steps in his direction. When he still didn't move, she took more until she could stretch her neck out very far and barely touch his hat to sniff it. At the first scent of him she had snorted and retreated, but when he continued to sit in his corner of her stall she went back, and sniffed some more. Now his scent was familiar and not entirely scary. Now when he came into her stall she faced him instead of turning her back on him.

Robert had been excited when she had decided to check him out. He knew if he moved it would all be over so he sat as still as a statue. He knew he was making progress when she started to come to get the feed from his hand as soon as he offered it for the first time. He had begun to stroke her neck with his other hand while she ate the feed. After a few times of drawing away from him, she had accepted his touch. He knew that each passing day he spent with her made him less of a threat. Robert never went fast when working with a horse. He used to say anyone could train a horse if they had patience, but few people possessed the kind that Robert had with horses.

Robert heard the wind pick up and the rain began to rattle the tin roof of the barn. It was going to be a cold, dreary, Thanksgiving Day. That was only on the outside, though. Robert had been invited to the Hayes' house for Thanksgiving Dinner. Nobody in their right mind would turn down one of Maggie Hayes' meals, especially Thanksgiving.

Robert smiled as he thought of the feast that he would enjoy latter today. He was also looking forward to some good company with the Hayes and Michael. That kid was sure something.

Robert had decided to teach Michael to barrel race, because he feared Charlie would try to teach Michael if she found out Michael wanted to learn. Charlie had demonstrated her teaching abilities where horses were concerned. Now in the afternoons, when the weather permitted Michael, Doc, and Robert were in the arena practicing barrels.

When they had first started, Robert had been apprehensive that Doc would be too much for Michael to handle with barrels. Doc had always been so aggressive when he went in the arena to run barrels, Robert didn't know if Michael could stay on his back. More than one rodeo cowboy had called running barrels a "controlled runaway".

Robert still remembered when he and Susan had been at a rodeo and a cowboy was making fun of barrel racers saying anybody could do that. Susan had challenged him to ride Doc around the barrels when the rodeo was over and they could use the arena. The cowboy had eagerly accepted the invitation, although Robert had thought it was more to get to ride the big red horse than to prove his point.

The barrels had been set up and the cowboy climbed on Doc. As soon as Doc leapt into the arena, the cowboy knew he was in trouble. He wasn't prepared for the force with which Doc began his barrel pattern. The cowboy was off balance from the beginning and never had a chance to regain it. Doc spun the first barrel and took off for the second one. By this time, the cowboy looked like a rag doll being slung by a rocket. After the second barrel, Doc attacked the third and final barrel. When he turned the last barrel, he accelerated for the run "home' as the finish line was called. The cowboy had both arms around Doc's neck holding on for his life. When Doc completed his run and stopped, more from his training than his rider helping him, a very embarrassed cowboy got off and handed the reins back to Susan.

"Mam," he said, "I owe you an apology. That's one of the wildest rides I've ever been on, and you are one heck of a rider. I think I'll just stick to bulldogging." With that he had tipped his hat to Susan and walked away. When he was gone, both Susan and Robert had burst out laughing.

"Do you think he knows all horses aren't quite like Doc on barrels?" asked Susan.

"Yep, cowboys know horses, and now he knows what it takes to ride a barrel horse."

Remembering that cowboy's ride on Doc, Robert was still amazed at how easily Doc had taken Michael around the barrels when they had first begun to practice. It was as if the big horse knew his rider's limitations and was being careful of them. Robert knew that logically that was not the way horses behaved, but it sure seemed that way. Robert heard the barn rattle as rain began to fall more heavily on the tin roof. Michael would probably get soaked on his ride over this morning. As if on cue, the lights down the center of the barn hallway came on, and Robert knew that Michael had arrived. He was a little surprised because it was so early on a holiday from school and he figured Michael would want to sleep in, especially with the rain and the wind. It made for some good sleeping.

"What are you doing up so early on a holiday?" asked Robert.

"I couldn't sleep. This is my first real Thanksgiving."

"What do you mean? I know you've had other Thanksgiving holidays," said Robert.

"Yes, but not like this. Aunt Maggie had been cooking for three days. You can't believe the cakes and pies she has made. I get hungry just thinking about it. I've never been anywhere on Thanksgiving that's anything like Aunt Maggie's house, and you know something else, I think she likes doing all that stuff!" said Michael incredulously.

It took Robert a minute to focus on what Michael was saying. He was too busy imagining what kind of delicious desserts he would be enjoying later in the day.

"Well of course she likes it. That's just Miss Maggie for you. The most important things to her are taking care of her family and anyone else who needs it," said Robert remembering all the meals she had brought to his family when his wife had been so sick. Miss Maggie usually made up an excuse to stay and do some housecleaning or laundry while she was there to help out. It had been something he and Susan looked forward to because it helped to know someone cared when you were going through tough times.

"I've never known anyone like Aunt Maggie," said Michael.

"I'll tell you one thing, boy, the world would be a whole lot better place if there were more Miss Maggies in it and that's a fact," said Robert emphatically.

"She's sure made my world better," said Michael. He had never been hugged, loved, fed, and taken care of the way Aunt Maggie did. It made him grateful, and little afraid he could lose her.

Robert had exited the Black Mare's stall while Michael was lost in thought. "I guess we better get to work so we'll have all the chores done in time to enjoy Miss Maggie's good cooking."

They each headed to opposite ends of the barn to get busy. One of them was whistling, and it wasn't Michael.

Chapter 44

Max came stumbling into the kitchen rubbing his eyes. Granny Maggie was chopping celery on her cutting board at the sink.

"Good morning, sleepyhead. I see you did decide to wakeup today."

Max smothered a big yawn with the back of his hand. "What time is it?"

"It's almost 9:00. Michael has been gone for hours. Your Dad went to the grocery store for me because I ran out of milk and a few other things for baking. Your Grandpa has gone to invite Miss Twilla to eat Thanksgiving dinner with us."

Max let out a groan, "Oh no, Granny, not Miss Twilla AND Charlie. That's not Thanksgiving. That's torture."

"Now Max, everyone isn't as fortunate as we are to have a family to share Thanksgiving with. It'll be fun. You know, the more the merrier."

Huh, with Charlie and Miss Twilla, it's more like the more, the more miserable."

"My, aren't you a big ol ray of sunshine. Why don't you get a bowl of cereal? That should finish waking you up and hopefully improve your thinking about our company."

"I'll eat some cereal, but I think it will take more than that to change my mind, especially about Miss Twilla. Her cat tried to kill me, Michael, and Norm, and then she got mad at us. She's the grumpiest old lady I've ever known."

"Well, that's in the past. Just make today a new start and see what happens," said Granny Maggie as she picked her knife up and began to chop onion to go with the celery for the cornbread dressing.

"Okay but don't say I didn't warn you," Max replied as he took his cereal to the couch to watch the Thanksgiving parades on TV.

The kitchen door opened and Chuck came in carrying his bags of groceries. "Here you go Mom, three gallons of milk and the other stuff you put on the list."

"Thank you, honey. I just hope I have enough milk. I have potatoes to cream, another pie to make, rolls, and you know how much your Dad loves ice cold milk with his cake or pie, not to mention the rest of you boys."

"Don't you mean how much Dad loves milk with his cake and pie," laughed Chuck. "By the way I ran into Tessa and Charlie at the grocery store. She said to tell you she is bringing a casserole, and Charlie said to tell you she is bringing a surprise. She said they would be here about 4:00 this afternoon. I think she has some studying to do for her nursing classes."

"Hm, I wonder what Charlie's surprise is? That sweet little girl can be so misunderstood." As soon as she finished speaking, they both heard a loud groan from the den.

"I think you need to go and convince your son that Charlie and Miss Twilla will be good Thanksgiving company. I haven't been able to so far."

Chuck smiled and walked into the den where he found Max eating his breakfast and watching TV.

"I heard what Granny said, and the only way to make those two good company is to use hypnosis or maybe an exorcism," said Max glumly.

"Aw come on, buddy, it's not that bad. You can stand them for one afternoon. Who knows it might even be fun."

"Yeah, if your idea of fun is having your teeth pulled with wire pliers and no anesthetic."

"Max you don't have to like it, but you do have to be good company, and be polite," Chuck said in a way that Max knew was final.

"Okay, Dad."

"Good, now hurry up and finish your breakfast, because I need you to help me fix the stall in the barn so Billy can't get out. He hates Norm so much that he keeps climbing over the door to get at him. Of course, Norm caused it all by barking at him and aggravating him until that goat had enough. Now I don't know if we'll ever be able to keep him from attacking Norm, but I guess we have to try."

Billy was a goat that Joe had brought home because the people who had him weren't taking care of him. Joe convinced them to sell him the goat, brought him home and put him in a stall to fatten him up before he turned him out with the cows on pasture. There was only one problem, Billy could not be kept in the stall. He was the world's greatest escape artist and when he escaped he went looking for Norm. If he found him he would let out a big "Baa", lower his head and try to butt Norm. So far, Norm had managed to escape, but Billy was getting more accurate with each charge. After the initial fun of taunting the goat had worn off, Norm began to suffer from goat paranoia. Now if he saw or heard Billy he made a mad dash for the safety of being under Aunt Maggie's bed, where he would stay until he felt the coast was clear.

Michael was just pulling the four-wheeler into the barn. It was a little after 1:00 and he was glad to be getting out of the rain. He had been outside most of the morning helping Mr. Bradley fix a big section of his fence that was down. It was getting colder, and he was definitely getting hungry. Aunt Maggie's dinner sure was going to be good. When he finished parking the four-wheeler he saw Max and Chuck working on the stall where Uncle Joe kept his new goat.

"Has Billy been out again?" Michael asked.

"Yep," said Max, "and we've been working on goat proofing his stall all morning. Every time we think we have it done, he's out before we get back to the house."

"There, that does it. I think this will hold him," said Chuck.

"Wow, I've never seen a stall that is wrapped in chicken wire," said Michael. "I don't think a cat could get out of that."

"Come on and let's go to the house. It's getting colder and raining harder. I could use some hot chocolate. How about you two?" asked Chuck.

"I'll race you," Max told Michael and they were gone.

"I take it that's a yes," Chuck said to himself.

Max, Michael, Chuck, and Joe were all seated on the couch and chairs in the den drinking their steaming hot chocolate and watching football games. Aunt Maggie was putting the finishing touches on her dinner and checking on the turkey.

"Joe," Maggie called from the kitchen, "what time do you have to go and get Miss Twilla for dinner?"

"She told me to be back about 3:00."

"Don't be late," said Maggie, "You know how sensitive she is."

"I know, honey, I'll be on time," said Joe. "I don't think sensitive is the word for what Miss Twilla is, more like just plain ornery."

"Miss Twilla is coming for Thanksgiving with us?" said Michael.

"Yep, and it gets worse, so is Charlie," announced Max.

"What! This is supposed to be Thanksgiving. With those two it'll be Painsgiving."

"That's a good one," laughed Max giving Michael a high five.

"You two don't know the half of it," said Uncle Joe, "I had to go to Miss Twilla's house and beg her to come and have dinner with us. She reminded me of Norm and Sweetie Pie's little incident last spring and wouldn't even let me in her house. She said it would upset Sweetie Pie for me to come in. I had to stand on her porch and persuade her to come to dinner. I tell you what, the things I do for Miss Maggie! I have to be at her house at 3:00, and I have to make sure she is home by 5:50 so she can watch the 6:00 news on TV. Speaking of that, I better get going by the time I get ready and get over there it should be about 3:00."

As Joe was leaving the room, Michael asked, "What time is Charlie coming?"

"Charlie and her Mom should be here about 4:00," said Chuck.

"Oh, her Mom is coming, too," said Michael thinking to himself that Charlie's Mom was still the prettiest girl he had ever seen.

"I know what you are thinking, but that doesn't help with Charlie," said Max.

"Hey guys, Charlie is bringing a surprise so maybe it will be something really cool, and you'll both have a good time," said Chuck optimistically

"Somehow the words Charlie, surprise, and good time just don't seem to go together," said Michael.

"Well, I want both of you to be on your best behavior while Charlie and Miss Twilla are here for Mom because she has worked so hard on this dinner. Is that understood?" asked Chuck in a voice that made both boys quickly say, "Yes sir".

Maggie had the table all set and most of the food ready to eat. It was about 3:30 and her meal was coming together. She had all of her desserts on her mother's antique oak buffet table and it was loaded. The boys had requested something chocolate, so there was a cocoa-cola cake for them. Chuck loved lemon pies so she had made a lemon pie and a cherry pie because she knew that was his next favorite. She made a pumpkin cake because it was her traditional Thanksgiving cake. She had made Joe a coconut cake because that was his favorite. Maggie surveyed her dessert buffet with a smile as she thought how much each one would be enjoyed. Just then she heard the kitchen door open and Tessa came in carrying a casserole.

"Hello Miss Maggie, I know we are a little early. I hope that's okay," said Tessa.

"Of course it is. We are almost ready to eat. Miss Twilla is having dinner with us along with Robert Bradley. All I have left to do is cream the sweet potatoes and carve the turkey. Where's Charlie?"

"She's getting her surprise out of the car. I think she wants to make an entrance," laughed Tessa.

The kitchen door opened again with a lot of banging and groaning. It was Charlie wrestling with a huge pet carrier and an umbrella. She definitely made her entrance. Max, Michael, and Chuck had heard the commotion and come to see what it was all about. Norm had been under the bed when he heard the door. He poked his head out from underneath Miss Maggie's bedspread and picked up a strange scent. He quickly came out to investigate.

The closer he got to the pet carrier, the stronger the alien scent became. Norm lifted his hackles and began to bark furiously while running around the carrier, which Charlie had placed on the floor while she closed her umbrella. This caused high pitched shrieks to come from inside the carrier while it began to dance wildly on the kitchen floor. When she saw what was happening, Charlie began to use her umbrella like a fly swat to make Norm stop, as she chased him around the carrier yelling for him to "shoo". Luckily, Charlie's aim wasn't good, and Norm was very fast so she didn't connect with her swings. All the onlookers stood for a few moments watching the comical scene in front of them. Only Tessa knew what was in the carrier. Everyone else had no idea. They were mesmerized by the sounds coming from it, and by Norm and Charlie whirling around it like a cyclone.

Suddenly, Michael ran to grab Norm when he realized he was in danger of being flattened with the umbrella. He bent to scoop Norm up in his arms and in the process, felt Charlie make contact with her umbrella on his backside.

"Ow!" yelped Michael.

"Way to take one for the team!" yelled Max.

"It's your dog's fault. He started it all. Can't you control him?" Charlie yelled back at them.

"Charlene Nicole Jackson," said Tessa in a voice that caused everyone to stop, "put that umbrella down, apologize to Michael for hitting him, and to Miss Maggie for causing such a ruckus."

"But Mom," began Charlie only to get quiet when she saw the look in her Mother's eye.

"Now, now," said Maggie, "There's no real harm done. I think we need to find something to do with Norm, and then you can show us what's in the pet carrier."

"Don't worry Granny, I know what to do," said Max. "Put him down, Michael."

Michael looked skeptically at Max but did as he asked. As soon as Norm's feet hit the floor, Max did his best billy goat imitation. The loud "Baa" sent Norm right back under the bed.

"Now Charlie, show us what your surprise is," said Chuck.

Charlie began to smile. She bent down, opened the door of the carrier, reached in, and brought out the animal.

"Wow," said Max, as Michael just stood with his mouth open.

"Well I never expected that," said Chuck.

"Oh my goodness," said Maggie.

Charlie was happy with the reaction to her surprise. It was a monkey!

"Miss Maggie I feel that I should apologize for letting Charlie bring her "School Project". I think we should put the monkey back in the car and just go home."

"Nonsense, my dear. There's no harm done and I don't believe I've ever had a monkey for a Thanksgiving guest before, with the exception of Joe," laughed Maggie.

"Yeah," said Charlie. "Please, Mom, can Max stay?"

Michael couldn't believe his ears. This was too good! The monkey's name was MAX. "Well, well, Max the monkey huh?"

"You're real funny, Michael," said Max through gritted teeth

"Don't worry, I'm just getting started," laughed Michael.

"So Charlie, where did you get a monkey?" asked Maggie.

"He is our class pet. We are having a contest to see who can teach him how to tie shoestrings. A different student gets to take him home over the weekends, and this weekend it is my turn. The student who teaches him how to tie shoes gets 15 extra credit points, two homework passes and their picture in the school paper with the monkey, and that's gonna be me," explained Charlie.

"Then how are you going to tell which one is the monkey," laughed Max.

Granny Maggie's loud "Max" caused both namesakes to jump. The human Max uttered a quick "sorry", and the monkey Max let out a small shriek.

"So have you trained him already?" asked Maggie.

"Pretty much. Watch," said Charlie as she reached into the pet carrier once more and brought out an old tennis shoe. She set the shoe and the monkey on the floor and said "tie" to the monkey. It took several tries, but Max, the monkey, finally had a very ugly bow tied in the shoestrings. When he finished he reached up to Charlie and she gave him a treat.

"That's pretty good," Michael had to admit, "how did you do that."

"I just used my brain, but then you wouldn't know what that is since you obviously don't have one."

"Charlie"! snapped Tessa.

"Sorry," said Charlie, somewhat automatically. "I just give him a little piece of candy whenever he does it right, and since he really likes candy it didn't take him long to figure it out."

"I do have to brag on Charlie a little," said Tessa, "She has worked very hard on this and done a good job. Once Max, the monkey, figured out what she wanted, he has tied knots in everything with strings on it. He even tied knots in the fringe on my western coat."

There was a knock on the kitchen door, and in came Robert Bradley. He had smelled the delicious smells of the kitchen as soon as he opened the door, but he didn't have long to think about them because the sight of a monkey on Miss Maggie's kitchen floor caught him off guard.

"Hello Robert," said Maggie, "meet Max."

"I know Max. What did you do, put a spell on him or something?"

"No," laughed Maggie, "this is Max the monkey. He is Charlie's class pet and she is keeping him over the weekend."

"I see I guess. You do still have the other Max don't you?"

"Yes, He's watching TV. Now come in and take your coat off. When Joe and Miss Twilla get here we can eat. Go on in the den and help Michael, Max, and Chuck watch TV."

Robert had just sat down when Joe and Miss Twilla came in the kitchen door.

"Land sakes what a dreary day. It's not fit for anybody to be out in this weather. If I hadn't already promised Maggie I would be here I would have stayed home," fussed Miss Twilla.

"Well, we're just lucky for that," said Joe making a face to Maggie behind Miss Twilla's back.

Maggie walked behind Miss Twilla to help her take off her coat and swatted Joe with her dish towel to make him behave. Joe knew what she was doing and dodged her with a wink. As he was about to exit the kitchen, he saw the monkey sitting on the floor with Charlie.

"Hello Charlie, who's your friend?" asked Joe smiling.

This caused Miss Twilla to turn and look. When she saw the monkey she froze for just a moment then began to rant, "A monkey! Those things carry all kinds of diseases. I saw a whole program about it on TV! You can get rabies from them! Get that thing away from me! Joe Hayes is this your idea of a joke? You can just take me back home right now."

The last remark brought a smile to three of the four faces in the den watching TV. Chuck wanted to smile but he felt he had to set an example for the boys.

Maggie quickly came up to Miss Twilla and put her arm around her, "Its okay Miss Twilla, Charlie will put him in his cage. Honestly, you won't even know he is here. Isn't that right Charlie?"

"Yes mam I'll put him up." Charlie quickly got Max the monkey stowed away in his pet carrier, but not before the monkey noticed Miss Twilla had on old lady lace up shoes as Joe called them. Charlie put the carrier just around the corner in the hallway where it could not be seen from the dining room. She was in such a hurry that she forgot to put the lock on the door. Max had learned to get out of his carrier without it.

"There now, how's that, Miss Twilla?" said Maggie.

"I suppose it's alright as long as that creature stays caged. There's no telling what kind of germs have already gotten in the food from it. You can never be too careful with those nasty things," sniffed Miss Twilla with righteous indignation.

"Hey, Max isn't a nasty thing, he's a...," began Charlie only to be quickly silenced by her Mother.

"Charlie! Why don't you go and watch TV with the boys in the den while I help Miss Maggie finish up, and we'll eat." Tessa punctuated her statement with a look to her daughter that caused her to exit the kitchen.

"Now, Miss Maggie, what can I do to help?" asked Tessa.

"Well, how about carving the turkey and putting it on this big platter while I finish my potatoes."

"Sure thing," said Tessa as she began to slice the turkey.

"Are you going to slice it like that?" asked Miss Twilla. "I'd do it this way," she said as she traced a line on the turkey with her finger to show Tessa where to cut.

Tessa looked at Maggie and winked. She proceeded to do as Miss Twilla directed, and the two of them began the job of carving the turkey. By the time they were finished, so was everything else. When the turkey was placed on the table it was truly a feast. There was turkey and cornbread dressing, sweet potatoes with melted marshmallows on top, green beans from the summer's garden, scalloped potatoes, corn, deviled eggs, gravy, and Miss Maggie's homemade yeast rolls.

"Everyone, come and eat," called Maggie

In no time every one was seated at the big dining room table. Joe sat at the head of the table, Miss Twilla was seated on his right with Tessa, and Chuck next. At the other end of the table sat Maggie, and on her right side was Charlie, Max, and Michael. Robert was seated on Joe's left across from Miss Twilla. Joe said grace for the food, and everyone began to pass the dishes and eat.

None of them had noticed that Max, the monkey, had quietly gotten out of his cage and slipped under the table. He took notice of the number of shoestrings and set about untying them so he could tie them back for candy. Joe had on boots with laces which the monkey tied to Miss Twilla's little old lady shoes so that Joe's right shoe was tied to Miss Twilla's left shoe. The monkey then made his way around the table tying Chuck and Tessa's shoes together, skipping Maggie because she didn't have laces on her shoes, but tying one of Max's shoes to Charlie's and the other to Michael so that both of Max's feet were tied to different people. Robert escaped because he had on cowboy boots with no laces.

While Max the monkey was busy hobbling the Thanksgiving diners, a series of events had been set in motion. Just before everyone had sat down to eat, Maggie had opened the kitchen door, because all the cooking and baking had heated up the kitchen and dining room so much it became stuffy. The screen door let in fresh air that cooled both rooms and carried a scent to Norm under Maggie's bed. Norm immediately jumped up, with hackles raised and followed his nose until he found the source of the scent under the dining room table.

Norm hadn't made a sound, and Max the monkey, had no idea that the little dog was anywhere around. He was busy tying Joe's other foot to the table leg. When Norm saw the monkey attacking Joe's foot, he began his best guard dog barking tirade. It was a wonderful thing for such a little dog to make so much noise and never seem to take a breath. The monkey was caught totally off guard and almost jumped out of his skin. He did jump high enough to hit the bottom of the table with enough force to make the dishes on the top all jump, too. This caused the diners to momentarily pause because they were so caught of guard by the barking and the banging. They were quickly jolted into action because the monkey shinned up the table leg and was immediately sitting in the middle of the Thanksgiving feast.

Once the monkey had left, Norm began to run around and around the table continuing his furious barking. With the kitchen door open, the barking reached the ears of Billy, the goat, who was newly escaped from his screened in stall. Billy knew that bark. It was his nemesis, and he was going to find that bark and butt it into the next county.

Max the monkey was still in the middle of the table. He even stopped and ate a little bite of turkey while the diners sat in stunned silence. When he realized that Norm was on the floor and not able to get to him, he began to throw food at the little dog. He threw everything from potatoes to green beans, to rolls and even tried to throw gravy which didn't work too well.

"Oh no!" yelled Charlie.

"Get that thing off the table!" screamed Miss Twilla.

"Joe, do something!" cried Maggie.

"Wow Max," said Michael, "do all monkeys eat turkey?"

"What do I look like, a monkeyologist?" answered Max who was still more than a little upset to share his name with Charlie's "project".

Max the monkey had become agitated with all the dog barking, yelling, and gravy that he couldn't get off his arms and hands. He jumped on Miss Twilla's shoulder and began to rub his arms in her hair to get rid of the gravy. Miss Twilla screamed and jumped up to run not knowing that her foot was tied to Joe's foot under the table. Joe was almost jerked off his seat while Miss Twilla was jerked back to hers with such force that she fell face down into the melted marshmallows of the sweet potatoes.

As soon as Miss Twilla's face hit the marshmallows, Charlie and Michael both jumped up. Charlie to save her monkey, and Michael to grab Norm. Not knowing all their shoes were tied together, all they succeeded in doing was making Max do the splits which caused a loud, "HEY" from Max!

"Let go of my foot," yelled Charlie.

"I don't have your foot. You let go of mine!" exclaimed a very indignant Max.

"Wait a minute," said Michael, "that stupid monkey has tied all our shoestrings together."

"If he was stupid, he couldn't do that could he?" asked a defiant Charlie as she kicked off her shoe that was tied to Max.

Max and Michael tried to do the same thing but couldn't because the monkey had tied their laces in a knot and their shoes were on too tight. Charlie immediately began to chase Norm around the table which he was still circling and barking. Chuck and Tessa were involved in trying to get the knots out of their shoes to help Miss Twilla who was moaning something about monkey fever through her marshmallow mask.

Robert was laughing so hard he couldn't help anyone, and Joe was trying to figure out why both his feet were anchored to something. Maggie was in shock just sitting watching all her hard work go to the dogs and monkeys as it were.

"Max we gotta catch Norm before Charlie gets him," said Michael.

"Yeah, but we need something to catch him with and we can't reach his lease tied together like we are," said Max.

"Wait, have you still got those fake handcuffs we found that we were going to put on Charlie?" asked Michael. In the process of cleaning their room before the company came for Thanksgiving Dinner, Max had found an old pair of toy metal handcuffs. The plan had been to put them on Charlie when they found out she was coming to dinner so Max had stuck them in his pocket.

"Yeah, why?"

"Just give them to me," said Michael.

Max gave the handcuffs to Michael who quickly opened them as big as they would go and then clicked them securely shut. He now had two perfect circles.

"Now we use these to catch Norm around the neck when he runs by us again and we have him caught, just as good as a collar and a leash."

"Good idea," said Max, "get ready here he comes."

Michael expertly managed to get one of the cuffs around Norm's neck but he ran by so fast Michael couldn't grab the other handcuff. Now Norm was lapping the table barking with the handcuffs flopping along beside his head.

"Smooth move," said Max sarcastically.

"Shut up and help me grab him when he comes back around."

Suddenly, the screen door was almost ripped off its hinges as Billy the goat, butted through it. The sound startled Max the monkey and he jumped to the dessert table, and landed right in the middle of Joe's coconut cake.

"Nooooooo," said Joe as he lunged to save his cake, but since he was still tied to the table leg and Miss Twilla's foot all he succeeded in doing was jerking the table and spilling all the drinks and gravy. He also succeeded in jerking Miss Twilla around sideways in her chair but she couldn't really tell because she had marshmallows all over her glasses.

Billy shook his head and looked for the source of all the barking. When he saw Norm running around the table with his handcuffs on, it was all he needed to cause him to let out a loud "Baaa", lower his head, get Norm in his sights, and charge!

When Norm heard the "Baa", he stopped dead in his tracks. He looked behind him and saw a very angry goat headed right at him. Norm knew he had to get under Miss Maggie's bed, but he was on the wrong side of the table to get there. He would have to run around Joe and in between the dessert table to get there. Norm took off as fast as he could.

At the same time, Joe had startled Max, the monkey, enough with his lunge for the cake that the monkey jumped to the floor. Just as the monkey hit the floor Norm ran by and the empty hand cuff went right over the monkey's head and settled around his waist. Try and screech as he might, the monkey couldn't get loose from Norm who was still running full steam to hide under the bed. Since Norm was dragging him and he couldn't get away, the monkey jumped on Norm's back and began to ride him like a tiny horse.

"Ride em, Max," cheered Charlie.

"Did you see that?" Michael asked Max.

"Yep," laughed Max. Suddenly, Max went, "Uh oh."

"What do you mean, uh oh?" asked Michael.

"Look where Norm's headed."

Norm was running like his life depended on it because it did. The goat was right behind him, and the monkey was on his back. About that time the monkey looked up and saw that they were going under the bed. He also saw the side rail on the bed and how low it was. Max the monkey began to screech, "Eeeeeeeeee" loudly and try to get away from Norm. Nothing was working and as Norm flew under the bed there was a loud clang as the monkey went under with him. There was an even louder clang when the goat butted the side rail as hard as he could. What had been utter chaos became dead quiet.

Michael walked into the living room looking for Aunt Maggie. He found her sitting on the couch with her feet propped up. It was 8:00 at night and all the company had long since departed .Joe had managed to get his boot untied and usher the goat back to the barn. The whole time he was lamenting his ruined coconut cake. Luckily the rest of the desserts had survived intact with no monkey germs, so Joe had been able to get over the loss of his cake by eating some of each of them and having three glasses of milk.

Miss Twilla got the marshmallows off her glasses just in time to see and hear the crashes into the side of the bed. That did it. She passed right out, and Robert had fanned her until she came to. Robert was laughing so hard, he was crying while he was fanning her. The first time she came to and saw Robert crying so hard she thought she was dead and passed out again.

Chuck and Tessa never did get the knot out of their shoestrings. They didn't seem to mind having their shoes tied together, because they sure spent a long time working on that knot. They finally just cut the knot out.

Joe was so mad at the goat he said he was going to shoot him. He couldn't find his shotgun because Miss Maggie had hid it after the rooster incident. Instead Joe took the goat to the barn and tied him in a stall until he could try again to contain him.

Miss Twilla had finally come to and demanded to be taken to the doctor for a tetanus shot due to her contact with the monkey. When Joe told her all the doctor's offices were closed for the holiday, she made him promise to take her to the doctor the next day for her shot.

When Michael and Max had finally pulled Norm from under the bed, the monkey came with him. He was knocked out cold from conking his head on the bed rail. Charlie was able to get him out of the handcuffs and in his pet carrier before he woke up. When he came to, he appeared to be fine until he saw either Norm or the shoe that Charlie had for him to tie. If he saw either one of those he began to screech and shake wildly. Aunt Maggie had to finally put an old towel over his cage to calm him down.

Tessa and Charlie left right after that. Miss Twilla insisted that Chuck take her home because the whole thing was somehow Joe's fault and she was never going anywhere with him again, except to the doctor tomorrow. Robert said it was the most fun he had had in a long time, and asked to be put on next year's guest list. The only person who hadn't really said anything was Aunt Maggie.

Michael sat down beside her on the couch and said, "Are you alright, Aunt Maggie?"

"Of course, why wouldn't I be," she said as she put her arm around him.

"Well, you worked so hard on your dinner and it didn't turn out like you planned."

"Just because it didn't go as I thought it would is not necessarily a bad thing."

"I guess I just thought you would be mad about Norm, the monkey, and the goat."

"No sweetie. I like to look at things like today as making memories."

"I don't understand."

"Well, if we had just had an ordinary Thanksgiving meal, it would have been nice, right?"

"Yes Mam ."

"We probably would have forgotten all about that dinner in no time, but I don't think any of us will ever forget the time a monkey, a goat, and a little dog were at our Thanksgiving Dinner, do you? That's making a memory."

A smile spread across Michael's face as he understood what Aunt Maggie was talking about. He looked up at her and said, "I like making memories. Thanks Aunt Maggie."

Her response was a big hug that he added to his memory of this Thanksgiving Day.

Chapter 45

Michael was watching a beautiful sight. It was a cold, snowy, January afternoon. It had been snowing all day, and now there were almost five inches of snow on the ground. Doc had been cooped up in his stall all day and was anxious to get outside to stretch his legs. As Michael came down the barn hallway, Doc began to nod his head and neigh to him. He pawed his stall door as if to tell Michael to hurry up and let him out. Michael had quickly gotten Doc's halter and lead rope and taken him out to the corral and let him go. Boy did he go! He jumped in the air, bucked, reared, ran and spun. It was a snow dance that was as graceful as a ballet. How an animal as big as a horse could move so fluidly and effortlessly in the snow was amazing. Doc snorted as he played, and big puffs of air blew from his nostrils in the cold. The white snow, the gray day, and the big red horse all combined to make a picture that Michael knew would stay burned in his memory forever.

As he continued to stand by the corral and watch Doc, he thought about how far he had come in less than a year. He had been around plenty of snow in Michigan, but it had never seemed this beautiful to him. He smiled to himself as he thought about how much better his life was now. The first thing that came to mind when he thought about his life being better was Aunt Maggie, and the second thing was Doc. Even though one was a huge animal and the other a lady, they were both very powerful. Doc's power was obvious. His massive size and strength were undeniable. That he let Michael control him and his power was an awesome feeling to the boy. Aunt Maggie's power was the power of love. Once Michael had felt loved, he couldn't get enough of it. It seemed the more love someone had to give the more powerful they were, at least to Michael's way of thinking. He thought that somebody like Aunt Maggie who loved so much had to have a bigger heart than almost anyone else and be stronger, too, because she loved people in spite of how they treated her. She was one special lady to him.

Christmas had come and gone and it had been his best Christmas ever. The Thanksgiving feast had been nothing compared to all the food in the South at Christmas. He had never eaten so much in his life, or seen so many Christmas decorations. It was impossible not to have the Christmas spirit here. The presents had been more than he had ever had!

His two favorite presents had been Aunt Maggie's and Mr. Bradley's. Mr. Bradley had given him a new bridle for Doc. It had silver inlaid in the leather and was the coolest bridle Michael had ever seen. Aunt Maggie gave him a Bible. He liked the Bible, but what made it one of his favorite gifts was what she had written in it. It was a letter telling him how proud she was to have him in their family, and what a good person he was. He had never had anything in writing from someone who loved him, and he read it over and over. She said the Bible was the instruction manual for a happy life, and that whatever problem you had, you could find the answer for it in this book. She had put his name on the front of it in gold letters. He already knew he would keep it forever.

Doc came over to Michael breaking his train of thought. He rubbed his big head on Michael's arm as if to say he was ready to go back to his nice warm stall. Michael scratched his neck as he clipped the lead rope to his halter to lead him in to the barn. Michael put him in his stall and rubbed him down before putting the blanket on him that Chuck and Max had given him for Christmas.

"There you go Big Guy, you should be good until morning. You've played in the snow, got your supper of grain and hay, and got your pajamas on. I better head on home so I don't miss my supper." Michael gave Doc a final pat as he closed his stall door.

Brenda Dawson

Robert had seen Michael take Doc back to the barn from the corral. He began to gather up some empty dishes that Miss Maggie had sent over food in for him. He had to rewash some of them because he discovered he had missed a few spots the first time he washed them. This slowed him down quite a bit. He was just putting the last dish in a bag to give to Michael to take back to Miss Maggie when he heard the motor on the four-wheeler start up. Robert went running out in the driveway to catch Michael with his bag of dishes. He was so intent on hurrying that he didn't notice how icy the driveway had become. Before he could catch himself, he went down hard on the ice with his left leg bent at a bad angle underneath him. He knew immediately that it was broken and he couldn't walk. He looked up to see the red tail lights of the four-wheeler leaving the barn.

"Michael, Michael, come back! Help me, help me!" Robert cried desperately, but Michael couldn't hear him over the roar of the motor on the four-wheeler, and he disappeared over the hill out of sight.

Michael opened the kitchen door and was very happy to be home. The ride home had been cold and the speed of the four-wheeler made for an even colder wind hitting him in the face. He was shivering as he took off his boots and coat.

Aunt Maggie heard him come in and said, "I'm glad you're home, Michael. It's not a fit night for man or beast. This weather is terrible. You are the last one to come home so now all my family is in from the cold. My gracious, you are freezing! Come stand in front of the fireplace and warm up. I've got a big pot of chili on the stove for supper and it's almost ready."

Michael was quick to obey, except he decided to sit in the big rocking chair that was by the fireplace instead of standing. The rocker had a big comfortable pillow back and seat. It wasn't long before he was warm and getting sleepy. There was something about getting cold and staying cold for a while that made you tired when you warmed up. Just before he drifted off he heard, "Supper's ready, you boys come on." The ensuing clamor of Max, Chuck, Uncle Joe, and Norm heading for the table roused Michael and he joined them.

"Honey this smells good. There's nothing I like better on a cold day than a big bowl of your world famous chili and cornbread, except maybe one or two of your other dishes like chicken and dumplings, or pork chops and gravy, or …"

"Dad, we get the picture," laughed Chuck. "If we don't stop you we won't ever get to eat Mom's chili."

"Yeah Grandpa Joe and I'm hungry," added Max.

"Settle down boys," said Maggie, "Joe please say grace and let's eat."

Joe said the blessing for their dinner and Maggie began to ladle out hearty bowls of chili and big pieces of hot cornbread. Things got quiet for a while as everyone began to enjoy their meal.

"Michael, your face is so red it looks like a third degree sunburn," said Max.

"That a case of windburn and cold," said Uncle Joe.

"I'll give you some lotion to put on it, and it will be a lot better by morning," said Maggie.

"Thanks," said Michael, "because I have to go back to the barn in the morning on the four-wheeler, and the wind from the ride is pretty cold."

"The schools have already closed for tomorrow because of the snow so you won't have to go as early," said Aunt Maggie.

"Yeeessss," said Max with much emotion, "no school tomorrow. We can sleep late Michael. At least I plan to so don't wake me up or else!"

"No problem, Max, sleep as late as you want. Aunt Maggie, is Charlie coming to our house tomorrow, since her Mom has work and there's so school?" asked Michael smiling as he saw the look on Max's face at this news.

"Yes she is, and I'm sure you will all have a lot of fun in the snow. Charlie is such a sweet girl," said Aunt Maggie.

Max just groaned and rolled his eyes. He knew when he was beaten.

"Mom do you remember the time Charlie left the hose running when she watered your flowers and when we got up the next morning your chicken house was flooded? Your hens wouldn't come down from the roosting poles to go outside and Max and Michael had to go in and get them," laughed Chuck.

"Yes," said Maggie, "but anyone can make a mistake."

The talk around the table continued with more Charlie stories, but Michael had stopped listening. The incident with the hose left running had jogged his memory of watering the animals in Mr. Bradley's barn. For the life of him, he could not remember turning off the water at the barn. The harder he tried to remember the less he could. He knew he would have to go back and check. Weather this cold would make any water left running solid ice, not to mention that Mr. Bradley got his water from a well and Michael didn't want to run it dry or burn up his pump in the well.

"Michael, why aren't you eating? Do you feel okay? All this being outside in bad weather can give you a terrible cold," said Aunt Maggie anxiously.

"I have to go back to Mr. Bradley's barn. I'll be back as soon as I can," said Michael as he stood up to leave.

"Whoa now Michael. Hold on a minute. What's the rush to go back to Robert's barn? Whatever it is it'll keep till morning," said Uncle Joe.

"No, it won't. I think left the water on in the barn after I watered the horses. I have to make sure it's off. If it's not the barn could flood, the saddles could be ruined and the feed, too. I have to go!" said Michael becoming more agitated by the minute.

Joe saw how upset Michael was getting and said, "It's alright, Michael, I'll just call Robert and ask him to check the water to be sure it's turned off. I know he won't mind and your Aunt Maggie won't be worried about you being out in the cold again." Joe got up from the table and reached for the phone. He dialed Robert's number and listened as it rang repeatedly with no answer. He hung up the phone with a puzzled look on his face and asked Michael, "Was Robert going anywhere tonight?"

"Not that I know of," replied Michael, "why?"

"Because no one answered," said Joe scratching his beard thoughtfully.

Chuck had been listening to the predicament Michael was in and said, "Tell you what, Michael, Max and I will drive you over to the barn, and on the way home we'll check out the big hill by our pond to see if it will be good sledding tomorrow. What do you say?"

"That's great, thanks Chuck," said Michael.

"Yeah we can see if its gonna be slick enough to push Charlie down," said Max which earned him a stern look from his Grandmother.

"Alright boys, let's load up," said Chuck as he began to put on his boots and coat.

Robert was colder than he had ever been in his life. He knew he would have to stay where he was until Michael came back in the morning. He didn't even have his coat and boots on. Just his long sleeved flannel shirt, jeans, and his slippers that Miss Maggie had given him for Christmas. When he had opened them, he never thought he would wear them. He wore boots not slippers. He had thanked Miss Maggie and taken them home to put on the back shelf of his closet. He had made the mistake of trying them on and they felt so good he had worn them every day since, when he went inside and took off his boots.

He smiled to himself thinking that cowboys died with their boots on, but not this cowboy, and he was a cowboy. Horses, his land, and his girls had been his life. He knew his life would end this night. He would not survive the cold on the snow covered ground without protection and warmth. He felt strangely at peace with the realization. He thought about Tam and Susan, and his faith told him he would be reunited with them very soon. The thought caused his blue lips to turn upward in a smile, a smile that stayed on his lips as he drifted into unconsciousness.

Chapter 46

Michael, Max, and Chuck were all buckled in Chuck's four-wheel drive truck. They were going to need all four wheels pulling to make it to Robert's barn and back on the slick roads. It was still snowing hard and the wind was whipping the flakes into a swirling, white cloud that was hard to see through. The windshield wipers beat fast and steady in an attempt to keep the snow from blocking the view from inside the truck.

"Man, it's snowing harder now than it was earlier. I can hardly see," said Chuck as he navigated the winding country road.

"Yeah," chimed in Max, "isn't it great? We might be out of school for more than one day. Keep you fingers crossed Michael."

"I'm still getting used to the idea of no school when it snows. Not that I don't think it's a great idea, its just that we never got out of school in Michigan, and there was a lot more snow there than there is here," said Michael.

"The reason we close school for snow is because the people are a lot more spread out here, and we have so many country roads. Our school buses can't safely travel over them when they are icy so we just wait for it to melt enough to be safe. I remember snow days, and how much I loved them when I was in school," finished Chuck with a smile.

"Hey Dad, there's the hardware store parking lot and it's empty. Can we cut some donuts in the snow?" asked Max excitedly. They had traveled into town, and the local hardware store had the best parking lot for icing up and sliding in the snow.

"What are you talking about?" asked Michael.

"Good grief, I keep forgetting how underprivileged you are when it comes to having some fun. Donuts are when you slide really fast and turn circles in the snow in your truck. Dad's a world class donut cutter, right Dad," said Max.

"I don't know about that, but we better get to Robert's first to check on the water. Maybe we'll try a donut or two on the way home," laughed Chuck.

They continued their snowy mission and finally came to a stop in front of Robert's barn. When Chuck turned off the motor, everything became eerily quiet and white. Michael opened his door and stepped out onto the frozen ground. He stood for a moment and listened to the silence of the snowy night. There were no sounds of cars, barking dogs, or any other animal noises. It was as if everything had found a place to wait out the cold and was not coming out until the weather was better.

"If you want to wait, I'll check the water and be right back," said Michael.

Chuck was glad to agree, but Max was ready to get in the snow even if just for a little while. He climbed out of his Dad's truck, reached down into the snow, got a big handful, made a snowball, and proceeded to hit Michael in the back with it laughing at the "splat" it made on the back of Michael's coat.

"Max, truce until I check on the water then look out," warned Michael.

Both boys went into the barn as Chuck just shook his head and smiled. It was good to see the relationship that had formed between his son and Michael. Michael was way too serious and Max was way to not serious. They were rubbing off on each other, although it appeared that Max was having more of an impact than Michael. It didn't surprise Chuck, because Max was just like Joe who didn't have a serious bone in his body, except where Miss Maggie was concerned.

Michael turned on the barn lights, and laughed as a sleepy eyed and yawning Doc poked his head over his stall door. So did Tessa's gray horse Moz. Michael and Max walked to the other end of the barn to get to the water hook up. As they went down the barn hallway, they startled the Black Mare and she snorted loudly. Max jumped about two feet off the ground.

"Holy cow, what's that," asked Max as he peered into the stall, seeing nothing because the mare was against the back wall and didn't show up at first.

"That's Mr. Bradley's friend's horse," said Michael. "You remember, the one that's scared of everything."

"Oh yeah, the crazy one you told us about. Didn't you say Mr. Bradley was going to try and fix her?"

"Yep, and he's making progress, but he won't let anyone else work with her. He says she is still too dangerous. Hey look, I didn't leave the water on. Whew! I was afraid I had flooded the feed room already. Let's go see if your Dad will do those donuts in the snow. It sounds like fun."

"You're gonna love it. It's better than a ride at the fair."

Both boys began to walk back down the barn hallway to leave. "Don't you have to unhook the hose and straighten it out when it's cold like this?" asked Max.

"What do you mean?"

"Well, at our barn when it's cold we drain all the water out of the hose so we can use it the next morning, and not have to carry water. If you don't the water in the hose freezes and you can't use it. You know Granny Maggie, her chickens have to have fresh water every day."

Michael thought about what Max said about carrying water, and quickly decided that he didn't want to carry enough water for three horses to drink. "Show me how you do that."

"Well duh, you just unhook the hose like this," Max said as he unscrewed the hose from the faucet. "Now you stretch it out straight with no kinks downhill so all the water runs out. We'll have to go toward Mr. Bradley's house with it because the other way is flat ground. Come on, help me pull this thing. What is it a fire hose? This is the heaviest hose I've ever seen," groaned Max.

Michael laughed, "Mr. Bradley is very proud of this hose. He said he has had it for a long time because it's so heavy duty. I think it's just heavy!"

Michael and Max managed to wrestle the hose in a straight line so that it was running downhill. They stood watching with satisfaction as water began to run out of it.

"I guess we're done Max, let's go," said Michael.

Max was looking at Mr. Bradley's house, "Hey Michael what's that lump in front of Mr. Bradley's back door?"

Michael turned and looked and began to frown. "I don't know, but it wasn't there when I left earlier. Let's go check."

As they approached the house Michael bean to run. He didn't realize it but he started saying, "Mr. Bradley, Mr. Bradley, oh no, oh no," over and over. As he reached him and dropped down to check on him, Michael saw that he was unconscious. Fear raced through him.

He looked quickly at Max and said, "Go get your Dad to call 911, and hurry because I think Mr. Bradley may be dead!"

Chapter 47

Maggie was looking out the kitchen window wondering what was taking her boys so long. They should have been back from Robert's by now. It was snowing harder and getting colder. The thermometer on the porch said it was already 17 degrees. Maggie knew she was like an old mother hen who wanted all her chicks home when it was bad weather outside. She couldn't shake the feeling that something was wrong. She listened carefully because she thought she heard something. Yes, there it was, sirens howling loudly and piercing the white stillness of the night. Oh my, she thought, that is never a good sign. Someone must be hurt badly or very sick. Frowning, she turned and looked at her husband. Joe was dozing in his big chair close to the fireplace. She wasn't surprised, because he never worried much about anything.

"Joe, don't you think they should be back by now?" she asked.

"Now honey, Chuck is a big boy and perfectly capable of getting to Robert's house and back. They are probably just playing in the snow."

"I know, but did you just hear those sirens a little bit ago? I just want them home when the weather is like this."

"Sweetie, trust me, they are fine and there is no need to worry your pretty little head about those three. Why if anybody was to mess up and kidnap them, they would bring them home by morning just to get Max to leave them alone," laughed Joe.

Just then the phone rang and caused Maggie to hurry to answer. Maybe it was Chuck. She picked up the phone and said, "Hello."

The voice on the line was Chuck and Maggie breathed a sigh of relief until she heard him say, "Mom, can you and Dad meet us at the hospital?"

Maggie's heart seemed to stop, "Of course we can, but what's wrong honey?"

"Don't worry, Mom, we are all fine. It's Robert, we found him unconscious in the snow. We don't know how long he had been there, but he was covered in snow and blue with cold. It doesn't look good, Mom. Michael is pretty torn up and I think he would like to see you. We are on our way to the hospital now behind the ambulance."

"I'll get my coat and your Father. Tell Michael I'm coming," said Maggie. She hung up the phone and called to Joe as she grabbed her coat and purse, "Joe hurry, we have to get to the hospital. Robert is in an ambulance on the way to the emergency room. The boys found him outside, unconscious." Maggie rushed past Joe's chair on her way to the car, "I'll be waiting on you. Hurry!" For a big man, Joe sure could move fast when he wanted to.

Michael watched as Robert was wheeled into the emergency room and the doors closed. He had never been in a hospital before, much less in the circumstances he found himself in now. He looked around wondering what to do.

Chuck could tell Michael was a little lost so he said, "Come on guys, let's go to the waiting room. Maybe Mom and Pop are there by now."

That sounded great to Michael. If anybody could make this better it was Aunt Maggie. He walked eagerly to the waiting room and wasn't disappointed. There was Aunt Maggie and Uncle Joe. Michael ran to her and put both arms around her in a big bear hug. He didn't think anything had ever felt so good in his life.

Maggie knew Michael was scared and she returned his hug along with patting his back and saying, "Don't worry honey, everything will be okay. Now fill me in on what has happened."

All three recounted the events that had happened at the barn with Chuck doing most of the talking. By the time he had finished, the door to the waiting room opened and a doctor was standing there.

"Are any of you the family of Mr. Bradley?" he asked.

"Why! What's wrong? Is he going to be alright?" asked Michael not waiting for any of his questions to be answered before asking another one.

"Well Doc," began Uncle Joe, "I guess we are his family, at least all that I know of. Do you know what's wrong with him?"

"Mr. Bradley is suffering from a mild case of hypothermia as well as a broken hip. We have him stable and regaining consciousness but we may have to do surgery on his hip."

"What do you need from us Doctor? Whatever it is we will be glad to help," said Aunt Maggie.

"Hopefully nothing if he comes around enough for us to get his signature on permission forms to operate, and it looks like that will be the case, but in the event he doesn't we just need someone to give us that permission."

"We are only close friends, not relatives, but if we can do that we will," said Maggie.

"We really need a family member for that, but maybe Mr. Bradley will be able to do so. I'll keep you informed."

The doctor left and Michael began to frown, "What's hyo, hypo, hyper…?"

"Hypothermia," Chuck finished for him, "it means Robert's body temperature was lower than it should be because of being outside in the snow without warm clothes on, and from what the doctor said I don't think it is a problem."

"His real problem is going to be his hip, Michael," said Aunt Maggie.

"Why? Can't they just put a cast on it like a broken leg or something?"

"I'm afraid not honey. A broken hip doesn't work that way and if it's bad enough they may have to do a hip replacement. Either way Robert is going to be off his feet for a good length of time. He's going to need a lot of help just taking care of himself. As far as I know he doesn't have any other family, but we will check to be sure," said Maggie.

"That's awful! What will he do? He can't take care of his barn, and Black Mare, and everything if he can't walk," worried Michael. He was also thinking of Doc.

"Oh honey, don't worry about that. If there's one thing I can do its help sick people get well, and I figure you boys will come up with some way to take care of everything else. After all there's only one of Robert and five of us so it won't be a problem."

Joe just shook his head. He knew exactly what would happen. Maggie would take care of Robert and get him back on his feet and that would be that. Getting in front of his wife now would be about as smart as jumping in front of a moving bulldozer and do about as much good. Maggie sure was something!

Michael felt a huge weight leave his shoulders. He had no idea what to do, and Aunt Maggie made it all so simple. He smiled as he looked at her and thought, Aunt Maggie sure is something!

Chapter 48

It was a sunny day in the middle of February. The sun was shinning, a breeze was blowing, skies were blue, and it seemed that spring must be just around the corner. It wasn't all that warm. The thermometer on Aunt Maggie's porch said 60 degrees but compared to the cold weather of January and the first part of February, it was positively tropical. Everyone in the Hayes family had spent the better part of the last week getting ready for Robert to move in with them.

The doctors had been right when they said that Robert might have to have surgery, and Aunt Maggie had been right when she said Robert might need a hip replacement. Michael had never heard of parts like hips being replaced but he was glad that Mr. Bradley could be fixed as Aunt Maggie said "better than new". They found out his hip had been bothering him for a long time, but he hadn't gone to the doctor to see about it. Michael thought that if you had to have something break it was good for it to be something that was already messed up to begin with.

It had been a month since that night they found Mr. Bradley out in the snow. After his operation he had to stay in the hospital for a week, and then he had to go to a nursing home to do therapy on his new hip for three more weeks. When he left the hospital, he had been walking with a walker, now that he was getting out of the nursing home he was walking with a walking stick that had four little legs on it. He was still very slow and a little unsteady. That was why he was coming to Aunt Maggie's house.

When Joe told Robert he was moving in with them when he got out of the hospital, Robert had been adamant that he would go home and be fine. He said he didn't need a babysitter. Joe and Robert had been discussing it and had gotten pretty loud when Miss Maggie walked into the room at the nursing home. When she found out what all the commotion was all about she told Robert that she was looking forward to helping him get better and had already gotten the groceries to make most of his favorite meals complete with his favorite desserts. Apparently, Robert was the type of person who hated for groceries to go to waste, because when he heard about what Aunt Maggie had done, he quickly agreed to stay for a little while. Joe had just shook his head, and Maggie had smiled a very big smile. Tomorrow was the big day that Robert would get out of the nursing home.

Michael had been sitting on the corral gate at Robert's barn while Doc and the Black Mare had been playing in the corral. They had been outside most of the day enjoying the nice weather. It seemed they were as eager for spring as their human counterparts. It had taken a little while to figure out how to keep the barn going, but it had turned out fine. Michael had been taking care of everything but the Black Mare, and that was because Mr. Bradley told him to stay away from her.

At first, he had just fed and watered her and not gone in her stall, but he began to feel sorry for her being cooped up and her stall needed cleaning badly. He came up with the idea of closing the big doors on both ends of the barn and letting her out in the hallway while he cleaned her stall. The first time he tried it, she came charging out and ran up and down the hallway looking for a way out. When she couldn't find one, she stopped at Doc's stall and began to sniff at him and check him out. Doc wasn't too happy with her and after a lot of snorting and squealing she was glad to go back into her freshly cleaned and bedded stall. This turned into a daily routine, and she and Doc began to be buddies. Michael was happy to see that they got along. If ever an animal needed a friend, she did.

Michael remembered the day she got out of her stall, and the big hallway doors were open. He had put fresh water and feed in her stall and must not have fastened the latch on the stall door completely. He was leading Doc out to the corral when Black Mare came racing by them. Doc began to run in circles around him at the end of his lead rein. He wanted to run, too.

Michael began to panic, wondering how he was ever going to hold onto Doc and catch the Black Mare before she ran away. He quickly decided he needed to put Doc back in his stall so he could concentrate on getting the Black Mare. As he was closing Doc's stall door, an amazing thing happened. Instead of the Black Mare continuing to run down the driveway, she came running back into barn calling loudly to her friend, Doc. Doc answered and while they were sniffing noses, Michael ran to close the hallway doors. Before he had time to think what to do next, Black Mare walked back into her stall and began to calmly eat her hay. Michael was nowhere nearly as calm as she was when he closed her stall door and double checked the latch. He looked at Doc. He never ceased to be amazed by the big red horse. He knew that Mr. Bradley would just say it was the herd instinct thing, but it sure seemed like Doc always came through for him when he need him.

From then on when Michael took Doc to the corral he opened Black Mare's door and let her follow them. It worked out great, and once both horses became accustomed to going outside and coming back in, Michael never had anymore trouble. Black Mare went wherever Doc went.

Michael jumped off the corral and called to Doc. The big horse lifted his head and looked in Michael direction without moving. It was as if he was saying "just a few more minutes, please". Michael laughed and waited a little longer.

"Sorry Doc," he said at last, "but we gotta go back inside. Aunt Maggie will be waiting for me to have supper." Doc began to walk toward Michael, and Black Mare was right behind him. Michael put them both up for the night and headed home.

Chapter 49

Early the next morning Robert was sitting in the doorway of his room in a wheelchair. He didn't need a wheelchair, as he had told the nurse, but she said it was hospital procedure when someone was released to go home. The problem was, he wasn't going home. He was aware that he was more nervous than he had been in a long time. He had always lived with his own family in his own house, and since his family had been gone he had stayed in his house. Now he was going to someone else's home, and he had no idea of what to expect or how to act.

When the doctor had told him he could only be released from the nursing home if he had someone to stay with him, he had racked his brain to try to think of some way to trick them into letting him go home. He almost had them convinced, too, and then the doctor had talked to Maggie about giving the instructions for his care to his sister who would be staying with him. He had known he was in trouble when she walked into his room with a very unhappy look on her face. Maggie proceeded to tell him there was no way she was going to let him go home with his imaginary sister and that if he wanted out of there, he would be going to her house.

Robert had argued long and hard with her, but she paid absolutely no attention. She quickly talked to the doctor, to her family, and then came back to talk to him. She basically laid the law down that he was going to her house until he was fully recovered, and that was the end of it. To be such a kind, little, southern lady she sure was hard headed. So, here he was waiting on Maggie and Joe to come and get him. He knew that if he had to go anywhere but his home, Maggie's would be the best place to be, but that didn't make him any less anxious. A person needed their own privacy and their own space. As far as he could tell, Maggie's house was full to the brim with Chuck and the two boys. Where was he going to stay, in the living room!

Robert was lost in his worrying and didn't hear them approach until Joe said in typical Joe fashion, "Taxi service for Mr. Robert Bradley unless you want to stay here."

"Good morning, Robert. Are you ready to go?" asked Maggie.

"I was ready to go three weeks ago, but they wouldn't listen to me."

"Well, I think that was a good thing," said Maggie. "Do we need to wait for the doctor or has he been here already?"

"He's been here and given me a paper that says I can go. He said he talked to you last night, and I just have to get a nurse to roll me out. I told them I didn't need this danged wheelchair, but they wouldn't listen to me. There's a lot of that going on around here lately. I'm beginning to think I'm not speaking the same language as everybody else," said Robert as he gave Maggie an accusing look.

Joe let out a big laugh, "Look's to me like you met Maggie Hayes, woman of steel. It's a side of her most people never see. Doesn't pay to argue with her does it, buddy?"

"Humph," snorted Robert, "I'd have more luck arguing with a grizzly bear!"

"Nonsense, both of you are exaggerating. I'm going to find a nurse to wheel you out so we can go home." Maggie turned and went to the nurse's station.

The ride home was short and quiet. Robert was still worried about how all this was going to work out. Once they got home, Robert was able to walk by himself with his cane even if it was very slow. Maggie opened the door and he was relieved to see he didn't have a bed in the middle of the dining room table. He finally had to ask, "Uh, where do you want me to go?"

Maggie looked up quickly and realized what had been troubling her friend. "Why anywhere you want to go. I want you to treat this just like your own home. If you mean where is your room, it's right out here."

Maggie walked him through the dining room to her sunroom. She had converted it to his bedroom. It had navy blue plaid curtains over the windows. A big, comfortable bed with a navy blue, down comforter had replaced her sofa. There was a night stand with a lamp and a bookshelf underneath. Maggie had placed a recliner by one of the windows. Directly across from his chair was a bureau with a TV on top of it. There was also a chest of drawers with a mirror on top. Maggie had left one of her big plants in the corner. It was the most inviting room Robert had seen in a long time. He should have known Maggie would do something like this. He was glad he hadn't voiced his concerns about sleeping on the dining room table. He suddenly felt very foolish.

"There is a bathroom just across the hall that no one ever uses, so just consider it you own. The boy's bathroom is upstairs, and Joe and I have one in our bedroom," finished Maggie.

Robert gave Maggie a sheepish smile and said, "This is great, but I'm sorry you went to so much trouble, and had to give up your sunroom."

"It was no trouble at all, Robert."

"Well I guess not. Who do you think did all the hard, backbreaking work of moving the furniture?" asked a very indignant Joe.

Without missing a beat and at the same time, both Maggie and Robert laughed and said, "Chuck!"

"I can see who you two think does all the hard work around here. I feel very underappreciated , and the only way I will feel better is if I have a big slice of Miss Maggie's lemon pie with a nice, big glass of milk," Joe said as he turned to go to the kitchen,

"Joe, that pie is for supper and you know it," said Maggie.

"But honey," said Joe, "we have a sick man who could use a little something sweet to make him feel better."

"Thanks, Joe, a piece of pie and a glass of milk would be nice. I'm really sick of hospital food," said Robert.

"I was talking about me," said Joe, "but I'm sure Maggie won't mind if it's gonna make you feel better, too."

"Joe Hayes, you are hopeless," laughed Maggie. "Come on in the kitchen both of you and I'll get you some pie."

After pie, and some good conversation, Joe had gone to the barn to work on his tractor brakes. With spring around the corner, the tractor would be needed a lot. Maggie had begun to make another pie for supper. This time it was going to be a peach cobbler by request from Robert and Joe. Robert had gone to "his room" and settled into the recliner with the T V remote in his had to watch the afternoon news. Before he knew it he was asleep. Maggie peeked in on him and smiled when she saw him fast asleep. She quietly closed the door and humming softly as she went, returned to the kitchen.

Robert awoke with a start! At first, he didn't know where he was, then he remembered and relaxed. He heard voices down the hall, and knew what had awakened him. He heard Michael's voice and as fast as a man with a newly replaced hip could go, went to find Michael. He was anxious to see him. He hadn't seen him much lately, since he had been doing therapy. Joe had told him how Michael was taking care of the barn while he was sick.

Robert had thanked God for Michael, because without him he didn't know what he would have done for the last month. More than once, Robert had been hit with the thought that God had placed Michael in his life for a reason. Every time he thought he knew what the reason was, it changed. He had thought it was to get him out of his house and back into life. Now it seemed as though God had known he would need help with his barn and horses that only Michael could give because he had been working at the barn so long. It was as if God was working a jigsaw puzzle with his life and there were new pieces to be fitted in until the picture was complete.

Robert entered the kitchen and saw Michael sitting at the kitchen table drinking some hot chocolate. Charlie sat next to Michael with her arms folded on the table and her head on her arms. She had a very dejected look on her face.

Michel looked up and saw Robert, and a broad grin spread across his face. "Hi Mr. Bradley, it's about time you got out of that place. Just wait, Aunt Maggie will fix you up as good as new!"

"I'm sure she will," said Robert smiling, "but I think she needs to work on Charlie first. Why the long face young lady?"

"I found out today that Max has been put in a petting zoo," Charlie said without looking up.

"That seems like a bad way to treat a boy. What did Max do?"

"Not Max the boy, Mr. Bradley, Max the monkey. You know, the one that came to Thanksgiving dinner with us," explained Michael.

"Oh I see. I thought he was your class pet, Charlie. What happened?" asked Robert.

"He was the class pet, but he never got over that Thanksgiving with Norm and the goat. Our classroom has big windows and right next door is a farm house. They have a little white dog that kinda looks like Norm and every time the monkey sees the dog he starts hollering and screaming so loud that Miss Lacey can't even teach. If that wasn't bad enough, the farmer got a bunch of goats and now when Max sees them he screams and spits in his hand and throws it at the windows where the goats are. Last week he was throwing his spit bombs and he hit Miss Lacey right in the face. It was really bad because she tried to catch him to put him in his cage and he kept running around the room, screaming and throwing spit and a whole bunch of kids got hit with it. A lot of parents complained and now he's in a petting zoo," finished Charlie forlornly.

"At least he learned to tie shoes," said Robert remembering how everyone's shoes were tied together.

"No, he won't even look at shoestrings anymore. Every time we gave him a shoe to tie after that he just sat down and shook. I think he had one of those nervous breakup things," moaned Charlie.

"I think you mean he had a nervous breakdown, honey," said Aunt Maggie.

"Yeah, I guess. It's just very sad that he's gone. Miss Lacey did say that he's much happier in the petting zoo. There aren't any dogs or goats for him to see. She said he hardly ever shakes anymore. She said they have a monkey doctor that gives him some good medicine, and he sits in his little tree house there and naps a lot. I guess nervous break downs make you pretty tired," sighed Charlie.

"I'm sure he will be fine," said Maggie, "now how about some hot chocolate for you Charlie, while we wait for your Mom to come and pick you up." Maggie didn't wait for an answer, she just began to make Charlie's drink.

Robert looked out the window and realized that he had slept most of the afternoon. The shadows were getting long and it would soon be dark. He looked at Michael and said, "I'll go to the barn with you and help you with the horses, Michael, just let me get my coat."

Before he could turn around, Aunt Maggie said, "Oh no you won't, Robert Bradley. In the first place, Michael is already finished at the barn for today, and you are not going to that barn any time soon. I talked with your doctor and he said you can only walk around the house and the yard for the next few weeks, and I intend to see that you do it."

Michael looked at Robert and said, "I think you better do what she says. Mr. Bradley."

Robert had to laugh. It looked like he was going to be at Miss Maggie's mercy for a while. He guessed he could force himself to take naps in that big comfy recliner and eat some really good food if it would make her happy.

Chapter 50

It was a beautiful spring day in mid March. Buttercups were blooming everywhere, grass was getting green and the sky was full of white, puffy clouds and blue skies. Robert and Joe were riding home from seeing the doctor. Robert's appointment with the doctor hadn't taken long at all. He was doing great, and had traded his four legged cane in for a regular walking stick. What had taken a long time was Robert's appointment with the hospital billing office. Robert didn't have any health insurance. Once he lost Susan he quit worrying about things like that. He had never needed any until he broke his hip, and now he was looking at a very large bill.

He had paid the bill the hospital said he owed them, and he still had to pay his doctor. His bank account was getting low. He hoped he had enough to pay the doctor. He should know by the end of the month, because he would get the bill by then.

Robert had spent most of his life farming and horse training. He still got a small check once a month from some investments his wife had made while she was working, but that was just enough to get by, not enough to pay bills. Any time he had needed extra money he had always worked enough side jobs to get it. That was before his accident, and now he couldn't do extra work. He was anxious to get home and balance his checkbook. He had never been very good with money. Tam had always taken care of the finances in the family. Now he realized that he would have to keep an accurate account of his money since so many people were apparently going to want it.

"I didn't ask you what the doctor said. Did he give you a good report on that new hip of yours? Did he say you could get out of the yard? If he didn't don't try to fool Miss Maggie. She's pretty sharp where her patients are concerned," laughed Joe.

Joe's questions took Robert's mind off his money dilemma, and he smiled thinking about how Miss Maggie had hovered over him like a mother hen over chicks. "Lucky for me, the doctor did say I could do more. I asked if I could go to the barn with Michael, and he said it would be fine. I can even drive now so I can drive us both, and Michael won't have to ride the four-wheeler," Robert said.

He grinned as he thought of the look on the doctor's face when he made him put it in writing so Miss Maggie would believe it. He didn't add that he had asked to doctor if he could go back to living at his house, and the relief he had felt when the doctor said no. He was enjoying the company and all the things the kids did at Joe and Maggie's place. He was a little afraid his house would seem downright dull when he did go home, but he decided to worry about that when the time came.

"I don't think Michael minds riding the four-wheeler but I know you are anxious to get back to your barn. I glad everything is going so good. I figured it would, and that we would need to celebrate, so in honor of the occasion, how about a nice, big, juicy, cream filled, chocolate donut still warm from the bakery," with that Joe reached over the seat and produced a box of a dozen donuts that made Robert's mouth water.

"Joe, what's Miss Maggie gonna think about this? I thought she told you no more eating between meals, and it's almost supper time now," Robert asked as he helped himself to a warm donut.

"That eating between meals was only if there was nothing to celebrate. Besides, the bakery was next door to your doctor's office. Where do you think I went while you were waiting on the doctor? Why it would have been criminal to be that close to fresh baked donuts and not had one or maybe two or three, but that's not the point. The point is to celebrate your good news. By the way when is your next doctor appointment, because I'll be happy to drive you again just to check and see if that little bakery is maintaining its standards. Oh, one more thing, I don't see why we can't keep this little celebration to ourselves. I just don't want Maggie to worry," said Joe as he licked the last of the chocolate from his fingers.

Robert laughed out loud. "I don't think that Maggie worrying is what you are concerned about. I think you are worried about what she will do to you if she finds out about your donut eating between meals, but I guess it wouldn't hurt if we didn't mention it," said Robert as he finished off his donut.

"That's the spirit," said Joe, "we men have to stick together. Joe quickly hid the donuts under the front seat of the truck as they turned in the driveway.

Robert was grinning to himself as he closed the door of Joe's truck. He wouldn't say anything about the donuts to Miss Maggie, but he was pretty sure the chocolate Joe had dribbled down the front of his shirt would. He couldn't wait to hear Joe's explanation of this one.

Joe reached down to get the bag that had Miss Maggie's vanilla flavoring and butter in it. As he closed the truck door he didn't see his yummy donuts hit the ground. The box had gotten caught on the corner of the grocery bag and drug out of the truck. Joe's mid-morning snack for tomorrow of coffee and donuts would no longer include donuts.

"We're home Miss Maggie," said Joe as he closed the kitchen door.

Maggie dried her hands as she finished washing the mixing bowl she had used to make a chocolate cake for supper. It was in the oven and almost done. It only needed to cook about 15 more minutes. They were having salmon patties with buttered rice, pinto beans and cornbread for supper. Ice cream and warm chocolate cake were dessert. Everything was done except the cake. As she waited on the timer on the oven to go off, Maggie sat down at the table for the full report from the doctor. Robert told her everything the doctor had told him and then sat back and waited for her verdict.

"Hmmm," said Maggie, "I'm not so sure about this barn thing. I think that may be rushing it just a bit."

Robert quickly spoke up, "Now Miss Maggie, the doctor said I could go to the barn. Its fine, I promise. Come on, you have to let me go, please!"

Joe was drinking a big glass of cold milk to wash down his donut snack. When he heard Robert pleading with his wife, he laughed so hard milk came out his nose. "You should hear yourself, Robert. If I didn't know better I would think Max or Michael was talking to Maggie!"

This caused Maggie to turn her attention fully on her husband for the first time since he had come in the door. She immediately saw the chocolate on the front of his shirt. She smiled sweetly as she asked, "You poor dear, are you starving for supper? I know you just had a sandwich for lunch before you took Robert to the doctor. I'm so proud of you for not eating between meals, but I know you must be very hungry now. Are you, honey?"

Uh-oh, here we go thought Robert as he got ready to see a big man squirm.

"Aw, sugar, it's not all that hard on me. I'm getting used to it. You just have to put your mind on it and be determined. I am pretty hungry, but the milk kinda took the edge off of it for me."

Like a good fisherman, Maggie knew her bait had been taken and was about to set the hook to reel a big one in, when suddenly Michael and Max burst in the kitchen door.

"Come quick, Grandpa Joe, it's awful!" said Max

"I'll say," yelled Michael, "we need help."

With that both boys ran back out the door. Joe looked at Maggie and hurried out the door followed by Maggie and Robert. The sight that was before them was hard to comprehend. As they looked at the truck parked in the driveway, Roho, the rooster was going up and down in the air on the other side of the truck. While he was airborne a big boom was heard coming from that side of the truck, too. Every time he was up in the air, a BOOM was heard from the truck. All three spectators rushed to the other side of the vehicle to see what was making the noise.

Max and Michael were standing a safe distance away as a major battle was going on between Roho, the rooster, and Billy, the goat, over Joe's chocolate cream filled donuts. Roho had found them first, but Billy had decided those donuts had his name on them. Roho wasn't giving up without a fight. The rooster dropped his wings, ran sideways at the goat, jumped up, and used his sharp spurs to scratch the goat in the face. This made Billy mad, and he tried to butt the rooster with his big horns. The only problem was the rooster was airborne when Billy butted at him, and he kept hitting Joe's truck. The loud booms had resulted in a series of dents in Joe's truck door. When Joe saw what was happening to his truck, he let out a roar, and jumped into the middle of the battle. Max and Michael looked at each other and shook their heads. They had already tried to break up the fight, but they had both been butted enough to concede defeat.

Joe managed to catch the rooster in mid-air and tuck him under his arm. With his other hand, he got hold of one of Billy's horns. Joe quickly saw that he had a problem. The rooster was secured under Joe's arm and couldn't spur, but with Joe holding the goat, the rooster was pecking as hard as he could at Billy's nose. This made Billy extremely angry, and he began to "Baa" and butt as hard as he could while having one of his horns held by Joe.

Joe managed to stay on his feet longer than any of the spectators thought he would. Even though he hit the ground he managed to hold onto both of his captives. This really wasn't a victory because now Joe was flat of his back with a mad goat's head in his stomach and an angry rooster pecking holes in his arm. Roho managed to pop loose and began to attack both Joe and the goat. Joe used his free hand to swat at Roho, while the goat used the chance to renew his attack on Joe's stomach. The sounds coming from the melee were remarkable. There was squawking and crowing, baas and grunting, and from Joe there were "oofs, ow's, and threats to both barn animals.

Suddenly, Roho was swatted off of Joe and back toward the barn, Joe let go of Billy, and the goat also felt the business end of Maggie's broom. Joe looked up to see his wife poised over him like an avenging angel, or so he thought until his angel spoke.

"Joe Hayes, just look what your snacking on donuts has caused. Your truck has enough dents to qualify as a wreck, you have donuts all over your back, and worst of all you didn't tell me the truth. I just hope you enjoyed those donuts because I'm not making any more desserts for the next two weeks!" With that, Maggie threw her broom down and stomped off to the house.

"Thanks a lot Grandpa Joe!"

"Yeah, Uncle Joe, we don't get any dessert either."

"Way to keep a secret Joe!"

All three turned and followed Maggie back into the house. Joe sat on the ground by his dented truck. He could only imagine how much joking he would have to endure from the guys at the body shop when he took his truck to be repaired with "goat dents" in it. Not to mention that everybody was going to be mad at him for at least two weeks. There was no telling how long Maggie would be upset with him for not telling her the truth. As Joe sat there, he did some thinking and knew where he had gone wrong. He should have put the donuts behind the seat instead of under it.

Chapter 51

Doc had his head over the stall door eagerly watching for Michael to come walking down the barn hallway. It was the first Saturday in April, and spring was making itself known. The birds were singing, the sun was shining, and the sky was a glorious color of blue. It was like nature was rejoicing in the bad winter weather being a thing of the past. Doc also felt the renewal of spring. Michael had brushed his copper coat until all his long, winter hair was gone. The care he had gotten since Michael had come, had given him a new lease on life. He felt better this spring than he had since Susan had gone. His knees weren't swollen with arthritis like they were last spring. They were still a little stiff, but after he loosened them up, they felt fine. Michael was riding him almost every day, and the exercise made him fit and strong. Doc was ready for his breakfast and then some time to run and play in the corral.

Doc began to nod his head and snort in anticipation, and as if on cue he saw Michael coming toward his stall. Doc let out a loud neigh of welcome that almost burst Michael's ears.

"Well good morning to you, too, big guy. Are you hungry or happy to see me? I've got your breakfast right here," said Michael with a smile as he filled Doc's feed bucket.

He gave Doc a quick pat as he went to feed Black Mare. He was pleased that she didn't run to the back of her stall anymore when he approached. She still didn't fully trust him, but she was a lot better. Michael wished she could talk so she could tell him what had happened to her. He knew what it was like to be mistreated, and it made him sad that she was still afraid. He poured her feed out and stood watching her as she began to eat. He put his face against the wire front of her stall next to her bucket and she tentatively reached her nose up to his face and sniffed him. Michael didn't move and she calmly went back to her feed.

"We've come a long way, haven't we girl," Michael said as he went back to Doc's stall. He went inside and began to stroke Doc's big neck. Doc turned, nudged him with his head, and returned to his breakfast. Michael leaned his face against Doc's shoulder, enjoying the feel and smell of his friend. His thoughts turned to last night's conversation before supper and he began to smile.

Joe, Robert, Chuck, Max, and Michael were all sitting around the table as Maggie was finishing their supper. No one was very excited to eat, but all of them were looking forward to the next night's supper.

"It's a good thing we get back to normal with our food tomorrow. I don't know how much more of this bread and water I could stand," said Joe.

"I think you are being a little dramatic, Dad," said Chuck.

"Humph, I don't think so. Why I've lost almost ten pounds in two weeks. If this kept up much longer, I'd waste away to nothing. I already feel weak and light headed. A man needs real food, not bread and water," Joe finished with a flourish by banging his fist on the table.

"Now Joe, you can't call Maggie's soup and salads bread and water. She just said since she wasn't going to make desserts for two weeks that we might as well eat healthy all the way around, and soup and salad would be good for all of us," said Robert.

"Dad burn it, Robert, there you go, taking her side. We men have to stick together. Show some backbone. I know mine is probably showing right through my shirt, as skinny as I'm getting."

"I think we all know who got us in this mess," said Chuck looking accusingly Joe, "and for goodness sakes don't tell Mom you've lost ten pounds or she may just make this menu permanent!"

Maggie was in the kitchen listening to the conversation, smiling. A person would think that Joe was being starved to death. She had made homemade soups and stews every night to go with a salad, but no breads or desserts. She also limited Joe to one portion of everything, which added to his feelings of starvation. She intended to make him think twice before he was less than truthful with her again. Between his bread and sweets withdrawal and the other boys reminding him that this menu was his fault, Joe had been miserable for the last two weeks. Tonight was the perfect end to her menu, because it was broccoli soup and Joe hated broccoli.

Doc finished his meal and turned to look at Michael, causing him to return to the present.

"I don't know how grass tastes, Doc, but if it's anything like broccoli, I'm sure glad I'm not a horse," said Michael. He reached up and put Doc's halter on to take him and Black Mare out to the corral while he cleaned their stalls and did the rest of his chores. He was anxious to finish so he and Doc could go for a ride. Robert wasn't with him today. He was going to town with Joe to get a letter that was at the Post Office. Michael figured it must be pretty important if he had to make a special trip to get it.

"Come on, Doc, let's go get your girlfriend and go outside."

Robert and Joe were on their way home from town. It was early afternoon, but Joe was already looking forward to supper.

"What do you think she's fixing, Robert? I sure hope its fried chicken. That little woman can make the best fried chicken I ever put in my mouth. It might be pork chops with potatoes and gravy, that would be good, too."

"Stop Joe, you are making me hungry and it's just a little past lunch," laughed Robert as he began to open his mail. He hadn't picked it up since he had his accident. He usually never got anything important so he hadn't worried about it. It looked like he was right because as he was leafing through it, most of his mail was junk. Suddenly one letter caught his eye. It was marked "Urgent Important Document Inside". He was still smiling at Joe as he opened the letter. After reading a few lines, his smile disappeared, all the color drained from his face, and heart began to race in fear.

Michael's heart was racing and he was breathing hard. Doc's neck was arched and he was prancing like he knew he had just done a good job. It was the best barrel pattern they had ever run, and Michael knew it! Apparently Doc did too, from the way he was acting. Michael had no idea running barrels was so fast, terrifying, exciting, and so much work.

Michael had kept practicing on the barrel pattern after Robert had gotten hurt, and been unable to come to the barn. He hadn't told anyone, because he was worried they wouldn't want him to without Mr. Bradley being there. This way he could still practice and keep learning on Doc. Boy, did he ever learn on Doc today! He and Doc had spent some time on the trail, and finished their ride by going to the barrels in the arena. He was still going around them at a canter, and he had begun to feel very confident. On his last barrel run for the day, he decided to give Doc his head and let him run as fast as he wanted to go. WOW!

As Michael had lined him up with the third barrel to begin his run just as Mr. Bradley had taught him, Michael had leaned forward, given Doc the reins and said, "Let's go Big Guy." That was all Doc needed. He jumped so hard taking off that he broke the leather strap holding his breast collar in place, which was the least of Michael's worries. He had never seen the first barrel come and go so fast. About the time Michael was set to make the turn, it was over and Doc was on his way to the second barrel. As they spun around it, Michael lost a stirrup, and was almost left in the dirt as the big red horse took aim on the last barrel. Michael didn't know how he managed to stay on Doc's back, (it might have had something to do with one of those angels that Aunt Maggie was always talking about) but he did. As he saw the third barrel coming closer, he managed to find his stirrup just in time to set up for the final turn. Once Doc had turned the last barrel, he kicked in a gear that Michael didn't even know he had for the run "home". By the time

Michael managed to get the big horse stopped, his eyes were watering from the speed of the run! Michael was pretty sure that his face must have looked like those astronaut's faces did on lift off when they were pulling some G's.

As the impact of what had just happened sunk in, because it was all over in less then 16 seconds, Michael's breathing began to slow a little but not his heartbeat. The excitement he felt was unbelievable. He didn't want to repeat the ride again today, but he knew he would the next time he rode Doc. He had never felt so alive in his life. It was the most awesome feeling he had ever experienced. Michael began to pat Doc and brag on him. Mr. Bradley had taught him that horses are very perceptive animals. They can tell by your actions, body language, and the sound of your voice if you are praising them or are unhappy with them. It must have been true, because Doc pranced all the way back to the barn.

Michael even liked the prancing. He couldn't help it he began to repeat, "Yeah, we're bad, we're bad," until he dismounted to take Doc's saddle off at the barn.

When he dismounted, Doc was still pumped up and reached out and pushed Michael with his head. It was something the big horse always did with Susan when they finished a winning run. Michael had no way of knowing that Doc had just paid him the ultimate compliment. Michael wasn't the only one feeling awesome and after a long, long time, very alive.

Michael felt like he was floating on air the rest of the day. He had finished cooling Doc out, putting the horses to bed for the night, and headed home. He knew he had to tell Mr. Bradley about his experience. It had to be Mr. Bradley because he was the only one who would understand just how great it was. He bounced across the fields on the four-wheeler replaying the run in his mind over and over. He parked the four-wheeler at the barn and walked into the kitchen. He was greeted with the most heavenly aromas he had smelled in two, long weeks. In his excitement, he had forgotten that today was the end of the "bread and water" meals as Uncle Joe called them.

Michael surveyed the table and saw fried chicken, creamed potatoes, gravy, green beans, corn, and biscuits. On the counter, he saw a steaming peach cobbler. He stopped grinning long enough to lick his lips and ask, "When's supper, Aunt Maggie? I sure hope it's soon, because I'm starving!"

"As a matter of fact it's right now. Go call everyone else to come and eat while I get our tea poured."

Michael's call to supper consisted of sticking his head in the den and announcing "supper" to the waiting crowd. If he had yelled "fire" no one would have moved faster.

When they were all seated around the table, Robert's place was empty.

"Where's Mr. Bradley? I know he doesn't want to miss this meal," said Michael, still wanting to talk to him about his barrel run.

"He's napping. He said he needed to rest when he got home from town with your Uncle Joe. He told us not to wait supper on him. I just hope he isn't doing too much too fast," worried Aunt Maggie.

"Now Sweetheart, Robert will be just fine, but I'll tell you one thing, nothing could make me late for dinner tonight. Chuck say grace and don't tarry saying the "Amen".

Maggie just shook her head thinking for the millionth time that her husband was a ten year old trapped in a sixty-two year old body.

Chapter 52

Robert was in his room with the door closed. He was so agitated, he didn't know what to do. He paced a while, read the letter a while, and sat and thought a while, but nothing helped. The situation facing him was so monumental that he could see no good solution to it. He stopped pacing to shake his head and grin a sad smile. It was ironic that until he had opened the letter he was happier than he had been since Susan had been gone. He had just made his last payment to the doctors and hospital for his surgery and was incredibly grateful to have had enough money to do so.

It had totally wiped out everything he had left in the bank, but in a few more months he knew he would be well enough to go back to doing odd jobs to rebuild his small savings. He was already thinking about fixing the barn back up and making some much needed repairs around the farm. He had decided to teach Michael everything he could about horses. The boy was like a sponge where horses were concerned, and Robert found himself drawn to him more and more. Now, a single piece of paper had changed everything.

The letter was a notice from the property tax department of the state. When he and Susan had been trying to start a place for troubled teenagers, they had to apply to change their property from a residential property to a commercial one. Susan had been taking care of all the paper work and it had been changed without Robert realizing it. He always had his property taxes taken out of his account at the bank so that he didn't have to worry about paying them himself. The amount was the same amount he had always paid. What he didn't know was that the taxes had gone up almost $1000 a year. That meant that he hadn't been paying the full amount for several years now, and the amount he owed had reached the point that it had to be paid within 90 days or his property would be sold at auction to the highest bidder.

Robert looked at the $9787.22 tax bill, and shook his head. It might as well be 9 million. He was flat broke. He had nothing he could sell, no job, no savings, and no rich uncle to help. He had always been a self made man who put most of his money back in his farm. When he lost his family, he had no desire to do anything, so he didn't. A broken heart can do that to a person. Just when he decided to live again, it felt like he had been punched in the stomach. He knew it was his fault. He had never been the one to take care of business. Tam had always done it, and after her, Susan had taken over. With both of them gone, he just didn't care. The letter he held in his hands proved what a foolish and bad decision he had made.

He couldn't let Maggie and Joe know about this. He knew they would want to help him and they had already done enough for him. He wasn't a charity case, and he didn't want anybody to think he was. Robert stopped pacing to sit down and write his own letter. At least he knew one thing to do.

Michael sat on the porch swing by Aunt Maggie. After supper and lots of appreciative sighs and mummers, Joe had hit his recliner like a contented cat curling up in its favorite chair to purr. Chuck and Max had gone to take Miss Twilla a plate Aunt Maggie made for her and some peach cobbler. Someone had to go with Chuck to hold the tea Aunt Maggie was sending so it didn't turn over. Michael and Max did rock, paper, scissors to see who the lucky one would be. Max lost, and was a very sore loser.

"Come on Dad, don't make me go. She has that monster cat that tries to kill me every time it sees me. I know it eats human flesh. It's gotten enough off me to prove it. Poor Norm is still traumatized. All you have to do is meow like a cat and he runs under the bed. It's just plain pitiful. I'm starting to suffer from flashbacks myself."

"Forget it Max. You lost fair and square so you're going. Now come on or I'll tell Charlie that you are afraid of kitty cats," laughed Chuck.

"I don't care, tell her. That cat scares me more than Charlie. I think I need some therapy."

"Max get in the truck or I'll give you some therapy myself."

"Okay, but if I turn into a mass cat murderer don't say I didn't warn you. This could push me over the edge!"

Michael still wanted to talk to someone about his barrel run on Doc. He hadn't been able to talk to Mr. Bradley because he had stayed in his room. Aunt Maggie didn't disturb him for supper, because she said she wanted to let him rest. Aunt Maggie's question to him made him wonder, not for the first time, if she could read minds.

"So tell me, how's Doc doing? You haven't said much about him in a while."

"He's good. Nope, he's better than good, he's great. I think he's the best horse there's ever been. He's smart, too. Sometimes I think he speaks English or at least understands it."

"So are you going to tell me how you really feel about your horse?" laughed Aunt Maggie.

"I guess I am a little prejudiced where Doc's concerned," grinned Michael, "but I just can't help it. Aunt Maggie today was the most incredible ride of my life."

"Tell me about it."

"Remember Mr. Bradley gave me some barrel racing lessons?"

"Yes."

"Well, today after I finished my work at the barn, Doc and I went trail riding. Mr. Bradley says trail riding is the best way to condition a horse, and it's good for Doc's arthritis."

"Doc has arthritis? Well, bless his heart."

"Yes mam, but you can hardly tell it anymore because he gets exercised every day. Mr. Bradley has a saying, "move it or lose it" about how important exercise is to a horse."

"I agree. There's a big, ol mule in the recliner that could use the same saying," giggled Aunt Maggie.

"After we came back from trail riding, we ran some barrel patterns in the arena. On the last one I gave Doc his head and let him run as fast as he wanted to go. It was great! You can't imagine what it felt like to be sitting on top of that much power. It was like I was riding a bottle rocket! We just zoomed the barrel pattern, without touching a single barrel. It was AWESOME. When it was over, I was out of breath like I had been the one doing the running," finished Michael.

Maggie shifted in the swing to get a closer look at Michael. She could hardly believe he was the same child that came into her life a little more than a year ago. The frightened, angry, unsure, and untrusting boy had transformed into a boy, no a cowboy, who was bubbling with excitement about a wild barrel ride on a huge horse. I sure didn't see this coming, Maggie thought to herself. She had hoped he would adjust to country life, but Michael had done more than adjust, he had found his niche. She said a quick, silent prayer of gratitude to God for placing this child in her path.

"Isn't it a little dangerous to go that fast?" asked Maggie.

"Oh no mam, Doc knows exactly what he's doing," Michael assured her.

Maggie laughed, "I wasn't talking about Doc, I meant you."

"Doc takes care of me real good, Aunt Maggie. Besides Mr. Bradley says that if you are gonna ride, you are gonna hit the ground eventually. It's important to know that and get right back up on your horse. He says "there ain't ever been a cowboy that couldn't be throwed.""

"Yes, well now you know why I don't ride horses," smiled Maggie.

"I felt like I was in heaven after that ride, Aunt Maggie. Chuck told me that heaven will be the best place ever when we get there, but I don't see how it could be better than my day with Doc today. What do you think heaven is like Aunt Maggie?"

"Oh my, we are getting into a deep discussion now," she said as she put her arm around Michael and hugged him close.

"No really, will there be trees and grass and stuff like there is here or what? Will I get to ride horses when I get there? Will we be together for always?"

"Well, all I can tell you is what I think after reading what the Bible says about heaven. It says there will be a new heaven and a new earth, so I think that this world we are in now must be just a beginning for God. When I think of all the beauty of nature we have now, the mountains, streams, trees, meadows, and flowers, I can only imagine how beautiful everything will be. I think that whatever makes us happiest here on earth, we will get to do in heaven, so if it's riding horses I think there will be horses in heaven. The Bible also says we will know and be known in heaven, so I think maybe we will be together always."

"Will we look just like we do now?"

"Whew, you sure ask some hard questions. I don't really know what we will look like. The Bible says we will have new bodies. I've often thought what if the beauty of our spirit here on earth determined the beauty of our heavenly bodies, and if it did I bet a lot of people would be a lot nicer," smiled Aunt Maggie.

Michael sat back and just stared at her.

"What are you looking at, honey? Do I have peach cobbler on my chin?"

"No mam," said Michael as he settled back into her embrace. If what Aunt Maggie said was true, he knew he was looking at the most beautiful lady there would ever be.

Chapter 53

Michael had been awake for some time. It was just beginning to get daylight. He had tossed and turned all night, but not because he was upset about anything, he just couldn't stop replaying his ride on Doc around the barrels. It was the single most exciting thing that had ever happened in his life! Yesterday he had been willing to just make one fast run on Doc. Today he could hardly wait until this afternoon when he and Doc could run again as fast as yesterday. Just thinking about it made his heart beat faster and his breath quicken.

Michael threw his covers off and quietly got out of bed. It was so early that even Aunt Maggie wasn't up yet. He didn't want to wake anyone else, so he dressed and tiptoed down the stairs. Mr. Bradley's light didn't show under his door so he knew he was still asleep, too. He sure must have been tired because he didn't come out of his room at all last night. Michael was still anxious to talk to him about his barrel run. Today was Sunday so they would all get dressed and go to church. After church, Aunt Maggie always made a big lunch and then everybody took it easy the rest of the day. It was a tradition for the Hayes family and it was one that Michael had come to enjoy. Aunt Maggie said Sunday was the Lord's Day and a day of rest. She said everybody needed time to rest, count their blessings, and enjoy life. She said if more people did that they would be a lot happier. Michael thought Aunt Maggie must be one of the smartest people ever.

Since it was Sunday, Michael would have to get back from the barn sooner to get ready for church. He was glad he had gotten up so early because he would have some extra time at the barn. He slipped out the kitchen door and stood for a minute listening to the sounds. It was between day and night so the frogs and crickets were still singing and the birds were so happy it was springtime that they were chirping announcing the coming of a beautiful day. Michael smiled and thought how much he loved the farm and the life he had now. Aunt Maggie would have been proud because he was already counting a blessing. He coaxed the four-wheeler to a start and began to bounce over the fields to another blessing, the horses at the barn and a big red one in particular.

As Michael stopped the four-wheeler at the barn he frowned slightly. Mr. Bradley's truck was in his driveway, but Mr. Bradley was at his house, wasn't he? Oh well, he would feed the horses their breakfast then figure out what was going on. Doc and Black Mare were surprised and happy to see him so early. Breakfast was fine at any time for them. When they were contentedly eating their grain, Michael decided to walk up to Mr. Bradley's house.

Robert was sitting at his kitchen table. He would have felt better if he could have paced around the room, but his hip kept him from doing that. He had gotten to his house in the middle of the night. He had left Maggie and Joe a note thanking them for all they had done for him, but he thought it was time for him to go back home.

He didn't say anything about the letter he had gotten, or the money he owed, or that he couldn't pay it. He had been at his kitchen table since he came in the house except for taking a few minutes to open the windows to let in some fresh air, since his house had been closed up for several weeks. He had been trying to figure a way out of the mess he was in, but he kept coming up blank. He was worn out from worrying about it. Robert read the letter from the tax office again, and then in frustration he wadded it into a tight ball and threw it out the open window. He finally just dropped his head in his hands and began to pray out loud.

"Lord, I need help that only You can give me. I know without You I am going to lose my farm and my home. I've never wanted lot, but please show me a way to keep my farm. I'm willing to work for it, but with this hip I just can't do the things I know how to do to make money. You are going to have to show me another way. I know You are always with me, even when I don't deserve Your love, because You told me that in the Bible. I know that when I ask You for help You always hear me, so with faith I believe you will provide a way out of this mess for me, even though I can't imagine how."

Michael had almost reached the house when he saw something come sailing out Mr. Bradley's kitchen window. Instantly curious, he walked over and picked it up. His eyes widened as he read it. From what he could tell, Mr. Bradley's farm was going to be sold! Michael heard Mr. Bradley when he began to pray through the open window. Now he knew why his truck was in the driveway. He had come back to his farm.

Michael ducked down under the window. He didn't feel right listening to Mr. Bradley talk to God, but he was afraid to move, because he didn't want Mr. Bradley to see him and think he was spying on him. As he listened, Michael heard the desperation in Mr. Bradley's voice. Michael put the crumpled letter in his pocket and silently made his way back to the barn. Once there, he raced to the four-wheeler. He had to get home and think about what to do!

Chapter 54

Charlie was at the barn cleaning Moz's stall. She had smarted off to her Mom when she told her to take out the trash, and now she was cleaning a stall so she could "think about her behavior". Charlie felt like she could think about it while she watched TV, and had told her Mom so, but that got her another day of stall cleaning and she still had to take out the trash. Sometimes she decided you just couldn't win for losing. They had gone to church, and sat with the Hayes as usual. She had tried to cheer herself up by needling Michael, but he was acting all weird. No matter how much she insulted him, he just sat there and looked at her without saying a word. While she was thinking that Michael must have suffered some brain damage when she hit him in the eye that time, she heard the four-wheeler stop at the barn.

Michael was deep in thought as he walked to Doc's stall. He had been so worried this morning that he had forgotten to turn Doc and the Black Mare out in the pasture. He still hadn't gotten to talk to Aunt Maggie. They had been in a hurry to get to church for the Sunday morning service, and after church, Aunt Maggie and Uncle Joe had gone to take some food to a family who's father had died. They still weren't home when it was time to go back to Mr. Bradley's barn. Chuck had told him that Mr. Bradley had left a letter thanking Aunt Maggie and Uncle Joe for all they had done for him, but he wanted to go home. Michael knew from the letter that had sailed out of Mr. Bradley's window why he had really gone home, but he wanted to talk to Aunt Maggie before he said anything. She always knew what to do.

Brenda Dawson

"Hello half-wit."

Michael was just about to open Doc's stall door when he heard the one voice that drove him crazy. He had ignored her all through church and now she was at the barn.

"Shut up, Charlie. I've had enough of you today. Why don't you go find some flies and pull their wings off or something? Just leave me alone!"

"Well, so you can speak. You didn't say anything this morning at church. I guess you were just too dumb to think of anything to say. And for your information, if I wanted flies, all I'd have to do would be hang around you because you draw them worse than what I'm shoveling in this stall," Charlie said as she pushed her glasses back up on her nose. She noticed a piece of paper sticking out of Michael's back pocket. She reached and grabbed it saying, "Well, well. What have we here? A looovve letter?"

When Michael saw what Charlie had done he lost it. He had been stewing all day trying to get to talk to Aunt Maggie to see what to do, and now Charlie had the letter he didn't know if he should have taken or not. He had to get that letter back! He lowered his head and hit Charlie hard in the stomach. They both fell down and Charlie began to gasp for breath. Next, to Michael's utter amazement, she began to cry. Charlie never cried. What was she trying to pull now?

"Get up Charlie, it's not working. You aren't hurt."

Charlie only gasped harder and cried louder. Michael was beginning to think maybe something was wrong with her.

"I…. can't … breathe. Just… wait… until… I… tell… Joe!" gasped Charlie.

The mention of Joe caused Michael to remember Joe's rule about hitting girls. Now he was worried.

"Okay I'm sorry, just give me my letter back."

Charlie had begun to get her breath back and stop gasping. Michael apologizing so quickly made her wonder what was in the letter. Before she could look at it Michael had grabbed it out of her hand.

"Take your stupid letter. I'm still telling Joe what you did," said Charlie as she scrambled to her feet.

"Charlie, please don't say anything. You don't understand what this letter is about."

"Then if you want me to keep quiet I guess you better tell me what's in the letter. Otherwise, I'm leaving right now to go and find Joe. I'll bet he won't be too happy with the way you treated me," finished an indignant Charlie.

"Charlie, some things are just none of your business."

"So long, loser, I'm outta here."

"Wait. I'll tell you, but you have to promise not to tell anyone, or I'll never talk to you again." Michael knew it wasn't a very good threat, but it was all he could think of at the time.

"Wow, that's scary," said a sarcastic Charlie. "Now, what's in the letter?"

Michael told Charlie the whole story finishing with, "You can't say anything about this. I have to talk to Aunt Maggie. She'll know what to do."

"Wow, that's a lot of money. It's too bad Susan isn't here. My Mom has told me she used to win lots of money barrel racing Doc."

"Well, she's not here. Just keep quiet about this until I know what to do," Michael said as he took Doc out of his stall to begin his afternoon chores.

Charlie stuck her tongue out at Michael's back as he walked away. The more she thought about it, she decided he probably was brain damaged like all the other boys she knew!

Chapter 55

It was late and the house was dark except for the light in the kitchen. Michael had talked to Maggie about the letter he found outside Robert's window. He had been anxious to know what the letter meant. When Maggie had told him it was about Robert's property being sold if the back taxes weren't paid, Michael became frantic with worry about what would happen to Mr. Bradley and Doc. Maggie had told him to go to bed and she would think about it, and they would talk some more in the morning. Now, Maggie and Joe sat at the kitchen table trying to decide what to do.

"I just wish we could give Robert the $10,000.00 to pay his bill," said Joe.

"I know. I do too, but we don't know if that hard head would take it if we did, even if we had it to give. You know how independent he is, and he didn't say anything about this in the note he left us when he went home, so he may not want us to know about his problems."

"What does our savings account look like, honey? How much money do we have left in it?" asked Joe.

Maggie reread the savings statement and shook her head. She and Joe were in the process of adopting Michael. They wanted him to know that he was a member of their family in every way and he would never have to leave. They hadn't told Michael yet. They were waiting as long as possible so if something went wrong, he wouldn't be disappointed, and they wanted to surprise Michael with a party. The adoption process wasn't cheap. It had taken their savings account from $16,000 down to $437.62.

"We don't even have $500 left. That isn't even a drop in the bucket on Robert's bill," said Maggie.

"This is one of those times when I wonder if I should have retired. If I was still working, we could just go make a loan to help Robert and I could pay it off."

"Nonsense, Joe, it was time for you to take things a little easier, and knowing Robert as I do, I don't think he would let us do that. We are just going to have to think of another way."

"Well sugar, I sure hope that pretty little head of yours can come up with something, because for the life of me, I can't." Joe reached over to give Maggie a kiss, "Goodnight honey, I'm going to turn in and sleep on it. I do some of my best work when I'm looking at the back of my eyelids."

Maggie smiled as she watched the big man head for the bedroom. Not only did he mean the world to her, he was her best friend. When Michael had told her about Robert, her first thought was to talk it over with Joe. Even though he sometimes made her crazy with all the things he got into, he was the smartest man she knew, and she valued his advice. If Joe couldn't help her find a solution, she knew there was only one place left to go. Funny, she thought, that should always be the first place to go when life hit you right between the eyes with a problem!

Maggie bowed her head and began to pray," Lord You know every twist and turn our lives will ever take, and if we ask for your help and guidance You are faithful to help us. I can't see how Robert can keep his farm, but I know You can make a way where we don't know how. Please show us the way, Lord that will be good for Robert and all of us. Please let us be wise enough to go through that door when you open it. In Jesus Name, Amen."

Maggie rose from the table and turned off the light to go to bed. She always felt better after she prayed. It was the same feeling she used to get as a little girl when she took a problem to her Daddy to fix. She knew her Father in heaven had heard her and would take care of her just like her Daddy did all those years ago. She stood in the dark for a minute and shook her head as she wondered how people who didn't know the power of God made it when they had troubles. All you have to do to have God use His power to help you is pray. She thought again of one of her favorite verses in the Bible. It was Matthew chapter 21 verse 22 where Jesus said, "Whatever things you ask in prayer, believing, you will receive."

As Maggie climbed into bed beside a snoring Joe, she was already thanking God for what she knew He would do for Robert.

Chapter 56

Michael had tossed and turned all night. He wasn't just worried about Mr. Bradley, he was worried about what would happen to Doc if the farm had to be sold. He made his mind up to talk to Mr. Bradley about it today. It was the first day of spring break so he could spend a lot of time at the barn today. He would wait until he could get his courage up and the right time presented itself and he would tell him about finding the letter. Together maybe they could figure something out, unless Aunt Maggie had already come up with an answer.

Michael made his way to the kitchen where he found Aunt Maggie cooking breakfast. She looked up at him and smiled.

"Good morning. You're up early for a vacation day."

"I didn't sleep very good. I'm worried about Mr. Bradley and Doc."

"I am too, honey. I wish I could tell you that I have a solution to Robert's problem, but I can't. I talked to your Uncle Joe last night, and we don't have the extra money right now to pay Robert's back taxes. Even if we did, I don't think Robert would let us do it for him. I'm afraid the only way out of this mess is going to have to come from Robert."

"But he doesn't have the money either. Remember I heard him praying about it," said Michael sadly.

"That's right. Robert was praying, and so have I. This is something that's too big for us to handle on our own. It's one of those things we have to put in God's hands and have faith that He will take care of

Robert, Doc, and everything else in a way that is best for all of us, even if it might not seem like it at the time."

"I don't know Aunt Maggie. What if God doesn't hear us asking for help? How are we going to know?"

"Honey, God always hears our prayers, and we know this by faith in what He has told us in the Bible. We just need to stay out of His way and listen to His voice in our hearts tell us what to do. I know from experience it works every time. You just have to pray without ceasing and listen."

"I'll try," said Michael skeptically as he got his jacket and headed for the door.

"Are you leaving before breakfast?" asked Aunt Maggie.

"Yes mam, I'm just not hungry this morning. I'll see you this afternoon," said Michael as he opened the door and went to start the four-wheeler.

Michael had been at the barn all day. It was almost time to go home, and he hadn't seen Mr. Bradley yet. His truck was in the driveway, but there was no sign of him. Michael had watched for him while he had done his barn chores. He didn't ride Doc for fear of missing Mr. Bradley if he did come to the barn. He put Doc and Black Mare in the pasture to enjoy a day in the sun and green spring grass. He made sure they were only out on the rich grass for three hours, because Mr. Bradley had taught him that horses could eat too much spring grass and colic or founder. Both of which were potentially deadly for them. Michael moved them off the grass to the corral about noon, and kept working in the barn. He even cleaned Moz's stall, not to help Charlie, but to keep him occupied.

He had been praying all day, just like Aunt Maggie had told him. He would pray a while, and try to listen for the answer to his prayer a while. He kept it up all day but nothing had happened! How long could they wait for an answer? Didn't God know this was an emergency? Michael closed his eyes and leaned his head on Moz's stall door to try and listen again for his answer.

When he did hear it, he was so startled that he jumped backwards and landed on his backside in the hallway of the barn.

"Just what I'd expect from a loser like you! Standing up taking a nap when you should be working. Get up and get out of my way. I have to clean this stall," said Charlie in her best ranch foreman voice.

Michael certainly hadn't been planning on Charlie's voice being the one he heard, but it did take his mind off his problem for a minute. He got up and dusted off his jeans. "Look, Charlie, for your information, I wasn't sleeping. I was thinking, so just shut up and go home."

"I don't think you can tell me what to do. I have to clean Mom's horse's stall, but I don't have to talk to you so get lost," ordered Charlie as she pushed her glasses up on her nose and turned to Moz's stall.

"Fine, but I already cleaned Moz's stall."

Charlie looked over the stall door and saw that Michael was telling her the truth. For a moment she was puzzled, but then her eyes narrowed and she turned on Michael

"What are you trying to pull? Are you trying to get more insurance so I don't tell Joe you punch defenseless girls?"

"You're just about as defenseless as a rattlesnake, and not near as good looking, besides…" It was all Michael got out before Charlie hit him with everything she had by jumping on his back. The force of her assault knocked him to the ground, and she started to yank his hair with both hands.

"A rattlesnake, huh? Let's just see how good looking you are BALD!"

Michael was face down in the sawdust. Charlie was sitting on his back pulling out patches of hair with both hands and screaming like a wild banshee. They had fallen with Charlie's weight positioned so that Michael couldn't get his hands under him so he could push himself up. He knew he had to do something soon because she was plucking him like a chicken!

"Charlene Nicole Jackson! What on earth are you doing? Get off Michael right now!"

Michael and Charlie both froze when they heard Tessa's voice. Michael was relieved to have his scalping stopped, and Charlie had both hands full of Michael's hair. She thought wildly for a moment and then said, "Bugs! Michael was being attacked by bugs and I was saving him!"

Michael looked up at Charlie who by this time had stood up and was trying to convince her Mother that she had come to Michael's rescue. From the look on Tessa's face, she wasn't sure what to think. This is just great thought Michael. Her Mom will probably make Charlie clean stalls for a month when she finds out what really happened and I'll have to put up with her. I've got enough trouble without Charlie around. Michael made a quick decision.

"It's true," he said, "I've got bugs." Once he said it Michael knew it didn't come out right.

"Really," said Tessa. "What kind of bugs do you have that make it necessary to pull out your hair?"

"Big ones," came the very intelligent reply from Charlie.

"Funny, I don't seem to see a single one. You would think if they were that big, I'd see at least one," said a still disbelieving Tessa.

"I must have got them all. It sure is a good thing I'm fast. Right Michael," said Charlie as she poked Michael in the ribs.

Michael's grunt must have sounded like a yes to Tessa, because she just shook her head and said, "I think you two are up to something. Charlie, I forgot to tell you I'm going to the store for a few things while you clean Moz's stall. I'll be back in about half an hour." With that, Tessa turned and left.

Charlie turned and looked at Mchael,"What's up with you? First you do my stall cleaning, and then you don't rat me out to my Mom. Are you planning on blackmailing me or something?"

"Before you blackmail somebody they have to have something you want, and trust me Charlie, I don't want anything from you," said Michael.

"That's not what you said when you wanted me to teach you to ride and barrel race," shot back Charlie.

"You teach me to ride! You teach me to barrel race! You are outta your mind! Mr. Bradley taught me to ride and he taught me to barrel race you….. ," Michael didn't finish. He had heard the answer to his prayer, and never would he have thought it would take Charlie to bring it to him.

Suddenly Charlie found herself wrapped in a bear hug from Michael. When he let her go, he took off jogging down the hallway and whistling. Charlie shook her head as she thought to herself, I've really done it this time. I must have pulled something important loose from his brain! I sure hope whatever it is, it grows back!

Chapter 57

Michael was so excited that he could hardly keep from running straight to Mr. Bradley's house to tell him his plan. He knew not to do that until he had everything worked out, and to do that he needed to talk to Charlie's Mom. He hung around the barn as far from Charlie as possible while he waited for her to come and get Charlie He needed time to think about what he would need for his plan to work. Now that he knew what to do to help Mr. Bradley keep his farm, he couldn't believe he hadn't thought of it sooner. Michael decided to go and get Doc and Black Mare and put them in their stalls for the night. Just as he was closing the stall doors he heard Tessa pull up and honk for Charlie. He took off running and even beat Charlie to her Mom's car. He was running so hard that he had to slide to a stop in the gravel, and would have fallen if Tessa's car door hadn't stopped his forward motion.

"Well Michael, I'm glad to see you, too!" laughed Tessa. What's the hurry?"

Michael turned a bright shade of red when he found himself staring into Tessa's beautiful face almost nose to nose.

"Uh, uh, uh," he stammered as he tried to remember exactly why he was hurrying. It took him a minute, but slowly he did regain his composure.

Charlie had come out of the barn and gotten in on the passenger's side of the car while Michael was bright red and grinning stupidly at her Mom. Oh boy, she thought again, I'm pretty sure Michael has something wrong with him, I just hope I don't get blamed for whatever it is. She pushed her thick glasses back up on her nose, leaned over to her Mother and said, "See Mom I've been telling you he wasn't all there, now do you see what I mean?"

"Sush, Charlie, Michael can hear you. Don't be rude."

"Mom, look at him, he's just about as bright as a small appliance bulb, his evevator doesn't go all the way to the top, if he was a fish you'd throw him back, if he…"

"That's enough Charlie. When are you going to remember not to say unkind things about people even if you don't mean them?"

"Why do you think I don't mean them," muttered Charlie under here breath as she folded her arms and stared straight out the car window refusing to even look at Michael, who by this time was no longer bright red and able to talk in complete sentences.

"Mrs. Jackson, Charlie told me about how you used to barrel race on Moz, and I was just wondering where the barrel races are held. I haven't heard of one since I've been here."

"Well, they are held lots of different places, and you haven't heard of any here because I'm afraid Cedar Grove doesn't have any barrel races."

"Well, how did you find a barrel race to go to and compete for money?"

"It was word of mouth mostly, and when you were running at a barrel race there would be flyers advertising other barrel races that were coming up. Sometimes, I would find a barrel race I wanted to go to in one of my barrel racing magazines. They tell you where, when, what time, and how much the entry fee will be for the race."

"You mean you have to pay to run in a barrel race?" asked a disappointed Michael.

"You sure do if you want to win money. That's where part of the prize money comes from, the entry fees."

Michael thought about this for a minute and then asked,

"Where do you get these magazines?"

"Just about anywhere they sell magazines, and most farm stores carry them. Barrel racers have to buy their horse feed so when they do they can pick up a magazine. Why, are you trying to find a barrel race?"

Michael was caught off guard by her question. Thinking quickly he said, "I don't even have a horse. I just wondered where they were held."

He hadn't told a lie, he just hadn't completely answered the question.

"Are you sure you and Doc aren't going to hit the barrel racing circuit? Doc was a champion, you know," smiled Tessa.

"Yes mam, I know."

"Maybe I'll try and find one for us to go watch. Would you like that?"

Tessa's question was followed by two very enthusiastic answers. One was yes and the other was a groan.

Chapter 58

Michael couldn't sleep. The rest of the house was filled with the sounds of slumber. Max was breathing deeply and evenly in the bunk bed across from him, the grandfather clock was dutifully chiming out the hours as it did all day, only now it was quiet enough to hear, and Uncle Joe's snores drifted up the stairs. It had been two weeks since he had found Mr. Bradley's letter, and a lot had happened since then.

Michael had gotten the magazines Tessa had told him about and poured over all of them. He was getting discouraged because there were lots of barrel races with lots of prize money, but by the time it was divided up between four or five divisions of winners none of them paid enough money to one winner to take care of Mr. Bradley's tax bill. Finally as he was looking through the last magazine, he found it!

It was called a Big Run Race, and it was in Memphis, Tennessee, which made it even better. First place paid $15,000.00, second place paid $12,000.00, third place paid $10,000.00, fourth paid $9,000.00, and it kept going until there were ten winning rides. Michael was only concerned with first place because he just knew that was what Doc would win. They would pay off Mr. Bradley's bill and have money left over. As he kept reading he saw something he hadn't counted on, the entry fee for this race was $1,200.00, and it could be paid all at once, or in three installments of $400.00 each. The first installment was due by the end of April, the second by the end of May, and the last one on the day of the race on June 28.

Michael hadn't told anyone about his plan to run Doc in a barrel race to win money to help Mr. Bradley. He had wanted to get Doc entered in the race and then tell Uncle Joe, Aunt Maggie, and Mr. Bradley because that way he figured they would have to let him do it. Now his problem was getting $1,200.00 before the end of April, and he only had about ten days left. He was desperately trying to think of a solution, but none would come. How in the world was he going to get $1,200.00? He wished he could talk to Aunt Maggie about it, but he couldn't risk that yet. He thought he knew what she would tell him. It's what she always told him to do with problems, pray. She sure believed in it, and at this point there was nothing else he could do

Michael closed his eyes and silently prayed, "Lord, I'm not even sure I know how to ask You this, but I sure need some help. You are the only one I can talk to about getting the money for that barrel race, and I only want it to help Mr. Bradley, and to be sure I don't lose Doc. Aunt Maggie always tells me "anything is possible with God", and she's always been right about everything else she's told me, so I'm counting on you to show me what to do. In Jesus Name, Amen."

Michael felt like he should have said something else but he didn't know what. He hadn't told God he only had a few days to get the money, but Aunt Maggie said God knows everything, so he guessed God knew that, too. Michael turned over to go to sleep. He didn't know why, but now he was sleepy and more peaceful than he had been since he saw the $1,200.00 entry fee.

It had been two days since Michael had prayed for help in getting the entry fee for the barrel race, and nothing had happened. He was still a kid with no money trying to find a way the help a friend with no money. He was worn out with worry about Mr. Bradley, Doc, and what would happen to them. He just couldn't lose Doc now, and even though Mr. Bradley hadn't liked him at first, he didn't want to lose him either. He loved being at his barn and watching him work with the

Black Mare. It was amazing what he was doing with her, and Michael wanted to keep learning.

Michael's frame of mind showed in his face when he came home from the barn and sat down for supper. He was the last one to come to the table so everyone else looked up at him.

"Oh my, is everything all right, honey?" asked Aunt Maggie.

"You look like your dog died," teased Max.

"Shush, Max," said Aunt Maggie who thought she knew what was bothering Michael.

"It's okay, I guess I'm just tired," was all Michael said.

Aunt Maggie let it go at that and everyone dug into supper. Michael wasn't very hungry and just pushed his food around on his plate while he continued to think about Doc. Uncle Joe had been talking, but he said something that made Michael stop and listen intently.

"Wait till you use it, Chuck. I'm telling you I found this new air hammer at the pawn shop in town, and it's just like brand new. I've been wanting one for a long time, but I didn't want to pay the new price for one. It works great. No more hammering for me, I'll just push the trigger and BAM it's done. It's a real man's hammer."

Maggie stopped with her fork in mid-bite. The thought of her husband with a high powered hammer was scary. He could do enough damage with a weed eater. What on earth could he do with a power hammer?

Chuck was thinking the same thing, but he was laughing about it, "Isn't that like giving a monkey a hand grenade and hoping nothing blows up?"

Joe just replied with his standard, "Shut up."

"What's a pawn shop, Grandpa Joe?" asked Max.

"A pawn shop is a store where you can buy or sell something. People can take something they have no more use for to a pawn shop if they need money. The owner of the shop will give you money for whatever you bring in. You can either pawn it, or sell it."

"What's that mean?" asked a confused Max.

"Take my new manly hammer for example. The guy who brought it to the pawn shop wanted to sell it, because he was moving out west and needed money to get there. The shop owner gave him a fair price for it and sold it to me the next day, which just goes to show you how smart your grandpa is, because when I saw it I snapped it up. Yes sirree, I know a good deal when I see one."

Maggie rolled her eyes and shook her head as she thought of some of Joe's other "good deals", most of which were in the shed out back collecting cobwebs.

"What does it mean to pawn something?" asked Max.

"That's when the pawn shop owner will loan you money on whatever you bring in, and hold it for a certain amount of time, usually about 90 days. If you want it back, you can come in, give the store owner his money back, and you can have your stuff back. If you don't come back for it in 90 days, or whatever time he gives you, he will put you stuff out in the store and sell it to whoever wants it. The catch is you don't get as much money if you pawn something as you do if you sell it, because the store owner has to keep it for so long before he can sell it."

"If you can get more money why would anybody want to pawn something when you didn't want it anymore to begin with?" asked Max.

"Well, sometimes folks need money and they have to sell something they really don't want to lose, like a piece of jewelry, a watch, or a wedding ring, and they hope to get it back. That's when they pawn it," said Joe.

Max kept talking, but Michael had stopped listening. His mind was replaying what Uncle Joe had just said. Money, pawn, sell, ring that was it! He had his answer!

As soon as supper was over, Michael rushed up to his room. When Michael had left Michigan to come to live with Aunt Maggie and Uncle Joe all he brought with him was a few clothes, and what he had always called his "bag of treasures". He had kept it as long as he could remember. It was an old blue velvet bag that had a few baseball and basketball cards in it, a picture of a dog he had torn out of a magazine when he was much smaller thinking one day he would get a dog just like it, a lucky penny, and an old photo of his Mother. He used to take it out and look at it so he could remember what she looked like, but he hadn't done that in a long time. She looked like she was about nineteen or twenty years old. It was faded and wrinkled, and the only thing he had left of her. At least it was until he left Michigan.

Michael had many case workers, and lots of foster families. The only reason his bag of treasures wasn't stolen during those times was no one wanted his "treasures". That was due to one very kind social worker. Her name was Jeanette, and Michael used to wish she had been his mother. She had been the first person to come and get him after his Mother had died. She took him to her home that first night because there were no foster homes available. She had been his case worker for three years, but she got sick and had some kind of operation, so he got a new case worker. That one didn't last long then he had another, and another. He didn't even know most of their names, but he never forgot Jeanette. He didn't know that she had never forgotten him until the state found his aunt and uncle.

Jeanette had made sure she was the one to do all of Michael's paperwork to leave Michigan. She had gone and gotten him the day he was to leave and go to Tennessee. Jeanette took him to her home and told him she had something very important to give him. Michael couldn't imagine what it was, because no one had ever given him anything. She brought him a tiny box and told him to open it. Inside he found a pretty gold ring with a shiny glass stone in the center surrounded by smaller red stones. When he saw it he vaguely remembered having seen it before.

Jeanette told him it was his Mother's ring. Jeanette had spoken with his Mom's best friend after she died and she told her the story of the ring. It was a family heirloom that was passed from the eldest daughter to her eldest daughter. It had come from a lot of great, great, great grandmothers, starting even before the family had come to America. Jeanette didn't know what country they had come from, but she knew the ring was very valuable. That was why she had kept the ring instead of giving it to a three year old who was going to foster homes. She knew the odds of Michael keeping the ring were nonexistent. That was also why she kept up with him and where he was. She wanted him to have it when he was old enough to keep it. Since he was going to his real family in another state, she was giving it to him now. She kept telling him not to lose it and to always keep it in a safe place.

Michael had listened to her and had done as she said. The safest place he had was his bag of treasures. When he arrived at Aunt Maggie's house he hadn't known what kind of place he was in so he hid his treasure bag in the very back of the closet Aunt Maggie had given him for his clothes. He had actually forgotten all about the ring and everything else once he had gotten used to living here, and loving it.

Michael found the blue velvet bag and opened it. He took out the tiny box and looked at the ring. Jeanette had said it was a diamond and ruby ring. She had told him to keep it and give it to his kids when he grew up. Right now, that thought was a million miles away, but Doc and Mr. Bradley were right here, and thanks to this ring and a pawn shop, they just might get to stay here.

Chapter 59

Michael felt the cool air come through the open window of Mr. Bradley's pick-up truck. It was Saturday morning, and they were on their way into town to get horse feed. They got feed every other Saturday. Michael went along to help load and unload the bags of feed, because Mr. Bradley didn't need to put the extra weight on his new hip, yet. Michael was so nervous he could hardly sit still!

He had the ring in his pocket that he had retrieved from the closet last night. Mr. Bradley liked to go the little café in town when he finished getting feed and doing any other errands. He would sit, drink coffee with his farmer friends, and "jaw" with them as he called it. Michael didn't mind because that gave him time to look around town and go to the tack shop to see what Doc might need. He wouldn't be going to the tack shop today. He was going to the pawn shop. Michael knew where it was, but he had never been in it. It was across the street and a little way down from the café Mr. Bradley liked.

When Michael and Mr. Bradley got to the feed store, they ran into Uncle Joe. He was getting a back rub for his cows to keep the flies off of them, and Miss Maggie's weekly order of chicken feed.

"Look what the cats drug in," laughed Joe as he slapped Robert on the back, "We've been missing you old buddy. How're you doing?"

"Good, good, I guess," lied Robert. He didn't know that Joe was aware of his problem with the taxes.

Joe studied his friend and said, "Let's you and me go over to the café and have us a big slab of pie, or cake, or maybe a donut and visit a while. How about it?"

Robert couldn't help but laugh, "I remember the last donut incident with you and it didn't turn out too well."

"Aw now you can't hold that against me. Besides we might need to run a taste test to see who has the best desserts, the café or Miss Maggie."

Robert was still smiling, "You might be right. Kind of a community service thing. We both know the answer to that question, though."

"Yep, but in the interest of fairness and to keep me from having to clean out the chicken house if I get home too early, how about it?"

Robert nodded his consent and the two men headed for the café. Robert told Michael to meet him there in about an hour to go back to the barn.

Michael waited until he saw them go inside the café and made a bee line for the pawn shop. The sign above the door said Big Al's Pawn Shop If You've Got It We Buy It! Michael thought Big Al must be a giant if that was his name. Uncle Joe was one of the biggest men he had ever met. He wondered if Big Al was bigger than Uncle Joe. Michael took a deep breath and pushed the door open.

What he saw inside was a little bit of everything. There were tools, lawn mowers, TV's stereos, appliances, guns, gadgets of all kinds, toys, computers, lots of other stuff, but when he saw jewelry, Michael stopped looking. He looked at the counter and there was a man there who could barely see over the counter. The name tag on his shirt said Big Al.

Michael was giving Big Al some serious thought when he said, "Can I help you, young man?"

"Yes sir, are you Big Al?"

"I sure am, and I know what you're thinking. They call me Big Al cause that's the size of my heart not my height. Now what can I do for you?"

Michael fished the ring out of his pocket and gave it to Big Al, "I'd like to pawn this ring, please."

Big Al took the ring and looked at it. He hated to tell the kid he didn't take costume jewelry. A ring this size couldn't be real. The kid had a kind of hopeful, desperate look on his face. Big Al made a show of getting out his jeweler's glass, putting it to his eye, and looking at the ring, while he was putting off telling the boy it was worthless. He held the ring closely and what he saw made him lose his breath and have a coughing fit.

Michael watched as Big Al went pale then red with coughing, "Are you okay Mr. Big Al? Do you need some water or something?"

Big Al was nodding "yes" to the first question and "no" to the second. He had been in the pawn business a long time and NEVER had he had a piece of jewelry this exquisite brought to him. When he had recovered enough he asked, "Where did you get this, son?"

"It was my Mom's. She died and gave it to me."

The boy's answer sounded reasonable, but he needed more information. He made it a practice to never take in anything that might be stolen. He ran an honest pawn shop.

"Aren't you the boy that moved in with the Hayes a while back?" Big Al asked.

"Yes sir. How did you know that?" asked Michael.

"Oh, that's just part of the pawn business, knowing folks around town. Joe Hayes comes in here fairly often to look around and see if I have anything he needs. I tell you what, I'm gonna need a little while to see exactly how much this ring is worth. Can you leave it with me for about thirty minutes or so?"

"I guess, but I have to leave to go home pretty soon," said Michael a little skeptically.

"Fine, I'll see you in about half an hour."

Big Al watched Michael leave then picked up the phone to call the café across the street. He had seen Joe Hayes go in there right before the boy came in his store. He needed some answers for how a kid got a ring this valuable.

Joe hurried over to Big Al's Pawn Shop. He wondered what all the fuss was about. Big Al said he needed to see him right away. Something about Michael having something he was trying to pawn and Big Al thought it might belong to Joe.

"Morning Big Al, what's going on?"

"Hi Joe, come take a look at this," said Big Al motioning for Joe to come and look at the ring.

Joe picked it up, studied it closely, and then let out a low whistle, "That's one of the prettiest things I've ever seen, next to Miss Maggie of course. Whose is it?"

"That's what I was hoping you could tell me. The boy who came down here last year to live with you brought it in."

"Michael!" exclaimed Joe. "Where in the world did he get it?"

"I don't know. That's why I called you to come over here. I thought he might have taken it from you or your wife."

"Are you saying Michael stole this? Dad burn it Big Al, Michael is a good boy. He's not a thief, and I don't appreciate you saying he is. Now if I was you I'd think twice before saying something like that again. I like you Big Al, but nobody talks bad about my family," said Joe who punctuated his words by hitting the counter with his fist making everything on it jump.

Big Al was getting a little nervous. He hadn't meant to insult Joe. "Take it easy, Joe. I just wanted you to know what was going on. This is the most valuable ring I have ever had in my store. Why the best I can tell, it's worth at least $30,000.00. If I just gave him ten percent of its value to pawn it, I'd have to give him $3,000.00, and that's a lot of money for a kid to carry around. What do you want me to do? Michael is coming back in about fifteen minutes.

"I'm sorry for getting a little riled up. I appreciate you telling me what's going on. Heck, if you weren't honest, you could have taken the ring without anyone knowing its real value. I don't know what Michael wants the money for, but I have my ideas. Tell you what, how about you give me the ring and tell Michael you'll give him $1,500.00 for it. That's half of what you said ten percent would be. I'm a little short on cash myself right now, but if you still want that hay baler I got last year at the Pearson auction, I'll give it to you for the $1,500.00, and that's $300.00 less than I paid for it. You know that because you were bidding against me. I'll find out where this ring came from and I'll let you know. What do you say?"

Big Al thought a minute and decided this was his lucky day. He did still want that hay baler, and would be happy to get it at such a bargain.

"I'll take you up on that, Joe. Now you better take this ring and get out of here before Michael comes back. I'll send someone over to pick up my new baler."

Joe nodded, took the ring and left. He needed to get home and talk to his best friend about this!

Joe walked into the kitchen to find Maggie just finishing organizing the pantry that held all her homemade jelly and jam. Strawberries would be coming in soon and she needed to know how much was left from last year. There was no strawberry left, five grape, four blackberry, six pear preserves, one apple butter, and three peach. Her brood had certainly eaten a lot of jelly last year. Now she knew about how much to make for this year.

Maggie turned around smiling to greet her husband. When she saw what he was holding in his hand, she went white as a sheet and had to sit down. Tears began to stream down her face as she asked Joe, "Where did you get my Mother's wedding ring!"

Chapter 60

Michael hurried back to the pawn shop. It was almost time to meet Mr. Bradley and he was getting nervous. He still had to get the money for the ring, and go to the post office. He had filled out the entry form for the barrel race, and was ready to send it in as soon as he got the entry fee. The post office was only about two blocks down from the pawn shop, so he could still make it back to the café on time. He had to mail the entry form today. It was due by Monday and the post office was closed on Sunday.

Michael saw Big Al as soon as he walked in the shop.

"Come in, I've been waiting for you. I've got a deal for you on your ring. I want to buy it from you instead of pawn it, if that's okay with you. I have someone who wants it, and I'd like to sell it to him."

Michael asked the question he had been worrying about,

"How much will you give me for it?"

"Will you take $1,500.00 for it?"

Michael couldn't believe his ears! That was enough for the whole entry fee and some left over.

"Yes sir, I sure will."

"You have to promise to be careful with all that money. It's a lot to carry around," said Big Al as he counted out the money.

Michael had never seen so much money much less held it in his hand. "Don't worry, I'll be very careful. Thanks Mr. Big Al."

Michael went straight to the post office. He got a money order for the $1,200.00 and mailed the entry for The Big Run Race. He was so happy. Now he just had to figure out how to tell Mr. Bradley and Aunt Maggie and Uncle Joe. He decided to think about that later. Right now he had to meet Mr. Bradley.

Joe was at a loss for words, and that was an unusual event. All he did was show his wife a pretty ring and she started crying. Joe hated it when Maggie cried. I broke his heart, and made him want the tackle whatever hurt her. He had been so surprised by her reaction he hadn't even heard her say it was her Mother's ring. Now Maggie was crying harder than ever. Joe got down of his knees in front of her.

"Sweetheart, what's wrong. You've got to quit crying and talk to me. Come on, honey, calm down and tell me what's wrong. I promise I can fix whatever it is."

Maggie looked at Joe with watery eyes and said, "Oh Joe, I'm not sad. You don't know how happy I am to see that ring. It was my Mother's wedding ring. I haven't seen that ring in over 30 years. I thought it was gone forever. I don't know how you found it, but you are the most wonderful man in the world."

Joe definitely heard the most wonderful man part. "Aw shucks honey, it was nothing."

"Joe, you have to tell me how you got it," said Maggie as she began to calm down.

"Well, the truth is, Michael found it. He had it at Big Al's pawn shop wanting money for it. Big Al caught me in town and asked me if it was stolen. I told him to give Michael some money for the ring, and he could have my new baler I got at the auction last year. I would take the ring to sort the whole thing out. It looks like all I had to do was show it to you. Now tell me about it."

"This ring has an amazing history. It has been in our family since the 1600's. According to the story our Mother told us, our family lived in Europe, in Austria, I believe. At one time this branch of the family was very wealthy, complete with mansions, fine art work, and things like diamonds, rubies, emeralds, and gold. I don't know what happened,

Brenda Dawson

but the only thing left to prove it, is this ring. It was given to the eldest daughter for her wedding ring when she married, and had been passed down through the generations. I don't know how the family managed to keep it when they went through hard times, like coming to America as immigrants, or going through the depression of the 1920's, but they did.

My grandmother gave it to my mother when she married in the late 1930's. Mother never wore it much because she was afraid something would happen to it. She gave the ring to my oldest sister, Mary, who was Michael's grandmother. She gave it to Michael's mother, a fact she came to regret. When Michael's mother became addicted to drugs and eventually took off, she took the ring with her. I always figured she sold it or traded it for drugs. It made me sad that my generation was the one to lose the heirloom. I never expected to see it again, but Joe you found it!"

Joe was eating all this praise and gratitude up. Now that he thought about it he guessed he was pretty special. Sometimes he just couldn't help himself.

"Do you have any idea how much that thing is worth?" asked Joe.

"Not really. Which ever family member had it usually tried not to let anyone know about it for fear of someone stealing it. I don't know if it's true or not, but I've been told the diamond in the center is five carets and the rubies surrounding it are a half caret each. These are very old, excellent quality, stones and the gold work in it is very pure. To think you got this ring back for a hay baler is unbelievable."

"I'm just glad I did if it means so much to you," said Joe filing this away for future use the next time he got in trouble. "Michael is going to have some explaining to do."

"Joe, I'm sure he wanted that money to help Robert. Michael has been worried sick about Doc. Let's don't say anything to him about it. I think he will come to us. Let's give him that chance."

"All right, but I don't like the thought of him carrying around all that money. I hope he says something soon. Oh, uh sweetheart, I sure have been craving one of your chess pies. Do you think we could maybe have one for supper tonight?"

"For you, after all you've done, of course you can," Maggie said sweetly. Joe began to grin and head for his recliner. This was going to be great!

"I'll make it just as soon as you clean out the chicken house like you promised."

Chapter 61

Michael had just finished another great run around the barrels on Doc. Mr. Bradley was standing by the fence ready to critique his riding. Doc was prancing and snorting. He had his neck arched, and his muscles bunched ready to go again. Adrenaline was flowing through both horse and boy. Michael had never felt so much power underneath him as he felt when he asked Doc to run. Mr. Bradley still hadn't let him open him all the way up. He said he wanted to be sure Michael could stay with him when he did.

Michael had told Aunt Maggie and Uncle Joe what he had done about entering the barrel race. He was surprised that they didn't seem very surprised. He told them about how he got the money for the entry fees and that he had $300.00 left over. He gave it to Aunt Maggie for safe keeping. Then came the hard part of telling Mr. Bradley.

They had all gone to his place and Michael repeated everything he had told them to Mr. Bradley. At first he just sat in his chair and didn't say a word. Michael was scared he was mad and wouldn't let him ride Doc. Finally Robert asked Maggie and Joe if they were okay with Michael riding Doc in a barrel race. They both said yes. Robert said the whole thing was a huge long shot. A barrel race like the one Michael had entered would draw the best of the best barrel horses. Doc hadn't run barrels in over ten years. He was nineteen years old, and Michael had never run in a barrel race. This race would be his first competitive ride. Robert also said if the entry fee hadn't already been paid, he would not have gone along with it.

Running for Home

Robert had two conditions that they all had to agree to. One, Michael had to wear helmet, and they all agreed. Two, he would put both Doc and Michael in training so that they would be as ready as possible, and if he didn't think Michael could ride Doc safely he would not allow them to compete. Maggie and Joe were fine with that, Michael not so much, but he had no choice.

That had been nine weeks ago. Mr. Bradley had taught him so much about the sport of barrel racing. Everything from sitting down in the turns, tipping you horse's nose so his shoulder doesn't hit the barrel, which hand to use for which turn, how to rate your horse for the turn, and on, and on, and on. Michael was also learning that barrel racers have to be in good shape, because it's a very physical ride. After a run like he had just finished, he was always breathing harder than Doc.

He was also learning that Mr. Bradley expected a lot of both him and Doc, but mostly him. Michael rode over to see what he thought about their last run. He had to have liked it, because it felt great.

"That wasn't worth a dime, boy. You did fair on the first two barrels, but that third barrel was awful. You ran him at it too straight. When you leave that second barrel position him farther over so he is already bent when you get ready to turn that last barrel. The kind of horses you will be up against won't make that kind of mistake so you can't either. Now walk him a few minutes and I want to see you do it right this next time."

Michael took Doc around the arena at a walk just like Mr. Bradley said. He patted Doc's big neck. "It's okay Big Guy, he's just trying to make us the best we can be. I still think we did pretty good, but he says good isn't good enough for this race. The barrel race is two weeks from today, so I guess we better work harder."

Robert again wondered what he had let that boy get into? He didn't know if he could control Doc when the actual barrel race began, and the big horse knew where he was and what he was about to do. Barrel horses are like any other athlete, they know when they are practicing and when they are running the real race. A whole new level of intensity kicks in, and with horses like Doc, a whole new level of power. A disturbing picture kept popping up in Robert's mind of Michael being thrown around like a rag doll and hitting the ground. He also kept thinking about his daughter. Was his farm worth possibly letting something happen to Michael? He knew the answer to that was no.

If Michael just hadn't spent all that money on the entry fee, he would have stopped it in the beginning. If Michael had just asked him before entering he would have said no. If Michael wasn't riding Doc so well he would have said no. There were a lot of "ifs" that he could not do anything about. The truth of the matter was, Robert was scared to death for Michael. The fear was making him be harder on Michael than he should have been. He knew that an accident like Susan's rarely happened, but it had happened to her. Robert shook his head to get rid of the disturbing thoughts.

"Bring him back up here and make one more run on him. Turn him loose, but don't ask him for any more speed than he wants to give you. Remember to give him enough pocket to get around the barrel and line him up better for the third barrel. When he starts running home, don't pull him up until you hear me yell."

Michael grinned as Robert gave him his instructions. Not too long ago he wouldn't have known what Mr. Bradley meant by the terms pocket and home. Now he knew that pocket was riding your horse far enough away from the barrel so that he had room to turn it without hitting it, and turning it over. Home meant bringing your horse back across the finish line. Michael looked over and saw Mr. Bradley had his stop watch out.

Leaning down, he patted Doc's neck and said, "He's going to time us on this one, Doc. Let's make it good."

Michael lined Doc up with the third barred and waited for Mr. Bradley to say "go". When he did, Michael leaned forward, and Doc knew what he was supposed to do. Michael had learned to hold the horn when Doc took off, or he could find himself on the ground. Doc pushed off his huge hind quarters with enough force to jump out from under Michael if he didn't. The first barrel always seemed to appear instantly to Michael. He held the horn with his left hand and the reins with his right as he sat down in the saddle for the turn. When Doc rolled around the barrel to complete the turn, Michael leaned forward again to help push him to the next barrel. This time when he sat down to turn he swapped hands. He held the horn with his right hand and the reins with his left. As they left the second barrel, Michael did as Mr. Bradley said and rode Doc more to the center of the arena to put him in better position for the third barrel turn. Again he held the horn with his right hand and the reins with his left. When Doc completed the third and final turn and headed for home, he accelerated even faster. Michael kept riding until he heard Mr. Bradley yell "whoa".

Robert pushed the button on the top of the stop watch, and looked at it. He raised his eyebrows and decided he needed to check the accuracy of his old stop watch. If this thing was reading right, that old horse and that kid just might have a chance. Robert didn't realize it, but the nervous adult had left, and the trainer had kicked in.

Michael saw Mr. Bradley smiling as he took Doc over to the fence. Michael was breathing hard, and Doc was prancing and side stepping as if he was proud of himself.

"How did he do, Mr. Bradley?"

"He did fair, and you rode him a lot better. Now let's take him back to the barn and cool him out."

"He isn't breathing hard at all. Do you think those supplements we are giving him are the reason?"

"No, the supplements are just vitamins. The reason he is doing so well is almost a year of trail riding up and down hills and building up his stamina and muscle. A horse is like any other athlete. If you give a football player vitamins and he doesn't work out and lift weights, he won't be able to play well. The same thing applies to horses. A lot of people want to win, but they don't want to put the work in it requires to have a fit horse."

"How can anyone think riding a horse is work?" asked Michael incredulously.

Robert just smiled and knew that Michael's love of horses was akin to his own.

Chapter 62

Robert woke up with a start and a sense of unease. It took him a minute to figure out where he was. Robert looked up at the ceiling of the camper part of his horse trailer and knew why he felt uneasy. Today was the Big Run Barrel Race. He and Michael had come to Memphis yesterday so that Doc didn't have a long trailer ride the day of the race. Maggie, Joe, Chuck, and Max were coming later today to watch and cheer for Michael and Doc.

Robert was more apprehensive than he had ever been in his life. He admitted to himself that he loved Michael like he was his own son, and he couldn't bear the thought of something going wrong and happening to him. He could hear Michael gently snoring in his bunk. Without thinking, Robert began to pray.

"Lord I know I asked for your help to save my home, but I didn't have any idea you would use Michael and Doc to answer that prayer. I know I must have faith in You and in Your ability to protect Michael, but please Lord keep him safe. Lord, I ask that You ride with him and give Your angels charge to protect him from anything, seen or unseen, that would cause him harm. I want to thank You for putting Michael in my life, and I ask that even if I lose my farm, please give him victory in his ride today. Lord, you are going to have to help me with this spirit of fear. I won't be much use to Michael if You don't. In Jesus Name, Amen."

Robert drifted back to sleep after he prayed. He awoke again to Michael shaking him and saying, " Mr. Bradley, wake up it's 7:00, it's race day, and we're burning daylight!"

Doc was in a big box stall in a strange barn. He knew what he was there to do, because he used to do this a lot with Susan. Being in the barn with other strange horses had brought back so many memories that he found himself looking for her again. When he didn't see her he kept flaring his nostrils wide searching for her scent in the air. He even let out quite a few piercing calls for her, but she still didn't come. He became frustrated and began to paw at the floor of his stall.

"Careful big guy, you'll wind up in China," laughed Michael.

Doc startled at first, then settled down and was glad to see Michael. He saw Michael had his breakfast and eagerly waited for him to pour it in his feeder.

While Doc was eating his breakfast, Michael looked around and noticed that a lot of other horses had come in during the night. He was surprised to see so many.

"How many horses do you think are running in this race Mr. Bradley?"

"There are 72. I checked last night when we pulled in while you were putting Doc in his stall. Most of them are here by now. The barrel race starts at 2:00, so a few more will come in. You and Doc are number 68 to run. Your number is based on when your entry was received, so four people entered after you did."

"What time do you think we will run?" asked Michel.

"With that many riders and that may drags it will probably be around 6:00 I imagine."

"What are drags?" asked Michael.

"That's when they clear the arena and bring the tractor in to drag the dirt smooth around the barrels. If they didn't there would be a big path dug out around the barrels and it wouldn't be fair for the horses running last like Doc. They pick a set number of riders and drag after they have run. It's usually anywhere between seven and ten. Come on, let's refill Doc's water bucket and then I want to show you the arena and practice pen where you'll warm your horse up."

Maggie and Joe were almost at the barrel race. They had been driving about three hours. Chuck, Tessa, Max, and Charlie were right behind them in Tessa's car. Maggie smiled as she thought of the look on Max's face when he found out he had to ride in the same vehicle all the way to Memphis with "Hurricane Charlie" as he called her. He had begged to ride with Maggie and Joe, but Chuck told him that would hurt Charlie's feelings. Max had said "what feelings" which had sealed his fate.

Maggie looked down at her hand and saw her Mother's ring. It felt good to have it on today. She felt sure that it had been around on lots of momentous occasions, and this was certainly one. Michael didn't know she had the ring. She wondered if he would notice it. She had been praying for Michael's safety ever since she gave her consent for him to ride. She couldn't imagine riding a big animal that fast and staying on. As much as she wanted Robert to be able to keep his home, she wanted Michael's safety more.

"Here's our turn, and there's the fairgrounds where they are having the barrel race," announced Joe as he checked his mirror to be sure Chuck was turning, too.

"I don't think I've ever seen so many horse trailers. I didn't know there would be this many riders. Do you think Michael has a chance at winning something Joe?"

"Sweetheart, your guess is a good as mine, because this is all new to me, too. Well here we are," said Joe as he put the car in park and opened the door.

Chuck parked beside them, and the first person to exit the car was Max. His hands were shoved in his pockets, and his face had a very aggravated frown on it.

"Granny if I have to ride home with Charlie I just may kill her. She repeated everything I said all the way down here. When she wasn't talking she was poking me in the ribs, or making noises that Dad thought I was making and got me in trouble. I mean it Granny, you've got to help me!"

Maggie smiled. Max looked like his next move was going to be pulling out hunks of his hair. "I'll see what I can do. Why don't you go find Michael and Robert. We'll be right behind you."

"Anything to get away from HER!" said Max as he trotted off.

Michael saw Max before Max saw him. "Max, over here."

Max hurried over and said, "I hate to tell you this but Charlie came, too," as Michael cringed he said, "I had to ride in the same car with her all the way here. You have to let me hang out with you. I can't take any more."

Before Michael could say anything, there was Charlie along with everyone else. Michael grabbed Aunt Maggie in a big hug.

"Hi honey, I'm glad to see you, too. Are you nervous?"

"No mam, not so far," said Michael.

"Good you'll do better that way." She didn't add that she was nervous enough for both of them.

"Come on, let's go get some seats. The barrel race is starting," said Chuck. "Good luck Michael, we'll be cheering for you."

As they walked off Max hung back. Chuck saw that his son was missing and said, "You too, Max." Max gritted his teeth and followed.

That had been over four hours ago, and if Michael hadn't been nervous then, he sure was now. He had just finished warming Doc up. Number 65 was running now and he was number 68. Mr. Bradley had told him to ride up and be ready to go in the gate when his name and number was called. Michael had never seen so many fast horses and good riders. It was just like Mr. Bradley said it would be. The winning time was a 16.495 second run. Michael could feel his heart beat. It felt like it was going to jump out of his chest. He mentally replayed everything Mr. Bradley had told him to do, especially not stopping Doc until he heard Mr. Bradley yell.

Then he heard it! The announcer said, "Our next rider is number 68, Michael Hayes riding Sparks Twister Doc. Michael come a ridin."

Michael took a deep breath and sent Doc toward the entry gate. Once inside, he lined him up with the third barrel and gave him the signal to go.

Doc knew what he was going to do. He loved it and had been missing it for a long time. When Michael gave him his cue, it looked like he had been shot out of a cannon. Robert was ready and pushed his stop watch as Doc triggered the electronic timer.

Doc got to the first barrel and spun it in one fluid motion. He finished his turn and leaped toward the second barrel.

Suddenly the announcer said, "Michael, pull up, pull up. The timer isn't working! Pull up!"

Michael was in another world. He didn't hear the crowd, the announcer or anything. He was flying. Never had Doc run like this! Michael was around the second barrel and headed toward the third. He positioned Doc just like Mr. Bradley had told him to, and Doc turned so quickly, if Michael hadn't been holding the horn he would have been slung off. As Doc turned for home, they were going so fast everything was a blur. Michael waited to hear Mr. Bradley yell, but he didn't hear anything. Doc stopped on his on, and Michael looked up at the clock to see his time. It was blank!

Michael looked at the announcer for an answer and heard, "A little tough luck, Michael. The timer didn't start. We'll give you a re-ride at the end. You'll be number 73."

Michael couldn't believe it. They had a super barrel run and it didn't count! He rode a still pumped up Doc out of the arena to Mr. Bradley.

"Now what, Mr. Bradley?"

"Well, you are going to have to run again. Timers sometimes fail and there's nothing anyone can do about it. I wish you had more time between your runs for Doc. I probably shouldn't tell you this, Michael, but according to my stop watch your run was a 16.368, and if that is right it would have taken first so far," said Robert grinning the biggest grin Michael had ever seen on his face.

Running for Home

"Wow. I knew it was fast! I knew Doc could do it Mr. Bradley! Don't worry he can do it again! Do you want me to keep walking him until they call us to run again?"

"Yes, and Michael…"

"Yes sir?"

"Great ride".

Now Michael had the same grin on his face.

Robert didn't tell Michael, but Doc probably wouldn't be able to duplicate his same run again. The horse needed more time to settle down and collect himself, and burn off some adrenalin.

Michael kept walking Doc and trying to get him to calm down, but he didn't have much success. He didn't have long to wait.

"Michael Hayes, we're ready for your re-ride. Michael had some bad luck with the timer on his first ride, but he had one heck of a ride from the way it looked up here, so Michael and Sparks Twister Doc, come on in."

Michael brought Doc back to the entry gate, and before he got Doc positioned like Mr. Bradley said, he took off! Michael managed to get set and turn the first barrel. Once around the first barrel, boy and horse regained their rhythm. They spun a beautiful second barrel and the crowd was on their feet, cheering for a kid on a big horse that got a bad break. Michael heard them this time and Doc did too. Once again he executed a perfect third barrel, and turned for home. Doc felt a small pinch in his chest but he didn't let it stop him from a blazing run to the finish… to home! Michael pulled him up when he heard the familiar "whoa". He looked up quickly at the timer and saw 16.702. His heart sank because he was hoping for the time Mr. Bradley had said Doc ran before. Michael exited the arena and dismounted. He led Doc back to the trailer, tied him, and loosened his girth. Doc pushed Michael with his head like he was giving him a high five. Michael smiled, and put both arms around Doc's neck.

"You are awesome, Doc. Thanks for giving me the time of my life. I bet we can talk Mr. Bradley into letting us run in some more barrel races."

"Michael, Michael." It was Aunt Maggie rushing to see him. Michael ran to her and was immediately wrapped in a big hug while Uncle Joe came up and was patting him on the back.

"Good job, buddy. We're proud of you," said Uncle Joe.

"Way to go," said Max.

"I guess you'll thank me now for teaching you how to ride a horse," said Charlie.

"Michael, Michael, come here," it was Mr. Bradley waving for him to join him. Michael and everybody else went to see what he wanted.

"Michael, they are tallying up the times, and I'm not sure, but I think you and Doc have placed," said Mr. Bradley.

Before Michael could reply, the announcer said, "Ladies and gentlemen, we have your results. It goes like this, 10th place goes to...."

Charlie couldn't stand it, "Mr. Bradley are you sure Michael placed? What was his time? Do they always start telling the winners with last place? Do you know what the winning time was? Who was it? I think Michael...."

A whole chorus of "Charlie, shut up" finally silenced her. When they could hear the announcer again he said, "… and third place with a time of 16.702 goes to Michael Hayes riding Sparks Twister Doc."

Everybody was yelling and clapping. Michael couldn't celebrate until he asked Mr. Bradley, "How much did we win? Is it enough?"

Robert put his arm around Michael's shoulders and said, "Michael, you and Doc won $10,000! And yes, it's enough. Thank you, Michael."

Before he could say anything, as man came running up to Robert and said, "Mister isn't your trailer parked in slot 126, with a big red horse tied to it?"

"Yes," replied Robert. "Why?"

"You better come quick. Your horse just went down."

Michael was running to Doc before the man finished talking. While he was running he was praying frantically, "Please God, Please God, Please God….."

Then he saw him! Doc was on the ground beside the trailer! Michael rushed to untie his head and let him stretch all the way out. He reached down to pat his face and stopped as still as a stone. The full realization of what had happened hit him. Michael couldn't breathe. This couldn't be real! This couldn't be happening! Doc was gone! Michael collapsed in sobs on Doc's neck. Not Doc, not his horse, not his friend. He couldn't imagine not having Doc anymore. Of all the things that had happened to him in his short life, this one hurt the most. He couldn't stand it!

Michael felt strong arms lifting him off Doc. He fought because he didn't want to let go of his horse.

"Let me go! Let me go! Don't anybody touch my horse! Don't touch him!"

But they didn't let him go. Robert put him in Aunt Maggie's arms. When he saw her he stopped struggling and sobbed like he had never cried before. Maggie sat with his head in her lap stroking his hair and telling him she was there and would take care of him. Michael sobbed until he couldn't make any more sounds.

It had been two weeks since the barrel race. Michael felt like he had been in a fog. He still couldn't believe Doc was gone. That awful night, a vet had come and said that Doc's big heart had just exploded. He said there was nothing anyone could have done. Michael was oblivious to everything that happened after he got in Aunt Maggie's arms.

They had brought Doc home to bury him. Mr. Bradley had let Michael pick the spot. Michael wanted to put him in the pasture by the creek where they had spent so much time together. Mr. Bradley agreed and Michael had helped bury his horse, his friend. Michael had been to see him every day since.

Michael was sitting on the front porch swing after getting home from Mr. Bradley's. Aunt Maggie came out and sat down next to him. She didn't say anything for a while. She just held his hand and rocked in the swing with him.

"I can't stop missing him and thinking about him. Aunt Maggie."

"I know, honey, that's normal. You loved him. It's hard to let go of the things we love. Time will make things better, but you will always miss him."

"How can it get better if I will always miss him?"

"Because now, since it's so soon after you lost him, when you think of him, it's with tears. As time goes by, when you think of him you will smile because of all the good memories you have of him and the times you had together."

"I don't know about God, Aunt Maggie."

"What do you mean, honey?"

"I prayed to win the barrel race, and I prayed that Mr. Bradley would keep his farm, and when I saw Doc on the ground I prayed the hardest I've ever prayed, but God didn't save him. You said God could do anything, but he didn't save Doc," Michael said as he wiped a tear away.

"Michael, I can't begin to know the ways of God, but I can tell you what I've learned from studying the Bible for a long time. God hears all our prayers, and He answers them whether we know it or not. God put a natural order here on this earth, and part of that is we all die sometime. We are never ready to let go of those we love, but we know we have to. I believe that everything that happens to a child of God is for their own good. It might not seem like it at the time, but usually if we wait long enough we will see it. I don't know why God didn't save Doc, but I do know He used Doc in a mighty way. Before God put you and Doc together, Robert Bradley might as well have been dead. Before God put you and Doc together, you had no sense of purpose or belonging or knowing how happy you could be. You prayed to win the barrel race. God answered that prayer. You didn't win first place, but you won enough to enable Robert to keep his home, which was your other prayer. God used Doc to answer both those prayers."

"I want you to remember Doc dancing and prancing as he finished his last barrel race. That's the Doc you always need to think of, and remember before Doc met you, he was a forgotten horse in a back pasture. You put life back in him. I think Doc died like we would all want to, having done something he loved doing so well he just had to prance about it, and then he went to sleep."

Michael sat quietly for a few minutes, and said, "Do you think there are horses in heaven?"

"Oh my yes, I know there are, because the Bible says Jesus is coming back on one."

Michael thought about what she said and smiled for the first time in two weeks, "I bet He'll be riding Doc."

Epilogue

Doc opened his eyes and he was lying in the softest field of lush, green grass he had ever seen in his life. He sat up on his belly and looked around. He had never seen such beauty. The sky was the bluest blue, the flowers were beautiful with colors never seen before, and the air, the air was so sweet he could almost taste it.

Doc stood up, and for the first time in years nothing hurt. His knees, his back, nothing hurt! He shook his head and snorted. Then he jumped straight up in the air and bucked and kicked like a colt. It felt wonderful! He ran and ran and never got tired. He came to a clear, flowing stream, and drank the sweetest water he had ever tasted. He began to eat the sweet, lush, grass. After a while, he dropped and rolled just because it felt so good. He jumped up again, and gulped in big breaths of sweet, sweet air. Wait! There it was! The scent he had been searching for all this time! Doc lifted his head and neighed as loud as he could. He turned into the wind to find the scent. Suddenly, he saw her!

"It's about time you got here, Mr. Big. I've been waiting for you. We got some serious riding to do," she said laughing.

Doc ran to her, and she swung up effortlessly on his big back. They flew across the green pastures with his mane and her hair streaming in the wind.

A woman sitting by the stream watched them and smiled. Doc was home.

Hickman Co. Library System
East Hickman Public Library
Lyles, TN